ROCCO

SARAH CASTILLE

St. Martin's Paperbacks

This is a work of fiction. All of the characters, organizations, and events portrayed in this novel are either products of the author's imagination or are used fictitiously.

ROCCO

Copyright © 2018 by Sarah Castille.

For information address St. Martin's Press, 175 Fifth Avenue, New York, NY 10010.

ISBN: 978-1-250-10407-6

Printed in the United States of America

Our books may be purchased in bulk for promotional, educational, or business use. Please contact your local bookseller or the Macmillan Corporate and Premium Sales Department at 1-800-221-7945, ext. 5442, or by e-mail at MacmillanSpecialMarkets@macmillan.com.

St. Martin's Paperbacks edition / January 2018

St. Martin's Paperbacks are published by St. Martin's Press, 175 Fifth Avenue, New York, NY 10010.

10 9 8 7 6 5 4 3 2 1

Praise for Sarah Castille's Sinner's Tribe series

"The exploration of the hardcore society of a motorcycle club (MC) is fascinating and chilling. Strong personalities populate this world and take no prisoners. Crafting a love story out of this combination is admirable."

>—*RT Book Reviews* (4 ½ stars) on *Rough Justice*

"A sexy and dangerous ride! If you like your bad boys bad and your heroines kicking butt, *Rough Justice* will rev your engine. A great start to a new series!"

>—Roni Loren, *New York Times* bestselling author

"Put your helmet on and hold tight for the ride of your life!"

>—*Romance Reviews Today* on *Beyond the Cut*

"Castille continues to raise the stakes in her visceral, violent series, offering her biker heroes plenty of pulse-pounding action, and giving readers the compelling romance they crave."

>—*RT Book Reviews* (4 ½ stars) on *Beyond the Cut*

"Castille takes the MC genre and lights it on fire! I want my very own Sinner's Tribe Motorcycle Club bad boy!"

>—Julie Ann Walker, *New York Times* bestselling author

"Castille emphasizes the darkest aspects of motorcycle gangs in the gritty Sinner's Tribe Motorcycle Club [series] . . . for the reader who doesn't believe bad boys need redemption and hungers for the story of a couple whose love survives despite dangerous times."

>—*Publishers Weekly* on *Sinner's Steel*

To Tara,
For your friendship, your warmth, and your inspiration,
and for showing me how to appreciate the beauty
of each and every day.

ACKNOWLEDGMENTS

To everyone at St. Martin's Press, thank you for loving my mafia bad boys and making their stories shine. Thank you to my editor, Monique Patterson, who helped me make this book be the best it can be. Thank you also to my agent, Laura Bradford, for her patience and helpful insights. Thank you to Danielle Gorman who is always there when I need her, and to Casey Britton who has the uncanny ability to spot even the smallest mistakes and who loves my mafia men as much as I do! Thank you to Jennifer, Maggie, Jacqui and Reggi for your cheerleading, company and advice. Meeting up with you is always the highlight of any week!

A huge thank you to all the readers, fans and bloggers who have left reviews, spread the word, or taken the time to connect with me about my stories, Your support means everything.

And finally thank you to John, Kaia, Sapphira and Alysha. For everything.

For it is by grace you have been saved.
Ephesians 2:8

ONE

"He was a nice boy."

"Yes, Papa." Grace Mantini crossed herself as the pallbearers carried the coffin of Benito Forzani across the grass of the Las Vegas Shady Rest Cemetery. As the daughter of a high-ranking Mafia boss she had attended so many funerals over the years she could go through the motions of the formal burial service in her sleep.

"He would have made a fine husband."

"I'm sure he would have." But not for her. Was she a terrible person for being relieved that the Mafia soldier her father had wanted her to meet had been found dead in an alley the day after her father and brother arrived in Vegas?

"He wore a baseball hat so you couldn't see his missing ear," her father continued, with the faintest hint of a smile. Unlike many other Mafia fathers, Grace's dad had no interest in forcing his daughter to marry into the mob, but that didn't stop him from playing matchmaker any time they were together.

"Yankees?" she asked, hopefully.

"Red Sox."

"It wouldn't have worked out," she said. "I like winners."

Her brother, Tom, stifled a laugh and reached around their father to poke her in the side. Four years younger than her, he had been groomed since birth to take over the family business. One day he would become a "made man" like their father, Nunzio Mantini, now the underboss of the powerful New York Gamboli crime family. Grace hoped it wouldn't be too soon. Men changed when they became made, and once that line was crossed, the serious business of living in a world of crime and death weighed heavy on their souls.

She smoothed her expression when she caught a few people looking in their direction. The graveyard was filled with members of the Toscani crime family who made up the Las Vegas faction of the New York–based Gamboli crime family, all dressed in black despite the blazing sun overhead and the unbearable ninety-degree heat.

"You could have come home if you married him." Her father sighed. "He had a new job in New York. Don Gamboli asked Benito personally to handle all the family accounting."

"I like it here in Vegas," Grace lied. "I can buy a house, party twenty-four hours a day, sunbathe all weekend, and I have my career . . ."

In fact, she hated Vegas. A New Yorker, born and raised, she had been happy with her two days of nice weather a year, the postwar on First Avenue she'd lived in with her aunt, a wallet with no driver's license, and a man she'd loved with every ounce of her being. Now she had an old Mitsubishi Mirage with a pathetic 74 hp under the hood that she had to flog to get anywhere, a permanent sunburn, and instead of a postwar, she shared a characterless ranch house with her best friend Olivia, and two jazz musicians, Miguel and Ethan.

But that's what happened when your family was in the mob. You didn't get to choose the kind of life you wanted to live. You didn't get to do the job you had always dreamed about doing. You didn't get to live in the city of your heart. And you didn't get to keep the things you loved.

She scrambled for a new topic of conversation. The last thing she wanted was for her father to find out she wasn't actually making use of her psychology degree. Instead, she was making ends meet by recording radio jingles during the day, the closest she could get to her ruined dream of becoming a jazz singer. Her father had tolerated her decision to move to Vegas six years ago only because she had been so distraught after the attack that she'd told him was a mugging gone wrong that she could barely function. If he'd known the real reason she'd left—no, run—from New York, he would never have let her go.

The priest finished the last rites, and the crowd responded with the proper prayers. She felt the whisper of a breeze against her neck, the softest caress. A shiver trickled down her spine but when she turned slightly hoping to catch the soothing air, the breeze died away.

"You can always come home if things don't work out," her father said. "You can stay in the house and look after Tom and me like you did after your mother died. We haven't had a good meal since you left. Eight years is a long time to go without *braciola* the way your mother used to make it."

Grace didn't miss his emphasis on the word "left" or the undertone of judgment that went with it. Her decision to move to Vegas had been acceptable; her abandonment of the family two years prior had not. But everything had changed when, at sixteen, she discovered that her life had been a lie. Her kind, doting father was not actually an insurance salesman; the weekly funerals they attended weren't just because her family was unlucky; and her mother hadn't bled to death in the arms of her ten-year-old daughter as the result of an accidental shooting by an overzealous cop.

And while the revelation that Papa was in the Mafia explained some of her father's behavior—the respect he received when they went out, the small favors that were bestowed upon him that hinted at his real power and influence—she was unable to process some of the larger concepts. How could her loving father be a criminal and a murderer? How could she wear the clothes he bought her, eat the food he paid for, or live under his roof when he had blood on his hands and everything had been paid for with dirty money? How could she even begin to understand the horrifying things he had done to achieve his position as second-in-command of one of the most powerful organized crime families in the country?

After her father had told her the truth, she'd run away. Just as she'd tried to run away after her mother died. Her mother's sister had offered to take her in, and her father, distressed by her total and utter rejection, had agreed. She'd thought nothing could be as devastating as discovering her father wasn't who she thought he was, but it was nothing compared to the night her heart was ripped out of her chest.

She felt a tickle on her neck, not a breeze this time, but something she knew instinctively as a warning. Someone was watching her. She took a quick glance over her shoulder, but she saw only trees glimmering in the sunshine, beckoning her with the promise of a respite from the heat in their cool shadows.

"You can get *braciola* in any good Italian restaurant. You don't need me."

"I'm getting old." He sighed again. "I worry about you being all alone. I want to see you settled."

"Setting me up with your friends' sons isn't going to do it. You know how I feel about . . . what you're involved in."

Her father bristled and his eyes narrowed, reminding her that although his hair had turned gray and there were new lines on his broad forehead and crinkles in the corners of his dark eyes, he was no weak, kindly old man. His shoulders were still broad, his back straight, and he was trim and fit from years of running and eating in moderation. But more than that, he carried himself with the confidence and authority of a man used to being obeyed. She could pretend to herself that she had made the choice to leave New York and that she was free to live her life the way she wanted in Vegas. But in reality, she was here only because he allowed it. If she pushed him too hard, he would drag her back to New York and force her into a marriage with the mobster of his choosing and there was nothing she could do about it. Such was the power of the Cosa Nostra.

"It's not what I'm involved in." He bristled. "It's who we are. It's our family. It's our blood, our heritage. You may not like it, but it's part of you. You can't run from it forever."

"It doesn't mean I have to marry into it."

He shook his head as the first shovel of dirt thudded onto the coffin. "Poor Benito. An incredible coincidence he was whacked right before he was supposed to meet with us. Do you know anything about it?"

"Are you asking me if I killed him?" Her voice rose in pitch.

Her father shrugged. "Maybe you were afraid I would force you to marry him . . ."

Only in a Mafia family would a father ask such a

question. Yes, he had given her a gun and trained her how to shoot, but she would never have used it for anything other than self-defense, and her father knew that.

"I'm a pacifist."

Tom barked a laugh and then immediately tried to cover it up by feigning a fit of coughing.

Her father's lips curled in distaste. "I thought you got over that years ago."

"It's not a disease."

"It is in our family," Tom whispered.

"Well, I didn't kill him." Grace had no intention of ever getting married to one of the men her father proposed. After being betrayed and broken, her heart crushed and her body scarred, she had no interest in love and even less interest in finding a man who promised to give her the world only to snatch it away at the first sign of trouble. And even if she did find someone, she would marry on her own terms. She would find a man who loved her and could accept that she couldn't fully return that love because she had lost her heart six years ago and would never get it back.

"What about Father Patrick?" Her father gestured to the priest who was now giving the last rites. "He's a nice boy. Good family. He would make a good husband."

"Papa! He's a priest!" Father Patrick was one of the few mob-friendly priests in Vegas, which meant he heard the kind of confessions that would turn the stomach of a normal man, his coffers were overflowing, and his church was full to standing every Sunday morning.

"He came to the priesthood after his wife died. Since he has already had carnal knowledge of a woman, I believe he can marry again and you won't suffer in any way for his faith." Her father opened both hands as if welcoming the priest into their crime family.

"Papa. Please . . ." She looked to Tom to save her, but

he was doubled over with laughter and no help at all. She'd forgotten how brutally forthright her father could be, something that had been both a curse and a blessing the night she'd finally returned home seeking the truth.

She glanced around to see if anyone had overheard them and caught movement in the shadows behind Father Patrick.

That's when she saw him.

Tall. Dark hair. Black leather jacket snug over wide shoulders. Broad chest tapering to a narrow waist. Black T-shirt tight over hard ripples of muscle. Bandanna, worn jeans, thick-soled boots.

Beautiful. Her body heated in places it shouldn't. Who was he? She didn't know any man who would dare show up at a Mafia funeral wearing anything other than a suit and tie.

She squinted, trying to make out his face, but the sun was in her eyes and he was nothing but a dark shadow on the other side of the grave.

After the service ended, a heavyset, dark-haired man broke away from the departing crowd and approached them with a few companions and two heavily muscled bodyguards in tow. He looked to be in his early to mid-thirties and clearly had a fondness for bling. A diamond ring sparkled on each of his thick middle fingers, a heavy gold chain encircled his neck, and on his wrist he sported Louis Vuitton's Escale Time Zone, which gave the hour in twenty-four time zones simultaneously and had a kaleidoscope-like dial. Grace disliked him immediately and even more when he made a blatant perusal of her body as he shook her father's hand.

"Nunzio." His smile didn't reach his breast-focused eyes.

"Tony." Papa introduced her and excused himself to greet some friends.

Grace recognized his name at once. Tony Toscani was one of two self-appointed bosses of the now-divided Toscani crime family. After his father, Santo, was murdered, Tony had claimed the right of succession. However, his cousin, Nico Toscani, refused to accept his claim. In an unprecedented show of defiance, Nico had taken half the family capos, crew, and assets and proclaimed himself boss of a new splinter faction. Don Gamboli had sent Grace's father to help resolve the situation, either by confirming one or other of the cousins as boss, or brokering some kind of truce to bring the family back together.

Tom obviously knew Tony and they shook hands, but when Grace held out her hand, Tony pressed his slimy, cold lips to the back of her wrist and drew her away from Tom's side. "Why didn't I know Nunzio had a daughter?" he murmured so quietly only she could hear. "Shame about your face. You could have been almost pretty."

Grace's hand flew to her cheek, pulling her dark hair down to hide the long, silvery scar that marred the left side of her face from ear to chin. Although people often stared, few were cruel enough to mention the ugly scar that had destroyed her dream of being a singer.

She glanced over at her father to see if he'd heard what Tony had said. Not many people would have the gall to insult the daughter of the New York underboss, whose vicious and ruthless nature translated into a fierce protectiveness when it came to his family. When Grace was six, her first-grade teacher had informed her parents that she needed remedial-reading lessons. The next day her teacher was killed in a hit-and-run accident. At the time, she hadn't thought much about it. But later she realized it was only one of many incidences in her life where people had to suffer because of her connection to the mob.

Grace tried to yank her hand away, but Tony tightened his grip and pulled her deep into the shade of the trees that had seemed so welcoming only a short while ago.

"Looks like a knife," he said. "Am I right? Who did you piss off? Or was this a message?"

"Let me go." Years of Krav Maga classes meant she knew how to disengage, but the result would be a scene that would, no doubt, embarrass her father and cause a major political incident.

"You got a man?" He tightened his grip, studying her intently. "You'd be lucky to find someone who didn't mind damaged goods, although the alliance you would bring would make it worthwhile."

Grace fought for calm. Anger achieved nothing. Despite the consequences, she needed to deal with the bastard the way she'd learned how to do. After fleeing New York, she'd vowed never to let another man touch her without her consent and her Krav Maga training had been the way she kept that promise to herself.

Gritting her teeth, she raised her hand and grabbed his wrist with the other, turning her hips until he was forced to let go. Unfortunately, her attempt to be discrete meant she left her back exposed. Taking advantage, Tony circled a hand around her throat and pressed his big, sweaty body against her, the sharp edges of his ring digging into her skin. "Sheath those claws, kitten. I like my women to be seen and not heard."

"Release her."

Deep and dark, the power of that voice froze her in place, even as it slid over her skin like the brush of thick velvet. She knew that voice, heard it in her dreams, and imagined night after night that fierce rumble vibrating against her chest.

Even though it was coarser, deeper with maturity, she would never forget that voice.

A name worked its way through the barriers in her mind. A name she thought she had wiped from her thoughts as well as her heart.

Rocco.

No. It wasn't him. It couldn't be. Last she'd heard he was still in New York working with his psychopathic father, Cesare, boss of the brutally violent De Lucchi crew. The beautiful, dark-haired boy she had fallen in love with had become the Gamboli crime family's most feared enforcer, causing the kind of trauma she had dedicated her life to heal.

Tony released her and she turned and saw him—the man from the shadows.

"Rocco," she whispered.

God, he looked even better than she remembered. Beautiful and breathtaking. His angled cheeks and firm square jaw were lined and scarred, and his thick dark hair was cut military short. Gone were the softness from his face, the roundness of his cheeks, and the dimple at the corner of his mouth. But his sculpted lips were full and sensual, and gold still glittered in the whiskey-brown eyes so dark now, they were almost black.

Once upon a time those eyes had looked into her soul, and those lips had touched every part of her body. Once upon a time all that beauty had belonged to her, and then the mob had stolen it away.

"Frankie." Tony released her and spun to face Rocco. "What the fuck? This isn't your business."

Frankie? Why did Tony call him Frankie?

Rocco gave Tony the briefest of glances, as if he were unworthy even of that gesture. "She's not yours."

"Maybe she will be. Look at her. She's disfigured. No

one will want her. Nunzio would be grateful if someone took her off his hands. I'd be doing them both a fucking favor."

Wham. Rocco's fist slammed into Tony's face, sending Tony staggering back into a tree. He tried to rise and suddenly Tom was there, his fists flying, shouting something about the family honor. As the assembled mobsters rushed toward the fight, Grace turned and walked away.

"Tesoro." Her father hurried to catch up. "What happened?"

"The mob happened," she said bitterly, whirling around to face him, grateful for an outlet for her pain. "I hate this. I hate that you're part of this. I only came out today to spend time with you, and to give you support because you knew Benito and I know you'll feel his loss. I miss you and Tom, but I don't want to be involved. I can't deal with the violence and the politics and the games." And she definitely couldn't deal with seeing Rocco again and reliving all the pain from their past.

"Grazia, don't leave. We see so little of each other. I'll make sure no one bothers you again."

Grace shook her head. "I'm sorry, Papa. I've spent too many years trying to create a life away from all of this. I don't want to be involved."

"Always running away," her father said softly. "What happens when there is nowhere left to run?"

Rocco wasn't in the mood for breaking legs.

And especially not the legs of Danny Bagno, owner of the Stardust jazz club. Danny had borrowed half a million dollars from Nico Toscani's most senior *caporegime*, Luca Rizzoli, and failed to pay the *vig*. The interest had accrued and Luca had decided to call in the loan, which meant that Luca did the talking and Rocco did the breaking.

Except tonight all he could think about was the girl he had lost for the very reason Luca had called him out tonight.

"Hey, Danny. How's it going?" Luca leaned against the bar in the empty club. The Stardust didn't open until seven, which gave them all afternoon to get business sorted out. Luca's young associate, Paolo, had taken up guard position at the bottom of the stairs. The club was underground, with no natural light except the few rogue beams that filtered down the stairwell.

"Ah . . ." Danny froze half in and half out of the doorway leading to the kitchen, but there was nowhere to run. Rocco stood in the shadows beside the kitchen door, and Mike, one of Luca's most trusted soldiers, blocked the back entrance after making his way in through the service door.

"Good, Mr. Rizzoli. It's going good." Danny's hand dropped to his ill-fitting suit jacket and Rocco grabbed his arm and yanked it behind his back, pushing him toward one of the polished wood tables in front of the stage.

"Keep your hands where I can see them, Danny, at least until Frankie's got that weapon you're hiding under your jacket." Luca chuckled. "We wouldn't want you to hurt yourself before he has a chance to show you his special skills. You haven't met Frankie before, but when we bring him with us, it means your loan is overdue."

Frankie. He'd answered to that nickname for so long, he'd almost forgotten his real name was Rocco.

Until yesterday, when every painful memory came back in a tidal wave of longing for a past that had been ripped away, and a future he would never have with the only woman he had ever loved.

Danny whined as Rocco patted him down. "I don't want any trouble. You guys want to have a cup of coffee, and we can work things out? The wife just bought a new coffee maker for my office and some fancy beans from Brazil."

"I hope she didn't spend any of the five hundred grand you owe us or we'll have to take it with us." Luca walked around the bar and poured himself a drink, directing Paolo to check the stairwell with a lazy wave of his hand. Tall and lean, seventeen-year-old Paolo had just been made an associate after years of running errands for the Toscani crew. He'd struggled with a drug problem, but his quick thinking and courage when Luca had been kidnapped earlier that year, together with his lock-picking skills, had been enough for Luca to give him another chance.

Rocco relieved Danny of his .22 and a Swiss Army knife that had seen better days. He'd been doing collections and shakedowns as long as he could remember, and the only thing that made them bearable was the fact that the kind of guys who tried to cheat the mob were scumbags, just like him.

No, not like him. Danny was hustler. Rocco was a monster. No wonder Grace had run away.

Grace.

Her name twisted through his mind, opening doors that had been closed for the last six years, flooding his veins with the poison of desire. He hated her now as much as he had loved her. His adoptive father, Cesare, had tortured his body; but Grace had flayed his soul until there was nothing left for him but to embrace the darkness he had been fighting for years.

He had lived for her. Breathed for her. He would have died for her. He supposed, in a way, he had. There was no salvation for a Mafia enforcer. No redemption. Rocco went to church and confessed his sins, said his Hail Marys and offered his body for punishment, not because he expected God to forgive him, but because the emotional numbness that came with the pain of penance enabled him to make it through the work he had to do each day.

Work that had not included pulling a weapon on the acting boss of the Toscani crime family in a public place.

But fuck.

Grace.

Her hair had darkened since he'd seen her last. Once light brown, it was now a rich auburn, falling in thick waves to the middle of her back. Long, dark lashes framed her brown eyes, a startling contrast to her soft pink lips. He had savored that mouth, kissed the length of her slender neck, the bloom of each cheek, every inch of her oval face . . .

Scarred.

His gut twisted and he pushed away the image of that long silvery scar. He had never seen the outcome of the injuries she suffered the last night they were together. The last time he had seen her, she was covered in blood.

My fault.

Rocco's hand tightened into a fist and he forced himself back to the moment he'd recognized her at the cemetery. The total and utter shock of seeing her again. Her body had filled out in the years they'd been apart, her slim frame giving way to the rounded, sensual curves of a woman—a beautiful woman.

Even at ten years old, she had been confident and self-assured. At fourteen, the combination of looks and poise had drawn the boys like flies, and it was all he could do to keep them away. And by the time she turned sixteen, his possessive instincts had taken over. Even though he was ten years older than her, when she offered herself to him, he'd claimed what his heart desired.

Gracie. My Gracie.

She had been his savior, pulling him out of the darkness and into the light. Grace with her beautiful voice and musical laughter. Grace with her warm hugs and soothing hands. Grace with her compassion and her tears. Grace who had tried to save his tortured soul as his adoptive father, Cesare, dragged him further and further into the abyss.

Grace who had run away when he showed her the real monster behind the mask.

He touched the cross around his neck, given to him by his mother when he had received Holy Eucharist two weeks before his parents were brutally murdered. He still prayed for forgiveness for his sin that day—the cowardice he had shown as a six-year-old boy who had hidden under the stairs instead of trying to defend his parents. He had almost no memories of his mother and father. Trauma had erased their faces from his mind, along with most of the childhood memories that could have kept them close to his heart. All he had left of his family were the symbol of their faith and his Christian name. Two powerful gifts.

Faith had sustained him when he discovered four years later that Cesare De Lucchi, the man who had adopted him from the orphanage six months after his parents died, didn't want a son to love, but a tool to mould into the perfect enforcer.

Christ. He needed a cigarette. Luca's wife, Gabrielle, had convinced him to try and quit, but he didn't give a fuck if one of his few pleasures shortened his already wretched life. He'd sealed the deal on his fate in the afterlife long ago, and every life he'd taken since then was just another drop in the fucking well of flames.

"Yeah. About that . . ." Danny's voice pulled Rocco out of his reverie and he gave himself a mental slap for losing focus. One glimpse of Grace and he was already losing his touch. Cesare had been right. Women were a distraction an enforcer couldn't afford to have.

Danny swallowed so hard Rocco could hear him gulp. "I just need a few more weeks. Things haven't been so good, you know. There's a lot of competition in the city. It's hard to get a new club off the ground."

"You had a few weeks. And a few weeks before that," Luca said, sipping what looked to be bourbon. "Where's all the money gone?"

They knew exactly where the money had gone and why the club wasn't doing well. Danny had a gambling problem. He'd drained the business dry and then he'd come begging to the mob. Luca was always happy to lend out a few bucks to help guys in need, but he was firm about deadlines. When it was time to pay it back, he expected to see his cash. Plus interest. And a little something for his trouble.

"You maybe got the *vig* this time?" Mike dropped his sports bag on the table and made a show of unzipping it and removing the baseball bat and gear Rocco had asked him to bring for the lesson today. "Maybe if you pay up, Mr. Rizzoli might be forgiving. I'm telling you, the last thing you want is to spend any time with Frankie."

Damn Mike was getting soft. It was too late for Danny to pay the interest he owed on the money, but clearly if it had been up to Mike, he would have had another chance. A former boxer who now ran a chain of boxing gyms that served as a front for the Toscani family's underground betting operation, Mike was a big guy who used his size and muscle to intimidate the low-lifes who were stupid enough to borrow from the mob. He shaved his head and wore skin-tight T-shirts for effect, but inside he was all marshmallow. You'd think after he lost his two best friends—Big Joe, who turned out to be an undercover cop and Little Ricky who had been gutted by a drug lord obsessed with Luca's wife—he'd have hardened up some. But no, it was like he'd taken all the good out of his friends and sucked it up until he'd almost lost the edge he needed to do his job.

"I don't feel very forgiving today," Luca said coldly. "How 'bout you, Frankie? You feel forgiving?"

"I don't feel anything." It wasn't a lie. Cesare had trained him not to feel—no emotion, no pain, no longing, desire, loss, or regret. No love because love made you weak, and above all things an enforcer had to be strong—physically, emotionally, and mentally.

"How 'bout I comp you an evening instead?" Danny suggested, staring at the equipment on the table—hammers, saws, pliers, gags, vices, knives, ropes, bats, whips, and the other tools of an enforcer's trade. "You and your friends, your family. I can give you all a meal, free drinks, a good show. Call it even."

Christ. The last thing Rocco wanted was to spend an evening listening to the kind of music that had drawn him and Grace together when they'd first met. At first, he hadn't believed a ten-year-old would like Rat Pack songs, but when she sang for him, the lyrics word perfect, something had stirred in his soul. Years later, when they would lie in bed together, hidden from the world, and she sang the same songs in her liquid voice, he remembered that day as the first warmth he'd felt in his life.

"I've got my own restaurant." Luca idly knocked a bottle off the shelf behind him, standing aside when it smashed on the floor. "What I need is the money."

"I have five grand in the safe." Danny was sweating

bullets now, his collar stained dark blue. "You can take that and next time . . ."

"There is no next time." Rocco twisted Danny's arm back, forcing him to his knees. "Paolo, gimme the bat."

When no bat was forthcoming, he looked up to see Paolo staring at a poster of a nude woman reclining on a piano. Stupid kid wasn't paying attention to what was going on around him. Shit like that would get him killed, and he looked like he had a lot of living yet to do.

"Paolo! What the fuck?"

"I'm sorry." Paolo's face turned sheet white and he raced over to the sports bag. "I mean I'm sorry, boss . . . sir." He cast a frantic glance over at the box of straws on the bar counter as he grabbed the bat.

"Jesus. Fuck." Rocco knew all the rumors. How he'd killed someone with a straw because the dude looked at him the wrong way. Or how he'd heard someone disrespect the boss, and gutted him like a fish. Or how he only drank blood, slept on a bed of nails, and specialized in obscure Mafia tortures with names like Sicilian Necktie, Cement Shoes, and Power Drill.

Most of the rumors were true. Sometimes, even the toughest wiseguys couldn't stomach what they needed to do. That's when they called in the De Lucchi crew, a group of professional enforcers led by Rocco's adoptive father, Cesare. Whether they were required to beat, torture, threaten, or kill, there was no limit to what the De Lucchi crew would do. Every member was inducted into the crew at the age of ten years old, stripped of the burden of emotion, attachment, and moral codes, deprived of love and human affection, trained to withstand pain, and unleashed on the world as a vicious, cold-blooded monster who felt nothing beyond the satisfaction of a job well done. And yet no one could match Cesare for sheer brutality. Cesare would go above and beyond simply because he liked to watch people suffer, and he had no issue with killing innocent civilians who got in his way.

Rocco was nothing like Cesare, and his refusal to take the violence beyond the requirements of the contract meant he had been a constant disappointment to his adoptive father. Still, when stupid, young associates didn't pay attention, he didn't hold back on teaching them a lesson that could mean the difference between life or death on the streets.

And, of course, he had a reputation to protect, and a jazz club owner who needed to learn a lesson. The second most feared enforcer in the Gamboli crime family couldn't let the disrespect slide.

When Paolo brought the bat, Rocco smashed his fist into the kid's face with a precisely calculated blow that would inflict the most pain and bloodshed with the least amount of damage. Blood streamed from Paolo's nose as he scrambled to his feet. Luca helped him up and sent him to the restroom to clean up before reporting back for duty.

"Oh shit. Oh shit." Danny shook so hard, Rocco thought he was going to piss his pants. He was the type. Some guys were fucking tough, didn't make a sound. But others, like Danny, started to cry even before Rocco swung the bat.

"I have a wife. She's got no one to look after her. She's in a wheelchair. She's got a . . . disease. And . . . she's . . . blind."

Luca chuckled. "Then who was that blonde bombshell at your house when we stopped by looking for you just an hour ago, walking around giving us a wiggle, winking at Mike like she wanted in his fucking pants? Said she was your wife and you two were on your way to Hawaii in the morning for a two-week vacation."

Danny moaned and Rocco yanked his arm up higher.

"You got cancellation insurance, Danny? 'Cause I'm thinking you aren't going to make that flight."

"How 'bout the club?" Danny trembled in Rocco's grip. "I could sign part of it over to you. We could be business partners."

"You are gonna sign it all over to us," Luca said. "I've got the paperwork right here. All nice and legal. I had it prepared by our very own attorney, name is Charlie Nails."

Rocco pushed Danny over to the table while Luca spread the papers out. Luca handed Danny a pen and Rocco squeezed his elbow until the club owner shuddered in pain. "Sign."

"I don't understand legal stuff." Danny shook so hard, Rocco released him just to see if he would crumple to the ground. He took no pleasure in his work, but small amusements made it bearable.

Danny disappointed him by remaining upright. "I need a lawyer."

Luca grabbed his hand and held it flat on the table. Before Danny could process what was happening, Rocco bent Danny's little finger back until it cracked. Danny screamed. Luca grimaced. Rocco didn't even flinch. He had fully embraced Cesare's teachings only after losing Grace to the violence that was destined to be his life.

"That's the best fucking legal advice you're ever going to get," Rocco said. "Now sign the damn papers."

Cradling his injured hand, Danny signed the papers. "Is that all?"

"No." Luca folded the papers and put them into his pocket. "We're in business together now. You're gonna run the place for us to pay off the rest of your debt."

"But what will I live on?"

"Not our problem." Luca turned away, motioning for

Mike and Paolo to follow. "But you'll have lots of time to think about it while you're getting better."

"Getting better from what?"

Rocco grabbed the bat and put everything out of his mind—the despair of a ten-year-old boy forced to do things that would make even the toughest mobster weep, the brutality of the man he'd thought of as a father, the pain of his heart breaking when he severed his connection with Grace to save her from the life he would never escape, his inexplicable anger at her for actually doing what he wanted and running away, and the powerful wave of emotion that had unsettled him since he'd seen her again.

He lifted the bat and took aim. "From me."

TWO

She was being watched.

Grace looked back over her shoulder yet again but couldn't determine who or what was causing the hair on the back of her neck to stand on end, only that it was the same feeling she'd had in the cemetery when she thought she saw someone in the shadows.

She briefly considered asking one of her father's bodyguards to make a quick tour of the restaurant where she, Tom, and her father were having dinner with Nico Toscani, his wife, and the top capos in his crew. Her father's visit to Vegas was not without danger given that the two cousins who had split the Toscani family would do anything to seize control of the Vegas faction. Although an underboss like her father was considered untouchable—his murder could be approved only by the don himself—it was not uncommon for a powerful capo to challenge the status quo by launching a coup and whacking everyone who stood in his way. At its essence, the Mafia was about survival of the fittest, and if the challenger proved more worthy, the don would rarely intervene.

"Is something wrong?" Mia Cordano Toscani followed Grace's gaze to the back hallway.

"No. I just . . . It's nothing." She smiled at Nico's unconventional wife, dressed in punk clothes, with a pink streak in her dark hair. Although they had both been brought up in Mafia families, they couldn't have been more different. Mia was confidant and outgoing, her disregard for the traditional role of a Mafia wife apparent in everything from her appearance to her attitude. A shrewd businesswoman, she ran her own cybersecurity firm, and seemed to have no issues taking on clients from the mob.

By contrast, Grace wore a burgundy lace crochet mini swing dress, antique jewelry, knee-high black boots, and a black fedora which she had tucked in her oversize crochet bag when they sat down to dinner. *Boho chic*, her best friend Olivia called her look. And far from running her own business, Grace had been drifting since finishing her psychology degree, paying her rent with the money she made from voicing radio jingles as she tried to motivate herself to find a job as a trauma counselor.

Grace.

She heard—no, felt—her name whisper over her skin, and a shiver ran down her spine. Rocco was here. She knew it just as she knew the liquor in her glass was vodka, and the music playing over the speakers was Lana Del Rey's cover of Sinatra's "Summer Wine."

After searching the room to no avail, she excused herself to freshen up and walked through the restaurant hoping to find the reason for her sense of unease in the form of the man she'd never thought she would see again.

"Can I help you, Grazia?"

Luca Rizzoli, the owner of Il Tavolino, and one of Nico Toscani's senior capos, intercepted her after she'd made her way through the crowded tables and past the stage where a small jazz band was setting up for the evening show.

"It's just Grace. My father is the only person who calls me Grazia. He's pretty old school."

Luca laughed. "I didn't want to offend and possibly lose a few fingers." He looked over at the table where his wife, Gabrielle, was talking with Mia, and his face softened. "Gabrielle wouldn't be very happy. Our baby is due in a few months and she's lined up a few tasks for me to do before then."

"Your first?"

"Second. We have a son, Matteo. He's six."

"He must be excited." She felt a tug in her heart, remembering how excited she'd been as a kid when her brother, Tom, was born. She had always wanted children, but after the devastating night at New York's Newton Creek where she'd been broken in both body and soul, she didn't even dream.

Rocco. Her first. Her last. Her only love. It had been six years since she'd run away. And two days ago, she'd run again. Why was she looking for him now?

"Not as excited as me." A smile spread across his handsome face, and she felt inexplicably jealous of the woman who had a man like Luca to share her life. Once a police detective, and now a private investigator, blonde-haired blue-eyed Gabrielle had been warm and welcoming to Grace, and it was clear Luca totally adored her.

"I was looking for the restroom," she said by way of explanation for her wandering.

"Down the back hallway, last door on the right." He reached into his pocket and pulled out a card. "I overheard you telling Gabrielle you're in a jazz band."

"Not me." Her heart squeezed in her chest. "But my housemates, Miguel and Ethan, are in a five-piece jazz band. They're looking for a new vocalist and Mia mentioned she had a friend who sang jazz so I thought I might try and hook them up. They're called Stormy Blu."

Sunita had been Stormy Blu's vocalist for years, but when she hooked up with a guy who was big into drugs and started missing rehearsals, the band had to cancel gigs and bookings had slowed. Ethan, the band's manager, was actively looking for a new vocalist and had begged Grace to take her place, but there was no way she could sing on stage when she knew everyone would be looking at her scar.

"Well, let them know there's a club looking to book new acts." Luca handed her a card. "I've just acquired an interest in the Stardust, a few blocks from here, and I'm trying to fill the stage."

"Thanks. I'll let them know." She tucked the card in her purse. Luca's reference to "acquiring an interest" was mob-speak for taking over a business in payment for a loan that had gone bad. Most likely the owner was dead or in the hospital. How did Luca go home at night to his young son and pregnant wife after doing what he did? Probably the same way her father had done. Without any flicker of conscience or regret. Her father had been a different person when he was at home—a good husband, a great dad, and a well-loved member of the community. It was what he did when he was away that she couldn't handle.

After Luca headed back to the table, she followed his directions to the back hallway, feeling a curious sense of anticipation as she walked along the dimly-lit corridor. Grace's mother and nonna and all her female relatives on her mother's side were firm believers in a sixth sense that was passed down through the women in the family. No one laughed if someone "felt" something.

Coincidence was explained by karma. Portents and omens were taken seriously. Close calls and brushes with death were the work of angels.

And yet, no one could explain why that sixth sense, and all the angels in heaven, couldn't save her mother when Jimmy "The Nose" Valentino burst into Ricardo's Restaurant on the corner of Mott and Grand and sprayed the restaurant with bullets after finding out that Ricardo was having an affair with his wife.

There was nothing unusual in the hallway. Two kitchen doors with glass windows. Broom closet, door ajar. Storage room. Men's restroom. Narrow hallway on the left, leading to the exit. Women's restroom on the right.

She reached for the restroom door and the skin on the back of her neck prickled.

Turning, she saw a man in the shadows near the exit. Her heart skipped an excited beat and she took a step toward him. "Rocco?"

He stepped into the light. Tall. Dark. Dressed in a leather jacket, faded jeans, and a worn pair of boots. His jaw was dark with stubble, and the gold cross that he'd worn as long as she'd known him glittered against the pitch-black T-shirt that covered his muscular chest.

"Grace."

The soft beat of Otis Redding's "These Arms of Mine" drifted from the restaurant, and the sound brought up far too many memories, ones she had buried long ago. They had connected through music. Shared through music. Loved and lost through music.

She drew in a ragged breath, pushing away the bittersweet memories as she inhaled the scent of him, whiskey and leather, and something so familiar a wave of heat flooded through her veins, shocking her with its intensity. How could he affect her so deeply after all this time?

Grace swallowed hard, forcing her throat to work. "What are you doing here?"

"Security."

"I mean here in Vegas."

"I live here."

Her heart skipped a beat. "So do I."

He didn't answer and she had nothing else to say. Until yesterday afternoon at the cemetery, it had been six years since they last saw each other. Six years since he had made a choice that destroyed a friendship and a love that had grown slowly over time.

His gaze raked over her, from her hair to her breasts and over her hips to the bare expanse of thigh between the hem of her dress and the top of her boots, and then back to her face. She trembled beneath his scrutiny. This man who had been her friend, her soulmate, her lover. Her first.

He reached for her, his hand pushing back the hair that she always wore down to hide the scar on her cheek. His touch set off a cascade of memories. Eight years of beautiful destroyed in eight minutes of horror.

"Don't." Pain that she had locked away clawed at her insides, ripping open the emotional scars that had never truly healed.

His face twisted in a scowl and he jerked his hand back as if he'd been burned. Or maybe it was disgust. She wasn't the same girl he'd known in New York, inside or outside.

"So you hated all this so much, you decided to become part of it?" His voice was tight and tinged with cruelty. "You and Benito. A match made in fucking mob heaven until he got himself whacked."

She stared at him, confused. "I never met Benito. His father is my godfather and one of Papa's oldest friends. We were all going to have dinner together. I went to the funeral out of respect, not because I'm involved. And I'm here tonight because Nico invited me and Papa said I couldn't refuse or I'd dishonor the family."

"The family you ran away from."

She bristled at his accusatory tone. "Yes, I ran away. That's what normal people do when psychopaths kidnap them, drag them down to Newton Creek, slice up their face and force them to watch . . ." Her voice caught, broke, but she made herself go on because she might never get the chance again to say what she wanted to say. "When she discovers the man she cared for wasn't who she thought he was."

"You knew who I was," he said, bitterly.

"I didn't want to know so I didn't think about it. But even when I did, I never imagined . . ." She couldn't say those words, couldn't say out loud that he was a member of the De Lucchi crew, a brotherhood of assassins who were at once revered and reviled by everyone who knew them.

"If I'd known you'd be trolling the streets of Vegas looking for a wiseguy to spread your legs for, I'd have come after you."

She slapped him. At least she tried to slap him. He caught her hand before it made contact and slammed it against the wall above her head, pinning her in place. His face, as he stared down at her, was cold and hard, his eyes terrifying in their emptiness, and yet as she looked into the darkness, she saw a flicker of light.

In all the years she'd known Rocco, he had never once been cruel or unkind to her. He had never been rough as he was now. Maybe the face she'd seen that night on the banks of Newton Creek was the truth of him, and everything she'd known about him in the eight years prior was a lie.

"Do it." She lifted her chin, wondering who this bold, brave woman was and where Grace had gone. "Hit me back. Hurt me. That's who you are, isn't it? That's what you do. You don't feel anything so why not teach me a lesson? Then we'll both know that what we had in New York was a mistake."

His massive body shuddered and he took a step closer, caging her against the wall with his hard, muscular frame. He was so much bigger than he had been six years ago, so strong, so powerful. She had no doubt that even with her Krav Maga skills, he could end her life as easily as he used to flick the cigarettes she had convinced him to stop smoking as soon as she was old enough to kiss.

"It wasn't a mistake."

It was the last thing she'd expected him to say and for a moment she was at a loss for words.

"You're smoking again," she said, using the scent of nicotine on his breath to avoid a discussion she wasn't ready to have.

His eyes narrowed slightly, but he didn't respond.

"I thought you quit."

Silence.

"Nothing has changed in six years, Rocco. Smoking is still addictive. It still causes cancer. And you are still going to kill yourself if you don't stop." She swallowed hard and put the mental brakes on that particular topic of conversation. What the hell was she doing lecturing a De Lucchi enforcer on the dangers of cigarettes?

"Why the fuck do you care?"

Why did she care? He was an enforcer. He hurt people and took lives. And yet, what he did for the crew didn't reflect who he was, at least not the man she knew before she ran away.

"I never stopped caring." Just like with her father after she left the family home when she discovered he was in the mob. She'd never stopped loving him; she just couldn't accept what he did for a living. "You were a huge part of my life. You were my friend, my . . ." She trailed off unable to call him a boyfriend because he'd never been a traditional boyfriend. They hadn't been able to go out together or socialize together. She couldn't introduce him to her friends and family. They had only stolen moments—the short drives to and from school, secret rendezvous in hidden places, nights in the darkness of his small apartment wrapped around each other in the refuge of his bed. "You were everything to me."

He snorted in derision. "I believe that like I believe you're not involved with the mob."

"I don't care what you believe." She lifted her chin, met his gaze straight on. "I made a new life here. I'm a psychologist now, specializing in trauma. And I sing. Jingles. On the radio." Anger flared in her chest, surprising her with its intensity. Usually, she buried all her feelings deep inside and only showed the world the face people wanted to see. When things didn't go her way, she tried to move on. When people annoyed her, she turned the other cheek. Anger was destructive, not productive. Nothing got accomplished when people got angry. Dead mothers didn't come back to life. Fathers didn't morph from mobsters into insurance salesmen. Boyfriends didn't betray you. Scars didn't fade.

"And if this is the person you've become," she continued, struggling to free her hand. "This mean manhandling mobster, I'm not interested in getting involved with you either. Now, let me go."

Rocco released her and she turned to leave. "Dammit," she muttered, half to herself. "I should have known better. I try to do one nice thing for Papa, and look what

I get. Some crazy nasty mob boss assaulting me in the cemetery, and now you." She looked back over her shoulder as she walked away, only to see his lips twitch at the corners. "Good-bye."

Grace didn't know how he closed the distance between them so quickly. One minute he was near the restroom, the next he had his hand on her shoulder.

"Wait." He turned her to face him, the heat of his palm burning through her clothes straight to her core.

"Let me go, or you're going to regret it." Part of her couldn't believe the words coming out of her mouth, but the unfamiliar surge of anger felt good, powerful, like it could buffer her from any storm.

"Like you regret wasting all those years with me every time you look in a mirror?"

His cruel words sliced through her, deflating her anger in an instant, sending her crashing to the ground. Her hand flew to the scar on her cheek, and she gritted her teeth to fight back the emotion welling up in her throat.

"I didn't regret them until now. You've become a total jerk."

He released her shoulder, pain flickering across his face so fast she wondered if she'd seen it. "Fuck. Grace—"

"Go to hell." She squared her shoulders and walked away, taking a deep breath and praying no one would be able to read on her face how totally ripped up she was inside.

All these years, some little part of her had imagined that one day they would find each other again. That she would get a chance to explain that she'd run away, not because she didn't love him, but because she couldn't handle the chaos, brutality, and insanity that was the life he had chosen to lead. She couldn't handle knowing that there was a part of him she would never be able to touch. It had taken six years and a psychology degree to help her deal with that night at Newton Creek, but until this moment, part of her had never stopped believing that the man who had taken a life before her eyes wasn't the man she had loved from the moment they met.

She'd been wrong. It was finally time to move on with the life she had worked so hard to build in Vegas, and close the door on a past that had started when she was ten years old.

"Grazia. Come here, tesoro. Meet Rocco De Lucchi. He'll be driving you and Tomasso to and from school until we get something worked out."

"Mama drove us to school. Why can't you drive us?" Her mother had only been gone two weeks and the pain wouldn't go away.

"I have to work," Pap said gently. "The insurance business pays our bills. I can't be here the way your Mama was."

"Then I'll walk," she shouted. "I'm ten years old. I know how to get to school."

"Tom is too young to walk with you." His voice rose to an angry pitch. "We discussed this already. Downstairs. Now."

She knew better than to defy Papa when he had been pushed to the point of shouting, and he'd been angry a lot since Mama died.

Lips pressed tight together, she stomped down the stairs, pulling up short when she saw the driver in the hallway. She didn't really like boys. They acted up in class and played stupid tricks at recess. But Rocco was different. Not a boy, but not quite a man. Beautiful. She didn't know boys could be beautiful, but there was no other word to describe him. His eyes were the brown of the caramels Mama used to make candy apples at Hal-

loween, and flecked with gold, and his skin was tanned and glowed bronze in the morning sun. He was tall and his arm muscles flexed when he leaned down and held out a hand.

And then he touched her.

Electricity zinged up her arm and something clicked in her heart.

"Buongiorno, signorina." His lips were soft on the back of her wrist when he kissed her skin, and her face heated although she didn't know why.

Papa laughed, breaking the spell. "I see you can charm little girls as well as you charm the big ones."

Rocco dropped her hand as if he'd done something wrong and stood abruptly. "She will be safe with me, Mr. Mantini."

"I know she will." Papa patted her on the back. "And now I think Grazia won't mind so much the ride to school."

"My name is Grace." For some reason, it was important that Rocco call her Grace and not her full, formal, boring Italian name.

"I am honored to be your driver, passerotta."

Her lips twitched at the corners. Although he hadn't used her name, his term of endearment acknowledged she wasn't a little kid like Tom, but instead was "learning to fly."

Papa went to collect Tom, and she followed Rocco out to his car. It was shiny and red, and the front was long and round. "How old are you, anyway?" she asked. "Are you even legal to drive?"

"Twenty."

She studied him, pursing her lips as if deep in thought. "You don't look twenty."

"You don't sound ten."

"How come you're driving us around? Don't you have a job?"

"This is my job." His smile faded as he opened the front passenger door and ushered her inside.

Before she could ask what was wrong, Papa showed up with Tom and a few minutes later they were on the road.

"You got any music?" she asked, uncomfortable with the silence. Tom was in the back seat fully engaged in playing a video game.

"I don't know any kids' stations but you can try to find something you like."

"I don't listen to kids' music." She pulled out her MP3 player and held it up for him to see. "I like the oldies. Frank Sinatra is my favorite."

His hands jerked on the steering wheel, making the car swerve. "You listen to Frank Sinatra?"

"Yeah." She shrugged. "I'm not embarrassed about it either. His songs are cool."

He laughed out loud, and the sound made her grin. She wanted to hear him laugh again, watch his eyes crinkle at the corners, and the lines on his brow smooth with his smile. "Do you like Sinatra?"

"Maybe a little."

"My mom loved his songs." Her bottom lip quivered, her mother's death still a fresh wound in her heart. "That's how I know them all. When I listen to them I think of her." She turned to the window so he didn't see her tears.

"Lamento la muerte de tu madre." He reached over and squeezed her hand. His touch eased the ache in her heart, and she turned to study his face.

"I lost my mother, too. Both parents, actually. When I was six." His words came out stilted as if he had to force each one out. "I don't have very many memories *of them, but I remember my mother singing in church. She had a beautiful voice. Do you like to sing, Gracie?"*

Her bottom lip trembled. *"I love singing. I used to sing with my mom."*

"Let's see if we can find something for you to sing." He turned the radio to her favorite station and the first bars of Frank Sinatra's *"Strangers in the Night"* played through the speakers.

"That's my favorite Sinatra song," Grace said, blinking back her tears.

"Mine, too."

How could they have so much in common? He called her Gracie. Just like Mama. He liked her music and he wanted to hear her sing. His favorite song was Grace's favorite song, and he'd lost his mother, too.

It was all too much. She hadn't cried since the day Mama died, but this man, with his handsome face and his beautiful voice, his kind words and his gentleness, had touched the very essence of who she was. He saw the girl who missed her mother, and through their shared passion and experience, he saw something more.

She felt safe with him—safe enough to let go.

"I can't sing today," she whispered. And then she leaned against his big strong arm and cried.

THREE

Guilt drove him to "Hell."

Hellfire, a club for special guests with particular needs, had only just opened when Rocco parked his bike in the back alley, a few blocks away from the Freemont Street Experience in downtown Vegas. After checking the street to make sure he hadn't been followed, he slid his membership card through the reader beside the unmarked, black steel door and descended the well-worn stairs.

Rocco didn't come to the sex club to socialize. He had never had a drink at the bar, sat in the lounge, or enjoyed any of the play equipment on offer. He wasn't here for sex, and the only kink he had was a need for pain so great, only one man could give it to him without causing permanent damage.

Clay, the owner of Hellfire, and once a bounty hunter for the mob, specialized in pain. Only the lash of Clay's whip could give Rocco the numbness he needed to get through each day without self-destructing. And he had never needed that emotional void as he needed it tonight.

What the fuck had he been thinking? He had almost destroyed Grace's life before, and he was about to do it again. She hated the mob and everything that went with it. A good man would leave her alone and let her live the new life she had created for herself in Vegas.

But he wasn't a good man.

He was a self-centered bastard, and he couldn't stay the fuck away.

Not on his own.

By the time he reached the dungeon, he knew an ordinary session wouldn't be enough. Already, cracks had formed in the walls that kept his emotions at bay, and memories trickling out, a warning of the rising tide.

He pushed open the door and dropped his bag on a nearby bench. Clay had managed to squeeze him in to his busy Saturday-night schedule, and he was already checking his equipment at the back of the room. He knew better than to try and engage Rocco in conversation. Rocco came to Hellfire to suffer the way he made others suffer, and tonight he had come to atone for the sin of coveting something he could destroy with his touch.

After stripping off his jacket, shirt, and shoes, he crossed the floor in bare feet, lifting his hands to the shackles hanging overhead. Clay came up behind him and fastened the strong, steel cuffs around his wrists.

"Cuffs okay? Anything hurt?"

Rocco shook his head and steadied himself for the lash of the whip that would beat Grace out of his mind and return him to the state of numbness that had been his life since the last day he'd seen her in New York.

"Ready?"

"Yeah."

The hiss of the flogger echoed in the chamber and Rocco gritted his teeth in frustration. Clay always warmed him up first with a flogger or a light whip, but tonight Rocco wanted pure, raw, and unadulterated pain.

"Get something harder."

"I'm warming you up or I'll damage the skin." Clay struck again and Rocco hissed out a breath. "Fuck the warm up."

"Suck it up, buttercup," Clay said, not unkindly. "You aren't in a position to do anything about it. Someone has to save you from yourself."

"It's too fucking late to save me."

By the time Clay finished the warm-up, his body was hot and sweaty, his skin burning like it had been licked by fire. Clay gave him a minute to catch his breath, and then the real pain began.

Searing. Slicing. White Hot. Mind numbing.

Pain.

Pain that took his breath away.

Pain that wiped his memories.

Pain that demanded his full attention and swept everything from its path. Except this time the pain wasn't enough. Instead of blissful numbness, he was dragged into the memory of the first time he kissed Grace. His moment of weakness. The night he had sealed their fate.

"Don't take me home. I just want to drive." Grace slid into Rocco's car, and all he saw were legs. Long, tanned, toned legs going all the way up from a sexy pair of cowboy boots to a frayed pair of cut-off denim shorts. She was wearing one of those floaty tops she liked that he could see right through and some kind of leather vest with fringes.

Fuck. His hands clenched around the steering wheel as he pulled away from the curb. Why the hell did her aunt let her go out dressed like that? He didn't know

what the style was called but there was always some-
thing torn and something flimy and a hell of a lot of
skin and it drove him fucking crazy. She was only six-
teen for fuck sake.

"Thanks for coming to get me. I had to get out of
there." She pulled the door closed and leaned back in
her seat, running a hand through the soft, thick waves
of her hair.

Jesus Christ. It was better when she wore a ponytail.
And jeans. And big sweaters. Although the sweaters
were always hanging off to one side exposing the creamy
skin of her shoulder and the jeans hugged every curve
of her beautiful body.

Sweat beaded on his brow and he took a deep breath
and focused on the road, letting her words slowly sink
in as he got a grip of his out-of-fucking-control dick.
She was sixteen and the daughter of the underboss. He
was twenty-six and an enforcer, the lowest of the low.

"You're quiet." She looked over at him, her face soft
in the glow of the streetlights. She'd been drinking. He
knew her so well, he could tell how many drinks she'd
had by how many lines of worry had smoothed from her
beautiful face. Her mother's death still haunted her, but
nothing had affected her as much as finding out the
truth about her father. Now she lived in a postwar on
First Avenue with her maternal aunt, instead of the
big mansion in Tappan, New Jersey, where there were
guards patrolling the premises and her father could put
his foot down if she went out showing too much skin.

He couldn't answer her for the lust throbbing through
his veins. Something had changed when she turned six-
teen. His affection for the underboss's daughter had sud-
denly turned to desire when she climbed into his car one
day and he realized she wasn't a young girl any more.

"What are you listening to tonight?" She reached for

the radio and her shirt fell open revealing a pink lace bra. All his blood rushed downward, and the car veered wildly toward the curb. How the fuck was he going to get her home? Every inadvertent brush of her hand on his arm, every light touch on his shoulder, the scent of her perfume, and the heat of her body, so close and yet beyond his reach, all combined to create a torture worse than anything Cesare could have devised as part of Rocco's training to become an enforcer.

With his gaze fixed firmly on the road ahead, he shrugged. He didn't need to answer. She knew what would be on the radio. It was always tuned to the classic hits station—big band, Sinatra and the Rat Pack, jazz, and blues—because those were the songs she loved to sing.

"What happened?" he finally managed to get out.

"I don't want to talk about it." She leaned languid in the seat, arms over her head, legs apart, body swaying gently to the music. Rocco drew in a shuddering breath, forced his thoughts away from the beautiful girl beside him and back to the meal he'd had for dinner, the game he'd watched on TV, the last job he'd done for Cesare . . . anything but her.

"Your aunt okay with you being out this late?" Her aunt had become her guardian after she'd left the family home unable to deal with the fact that everything her father had given her had come from money he'd earned doing work for the mob—ironically, the same organization that paid for the car Rocco drove, the gas that fueled it, and the clothes he was wearing right now. Did she know he was part of the same organization? They never talked about what he did when he wasn't with her or how he came to work for her family, and she'd never told him why she'd left the family home. He knew only because her father had called him up the next day and

explained the situation. Then he'd asked Rocco for a favor. Protect her. Drive her anywhere she needed to go, anytime she called. She trusted Rocco, he said. And he trusted Rocco with her. It would be an arrangement outside Rocco's mandate as an enforcer. Cesare was not to know.

Even if he hadn't been tempted by the possibility of being owed a favor by the underboss, he would have said yes. He would do anything for her. It wasn't his first defiance of Cesare's rules. And it wouldn't be his last.

"Yeah. I told her a friend was picking me up. Things were getting out of hand."

His heart leaped like he'd been shot with adrenaline. "What the fuck happened? Did someone touch you?"

Her lips tightened and she looked away, her silence triggering his protective instincts. They were passing the park in Batsto so Rocco headed for the Warren Grove bombing entrance and parked the car in a shadowed area of the lot. This late at night, there was no one at the park although the lights kept vandalism to a minimum.

"Tell me." He turned off the car and stared at her in the silence.

"It's okay, Rocco. I'm okay." She opened the door and stepped outside.

Rocco drew in a ragged breath and tried to get a grip on the maelstrom of emotion that threatened to overwhelm him. Through a combination of torture, pain and deprivation, enforcers were taught to control their emotions. But when it came to Grace, Rocco couldn't contain them.

"Grace." He slammed open his door and rounded the car to where she was now leaning against the front bumper, looking out into the dark forest, the lights of the city twinkling in the distance. "If someone hurt you, I'll find him and—"

"Shhh." She put a finger to his lips. "No one hurt me. No one touched me. That's the point. I didn't want them to. I didn't want to dance with anyone or kiss anyone. I didn't want to fool around in one of the bedrooms like all my friends. I wanted you."

No. No. No. This wasn't happening. Not with the underboss's daughter ten years his junior, whose safety had been entrusted to him by her father. She might not understand, but in the Mafia hierarchy, he was nothing. Boss, Underboss, Consigliere, Capo, Soldier, Associate, and then outside, but beneath the structure, the enforcers. A necessary evil.

"You don't want me." He drew her fingers away but for the life of him, he couldn't let go.

"I think about you all the time." She pushed herself to sit up on the hood, licked her lips drawing his attention to the lush bow of her mouth. "No one knows more about me than you, Rocco." She leaned forward, put her hands on his waist and drew him forward between her parted legs. Her touch seared through his body straight to his cock, and his vision blurred.

"Grace . . ." His voice caught, broke.

"Do you think about me?" She looked up at him though those long, dusky lashes and he let out a groan. Cesare had beat him, so he would not feel—empathy, sympathy, guilt, desire, regret, longing, anger, fear, hate, love. He had to be ice, stone, cold and calculating to do the jobs no one else could do. But Grace had always been the chink in his armor. She was the crack that let the light shine through.

"No. I don't think about you." His words sounded unconvincing even to him. "Now stop this and I'll take you home."

"Liar." She pulled him closer until her arms were wrapped around his body and their hips were pressed

*together and her breasts were tight against his chest. "I
can feel you want me," she whispered, rocking gently
against an erection so hard it was beyond any pain Cesare had ever given him.*

*"I'm too old for you." He touched her, his hands on
her arms, his intent to push her away, and yet he couldn't
help but caress the softness of her skin, the narrow dip
of her waist, the sweet curve of her hips.*

"You're perfect for me."

*Everything Cesare had taught him about inner
strength and self-control fell away as his arms tightened
around her. She felt right, like he'd found something he
had never known was missing and in that moment he
knew he had been born to be hers and she was meant
to be his. And he knew something else. He would never
let her go.*

*"You're too young," he protested. "You should be
with a guy your age." Now that his hands were moving,
he couldn't stop. He slid them through the hair he'd
imagined holding so many times, tangled his fingers
through the silky softness.*

*"They aren't you, Rocco." She leaned up, slid her
arms around his shoulders and pulled him down until
their lips met.*

*And then he was lost, swept away in a tidal wave of
sensation. So soft. So sweet. So right. He hugged her to
his chest and kissed her until there was no breath left
in his body, and the world had narrowed to the girl in
his arms, the pounding of his heart, and the single most
beautiful moment of his entire wretched life.*

The pain receded and his vision cleared. He started,
jerked, coming fully to himself when the chains
clanked overhead. He tried to look over his shoulder to

see what the hell was going on. Once he established a rhythm, Clay never quit until Rocco passed out or went slack in the chains.

"What the fuck?"

"Your phone. You told me to stop if I ever heard Limp Bizkit's disastrous cover of "Faith.""

Fuck. It was Cesare.

"Bring it here."

Clay brought the phone over and used the quick release to free Rocco's wrists. He helped Rocco over to a bench by the wall and slid the phone into his partially bloodless hand. Always discrete, he left the room so Rocco could have privacy for the call.

"Cesare."

"I have a contract for you." Cesare didn't waste time with pleasantries and, as always, his gravelly voice made Rocco's stomach twist in a knot of hate. "Nunzio Mantini is in Vegas with his son. The don sent them to find out what the hell is going on with the Toscanis. They've only got two bodyguards with them. I want them gone. We have Luigi's permission for the hit."

Luigi Cavallo was the Gamboli family *consigliere,* a senior family advisor who was equal to the underboss in rank. His permission was the don's permission, and yet why would the don have sent Nunzio to Vegas to meet with the Toscanis if he didn't expect him to return? The Toscani situation had escalated to the point where the body count was sure to attract the feds, and no one wanted the feds sniffing around.

"They are having dinner with the Bianchi family before they leave," Cesare continued. "I'll call with the details. Do it then. The Bianchis are expendable."

"Don't tell me how to do my fucking job."

Fuck. Rocco rarely had any qualms about his contracts. The De Lucchi crew were usually only called upon to punish the most egregious of crimes or to send the most serious of messages, and their victims were almost always the worst of the worst, career criminals who had taken many lives. Nunzio Mantini would have whacked more than his fair share of men to achieve the position of underboss, but he had been a good, loving father to Grace, and as far as Rocco knew, he was loyal to the don. But it wasn't the right or wrong about whacking Nunzio that was tearing him up inside. It was what it would do to Grace. She had never gotten over her mother's brutal death. Losing her father and her brother would destroy her.

It would destroy him, because it would mean the end.

The end of hope.

The end of dreams.

The end of a future that didn't involve blood and heartache and pain.

But this was who he was. The monster Cesare had created. Grace had run from him once, no doubt she would run again. For the De Lucchi crew, every contract was do or die.

"I'll call you when it's done."

This time, he would cut her free forever.

"Hi Matthew. Is it lunch time already?" Grace kneeled down to hug six-year-old Matthew Jones on the floor of the Sunnyville Center for Kids, an orphanage and safe haven for neglected and abused children run by Father Seamus O'Brien. She had done her psychology internship at the center, counseling both children and caregivers as they sought to heal and empower the children and give them a fresh start in life.

Although the nonprofit did not have the funds to offer Grace a position after her internship finished, she stayed in contact with the kids by volunteering twice a week, helping out her roommate and bestie Olivia, who was one of the few permanent counselors on staff.

"I got out early because I was good in music class and didn't play with the drums." Matthew gave her a quick hug and backed away. After years of abuse, physical contact made him uncomfortable, but he had progressed during Grace's time with him from not even being able to hold hands with his caregivers to readily walking into her arms.

Olivia and Father Seamus joined them, and they chatted for a few minutes about the facility and programs. Tall and lean, with steel-gray hair and clear pale-blue eyes, Father Seamus favored jeans over formal attire and looked more like a model than a priest. He had opened the orphanage twenty-five years ago with an enormous bequest from a generous donor, but with so many children to help, and after so many years, the money had started to run out and he was now struggling to keep the center afloat.

Grace had been more than happy to offer her time as a volunteer after her internship. Not just to help Father Seamus and the kids, but because she wasn't ready to put her degree into practice. Every time she tried to fill in an application form, she felt like a fraud. How could she heal people when she couldn't even heal herself? How could she save people when she couldn't save the person who needed her most? She had been looking for something when she started her degree and she clearly hadn't found it.

"So, how was dinner with your dad on Friday night?" Olivia asked as they crossed the parking lot. "My weekend away with my old high school pals was a little bit crazy or I would have called."

Grace had met Olivia when she started her internship at the center and liked her right away for her openness and sense of humor, a direct contrast to the secretive world she had lived in until she left New York. Although gentle and caring with the children she worked with, Olivia had a wild side that she indulged with crazy weekend-long parties, high-risk sports, and an impulse-purchased motorcycle she parked on the front porch of the house they shared with friends, Ethan and Miguel.

"Rocco was there." She'd told Olivia about Rocco shortly after they met, describing him as an old boyfriend from New York who worked for her dad and was ten years older than her. They broke up, she'd said, after an incident that had been serious enough to cause her to leave New York. Even though as a woman Grace wasn't officially part of the Cosa Nostra, she was still bound by *omertà,* the code of silence that meant she couldn't reveal her ties to the mob on penalty of death. Her father had made that very clear to her on the night he had revealed the truth about his life.

"Rocco, the first-love, teenage-love, love-of-your-life, too-old-for-you, subject of the mysterious incident, ex-boyfriend from New York, who is the reason you haven't been able to have a stable relationship in six years Rocco?" Olivia pushed one of the many rogue curls from her mass of brown hair. She claimed she hadn't used a hairbrush since an incident when she was fifteen and her sister had brushed through her curls increasing their volume to such an extent her mother thought she'd stuck her finger in a light socket.

"Yes." She bit back a laugh. "That Rocco. I actually saw him at the funeral last Tuesday, but I thought—"

"You thought you wouldn't mention it to your best friend because . . . ?" Olivia pressed her lips together and glared, a look that came off as cute instead of fierce. Olivia was three inches shorter than Grace's 5'6" slim and petite where Grace was gently curved.

"I was processing it."

"Processing it." Olivia snorted a laugh. "That's psychology speak. Not best-friend speak. I might never forgive you."

"You will because you want to know what happened."

Olivia sighed and opened her car door. "Curiosity killed the psychologist. Okay. You're forgiven. Give me all the juicy details. And I mean all of them. What are the odds that you'd bump into him here in Vegas at a funeral of all places?"

"He worked for my dad, and the funeral was for my godfather's son, so I guess it isn't that remote a possibility. I just didn't know he was living in Vegas."

"Or hanging out in a cemetery," Olivia said when they were both in her car—a cherry red Ford Mustang that she'd bought with an inheritance from her grandmother. "I hope you didn't read anything into it—cemetery, death, tombstones—lots of symbolism going on there for you superstitious types."

"I'm not superstitious." She double-checked her seatbelt as Olivia pulled out of the parking stall. Olivia was an all-or-nothing kind of person, and when she was in her car, it was top speed all the way.

"Right. Not superstitious. When most people drop something on the sidewalk and bend down to pick it up seconds before a car runs a red light and drives right where they would have been walking, they think it is a fortunate coincidence. You think it's a sign."

Was that all it was? Bumping into Rocco in a cemetery was a fortunate coincidence? Maybe it was. Now that she knew it was totally over between them, she would be able to move on.

"So how was he?" Olivia asked as they peeled out of the parking lot.

"An ass."

"Well that makes it easy."

Grace sighed. "It would have been easy if he'd gained a lot of weight or lost all his hair, but he didn't. He looks even better now than he did before. If I didn't know him and saw him walking down the street, I'd probably throw myself at his feet and beg him to take me."

"So he was a devastatingly gorgeous ass?"

"Yes." Grace licked her lips. "But I don't totally blame him for his anger toward me. I left without saying good-bye after we'd effectively been together for eight years. It was just a horrific circumstance. I couldn't deal with all the chaos and insanity of his life, and one night it became too much so I ran away."

"How did you end it at the restaurant?" Olivia turned a sharp corner, and Grace's shoulder slammed against the glass.

"I told him to go to hell, and then I walked away."

Walked away. Ran away. The story of her life.

"Well, that's sounds pretty final." Olivia grinned. "I'd say you've got him out of your system. Time to move on with your life. I think you should bang Ethan. He's in love with you and I'm getting tired of sitting in the kitchen with him every night as he moans about how you don't notice him."

Grace's melancholy disappeared in a giggle. "What kind of counselor are you? What about the stages of grief? And there's no way I'm going to sleep with someone who lives in our house. Ethan's like a brother to me."

"There are no stages of grief when you don't see someone for six years and then he shows up and proves you were right to walk away in the first place," Olivia said. "The time for grieving is done. And as for Ethan, that dude is seriously hot. When you called from the re-cording studio last year and told me you'd found two guys to rent my two extra rooms, I wasn't expecting the Hemsworth brothers."

Grace laughed. "Miguel has dark hair, a hideous goatee, and he speaks with a Portuguese accent. He's looks and sounds nothing like a Hemsworth."

"Yeah, he does. The younger one." She screeched to a stop at a traffic light. "It's the bone structure. And that body . . . Take another look when you get home tonight. And the dark hair and eyes just make him look more mysterious."

"You can't lust after our roommates."

Olivia turned in to the parking lot of her favorite deli. "I can lust after whoever I want, and since I'm two months into the longest dry spell of my life, anything with two legs and a dick is looking pretty good."

"Well, then you should go hear Stormy Blu play next Tuesday night and you can stare at him to your heart's content. A friend of my dad's told me about a jazz club that was under new management. I gave the info to Ethan and he set up a gig. He said the club is well known and the gig might open some doors for them. I just hope Sunita doesn't mess things up."

"Why don't you sing?" Olivia suggested. "If this is a big opportunity, it will kill Ethan if Sunita fucks it up like she's done with their last few gigs."

"Get your body to Andy's AutoBody. Why fix your car anywhere else?" Grace sang the tune of her most recent jingle, and Olivia snorted a laugh.

"Not quite what I was thinking. How about the Sinatra songs you sing in the shower that make us all freeze in the kitchen in the morning because your voice is so amazing?"

"Everything sounds better when it's wetter," Grace sang softly, embarrassed at the thought she'd been overheard in the shower.

"What jingle is that?" Olivia turned to grab her purse from the back seat.

"Bert's Bathroom Fixtures. They couldn't come up with a catchy jingle that included the name Bert."

She pushed open her door, and Olivia put a gentle hand on her arm, holding her back.

"Don't you want to sing songs instead of two-line jingles? See the audience that is spellbound by your performance?"

"I don't sing on stage. Not since I left New York." Grace had never discussed her shattered dream of becoming a singer with Olivia, and her throat tightened in anticipation of Olivia's next question. Olivia wasn't the type of person to let something like this go.

"Why?"

Grace shrugged as she exited the vehicle, trying to put some distance between them. "Bad memories, mostly to do with Rocco."

"Well, you've dealt with that issue," Olivia said firmly. "You've finally put him to bed, and it's time to move on. Why don't you mark that occasion by doing something that empowers you? Take back your voice. Get on that stage just once and see how it feels."

Grace rounded the car and stood for a moment staring at her reflection in the plate glass-window of the deli. Her pulse kicked up a notch at the possibility of singing again—really singing, but the glare of reality brought it down.

"I can't." Her hand flew to her cheek. "The scar. Remember."

Olivia's face softened, and she closed the distance between them. "I know when you look in the mirror it's all you see, but your friends see you, Grace. Not the scar. Really, it's barely visible, and sometimes it just looks like light shining a different way on your cheek." Her lips curled into a smile. "I think it's kind of sexy, actually, like you're a little bad ass."

"I'm bad ass," she said deadpanning.

"Exactly." Olivia, who totally was badass, grinned. "Now, let's go get a badass lunch before I die of hunger, and I'll convince you to sing on stage by ordering an extra-large plate of your favorite nachos."

"Does this kind of manipulation actually work with your clients?" Grace asked as she pushed open the deli door. There was no way she was falling for Olivia's tricks. She'd taken the same courses, read the same textbooks, attended the same lectures. She understood about empowerment, and reclaiming the self after trauma. But she had only just decided to move on. Singing again after six years was too big a step.

"Only the ones with psychological issues."

"So that would be all of them."

Olivia laughed. "All of them, plus one."

Five days after his disastrous encounter with Grace, Rocco returned to the Stardust at Luca's request.

"Why the fuck do you need me here?" He pulled up a chair beside Mike at the same table where Danny had learned a lesson in not fucking with the mob, and glared at Luca who had arranged the meet.

He usually avoided going to jazz clubs. Invariably, the band would play Sinatra and the Golden Oldies that Grace loved to sing in his car, and the fucking memories were not something he wanted to relive.

"Danny just got out of the hospital and I wanted to make sure he understood how this new operation was going to work. I thought the new owner should be in attendance so, of course, I called you." Luca gave him a smug smile, and Rocco had an urge to punch that grin away. Luca smiled too much for a Mafia capo. Ever since he'd married Gabrielle, Luca had become a changed man. Rocco wasn't sure if it was for the better. No one wanted to be around someone who was fucking happy all the time, and it had become exponentially worse after he announced Gabrielle was pregnant.

Rocco couldn't imagine being married once, much less twice, and as for kids, he had absolutely no desire to involve anyone in his fucked-up life.

"What the fuck are you talking about?" Rocco pulled out his cigarettes. "You took over the business from Danny. My involvement was limited to making sure he learned not to screw us over."

Luca waved a waitress over and ordered drinks over the sounds of dueling pianos up front. "I can't manage another business," he said after the waitress left. "I've got two restaurants and the nightclub, a new wife, a little boy, and a baby on the way. Not to mention my mother across the street and the hordes of family in the city. I don't have time. I've signed it over to you in payment for your last few contracts."

"Jesus Christ. I'm not a businessman." Rocco leaned back in his chair and surveyed the club. He hadn't had a chance to really look around last week, but the Stardust, with its Rat Pack prints on the walls, shadowy corners, and plush purple booths, had a lot of character. A dark little cave, down two flights of stairs off the Strip, the club was the kind of place where a man could kick back, drink out of a mug, and forget about life while listening to whatever band was sweating away on the small stage up front. It was raw and filled with people who were there for the music and not the booze.

"You don't have to do anything," Luca said. "Danny will manage it, and you can hire people to do the rest."

He pulled a bundle of papers from his jacket pocket. "You just need to sign on the dotted line."

Although Rocco couldn't admit it, the idea of doing something that didn't involve violence was tempting. He didn't enjoy breaking legs and fingers, whacking guys or fitting them with cement shoes so they could have a permanent swim in Lake Mead. He did those things because it was his job, because he had no choice. Cesare had raised him to become an enforcer, and after he'd taken his first life, there was no going back. Only his decision to align himself with Nico had slowed his descent into darkness.

When Nico split the Toscani family and challenged Tony's claim to succession, Rocco, as the De Lucchi crew representative in Vegas, was forced to make a choice, and he'd chosen Nico. He admired Nico's determination to keep the family out of the drug trade and the sheer fucking balls it took to set up a faction in the face of fierce opposition. Nico wasn't interested in violence for the sake of violence like his cousin Tony, who would kill a man for looking the wrong way. When Nico or his capos called Rocco with a job, the target deserved what was coming to him. And that kind of work sat easier on Rocco's conscience than the mindless, gratuitous violence that had characterized his life with Cesare and men like Tony who shared Cesare's views.

The only downside to working closely with Nico's crew was all the fucking socializing. Nico's guys—and Luca in particular—liked to sit around, have a few drinks, and talk. And talk. And talk.

"No." He shoved the papers across the table. "It's not what I do."

"Life is short." Luca pushed the papers back. "You have to grab every opportunity that comes your way, and this, my friend, is an opportunity. Just look around you.

It's Thursday night and every seat is filled. This place has earning potential, atmosphere, and tonight I hear there's going to be a great band."

Damn Luca. Getting him worked up over something he couldn't fucking have. He was already in a bad mood after seeing Grace. What the fuck was wrong with him? Why did he keep seeking her out only to fuck things up even worse than he'd done before? He was torturing them both with his inability to stay away because once he whacked her family, those stolen moments would be just another memory.

"How about you pay me in cash and dump your fucking club on someone else?"

Rocco didn't actually need the money. He had his Harley-Davidson motorcycle and a place to sleep at night. Other than food and drink, he didn't have any other expenses. No house. No mortgage. No girlfriend needing expensive gifts. No trips to Hawaii to roast in the sun. He was paid in cash for every contract, and if he wasn't on a job, he was either at church praying for redemption or hanging out in the Toscani family clubhouse drinking away the pain of knowing redemption would never come.

"Because you're the best man for the job," Luca said. "No one knows this kind of music better than you. We didn't name you Frankie 'cause you were singing Death Metal that night we found you pissed out of your mind in the restroom of that fancy club."

Mike snickered, his smile fading when Rocco gave him a glare.

"What the fuck am I going to do with a jazz club?" Rocco tapped a cigarette out of the pack. He was down to three a day, not because he cared whether he lived or died, but because Gabrielle and the guys were constantly on his case to quit and he was tired of listening to them moan.

"I'm sorry. You can't smoke in here, sir." The waitress put down her tray and handed him a tumbler of whiskey, nodding in the direction of a bouncer who was heading over to their table.

"Hell, there isn't anywhere a man can smoke anymore." Rocco stared at the bouncer until the fucker backed off. Damn. With Grace constantly on his mind, and in the kind of place he had always imagined her singing, he needed his nicotine fix more than ever.

"Nothing has changed in six years, Rocco. Smoking is still addictive. It still causes cancer. And you are still going to kill yourself if you don't stop."

"Why the fuck do you care?"

"I never stopped caring."

She had never stopped caring. And he never stopped being a fucking ass.

He closed his eyes and imagined her gentle curves, her thick long hair, the swell of her hips, and the sound of her voice as she sang in the car every day when he drove her to high school, telling himself over and over he was too old and too fucked up and too tainted by the violence of their world to be messing with the sweet beautiful innocence of Grace.

It was because of her that he'd been given the nickname, Frankie. He'd gotten stone cold drunk only once since moving to Vegas, and that was because Luca had dragged him out to a club one night on the pretense of holding a meeting, much as he had done now, and the singer had looked and sounded so much like Grace that he thought his heart would fucking break. He'd poured a bottle of whiskey down his throat to numb the pain, and Luca had caught him singing Sinatra tunes in the restroom. He had never lived it down.

"So?" Luca persisted. "What do you think?"

Fuck. He couldn't deal with this. Own a jazz club and be reminded of Grace every fucking night?

"Give it to someone else." He finished his drink and walked out of the bar as the band started to play "The Impossible Dream" behind him.

FOUR

Mike couldn't believe the hotness of the vocalist on stage at the Stardust. All that thick, red hair, big tits, lush curves, and the bright orange dress that was so short it was more than a tease . . . He wouldn't mind her in his bed for a night. Too bad about the voice. She sounded like a dog with a cold.

He looked over at Mr. Rizzoli talking with Danny at the other table. What the fuck was that about? Mr. Rizzoli was up to something tonight, and he was pretty damn sure it had to do with the papers he'd offered Frankie. He hadn't seemed put out when Frankie stormed out of the club. Instead he'd just tucked the papers away, ordered another drink, and called Danny over for a meeting. Since Frankie had gone, Mike's job was to look out for Mr. Rizzoli and make sure Danny didn't get any ideas. Desperate men did desperate things, although with two casts and a face full of bandages, he didn't think Danny would be able to do much.

The vocalist left the stage and teetered through the crowd on her high heels. Mike held his breath, hoping she'd notice him, but she walked right past him and stopped in front of a dude in a dark suit. No big deal. She wasn't really his type. He liked blondes, small and petite, women with soft voices and gentle hands. He liked women who made him feel like a man, and who reminded him of his first love, Melinda, and the good times they'd had until his best friend offered to drive her home from a high school party and their car had gone over the side of a cliff.

Losing them both, and finding out they'd been sleeping together behind his back, had changed the course of his life. Unable to focus on what had been a promising boxing career, he'd started throwing fights in exchange for payouts from the mob, and eventually joined Luca's crew as an associate and then as a made man. It wasn't the life he'd dreamed about, but he liked hanging with the crew and using his skills to protect the bosses or rough people up when they tried to cheat the mob. He liked the prestige of being a made man, and the connections and money that came with it. With Luca's backing, he'd been able to set up a chain of boxing gyms so he could help others succeed where he'd failed.

When she got nothing more than a lukewarm smile from the man in the suit, the vocalist moved on, butchering a slow, stripped-down version of "Estate," an Italian song made famous by the bossa nova icon, João Gilberto. Gah. Mike wished Luca would finish up, too. He really wasn't much of a jazz man. He preferred the heavy beats of bands like Rammstein that could get his heart pumping when he was working out at his gym.

He felt a prickle of awareness only seconds before he caught a woman watching him from the bar. Long, blonde hair tumbled down her back in a riot of curls. She was small and slim with a waist he could swear he would be able to get his hands around, sweetly curved hips, snugly outlined in a tight, black dress, and the rack . . . Whoa. Why hadn't he noticed that bombshell walking in the door? It was like someone had taken his pornographic fantasy and made it real.

Her eyes widened when he caught her watching, and he could have sworn a blush rose up in her cheeks. She dropped her gaze, but seconds later her lashes fluttered and she looked at him again. He felt a jolt of heat in his groin at the obvious invitation.

"Gonna grab a drink," he called over to Luca. He waited for a nod of approval and made his way to the bar, wishing he'd worn something other than a worn pair of jeans and a T-shirt, although the T-shirt did show off his biceps and abs, tight and hard after the daily work-outs that kept him in shape. He might have failed as a professional boxer but that didn't mean he quit the sport. There was a lot of money to be made in underground fights, even when he didn't rig them.

"Is this seat taken?" He gestured to the conveniently empty seat beside the woman and was delighted when she licked her lips and smiled.

"Now it is."

She had soft, sultry voice, smooth and warm that brought to mind hot sticky nights in the Nevada heat, sweaty sheets, and sexy moans. He settled in beside her and flagged the bartender down for a drink. "You want anything?"

"Whatever you're drinking."

He glanced down and saw an empty highball glass in front of her, when he would have expected some kind of girly drink with an umbrella. A woman after his own heart.

"You like jazz?" she said after he ordered their drinks.

"Not really my thing. I came with friends."

"I saw you." Leaning closer, she traced a long, pink

fingernail over the back of his hand sending all the right messages to the wrong part of his body. "You were kind of hard to miss with all those muscles. Are you a fighter or a bodybuilder or something like that?"

"Yeah." A smile spread across his face and his chest puffed out of its own accord. "I own a chain of boxing gyms called Mike's Gyms. I've got three in the city, and I'm gonna open a fourth."

"I know them." A smile spread across her fucking beautiful face. "You've got a picture of Popeye on the sign outside the one in Centennial Hills."

Now didn't that just make his day. "You got a name, sweetheart?"

"Tiffany."

Pretty name for a pretty girl. And smart, too. And from the looks of her she liked to stay in shape, just like him.

"You here alone?" He gave a quick look around for dudes who might take offense to him hitting on Tiffany, but no one was paying them any attention.

"Yes. I just got off work. I was supposed to meet a friend, but she had an emergency at home and had to bail."

"That's too bad. Pretty girl like you shouldn't be spending the evening alone."

She looked up at him through her thick golden lashes. "I'm not alone now."

Holy shit. She was coming on to him. Play it cool. Play it cool. "I'll keep you company as long as you like."

"I'm not really into jazz either," she said. "I just came here because of my friend. Do you want to go someplace else? Maybe grab a bite to eat. I know a nice little Italian restaurant nearby."

Mike's heart did a little skip and he looked over his shoulder to see Mr. Rizzoli shaking Danny's good hand.

Thank fuck. He was done with the meeting and Mike was free. "Are you Italian?"

"On my father's side."

"I'm Italian, too," he said proudly. "Both my parents. And their parents before them, and back generations."

A beautiful smile spread across her face. "My father would love you. He's always wanted me to go out with an Italian guy."

Was she thinking of him as more than just a one-night hook-up? Mike didn't dare hope. A beautiful girl like her had to have guys chasing after her all the time. And yet, he was a good-looking guy. Sure he was big, but it was almost all muscle. Women liked muscles. They liked their men to be strong. No one in the Toscani crime family was stronger than him except maybe Frankie, but that dude was in a bad-ass class of his own.

"I'm not going to say no to an Italian meal with a beautiful woman." Swallowing hard, he gave a little push to see how far this might go. "Maybe afterwards . . ."

Tiffany wound her cool hand around his bicep. "Could we go to your place?"

Hell yes! This night was just getting better and better.

"Sure. I've got two dogs, though. Don't know if you're a dog lover. They're big, but they're friendly."

"I love dogs!" Her eyes sparkled. "My roommate has a rescue puppy. He's so cute. Maybe you could come and see him some time."

For a moment Mike was lost for words. She was perfect. Everything about her was fucking perfect. He had never imagined the perfect woman existed and there she was sitting beside him wanting to eat Italian food, go back to his place, and meet his dogs. "Let's go." He slid off his stool and held out his arm to help her.

Tiffany curled her hand around his bicep as they left the bar. "It will be nice to be with a guy who's so strong.

You make me feel safe. No one's going to bother me when I'm with a guy like you."

His smile faded and his protective instincts surged to the fore. "Is someone bothering you?"

She hesitated for the briefest of moments and then shook her head, but Mike had a feeling she was just being shy. No matter. He would convince her to talk and then he would make sure she never felt unsafe again.

He checked in with Mr. Rizzoli to make sure he was good to go, then he puffed out his chest and escorted the beautiful bombshell out of the bar. Imagine. Him with a woman like this.

It was almost too good to be true.

FIVE

Grace woke up with the worst hangover of her life.

She lay in bed willing the light to disappear, the traffic to still and Ethan to stop pounding on her bedroom door.

"Your phone has been buzzing," he shouted. "If you're decent, I can bring it in."

Was she decent? A quick check revealed she was more than decent. She'd fallen asleep in her clothes after letting Ethan and Miguel drag her out to a party the previous night. "Okay."

Ethan staggered in looking as bad as she felt, which for him took his handsomeness down to a nine point five out of ten. Tall and blond with a thick beard, pale blue eyes and a ripped muscular body, Ethan looked nothing like a jazz singer and everything like the missing Hemsworth brother Olivia insisted he was.

"Glad you made it to the party?" he asked, handing her the phone. "Wednesday is the new Thursday. Miguel and I plan to go out every Wednesday night so if you want to come again next week . . ."

"This is not the best time to ask." She checked the

screen for messages and groaned. "Oh my God. I've got a last-minute gig this afternoon, and I can barely talk." Jingle singing was a niche skill and she usually got her work through the production companies that hired talent for radio, movies, and television. For the most part, they were totally disorganized and more often than not she was called in at the last minute when someone was up against a deadline. Grace didn't mind the last-minute work, but delivering three to five words in a short and punchy way with real power was inordinately more difficult after spending a night drinking too much and shouting over loud music.

"You want me to make you some tea with honey?"

She pushed up on one elbow and raised her eyebrow. "You're offering to make me tea? Now I'm suspicious."

"Just looking out for our new vocalist." He gave her a hopeful look. "I don't want you to strain your voice before those talent scouts see us at the Stardust next Tuesday night."

Grace fell back on the bed. "I gave you the referral. I wasn't volunteering to sing."

"I'm worried Sunita won't show."

"I know she hasn't been there for you recently, but I'm sure she won't let you down." Grace patted his hand. "You told her that it's a well-known club, didn't you? That it could be the break you guys have been waiting for?"

"Yeah." Ethan sighed. "Even when she does show up now, though, her voice isn't the same. She's lost her range. I think it's from all the smoking. And she's usually high and forgets the lyrics. I auditioned three new singers this week and none of them were a good fit. But you . . ."

"No, Ethan."

"With your voice and Miguel's arrangements, and

maybe some of the songs I've written, the band could really go places, maybe even get a recording contract."

Uncharacteristically irritated by the pleading note in his voice, Grace threw back the covers and slid out of bed. "Look at my face, Ethan. Can you see this face on an album cover? On a video? On a promo poster? On stage? No one wants to see a scarred singer."

Guilt flickered across his face. "You can barely see it. The only time I ever notice it is when you bring it up."

"That's because you're my friend." She grabbed her bathrobe from the floor.

"You could wear a mask," he suggested. "Something mysterious. It would make us stand out from the crowd."

"Now you're getting desperate."

"Grace." Ethan groaned. "I am desperate. If she doesn't show or worse if she shows up and messes up, I don't know what I'll do. We're getting a bad reputation, and the jazz community in the city isn't that big."

"Cancel the gig then. Don't book anything until you get a new singer."

"I already told the guy we'd be there. I thought for sure one of the women I auditioned would work out, but none of them were very good."

"Then you'd better sit on Sunita's doorstep and keep her drug-dealer boyfriend away." She turned and gave him a sympathetic hug. "Olivia and I will come out to support you guys. Even if you have to go instrumental, we'll be there to cheer you on."

He sighed and brushed his lips over her forehead, the barest peck, but after what Olivia had told her, that small show of affection made her tense up inside.

"I'll get you that tea," he said quickly, moving away.

Grace followed him to the door. "You'd make someone a pretty good boyfriend. Why are you single, again?"

"Just waiting for the right girl to come along, and my

best chance of meeting her is if I'm in a band with an amazing vocalist who will draw crowds of people to come and see us."

"Ah. The truth comes out." She laughed despite herself. "You want me to sing so you can meet women because your charm and extreme good looks are just not working for you."

Ethan smiled, and Grace wondered why she never had taken that next step with him. They had a lot in common, an easy friendship, and there was definitely an attraction. Last night they'd danced together for hours, and she'd almost given into temptation when his lips brushed over her cheek. But then Rocco's face had flashed in her mind, and all she could think about was him. His touch. His scent. The heat of his body when he had pinned her to the wall. The deep voice that made her melt inside. Now that she'd seen Rocco again, moving on wasn't going to be as easy as she'd thought.

By noon she was in the studio and ready to record. It was a union job so she didn't have to worry about getting paid, which often happened with non-union jobs. She chatted briefly with the other session singer, before they reviewed the script and discussed phrasing, tone color, cut-offs, and glottal starts for vowels. Her voice was still rough from last night and she did a few extra warm up exercises with her partner before they let the producer know they were ready to go.

They had gone through a few takes of a catchy craft beer jingle when she noticed movement in the control room though the glass of the vocal booth. As she punched out the brand name with a long trill, her eyes focused on the newcomer who was shaking hands with the producer.

Rocco.

A thrill of excitement shot through her body and

suddenly she was sixteen again, and her breathtakingly gorgeous twenty-six-year-old boyfriend was waiting for her after school, leaning against an ancient black T-bird in a black leather jacket. What the hell was he doing here? And how had he found her?

Grace's tone wavered and she signaled that she needed a break.

"You okay?" her partner asked.

"Yeah. I just need . . . some water." She took a deep breath to calm her nerves and poured a glass of water. If she focused on her session partner, instead of the producer and audio engineer, she wouldn't see Rocco standing behind the glass with his arms folded, legs apart, dominating the control room with the force of his presence alone.

"There's no beer like Millcreek beer night, noon and morning . . ."

They did ten takes until the producer was happy with the jingle that seemed to advocate twenty-four- hour drinking. Grace quickly filled in the paperwork the union had sent her and took it to the control room to get it signed.

"Great job." The producer scrawled his name on the document. "Keep that up and we'll be requesting you for some national slots."

"That would be great." Her session partner had earned $12,000 from a single thirteen-week run of a national spot, more than enough money to keep her going for months if her other contracts dried up.

Once the paperwork was done, she glanced over at Rocco, standing in the corner like he had every right to be there. "Are you here . . . ?"

"To see you." He nodded at the producer. "Bob."

"Any time." The producer swallowed hard and dabbed at the sweat on his forehead with the back of his sleeve. "Give my regards to Luca."

"Will do." With a firm hand on Grace's lower back, Rocco guided her out of the studio she could walk through in her sleep.

"He knows Luca?" she asked as they walked to the elevator.

"He owes Luca money and he hadn't paid the *vig*. Now that he's done me a favor, he owes slightly less money and he gets to keep all his fingers." He pushed the button on the elevator and she was momentarily at a loss for words. "Was that a joke?"

"No."

"Oh." Her heart thudded in her chest and she pushed away the mental image of Rocco chopping off the producer's fingers with his knife. "So, what did you think?"

"I'd buy the beer."

Her lips quirked at the corners. Rocco had never been one to mince words. "You like pale ale?"

"Your voice. I felt it in here." He thudded his chest, and her amusement faded when she remembered their altercation on Friday night at the restaurant.

"Nice to know you can still feel."

"I'm not a monster, Grace." The elevator door slid open and they stepped inside.

Grace turned her head as the doors slid closed and deliberately brushed her hair away from the scar. "That's not how it looked that night at Newton Creek."

There. She'd said it. Put it out in the open. He had killed someone in front of her, and she would never be able to erase the image from her mind, never be able to accept that the man she loved could cross that line.

"It was you or him. I chose you. He was far from an innocent man."

"Don't." She held up a warning hand. It was hard enough to accept he could take a life; she didn't want to know he had done it for her. "That doesn't make it right."

Seeing him again made her realize that she had never truly healed from any of the experiences that had defined her life—her mother dying in her arms, discovering her father was in the mob, Cesare kidnapping and assaulting her and holding her hostage at knife point until Rocco did as he commanded. She still had nightmares of blades slicing through her body, still felt her mother's blood warm in her hands, still woke to see Rocco's face, twisted in anger and fear and helpless despair.

He shuddered, closed his eyes. "Nothing about this world is right. And if I'd had a choice—"

"There is always a choice," she said bitterly, cutting him off.

"You mean run away? That choice would have meant my death and yours. You know that."

She did know that. There was no running from the mob. No hiding. Once you became a made man there were very few circumstances in which you would be allowed to leave. Fewer still for a member of the De Lucchi crew. The enforcers saw too much, knew too much, had done too much.

"How did you find me?"

He shrugged and she knew she'd never get an answer. Not that she needed one. The Mafia owned this town.

"Why are you here?"

Rocco pushed the stop button and the elevator jerked to a halt. "I want . . ."

"Yes?"

"I thought you lied to me." He stroked a thick finger along her jaw, sending delicious tingles through her body. "I couldn't handle the thought of you with Benito."

"I've never lied to you, Rocco." She looked up at his handsome face and had a sudden urge to touch all his scars, run her fingers along his stubble, kiss his cheeks, his jaw, his sensual lips. She wanted to touch him, taste him again, relive the past that she knew should stay in the past. It was impossible not to be attracted to him. He oozed charisma and sex appeal. They had formed a connection fourteen years ago and time had not diminished his pull in the least.

"I can't handle the thought of you with anyone." He cupped her jaw, tilted her face so she stared into his beautiful dark eyes flecked with gold. The heat of his hand made her knees feel weak, and she had to remind herself that she had a new life now. One that was free of the mob and the drama that went with it. He was part of a world that had almost destroyed her, and the best thing she could do for herself right now was shut this down.

"What do you want?"

Rocco had never been a big talker, but he seemed to be struggling to express himself, almost as if he were overwhelmed with emotion, which was pretty much how she felt now.

"Gracie . . ."

She almost melted at the nickname he had used for her when they were together, and the sound on his lips brought back memories of hot, sweaty nights, his big hard body covering hers, whispers in the dark, gentle hands, soft lips, and his thick, hard cock. He had introduced her to sex as he introduced her to so many things: gently, softly, his entire focus on her pleasure until she was ready to fly.

"You're the only person who ever called me Gracie," she murmured softly, trapping his hand against her cheek with her palm. "I missed hearing it."

His growl of warning sent awareness sizzling through her, ripping the breath from her lungs. His gaze dropped, hot and hungry, to her lips as if he knew just what she was thinking.

"Okay." She let out a breath, tried to take control of

the situation. "How about we start again. Hi, Rocco. Nice to see you. I missed you." The last two words dropped from her lips before she could catch them, and her body moved almost of its own accord, closing the distance between them until they collided, mouths crashing together in a savage kiss.

His hands tangled in her hair, fisting the soft strands, pulling her roughly toward him. And then they were one again. Teeth and lips and tongues and breath reforming the connection they had lost six years ago. His kiss was everything, her world, her life, the beat of her heart, the rise and fall of her lungs, nectar for her soul. His tongue pushed through the barrier of her lips and she took him in, devoured him, hands fisting his shirt, pulling him close.

Out. Of. Control.

He groaned into her mouth, pressed his hard, lean body against her, pinning her against the wall of the elevator until every inch of him was pressed against every inch of her.

This close she could smell the whiskey on his breath, the hint of nicotine, and an undercurrent of something wild. He felt like he was made to fit against her, like she had finally been made whole.

"Rocco," she whispered when they finally came up for air, chests heaving, hands roaming, hips grinding.

"Don't talk." His hand slipped from her hair to cup her jaw, holding her still as he ravished her mouth, drinking her down as if he were dying of thirst. Her head spun, and she couldn't remember if she needed to breathe or why the red light in the elevator was flashing or if her legs needed to do something except wobble like jelly.

"Arms around my neck, *dolcezza*."

She slid her arms over his shoulders, clinging to him, pressing her body into his heat. He was so strong.

So big. So hot. His muscles so hard. He held her effort-lessly, kissed her desperately. She had never felt their age difference as she did now, but he was just so much more than the men her age, so much man.

For the first time in six years, she felt alive. Rocco was here. She could smell him, touch him, taste him. All the things she had imagined since she left, she could have right here, right now, and God, she wanted them all. Rocco's lips, Rocco's mouth, Rocco's tongue, all the beauty of his face looking down at her, the sweetness of the whiskey when he kissed her, the warmth of his breath, the softness of his tongue as he explored her mouth. It was like the first time all over again.

She wanted him.

She wanted a bit of the dirty and selfish bastard that he was, and he was happy to oblige. Catching her slim wrists, he pinned her hands to the wall above her head with one hand and fisted her hair with the other.

"You want this?"

"Yes," she said, without hesitation.

He took her mouth again, rough and hard. Electric-ity filled the space between them and he felt something snap into place—a connection—the bond he'd felt the first time they met.

Fuck. He hadn't expected that. He hadn't expected any of this. All he knew was that he had to see her one last time, had to try and end things in a way that would allow them both to move on after he did the one thing that would make her hate him forever.

His hand slid down her body, and he squeezed her breast so hard she made a soft noise in her throat.

It was the sound that did it.

Soft. Willing. Open.

Grace had always been soft. Sweet. Although she liked her sex rough, he had never been as rough as he knew he would be if he took her now. He was unmoored, lost in a sea of emotion, caught between desire and the need to let her go.

And suddenly it felt wrong. His thoughts felt wrong. This. Felt. Wrong.

But she wanted it, wanted this, wanted him. For these few moments, he could have her the way he had imagined every night for the last six years: in his arms, giving herself to him, as if that one terrible night at Newton Creek hadn't happened. He could take what she offered and then push her away. By the time he fulfilled his contract, their connection would be broken.

Resolved, he slid his hand between them and yanked up her dress. "You ready for me?"

"Why don't you find out?" She nipped his bottom lip, and his cock, already hard and aching, stood to fucking attention. Grace had always liked to tease.

A growl rose up through his throat as he shoved aside her panties and slicked a thick finger through her folds. "Dirty girl. You're soaked."

"And you're hard." She ground her hips against his erection and he almost came right then. His Grace had never been sexually aggressive and it fucking turned him on.

"Is this what you want?" His words came out harsher than he intended. "You want me to fuck you in your pretty dress up against this wall in an elevator where someone might see us? You want me to tear off those panties and shove my cock inside you so deep you forget your own name?"

"I want you." She nuzzled his neck. "Any way I can have you."

Fuck. No. Bold, aggressive Grace he could handle.

Soft, sweet Grace he could not. He wanted slapping and swearing and biting and scratching. He wanted her anger and her hatred. He wanted to suffer for the choices he had to make. He wanted passion, but more than that he wanted pain. He wanted her to make it easy for him to hurt her and walk away.

He didn't want to be reminded of Grace the way she had been before that night at Newton Creek when he ripped away the veil of her innocence and destroyed their bond.

"Fight me," he murmured as he palmed her breast in his hand through the thin fabric of her shirt.

"I don't want to fight you." She bucked against him, grinding her hips against his. "I'm not saying no, Rocco. I'm saying yes."

He nipped her collarbone, ran his tongue down her neck, tasting the familiar sweetness of her skin. When she shuddered in a breath, he moved lower, feathering kisses over the crescents of her breasts, tugging the filmy fabric down so he could pop a rosy nipple from beneath her pink bra.

Pink. Not red. Or black. No four inch heels and skin-tight, barely-there clothes that screamed "fifty for a hand job, eighty for oral" that would make it easy for him to take what he wanted without even the smallest emotion flickering in his chest.

Grace had never dressed in slutty clothes. Even though she could have pulled off any look, she always wore flirty little dresses or tiny cut-off shorts with tank tops and loose sweaters. She'd looked slightly hip, a little chic and always very sexy but in a teasing, not a revealing, kind of way. Her clothes hinted at the treasures underneath, but only one man could claim her bounty.

His hand hovered over the edge of her dress, muscles tightening as he prepared to tear the fine fabric and fully expose her breast for his viewing pleasure, leaving her to deal with the consequences when the elevator doors opened.

She whimpered softly, arched her back, willingly offered her breasts into his hands. Trusting. So trusting.

Hail Mary, full of Grace!

Christ. The last thing he wanted in his head when he was about to bury himself in the woman who had ripped out his heart, and walked away from eight years of memories without even a fucking good-bye was the goddam fucking Ave Maria. That was what he got for going to confession every two weeks to confess his sins to a mob-friendly priest.

He released her hands and drove his fingers into her hair, yanking her head back so hard her soft, sensual lips formed an "O" of surprise. He was going to bruise those lips with his kisses, mark the slender column of her throat with sharp nips of his teeth.

Blessed art thou amongst women

His mind skipped over some words, homing in on what it appeared to think were the relevant parts of the prayer, reminding him that she was a woman—a young woman—and he was bigger and stronger and older and that he could very easily harm her if he didn't take care.

Well fuck that. His body was tight and primed and ready to take her, and his stupid conscience could take a back seat on this ride.

He was going to yank her dress up to her waist, tear her panties away, and bury himself deep in her hot, wet cunt. He would fuck her hard and make her come screaming his name. And then he would leave her the way she'd left him and she would know how it felt to be betrayed by the only person who had ever meant anything in your life.

Except she'd only been a girl and he'd been a man. A man she had trusted with her body and her heart. A man she didn't know was a monster.

Holy Mary, Mother of God,
Pray for us sinners

Fuck. Fuck. Fuck. He couldn't do this to her. He couldn't take her like this in a public elevator with her pretty dress hiked around her waist while she looked up at him with those beautiful caramel-colored eyes like he was a fucking dream come true.

He was no fucking dream.

He was nightmare. And he had lied to her. He was a monster. The worst of men.

"I can't do this." He released her, unwound her body from his, and lowered her to the ground.

"What?" Dazed, she took a step toward him, and he shook his head.

"No, *dolcezza*. I can't do this to you."

"No?" Her cheeks flamed red, and her hand flew to her cheek, covering her scar. He knew what she was thinking, but he was beyond words, unable to assure her that it had nothing to do with the scar on her face and everything to do with the scar on his heart.

He hit the button and the elevator lurched to a start. Thank god it was a small building and no one had called maintenance about the stalled elevator. He gestured to the dress he had rumpled. "Fix yourself up."

She stared at him, stunned, making no move to cover the part of her breast that he exposed. The sight of her so disheveled and confused, so pale and beautiful in the hard fluorescent light of the dingy elevator hammered home the rightness of what he'd done. She didn't belong here. And not with him.

"Gracie," he said softly, pointing because he didn't trust himself to touch her again. "Fix your dress."

Her hand shook as she straightened her clothes, but she didn't look up, keeping her head tipped to the side, resting in her hand.

"I'll walk you to your car." He reached for her, and she slapped him away, fire replacing the confusion in her eyes in a heartbeat. And fuck. Didn't that just make him want her all over again.

"Get away from me."

The elevator doors slid open and she walked out into the lobby.

"Grace. I didn't want—"

"I don't want anything from you." She pulled open the front door.

And then she was gone.

SIX

"Whoo hoo. Hot babe alert!" Ethan turned down the volume on the TV and ogled Grace as she walked into the living room where he was spread out on the couch with his golden lab, Trevor.

"Too much? I'm having dinner with my dad and my brother and my dad's friends. They're leaving tomorrow, and it's my last chance to see them." She smoothed down the ethnic floral boho dress, black with red, pink, and green flowers and a deep V neckline. She'd paired it with black ankle boots and an oversized fringed bag.

"You might want to rethink the boots," Miguel piped up from the kitchen where he and Olivia were making dinner. "They scream 'fuck me.' Not sure if that's the message you want to be sending when you're out with your dad and brother."

"What's wrong with you?" Olivia gave him a swat with her tea towel. "They are perfectly respectable. Fuck me boots are white, or covered in laces and buckles, or they are black and shiny and go up to mid-thigh . . ."

"You got a pair of those boots?" Miguel licked his lips.

Olivia snorted. "If I do, you'll never see them."

"You look nice," Ethan said from the couch as she grabbed her bag. "Hot, but not in an inappropriate-for-a-family-dinner kind of way."

"Thanks, Ethan." She raised her voice by way of chastising Miguel and headed outside where Tom and her dad were waiting in a black Bentley limo with her father's two bodyguards.

She stared out the window as her father and Tom discussed the Vegas political situation. Maybe Olivia was right about Ethan. He was a nice guy, a great musician, and he'd been a good friend. He was devastatingly handsome, and they had a lot in common. He'd made it clear more than once that he was interested in taking their friendship to the next level, and of all the guys she'd been with since Rocco, there were none she liked more.

But best of all, he was normal. A civilian. With no ties to a criminal organization. Ethan's friends wouldn't meet unexpected and violent deaths that required a full black wardrobe and a funeral every Sunday. He wouldn't have dozens of "uncles" and "cousins" with strange nicknames, and he would keep his money in the bank and not in a hidden safe under the floorboards. He wouldn't mysteriously show up at her place of work uninvited, gain entry into a private studio by threatening to break the producer's fingers, and then kiss her breathless in an elevator, only to brush her off and walk away.

Ethan wouldn't kill a man to save her, and destroy himself so she could be free.

After her family left, she'd tell Ethan she was ready for that next step. Now that she knew Rocco had fully embraced the life that had taken her mother, she could finally put the past to bed and move on.

The limo slowed to a stop beside Carvello's restaurant, an out-of-the way hole in the wall, well off the beaten path in downtown Vegas. Grace had heard about it, but had never tried it out because it wasn't in the safest area of town, and with so many other options in the city, she didn't want to take the risk.

Her father's bodyguards got out first and checked the street before gesturing for her father to emerge from the limo.

Grace's skin prickled and she held out her hand, holding her father back. "Papa. Something doesn't feel right."

"I thought you'd gotten over the whole superstitious feeling thing when you became a psychologist," Tom said. "Did you ever think about why you believe that kind of stuff? It's not very scientific or logical."

"I don't analyze myself."

"Maybe you should," he suggested. "You might just discover something you didn't know."

"I think I know myself pretty well." She followed her father out of the limo, cutting off any further conversation about a subject she didn't want to discuss.

The owner of the restaurant, a middle-aged man with a salt-and-pepper beard, greeted them at the door. After the bodyguards checked the restaurant for potential threats, the owner led them to a table in the back corner where the Bianchi family—the capo, his two brothers and their two sons—were seated.

Grace sighed when she saw the two men who looked close to her age. "Papa. Please don't be trying to set me up again."

"What?" Her father shrugged his shoulders and opened his hands. "You don't want to meet people? Make some new friends?"

"I have enough friends."

"Relax, *polpetto.*" Her father patted her arm. "We're here for a meal. Not a marriage."

Tom snickered at the nickname. For some reason, her father had started calling her "meatball" when she hit her teen years and had never stopped.

"Shut up," she muttered under her breath as they made their way to the table. "Act your age."

"I am acting my age. Twenty-year-olds are allowed to laugh when their fathers call their sisters *polpetto*." His smile faded as the capo stood to greet her father. "The only thing that isn't funny is why Papa is meeting with the Forzanis. They are supporters of Tony Toscani, and Papa's meeting with Tony didn't go well. That dude has a couple of screws loose and he pretty much told Papa that if the don didn't appoint him boss of the Vegas faction over Nico, he wouldn't abide by the decision. He was incredibly disrespectful. So much so that I think Papa might ask the don to put a contract out on him."

"Maybe he's trying to get the Forzanis on his side in case that happens."

Tom nodded. "That makes sense. They run one of the biggest crews in Vegas. I think only Nico and Luca Rizzoli run bigger ones."

"Tom . . ." She swallowed hard. "If the don did put a contract out on Tony, would he use . . . the De Lucchi crew."

"He'd have to. Tony's too high ranked for an ordinary hit. And they have someone here—Rocco, that guy who used to drive us to school."

"Yeah." Her voice caught. "I remember him."

"He's almost as brutal as Cesare," Tom said. "I won't tell you the kind of stuff he's done because it would make your stomach turn, but he scares the living shit out of even the most hardened wiseguys. He's one of the most ruthless, cold-blooded enforcers in the entire crew. I guess it makes sense. He's Cesare's son, and he'll be the new De Lucchi boss when Cesare is gone."

Her hand trembled as she reached for her chair. "He's going to be the De Lucchi boss?"

"Yeah. That's how they work. Cesare's dad was boss before him, and then his grandfather and back to whenever the De Lucchis started. That's why they are required to initiate either a natural born or an adoptive son into the crew so that the De Lucchi crew never dies, and the leadership has the same training."

Well, didn't that make her decision easier. Good-bye Rocco and the mob. Hello Ethan and a normal life.

And yet . . . She touched her lips, remembering Rocco's kiss, the feel of his hard body against hers, that soul-deep connection that had snapped into place the moment they were in each other's arms. How could something that felt so right be so wrong? How could such a brutal man be so gentle?

How could she be with Ethan when only Rocco set her on fire?

Rocco smashed the butt of his revolver into the skull of the Bianchi family guard standing in the alley behind Carvello's restaurant. One of the first lessons Cesare had taught him was how to move undetected in the shadows, and he was always amazed how little attention people paid to the world around them.

He dragged the body a few feet away and out of sight of the main road. Something about this hit felt wrong, and it wasn't just because of Grace.

Enforcers were supposed to feel nothing. They were tools to be used at the will of the boss. And yet Cesare had not been as detached as he usually was when he called with an assignment. His impatience and show of temper were unusual, and that, together with Rocco's uncharacteristic emotional instability, meant he'd been standing outside the restaurant for the last quarter of an hour trying to decide what to do.

He heard footsteps on the sidewalk and pressed himself against the wall, sinking into the shadows. Moments later Grace walked past, her phone to her ear, her boots tapping a hurried rhythm on the pavement.

Jesus Christ. What the fuck was she doing here? A mob meeting was no place for a woman, much less the daughter of an underboss on dangerous ground.

"Ethan?" He voice carried down the alley. "My dad is trying to set me up again so I told him I'm with you." A pause. "Yeah. Boyfriend. I thought that would be the end of it but he insists on coming to meet you after dinner." She sighed. "No, you don't need to wear a suit, but you do need to lose the track pants. Your green cargo pants would be perfect. They're in the laundry room." A soft laugh. "Well it won't be hard since we've been living together for three years." A nervous laugh this time. "Okay. But it has to be a father-appropriate kiss. See you soon."

Ethan? She had a boyfriend? And they were living together? Christ. He hadn't even considered she would be with someone else. So what the fuck was she doing with him in the elevator? Was that her way getting closure?

His gritted his teeth and smashed his fist against the brick wall. Breathe. Breathe. He should be happy for her. This was exactly what he wanted. A final cutting of their ties. Why then did he have a sudden urge to find out where she lived and eliminate the competition with a few well-placed blows to that fucker's face?

He studied her as she walked down the sidewalk back to the restaurant. Goddam fucking sexy boots. And that dress. He could see the crescents of her breasts, the curve of her hip, and when she walked, the slit in the front opened to reveal her long, toned legs. Naughty dress. Even in frills and flowers, she couldn't hide that streak of rebel that had intrigued him from the first day they met.

He couldn't get a more perfect time for the hit. If he left right now, he could be in and out before she returned to the restaurant. She would never know it was him. And now that he knew what kind of woman she was—the kind who would kiss one man in an elevator and go home to sleep with another—he had no qualms about what he had to do.

Taking a deep breath, he searched for the darkness inside him, the cold, hard place where he had learned to retreat to escape Cesare's rage.

When he was certain Grace wouldn't hear him, he pulled open the back door and slipped inside. The air was rich with the thick scent of tomato sauce, and the floorboards creaked as he made his way down the hallway. From his vantage point near the restrooms, he could see most of the restaurant. Mantini was seated at a big, round table in the corner with the Bianchi family in front of him and a guard on either side.

Rocco didn't know much about the Bianchis except that they were aligned with Tony's crew. Interesting. Maybe Mantini had lied to Nico about the don's decision to favor Nico's claim. He made a mental note to let Nico know that Nunzio Mantini had been meeting with the Bianchis before he died.

He drew out his weapon and screwed on the silencer. But when he turned to take aim, he felt an unfamiliar tightening in his gut, and the walls he'd put up to protect his heart shuddered, cracking, splintering, letting a sliver of light shine through.

Jesus fucking Christ. How could he whack Grace's father and brother when she was standing outside? How could he make her suffer through the exact same circumstance in which she'd lost her mother and take away the only remaining family she had? How could he give her up forever, when she had just walked back into his life?

Fucking Cesare had destroyed everything he cared about to make him into the perfect enforcer. He'd burned all Rocco's toys and books when he turned ten, driven away his friends, and made Rocco watch as he took the life of the dog Rocco had raised from a pup.

And then the training began, and Rocco was reborn from the ashes of the bonfire that destroyed his childhood as a creature of torment and pain.

Ten years he had lived in darkness until Grace walked into his life.

Cesare had driven Grace away, and Rocco had allowed it to happen. He had sunk back into the darkness, hardened his heart, and accepted his fate. But now he had a second chance. A second choice. Cesare might have taken everything but he had not taken his will.

He lowered his weapon, waited until he heard the tinkle of the bell on the door that let him know Grace was safely inside.

As he made his way back down the hallway, he wondered how he could put things right. Start again. Rein in the fierce, almost desperate need he felt when he was with her and show her a different man for the short time he would have before Cesare came for him.

Because Cesare would come. A De Lucchi never failed to complete a job.

Do or die.

He was halfway down the street when he heard the screech of tires. Looking back over his shoulder, he saw a black SUV pull up in front of the restaurant. The doors flew open, and five men all dressed in black and wearing ski masks poured out, brazenly waving their weapons in the air.

Rocco's heart seized in his chest and he raced back the way he had come, slamming open the back door and plunging into the darkness of the hallway.

Gunshots cracked the stillness.

A woman screamed.

Grace.

The emergency lights flickered on and he kept to the shadows, racing through the semi-darkness toward the front door.

"Grace!"

He spotted her crouching behind a table and cautiously moved toward her. Relief flooded her stricken face when she saw him. He threw himself forward, taking her down to the floor as a bullet pinged over her head.

"Papa. Where's my father?"

He held her down, assessing the situation as gunfire ran out around them. Nunzio's bodyguards were doing their job, keeping the family safe behind an overturned table.

But *holy shit*. Had someone dared to try and whack the New York underboss?

"Let me up. I have to get to Papa." She squirmed away and crawled across the floor to kneel beside her father who was groaning on the ground beside an overturned table. Tom was curled against the wall cradling his arm against his chest. The bodies of the Bianchi family lay around him.

One of the guards screamed and went down, holding his stomach. Rocco took his place, helping the remaining guard protect the family keeping the enemy soldiers pinned near the door.

"Papa." Grace touched her father and her hand came away red with blood. "He's hurt."

The guard beside Rocco took a bullet to the chest and he fell, knocking over a table as he crashed to the ground. Glass shattered, and the table flipped over, giving Rocco a shield. One of the masked assailants walked over, his gun pointed at Grace's fallen father.

"No. Don't touch him." Grace rose to a protective crouch over her father, hands up in front of her in a warding gesture.

"Then you die, too."

Grace grabbed her father's weapon from beneath his jacket and rose to her feet. "Stay back, or I'll shoot."

Rocco's brow lifted in surprise. The Grace he knew would never have touched a gun, much less point it at someone with the clear intent to kill.

"Didn't your daddy tell you little girls aren't supposed to play with guns?"

"He taught me to shoot," she said, steadying her hand. "And he taught me not to miss."

Fuck. She would never be able to live with herself if she killed a man. Grace was a nurturer, a saver of souls. Rocco suffered the burden of every life he was forced to take, he couldn't image how she would bear the guilt. He had no idea what game these guys were playing or who they worked for, but it was clear whoever had hired the De Lucchi crew to take out Mantini wasn't the only person who wanted him dead.

"Did he teach you how to die?"

Rocco grabbed a water glass and threw it across the room. The glass shattered against the wall, drawing everyone's attention. Taking advantage of Grace's distraction, he shot the assailant in the chest, firing two bullets in quick succession before ducking behind the table again.

A scream. Shouts. A groan.

"Rocco." She stared at him aghast. "Why?"

"So you didn't have to." Rocco shot out the emergency lights and another gun battle ensured. When he heard the thud of a body hitting the floor, he dived into the darkness, looking for Grace.

He found her kneeling beside her father, her voice rising above the shouts as their assailants tried to find a light and tend to the man who was down. Clearly, they weren't professionals. A professional focused on the goal and nothing else.

"Gracie, it's me," he said quietly, touching her shoulder. "Quickly. We'll go out the back door."

"Get the fucking lights," the ill-tempered assailant screamed. "Find out who shot me. Was it the girl? Kill the fucking bitch."

"No." Another voice, low, commanding. "Just the *capo bastone* and his son. We need to take the girl alive."

Italian. He recognized the Sicilian accent. And they were Mafia because civilians wouldn't use the term *capo bastone* or know that it meant underboss.

"I'm not leaving him," Grace whispered. "And Tom. Where's Tom?" She pulled away and Rocco tightened his grip.

"There are five armed men in here, and some out back. This ambush was well-planned. How does it help your father and Tom if you get kidnapped or killed? I saw some of the staff run out. They will have called 911. The police and ambulance will be here in minutes. We need to get you out of here."

"They'll kill them."

"They probably think Tom and your father are already dead, and one of them has his own injuries to deal with." He pulled her back, and for a moment he thought she would come with him, but she struggled out of his grasp.

"What about you?" She backed away, her eyes glittering in the darkness. "What are you doing here? Are you part of this?"

Thank God, he could answer honestly. "No, *cara mia*. But you need to come with me."

Still, she hesitated. "I'm going to go call 911. I'll wait outside for the police to come. That's what normal people do."

Rocco shook his head. "If you stay here, you'll spend the rest of your life marked as being associated with the mob. We have our own way of dealing with these things. Our own way of keeping you safe. Someone is after you, Gracie, and you know the police won't be able to protect you."

"Do you have your own way of saving Tom and my dad?" she snapped.

Yes, he did. He had been taught how to use the darkness as a tool, to see where others could not. He could take out every man in the whole damn room before she took her next breath. But he wasn't going to do it. He would lose her forever if she had to witness that kind of bloodbath, and it wasn't a risk he was willing to take.

Sirens wailed in the distance, and his pulse kicked up a notch. "The police are coming. The shooters won't stick around. Trust me, Gracie. Trust me just one more time."

She hesitated, and he didn't blame her. Given how he'd acted since he'd walked back into her life, he was probably the last person worthy of her trust.

"Okay." She let out a long breath and grabbed her purse off the ground. "Let's go."

He grabbed her hand and they ran through the back of the restaurant and out the back door where the guard he had knocked out was still unconscious on the ground. He quickly dispatched a second guard at the end of the alley with a blow to the head, and led Grace at a quick walk to his bike a few blocks away as she made her call to 911.

Heart pounding, he helped her mount the bike, tucking her dress between them. As he sped away from the scene of devastation, Grace wrapped her arms around him and pressed her cheek against his back.

Safe. Grace was safe. His protective instinct sated, he considered the fallout of what had just happened. He had never failed to complete a contract, and once Cesare found out, he would be called to account. How easy would it have been to just let the shooters do the job for him and take the credit? He would have been able to pursue Grace with his conscience clear. And what about Grace? Someone was after her, and there was no way he could leave her now. He might have saved her family, but the price would be his life.

SEVEN

An icy chill settled over Grace as Rocco raced through the streets. She had no idea where they were going, but the effort required to talk seemed overwhelming.

She had just put her trust in the very organization that might have taken her father's life. *No.* In a mobster.

She tightened her grip, when he took a sharp corner, almost sliding sideways off the seat. Her hair whipped wildly around her and she realized belatedly that neither of them was wearing the required helmet. No wonder he was taking the side streets.

Even if she had been able to formulate words, talk became impossible when he picked up speed. Despite everything that had happened, she felt curiously safe with her body wrapped around his as they raced through the streets on one thousand pounds of shiny steel.

Safe but numb.

"I'm taking you to my place until we know how this is all gonna shake out," Rocco said, answering her unspoken question when they slowed to a stop at a traffic light. His voice was barely audible over the rumble of the motor. "Someone is after you, and it's not safe for you to go home."

She opened her mouth to tell him she could go to a hotel or stay with friends, but no words came out.

Papa had been shot. She had held his body on the floor of the restaurant just like she had done with Mama. His blood had been warm on her hands. And Tom. What happened to Tom? She couldn't lose them both.

Finally, they pulled over in front of a nondescript gray condo complex on Dumont Boulevard.

Rocco helped her off the bike, holding her hand as he led her down the sidewalk. Without his warmth in front of her, she felt the chill and a shiver ran through her body.

"Can't keep you safe at a hotel and you wouldn't want to put your friends in danger." He put an arm around her, pulling her against him. How did he know she was cold right to her core? How did he know what she was thinking?

I'm anti-violence. But apparently she wasn't. Not anymore. She was no different from any other member of the mob. If Rocco hadn't distracted her and shot the man in the restaurant, she would have pulled the trigger.

"You didn't kill him, *cara mia.*" He unlocked the glass door, all casual as if he hadn't just read her mind. "And it's unlikely I did either. He was wearing a vest. But until we figure this out, you can stay here and, after you're settled, I'll go find Tom and your dad."

I'm in shock, she suddenly realized when he stared at her as if waiting for her to speak. This is how it felt when Mama died. Cold. Numb. Lost.

"You okay?" He pressed the elevator button and the door slid open. The curious fog around her thickened as she stepped inside the small space. Fear seized her heart.

"No!" She pushed past him and ran back into the

hallway. Where was she? She didn't recognize the gray wallpaper, the pictures on the walls . . .

"Gracie." Strong arms wrapped around her from behind. A warm breath in her ear. "It's okay. I think you're in shock. We'll take the stairs. It's only two flights up."

His warmth soaked into her, beating back the chill. She knew that voice, that scent, that hard muscular body. Rocco. He would keep her safe.

He kept a firm hold on her as they climbed the stairs, sliding an arm around her waist when they stepped out into a brightly lit hallway dotted with teal-colored doors.

She brushed back her hair, stared at herself in the mirror at the end of the hall. Her face was streaked with dirt. Walking closer, she touched the marks with her finger and realized it wasn't dirt at all.

Blood. Blood on her hands. Her face. Her neck . . . Blood everywhere. A sound erupted from her throat, part whimper, part moan.

"Shhhh. Don't look." Rocco turned her to face him and wrapped his arms around her. "We'll get you cleaned up inside." Still holding her against him, he unlocked the door. "So what happens when a trauma psychologist suffers trauma?" he asked, half to himself. "How do you heal yourself?"

She didn't have an answer because she didn't understand the question. What trauma? All she wanted right now was to get the blood off her hands.

"Is it because of what happened the night down by the river? Is that why you chose psychology?"

Her mouth opened and closed again. Why was he talking so much? Rocco never talked. And she'd never thought about why she went into psychology, only that of all the professions that had interested her after a school trade fair, it was the one that had called to her, the one where she thought she could help people heal

the wounds that no one else could see. And her special-
ization? She wanted to heal the people who had been
blindsided by life. Just as she had.

Rocco's studio apartment reflected nothing of the man
she had left back in New York. Although it was fairly
modern, with painted exposed brick walls, gray carpet,
and a small galley kitchen with bright green walls and
white cabinets, the apartment was sparsely furnished.
Two metal stools were tucked into a small breakfast bar
in the kitchen, a black leather sofa sat in front of a big-
screen TV, and at the far end of the room, a king-size bed
sported a black and white duvet and a few pillows.

She searched for, but couldn't find, the things she remembered he loved. No magazines or sports equipment. No pictures of the Rat Pack or the old films he'd
liked to watch. No iconic black-and-white prints of New
York, Peanuts comics, video games, or collectible cars.
It was like his entire personality had been erased.

"Come, *dolcezza*. Let's get you cleaned up." He
clasped her fingers in his warm grip and led her to small
white-tiled bathroom across from the kitchen. "Here you
go. There are clean towels under the sink."

Grace looked around, unsure what he wanted her
to do.

"Your dress." He pointed to a stain she hadn't noticed
before. "You need to take it off and get in the shower.
That's the best way to get off the blood."

Blood.

Papa's blood. Staining her dress the way Mama's
blood had stained her white dress with the cherries on
it that she'd worn for their special lunch together. She
looked down and suddenly couldn't bear another second in the dress she hadn't wanted to wear to the dinner she hadn't wanted to attend with a bunch of mobsters
who had shot her father.

"Get it off. Get it off."

"Shhhh." Warm hands touched her neck, sweeping her hair aside. Sure fingers held soft fabric as he slowly tugged her zipper down. Grace closed her eyes as his rough fingers skimmed over her skin inch by slow, soothing inch. So strong. So gentle.

Even in the cocoon of numbness that was barely allowing her to function, her senses knew his touch. She felt like she was in a dream where Rocco held her safe in the shelter of his arms. She drew in a breath, filling her lungs with his scent, sinking into the memory of their very first time.

"Touch me." She had to tug his hand over to her breast as they took shelter under a tree in Prospect Park during a fierce rainstorm. What had started out as a walk had turned into something intimate when the rain chased everyone away and they had decided to wait it out in a dry little thicket while raindrops pattered around them.

"Grace . . . I can't." He tried to pull his hand away but she pressed it to her chest.

"Why? You kissed me the other night."

"That was a mistake." He groaned softly, and his fingers curved around her breast sending delicious tingles through her body. "I'm too old for you."

"We're not having the 'too old' conversation again." Now that his hand was busy, she took advantage of the opportunity to explore his body, running her hand down his chest and over the ripples of his six pack. She had never thought of how a man might arouse her, but Rocco, with his beauty and his tight, hard body made her stomach flip.

"You don't know—" he started again, but she cut him off with a kiss.

"*I know exactly what I want and what I'm doing and who I'm doing it with. It's not like I've never fooled around with anyone before . . .*"

His body stiffened. "*Who?*"

The question hung heavy like the gray clouds above that had not yet released all their tears.

"*I have a feeling if I told you, the poor guys wouldn't show up at school tomorrow.*"

"*Damn right,*" *he said quietly.* "*You're mine.*"

"*Then make me yours.*" *She slid her hands under his shirt, touched his warm skin. He was smooth and hard and she wanted to explore every muscle, every inch of his body. She wanted to lick and suck and devour this man who had somehow managed to fill the emptiness that had consumed her after her mother died. She wanted him with his quiet intensity, his dry sense of humor, his love of jazz, his passion for cars, and the way he made her feel like she was the center of his world when they were together.*

Rocco groaned, and she pushed his shirt higher, then leaned in to kiss his pecs. "*I've dreamed about touching you,*" *she murmured, breathing in the familiar scent of his skin, raw and musky, leather and rain.*

She could feel his heart pound in his chest, hear his breathing quicken. His hands slid around her, smoothing over her curves and down to her ass. And then he was walking her backward until she felt the rough bark of the tree through the soft cotton of her shirt. He tipped up her chin and stared into her eyes as if trying to convince himself to walk away.

"*You deserve so much more than me,* cara mia. *And your first time should be special. With someone you love, someone closer to your age. Not this. Not me.*"

"*What could be more special than this?*" *She waved vaguely at the thick, gray mist around them, the sodden leaves, thick on heavy branches, hiding them from view, the soft green grass beneath their feet, glittering as rain drops fell softly from the sky. "It's magical. I feel like we're in our very own cloud. I can't even hear the traffic. This is made for us. All that's missing is the music."*

He shuddered and leaned in to kiss her, soft and sweet. His lips feathered across her cheek to her ear and he sang her favorite verse of Sinatra's "All the Way," as his hands slid under her shirt to cup her breasts.

Unlike the boys she'd made out with at parties or behind the school, Rocco knew what he was doing. He squeezed her breasts gently, explored each soft swell until they felt swollen and sore. When he finally flicked the catch of her bra and cupped her naked breasts in his palms, his thumbs flicking over her hard nipples, she thought she might burst from the pleasure.

"Did you plan to seduce me, cara mia*?" One hand slid over her hip to the edge of the skirt that was now bunched up her thigh. "Is that why you wore a skirt?"*

"I've been trying to seduce you since I turned sixteen. Maybe even before." She let out a ragged breath as his finger stroked a slow path up her inner thigh. "I was hoping you'd get the hint before winter."

He chuckled and traced his finger along the edge of her panties. She had wanted him like this ever since she understood where that wanting could lead, how close it could bring two people together. They had a connection that she could feel in the center of her chest, but now she knew it could be more.

"Has anyone touched you here?" He stroked his thumb over her damp panties and she let out a moan.

"No. I didn't let them. I saved myself for you."

His eyes heated, the golden flecks sparking in their warm caramel depths. "And no one has touched you here?" He shoved her panties aside and slicked his finger across her wet entrance. She felt his touch like a deep throb in her groin, and her vulva felt swollen and hot.

"No." She breathed out a sigh. "Oh, Rocco. Do it again."

As if her words had broken down his walls, he yanked her panties away, tearing them from her body so violently, she caught her breath. So this is what lay beneath the calm, controlled exterior. Passion. Barely contained. Fierce and forbidding. She was greedy for it. She wanted him bared. Unleashed. Out of control.

Hands shaking, she undid his jeans and reached into his boxers. His shaft was stiff and hard, so thick she wondered if he would hurt her. She'd only ever touched two other penises . . . no . . . dicks, cocks . . . in her life and they had been boys, not men, and her touching had set them off so she didn't have much time to play.

She didn't notice the piercing until she had stroked her way to the top. Her hand froze and she stared at the silver barbell glistening just below the crown.

"What's that for?"

He wrapped his hand around hers, made her tighten her grip until a drop of liquid beaded on the smooth, rounded head of his cock. "For you."

"Me?" *With her free hand, she touched the piercing lightly.* "Do all guys . . . ?" *Her cheeks flamed. She'd fooled around because she didn't want him to think she was inexperienced, but nothing had prepared her for this.*

"No."

"Did it hurt?"

"Like a bitch."

"Will it hurt me?"

"I would never hurt you. This is for your pleasure." *He gently unclasped her fingers and turned her to face the tree.* "You must do what I say, cara mia." *His breath was warm in her ear.* "I've wanted you for so long it won't be easy to hold back."

"Okay." *She felt a bubble of happiness rise inside her. He had never told her he wanted her before. Even when he'd kissed her, he hadn't said anything that made her think the depth of his feelings came close to matching hers.*

"Hands on the tree. Legs apart."

She heard the soft rustle of clothing as she got into position, and then his shirt fell over a tree branch. Moments later, she felt his warm, hard chest against her bare back. She dropped her hands, intending to remove her shirt and bra so they weren't bunched up under her arms, but he growled a soft warning behind her.

"No, bella. *I won't take the risk that someone might come by and see what only I should see.*"

She felt his words vibrate through her body and settle as a warm pressure in her womb. His hardness slid between her legs, the piercing an erotic burn against her clit, and she instantly understood what the barbell was for.

"Oh." *Instinctively, she rocked her hips, chasing the slick sensation. Rocco's hands smoothed up her body to her breasts, and he pinched and tweaked her nipples through her clothes as he thrust between her legs driving her wild for a release from the storm of need that consumed her.*

"Rocco. Please. I can't . . . I don't . . . Not like this. I want to see you. I want to touch you."

He feathered kisses over her shoulder. "I won't last long. I need you ready for me."

"I've been ready since I understood what ready was."

With a low groan, he withdrew and spun her around. His hand delved down beneath her skirt, skimming over her clit to her entrance. She bucked at his touch, and he stilled. "Relax, dolcezza. I want to feel you."

She pulled her lip between her teeth as he pushed his finger inside. He felt thick and foreign, and she tensed around him. If his finger felt big, how would his cock feel?

"You're so wet. So tight. He pushed his finger, deeper and her eyes watered with pleasure.

"That feels good."

"This will feel better." He removed his finger and replaced it with two, crooking them slightly to rub against a sensitive spot on her inner wall.

"Oh." She gripped his shoulders, panted her breaths. "Don't stop, Rocco. Don't stop."

He thrust his fingers in and out, keeping a steady rhythm as he slicked moisture up and around her clit, adding sensation to sensation until she thought her knees would give out.

"I want to feel you come," he said softly. "I want you to come all over my hand."

She wanted it, too, wanted a release from the tension in her body. But not like this.

"I want you inside me the first time I come like this. I want to feel you. I want us to be close in a way no one else can be."

He pulled away, leaving her aching and bereft. As her heart beat a frantic rhythm, he pulled a condom from his back pocket and sheathed himself, carefully rolling it over his piercing. His hands slid under her ass and he lifted her, bracing her against the rough bark of the tree and she wrapped her legs around his hips.

"Sei la mia vita," he murmured. "Il mio unico vero amore. Sei più bella di un angelo."

"I like it when you speak Italian," she whispered, and she told him in Italian he was everything in her life, too.

She had never felt this sort of heat and longing for any-one. Since the day she met him, she had known he would always be part of her life.

The head of his cock nudged her entrance, and she widened her legs.

"You are mine, Grace Christina Mantini," he said softly. "And now you will be mine always." He pushed inside her, slowly, inch by thick inch, giving her a chance to get used to his size. But when his piercing touched the sensitive spot inside her that he had so tenderly stroked, she let out a loud gasp.

"My shoulder." His voice was rough, hoarse, strained with the effort of holding himself back, the cords standing out in his neck in sharp relief. "Scream into my shoulder."

"I won't scream."

His hands tightened on her hips and he pushed into her hard and deep. "Yes, you will. And when you do, I want to hear my name."

He pulled out again and this time when he thrust, her world shattered into a million stars, liquefying her body with pleasure. And she screamed. Just like he said she would.

"Rocco!"

"Gracie?"

She shook herself out of the memory, looked over her shoulder at Rocco's concerned face. "You need any more help?"

Rocco. He was really here. His hands were on her skin. His breath was warm on her neck. He was keeping her safe when the world had gone to hell and she might just have lost the only family she had left.

She must have made a sound because suddenly she

was in his arms, her face buried in his chest, his heart beating strong and steady beneath her cheek.

"I'll find them," he said softly, answering her unspoken worry. But she wasn't surprised. He knew her. He knew her, and he understood her like no one else ever had.

When she slid her arms around him to hold him tight, pressed her body against his, she felt his arousal, hard beneath his jeans. Maybe he was a colder, harder version of the man she had left behind, but she felt a small pleasure knowing that some part of him still wanted her, even though she was broken and scarred.

"You'd better shower." His voice was thick and hoarse when he released her. "I'll make some coffee."

And then he was gone.

Feeling slightly less disoriented, Grace slipped off the rest of her clothes as soon as the door closed behind her. She turned on the shower and stepped into the scalding spray. Keeping her eyes shut tight so she didn't see the blood, she scrubbed her skin with the body wash she found in the corner of the tub, wrapping herself in his familiar scent. The fog began to clear from her brain, but no matter how high she turned up the heat, the numbness wouldn't go away.

When she was done, she found an oversized T-shirt folded on the sink, as well as a large, fluffy towel. After drying off, she put on her bra and panties and tugged the T-shirt over her head. It fell to her upper thigh, just long enough to be decent, but too short to wear out.

When she came out of the bathroom, Rocco was on the phone, looking down on the street from the living-room window. There was no uncertainty in his stance, no apology, no questions about where he fit in the grand scheme of things. He owned this world. Dominated it in a way he hadn't before. The difference between a boy and a man.

He turned and his gaze skimmed over her body, lingering on the bare expanse of her thighs. "Change of plans," he said into the phone. "You're gonna stand guard at the door outside the hallway. Call Paolo and tell him to watch the street. You do not come inside the apartment. You got that?"

Grace found her purse on a table by the door and pulled out her phone.

"You letting your man know where you are?" Rocco asked, brusquely.

"I'm texting Ethan so he can bring me some clothes."

"Ethan." There was no mistaking the bitterness in his voice.

"Yes."

His jaw tightened. "Do you guys have someplace else you can go until I get this thing sorted?"

"Can't I stay here?"

A pained expression crossed his face. "He wouldn't have a problem with that?"

"No. Why would he?"

Rocco's face creased in a scowl. "Because if our positions were reversed there would be no fucking way I'd let you stay with him or any other man for that matter. No. Fucking. Way."

Grace sat on the cold, black leather sofa and scrubbed her hands over her face, trying to clear away the last of the fog that was making it so difficult to process everything that was happening. "Ethan has his own bed."

"He's a fucking idiot."

"He's my friend." She looked up, caught a flicker of hope in his eyes before his face smoothed to an expressionless mask.

"You're not fucking him?"

Grace sighed. "Not that it's any of your business, but

the answer to your crude question is no. That's what I meant when I said he was a friend. I don't sleep with my friends. I also don't swear or hang around with a lot of people who use fuck in every other sentence, so how about expanding your vocabulary?"

"Who do you fuck?" He folded his arms across his chest like he was bracing himself for bad news.

"This week, the closest I've come is you. And don't ask about last week or the week before that, because it's been a while."

He gave a grunt of satisfaction. "No man?"

"No. I don't do relationships." She swallowed hard. "Do you have a girlfriend? I don't have to stay here if it will cause a problem."

Rocco snorted. "No. And even if I did, I'd kick her out for you."

"That's nice in a cold-hearted, mean mobster kind of way." A shiver ran threw her body, and she wrapped her arms around herself, trying to beat back the chill.

Rocco's face softened. "You still in shock?"

Grace managed a ghost of a smile. "Not if I'm having a conversation with you about who I'm sleeping with."

"Never saw you like that before." He shook his head. "Just standing there, staring at the wall . . . nothing I could do. Felt like a knife was going through my gut."

Her hands trembled and she curled her feet under her. Rocco's apartment wasn't cold but she felt like ice inside. Still, their conversation was keeping her mind off what happened in the restaurant, and she was grateful for the few moments of respite before she tried to find her dad.

Rocco's brow creased in a frown. "You cold?"

"Inside."

"You need something warmer?"

Yes. That's exactly what she wanted. Warmth. An anchor. A safe haven. A port in a storm. "You." She uncurled from the couch and walked right into his open arms. Rocco wrapped her in his embrace, holding her until the heat of his body melted her inside, and she felt like they were one person and not two.

"I need to find Tom and my dad," she said finally, pulling away.

"I've got a guy coming to keep watch." He brushed a kiss over her forehead. "Then I'll hit the road."

"I'm not staying here while you look for them. We can go together."

"No." He walked across the room and grabbed his jacket.

Grace lifted an eyebrow. "I'm not asking permission."

"And I'm not letting you go. You heard the shooters. They wanted you. It's not safe for you to leave."

"I'm not your prisoner, Rocco." She folded her arms, wondering how far he would go to stop her. The Rocco she knew would never have hurt her, but this man, this Rocco, was an entirely different beast.

Mercifully, someone knocked at the door, breaking the stalemate. "Hey, Frankie! It's me."

Rocco tore his gaze away and pulled open the door, stepping aside for his heavily muscled friend.

"This is Mike. He's gonna be out in the hall guarding the door." His gaze slid to Mike, who wore a tight T-shirt that advertised a local gym and was cut to enhance his spectacular biceps. With his shaved head and tattooed forearms, he reminded her of a ruggedly handsome Popeye, minus the pipe.

"This is Grace Mantini. The fucking New York underboss's daughter." Rocco waved vaguely in her direction. Mike smiled, his gaze dropping to her bare legs, before lifting again to her face. "Nice to meet you—"

Rocco cut him off by slamming him against the wall, his hand at Mike's throat. "Don't fucking look at her."

"Sorry, Frankie." Mike's hands came up in a defensive gesture, although he was bigger and more muscular than Rocco and appeared to be more than capable of defending himself in a fight.

"Don't think about her. Don't even fucking breathe the same air as her."

"Apologies, boss."

"Get out." Rocco released him and shoved him out the door, his powerful muscles rippling with the effort. "Stay in the hall."

"I got it. I got it." Mike nodded with his head down. "Miss Grace, I'll be outside if you need me."

"Don't talk to her either," Rocco shouted.

So this was the new Rocco. Grace wasn't sure if she liked his hard-core attitude or the way he treated his friends, especially when only moments ago he'd given her a glimpse of the kind, caring man she knew from New York. "I think you were a little hard on him. He didn't do anything wrong."

"He's a man." Rocco pulled on his leather jacket.

"I picked that up."

"You. Looking how you look. Talking how you talk. Dressed how you're dressed. I don't trust anyone with a dick."

By habit, her hand went to her scar, but when she opened her mouth to protest, he held up a warning hand and shook his head. "Don't say it. Don't even fucking think it. Last time I'm going to say this, so listen good.

You are more beautiful now, Grace Christina, than you were the last time I saw you in New York, and you were so beautiful then it took my fucking breath away."

And then he pulled open the door, and left her standing with her hand still warm against her cheek.

EIGHT

Mike didn't know the protocol for consoling the beautiful, weeping daughter of the New York underboss
through a closed door, especially when Frankie had
looked at him like he wanted to put a bullet through his
head last night. Was he even allowed to knock? The
sound of her crying was ripping at his heart and he just
wanted to give her a hug.

A chaste hug.

Although, given she'd only been wearing a T-shirt
last night when Frankie left, maybe just a pat on the
back.

"You okay in there?" He opted for talking since that
seemed to be the best way to keep all his limbs intact
in the event Frankie returned unexpectedly this morning.
Frankie was one bad-ass motherfucker. No one crossed
Frankie. He'd as easily slit the throat of a man he called
friend as he would slit the throat of an enemy. Mike was
a big guy. Not much scared him. But Frankie . . . yeah
the guy gave him the shivers.

Still, it wasn't right to leave Grace crying alone in a
strange apartment. Only a cold bastard like Frankie

wouldn't understand the need to be with someone when shit went bad. Mike knew this because he'd been through more than his fair share, and the worst thing was being alone.

Mike had had his fair share of lonely times, but Friday night with Tiffany had changed that. She had been everything he had imagined in bed and more. Not only that, she'd given him her number and told him to call the next time he was out with his friends. He thought it was cute that she was shy to go out alone with him on an actual date when they'd been naked together for most of the night, but his plan to call her up for another round of hot sex had been foiled when he got Frankie's call.

No one said no to Frankie. He had made his bones under his dad, Cesare, one of the most brutal, vicious enforcers in the entire Cosa Nostra. He had a reputation for savagery and a history of resolving issues by shedding blood. Frankie was feared and sometimes loathed, but he seemed to like it that way.

Over the last year though, Mike had gotten to know Frankie a bit better. He'd been spending more time with Nico's crew ever since Tony's uncle, the former boss of the Toscani family, got himself whacked. He'd seen Frankie almost smile once or twice, heard him have a normal conversation, even had a drink with the dude at Luca's and Gabrielle's wedding. He'd begun to suspect that somewhere inside all the darkness, there was a regular guy. And last night, when he'd seen him with Grace, he'd realized it was true.

He heard the rattle of the chain and the door swung open. Mike quickly dropped his gaze, but not before noticing she was—thank God—fully dressed in a black flowered dress and a pair of kick-ass boots. "I'm fine. Thanks."

Mike stared at her boots and wondered if Tiffany had

a pair of boots like that. Damn. He'd liked to fuck Tiffany in nothing but a pair of sexy boots. "Are you sure, Miss Grace? You didn't sound fine."

"Mike?"

"Yeah?"

"You don't have to stare at my boots," she said. "I feel awkward talking to the top of your head."

Mike cleared his throat. "Frankie said . . ."

"You've already broken the 'breathing the same air as me' rule, so why not go for broke and look up? I promise I won't bite."

"It's not you I'm worried about," he said, lifting his gaze.

"I'll take the blame." She smiled, although her smile didn't quite reach her eyes, but she'd been crying only moments ago, so he figured she was probably still sad.

"It's okay, Miss Grace. I screwed up lots when I was an associate. I can take a punch."

"I'm sure you can, but if he punches you because of me, his life won't be worth living."

Mike barked a laugh at the thought of Grace giving Frankie shit. Damn he'd love to see that. But then she was a Mafia princess, the daughter of the New York fucking underboss. She would be used to bossing people around, and from the scar on her face she was no stranger to violence. He figured not many people would notice the scar, but it wasn't often he saw a woman with the kind of mark he usually saw on wiseguys. Not that it detracted from her beauty. Hell, it just made her look a little bad ass, and on a beautiful woman, badass was good.

"So you okay?" He reached to wipe a rogue tear from her cheek, and caught himself just in time. Talking and breathing were bad. Touching would be infinitely worse.

"Well, I was fine last night when I was calling hospitals

and police stations trying to find my dad, while waiting for Rocco to come back so I could tell him off for leaving me when he knew I wanted to go with him."

She sounded so fierce Mike almost couldn't believe this was the same woman he'd heard sobbing only moments ago. If he hadn't known just what a cold-hearted ruthless bastard Frankie could be, he almost would have felt sorry for him having to come back and answer to Grace for leaving her at home.

"I found him at St. John's Hospital," she continued. "He was in surgery all night and a nurse just called to tell me he'll be out of recovery in an hour, but things aren't looking so good so they're going to move him to ICU. No one has seen my brother, and I'm here and not where I need to be." Her bottom lip trembled. "Actually, to be honest, it's been a really shitty night, so you're right. At this moment, I'm not okay, but after we get out of here I will be." She turned around. "Can you zip me up?"

Whoa. Whoa. Whoa. Mike's head spun with too much information that he couldn't process all at once, and the warning bells screaming DANGER in his mind.

Too late, his brain registered the creamy skin of her bare back, the gentle curve of her neck, the sexy strap of her bra. *No. No. No.* He had not just seen Frankie's woman beneath her clothes. He'd just found his dream girl, Tiffany. Life couldn't be that cruel.

Unsee it. Unsee it. He tried to scrub the image from his mind.

"Maybe you could . . . uh . . . just use . . . a coat hanger," he suggested.

"Zip," she commanded.

So he said good-bye to the balls that had served him well when he'd brought Tiffany home to meet Ace, his pit bull, and Mitzy the mutt, and the heart that had thudded when she kissed him good-bye, and the muscles she had squeezed when they walked down the street, and the brain that couldn't think of a way out of this situation.

He zipped, trying not to touch her skin. And then he held his breath, waiting for the apocalypse to come.

"My friend, Ethan, offered to come here with some clothes, but I think it will be faster if I just go home and change because our house is on the way to the hospital." She pushed past him and walked down the hall. "Let's go. We only have an hour before I can get in to see my dad. I suspect things will be infinitely worse for both of us if you let me walk out of here alone."

Out of here? She was leaving? Who was Ethan? Where was home? Why was the front of her dress wet? And more important, had Frankie said this was okay?

He checked his phone. No texts. Christ. Frankie would freak the fuck out if she wasn't in the apartment where he'd left her. Mike moved quickly to intercept and stood in front of the elevator. "Well, I dunno, Miss Grace. Frankie thinks it's dangerous for you to be out right now. How about you just wait until he gets back—"

"I waited all night," she said, her voice wavering, and for the first time he registered the dark circles under her eyes. "My dad is on life support. He might not make it. I have to go. Now."

"Let me text Frankie and ask," he begged, pulling out his phone. "Maybe he'll get a few more guys to come with us."

"I don't want to go to the hospital with a bunch of mobsters in tow," she snapped, pulling herself up to her full height. And suddenly she looked every inch a Mafia princess, save for her tear-stained face and her sodden dress. "I want you. That's all."

"Me?" His voice rose in pitch.

"Yes. You. And you aren't going to tell Rocco yet. He

was always overprotective back in New York, but now he seems to have developed a very bossy streak and I can't risk him getting in my way. We'll go to my place so I can change out of these bloodstained clothes, then we'll go to the hospital and check the situation out. Once I know what's going on, then we'll let him know where we are."

Mike let out a shuddering breath. "You knew Frankie before Vegas?"

"Yes. But I know him as Rocco, not Frankie. Why do you call him Frankie?"

"It's a nickname," Mike said with a shrug. "You know like 'Louie Lollipops' or 'Vinny Carwash.' Guys call me 'Mikey Muscles' 'cause I own a chain of boxing gyms and spend a lot of time working out. My real name's Louis, but it's been so long since anyone called me that, I just go by Mike. I got off easy compared to some. There's one guy called 'Baby Dick.'"

"But why Frankie?" she asked.

"Happened before my time, but apparently he got totally shit-faced one night, if you'll pardon my French, and started singing Frank Sinatra songs in the restroom of a nightclub. After that everyone started calling him Frankie."

She stilled and her eyes watered. "Which song?"

"Don't know, Miss Grace. I wasn't there. Mr. Toscani or Mr. Rizzoli would be able to tell you, though. I heard you met them already." He gave her a half grin, hoping maybe she'd forget the crazy plan if he could keep the conversation going. "Is there a song special to him? Maybe I might spread it around . . ."

Her eyes got a faraway look and she sighed. "No. Nothing I can share." And then her faced tightened again. "Let's get going. What are you driving?"

Clearly, she wasn't going to change her mind and sit

quietly in the apartment waiting for Frankie to return. Grace had fire, and short of picking her up, which would require touching her, there was no way he could tell the daughter of the New York underboss what to do. He was a soldier, a faction soldier to be precise, and the only people lower than him in the Cosa Nostra hierarchy were the unmade associates like Paolo, and the De Lucchi crew. Of course, no member of the De Lucchi crew was treated like anything other than the equivalent of a capo—a dangerous capo who could slit your throat before you even knew he was there.

"I've got a pick-up truck," he said. "It's useful for hauling equipment to the gym. I've got a young associate with me. He's been watching outside all night. Name is Paolo. He'll be coming, too." No way was he going anywhere alone with Frankie's woman. He needed a witness who could testify that he'd treated her well when it came time to pay the price for his failure.

Thirty minutes and buckets of sweat later, he pulled up in front of Grace's ranch house in North Las Vegas and instructed Paolo to keep watch out front while he escorted her inside.

Larger than it appeared, the house was warm and homey, with two overstuffed red couches in front of a big TV, an easy chair covered in blankets, polished wood floors, and a big-ass kitchen leading to a dining area with a huge oak table covered in sheet music.

A German shepherd bounded over to him, barking and growling. "That's Trevor," Grace said. "He belongs to Ethan. Or, actually, Ethan belongs to him."

Mike let the dog smell his hand and gave him a pat. He'd had dogs all his life and there was nothing he liked better than to meet a happy, well-cared-for pet.

"This is Ethan," she said, pointing to a tall blond dude. "And that's Miguel over on the couch."

Grace excused herself to get dressed, and Ethan followed her down the hallway. At the back of his mind, Mike told himself he should probably follow her. Maybe the dude was up to no good. But he couldn't tear himself away from his position in the front entrance. If he couldn't guard the door at Frankie's place, he could at least guard it here.

He chatted with Miguel about the game on TV until Grace returned. She had changed into a loose flowery top, a pair of skin-tight jeans, and those fucking sexy boots. She looked feminine and bad-ass at the same time and if hadn't just met the woman of his dreams, and been scared as fuck of Frankie, he might have considered making a move.

"Let's go." Grace picked up her purse, but when she made a move to leave, Trevor pressed himself against her side and barked at the door.

"Sorry, Trev," she said, laughing. "I can't stay."

Trevor growled, and the skin on Mike's neck prickled. He knew dogs, and that wasn't Trevor wanting Grace to stay home and play. It was Trevor warning them of danger.

His hand drifted to the weapon he had holstered beneath his jacket. Where the fuck was Paolo and why hadn't he texted a warning?

Trevor's hackles rose and he growled again, a deep, low rumble that had Ethan and Miguel look over in alarm.

"Miss Grace, you'd better . . ."

Boom. The door splintered and exploded open. Mike drew his gun and ran to put himself between Grace and whatever force of nature had just bust down the door.

"Where is she?" Frankie stormed into the room, his leather jacket creaking with every stride of his long legs. Trevor surged forward, the sound of his barking echoing through the house. Frankie froze, dropped his gaze, and stared the dog down. Within moments Trevor was on the ground, nose between his paws, tail tucked between his legs.

Jesus H Christ. Mike had had dogs all his life and he'd never seen anything like that.

"What did you just do?" Grace shouted into the silence as the door swung loose on its hinges. Her friends stared open mouthed, and Mike reluctantly tucked away his gun. Trevor inched across the floor, pushing a squeaky toy toward Frankie's shoe.

"What part of 'stay in my apartment' did you not understand?" Frankie snarled.

Shit. He'd seen Frankie pissed before, but never like this. The dude was seriously going to explode, and Mike knew when the dust settled he would be the first casualty.

"The part where I was supposed to sit around waiting to find out what happened to my dad. I called around and I found him. I told Mike to take me here so I could change before we went to the hospital." Her hands found her hips and she glared.

Frankie's eyes sliced over to Mike. "You had one fucking thing to do."

"She wanted—"

"One. Fucking. Thing."

Mike's stomach tightened. He didn't mind the dressing down. Hell, when he'd been an associate, he made plenty of mistakes, and Luca called him out on every one. But he didn't want Grace to hear. She was the underboss's daughter. If she said anything to anyone about how he'd failed to do his job, whatever life Frankie left him with wouldn't be worth living.

"Don't yell at him. It's not his fault." Grace walked right up to Frankie and poked him in the chest. "And this is not okay. Not. Okay." She emphasized each word with a poke of her finger. If Mike hadn't been so worried about what Frankie was going to do to him, he would have laughed at the shock on Frankie's face. The most feared enforcer in the entire Gamboli crime family and she was in his face poking at his chest like he was a little kid.

"Following me is not okay. Breaking down my door is not okay. Blaming Mike when I'm the one to blame . . ." Poke. Poke Poke. "Not. Okay."

Frankie grabbed her hand, drew it away from his chest. "You were gone."

"I was gone?" Her voice rose in pitch. "That's your excuse? I was gone so you feel justified in hunting me down and turning into a one-man wrecking ball? Is that your way of saying you were worried about me?"

Frankie didn't answer. Instead he walked over to Mike and stared him straight in the eyes. "Get the door fixed."

"Sure, Frankie. I'll get someone over right away." He swallowed hard. Was this it? Was Frankie going to let him walk out of here with all his limbs attached?

"Paolo is outside. He needs medical attention."

Mike frowned. "What kind of medical attention?"

Wham. Frankie's fist slammed into his face. Mike staggered back from the force of the blow, lost his balance, and fell to the floor. It wasn't often he was knocked down, but Frankie knew how to throw a big punch, and exactly where to hit to cause maximum pain.

"That kind of medical attention," Frankie barked. "The fucking kind of medical attention you'll need after putting my fucking woman in danger."

"Oh my God." Grace grabbed a tea towel and knelt beside Mike. "Are you okay?"

"Yeah." He took the tea towel and held it to his bloody nose. "I'm good."

"That was also NOT OKAY," Grace snapped at Frankie, as she stood. "I can't believe you. I am so not your woman. And punching your friends in my house because they helped me out is NOT ACCEPTABLE."

Mike swallowed, tasted blood. How could she speak to him like that? Did she not have a care for her own safety? Or her life? He glanced over at Grace standing straight and tall, glaring up at Frankie who had at least seven inches on her. She didn't look afraid. She looked angry. Damn angry.

"Grace," Ethan called out softly. "Do you want me to call the police?"

Mike gave him an approving look. Ethan at least had some balls. Miguel was a pussy, cowering on the couch while a crazed Mafia enforcer broke down his door to find his woman.

"No. There's no need to call the police," Grace said without taking her eyes off Frankie. "He's just leaving."

"Not alone." Frankie held out his hand. "Come."

"Holy crap," Miguel said, finding his voice. "Are you with him Grace? A biker?" His nose wrinkled. "Isn't he too old for you?"

SQUEAK. Trevor's squeaky toy flew across the room and hit Miguel in the center of the forehead. Miguel staggered back, and his face turned red. Mike laughed through his pain. He hadn't even seen Frankie bend down to pick up Trevor's toy.

"ROCCO!"

Tension curled in the air between them. Mike thought it telling that not even ballsy Ethan dared interfere now. Frankie was the alpha dog in the room and even Trevor knew it.

"Come," Frankie demanded, making an abrupt gesture with his fingers.

"No."

Everyone in the room sucked in a collective breath. They clearly didn't know who Frankie was, but they'd all picked up that he was a very dangerous man. What they didn't understand was that they were witnessing something unprecedented. A De Lucchi had actually lost control.

"Grace." Frankie made an impatient gesture with his hand.

"I'm not going anywhere with you." Grace folded her arms across her chest.

Frankie froze and for the first time since Mike had met him, the enforcer didn't seem to know what to do. Mike hoped he lived long enough to tell the tale.

NINE

"You aren't going alone," Rocco said. "That's final."

It took Grace a few moments to identify the cause of the heat surging through her body.

Anger.

She was angry. Not just angry. Furious. She allowed the feeling to fill her, reveled in the sensation.

When her mother died, she'd been lonely and lost, but never angry. When the kids at school had given her a hard time—which didn't happen after she met Rocco—she turned the other cheek. And when Cesare had hurt her, harmed her, showed her who and what Rocco was, she'd felt nothing, until nothing gave way to a grief that wouldn't end. Her life had been dominated by loss and sadness. But anger was something new.

Powerful.

And Rocco had awakened it.

Her heart pounded in her chest, sending blood rushing through her veins. Muscles twitched and tightened. Her breaths came in pants. And hot. She was so hot. Burning bright like the sun. When she had counseled patients during her internship, she talked about anger. She taught people to control it, suppress it. But she'd never felt it. Never understood it's power. Never felt the need to embrace it and make it her own.

"Fuck off."

She felt almost giddy letting the words fall off her tongue—words she'd never said to anyone before. Harsh words. Swear words. Angry words. She felt almost drugged with the emotion, reckless. Rocco was a dangerous man, and yet when she looked at him, she remembered how he used to be. She remembered laughter and singing, whispered kisses and gentle touches. She remembered her first time and how hard he'd tried to make it good for her. Even after all these years, she knew in her heart that Rocco would never hurt her, and that gave her the courage to push back against a man who had a reputation for making even the most hardened wiseguys weep.

If she'd expected him to respond the same way, she was mistaken. Instead, he studied her for a long moment and then dropped his hand. "I'll take you to the hospital."

It was more than she'd hoped for, and yet she was reluctant to let go of the new emotion and the confidence it gave her. "No more violence."

His lips twitched at the corners. "Don't push it."

This time when he held out his hand, she threaded her fingers through his, and heat of a different kind sizzled through her body.

"You don't pull shit like that on me again." He yanked her forward toward the broken door. "You stay where I tell you to stay. You don't leave so I don't know where you are." He went on and on as they left the house. It was probably the most he'd said at once since she'd seen him again, maybe ever. Rocco had never been a talkative man and sometimes having a conversation with him was like squeezing blood from a stone. But she didn't need a psychology degree to read between the lines. He'd been worried about her.

He cared.

His hand tightened around hers. So warm. So strong.

They walked past a young man leaning against a vehicle parked at the side of the road holding a balled-up sweatshirt against his nose. She opened her mouth to ask if he was okay, but Rocco pulled her along.

He stopped in front of his bike and unclipped a helmet from the back of the seat. Their hands touched when he handed it to her, and he drew in a ragged breath.

"I'm okay," she said softly, straddling his bike.

His hand curled around the side of her neck, and he yanked her forward, his mouth crashing down on hers, his tongue skimming her trembling lips. Heat, desire, fear, and anger all coalesced in the fire of his kiss. His lips were firm and insistent, his tongue gentle. Responding to his need, she surrendered to him, letting him know with her body that she was okay. His groan vibrated through her as his tongue swept inside her mouth, possessing her. His hand fisted her hair, holding her still.

When he finally broke away they were both breathing hard.

"You were gone," he said.

Then he climbed on the bike, pulled her arms tight around his waist, and the engine roared to life.

St. John's Hospital was a maze of white corridors, speeding gurneys, the cloying scent of antiseptic, and people in scrubs and white coats rushing in all directions.

"Papa's in the ICU, but no sign of Tom." She pulled out her phone after filling in the paperwork at the front

desk and checked it for the hundredth time, hoping to
see a message from Tom. "Last night I tried all the police stations, hospitals, the morgue . . . I've texted and
called. I don't know where he could be. Unless . . ."

"Unless he's lying low," Rocco said quickly. He hadn't
told her where he'd been all night or what he had done,
only that he had also found her father at St. John's.
"Worry about him later and go see your dad. He needs
you right now."

They found the intensive-care unit, but were stopped
by a formidable looking nurse at the entrance.

"Are you family?"

"I am," Grace said. "And he's with me."

The nurse pointed to a chair in the hallway. "Your
friend will have to wait outside. Family only."

Rocco lifted an eyebrow in censure and Grace quickly
patted his arm. "I'll be okay. I'm pretty sure the ICU isn't
a dangerous place."

He gave an irritated grunt and folded his arms. "I'll
be right here."

After talking to the doctor about the operation to remove the bullet in her father's chest, Grace sat beside
her father's bed and held his hand, careful not to touch
the tubes or wires. Not for the first time did she wish she
could have spent more time with him over the last eight
years, but he was part of something she couldn't accept.
From the death of her mother to the brutal night on the
bank of Newton Creek when she'd lost Rocco, the mob
had destroyed everything she loved.

Grace adjusted her father's bedclothes and smoothed
his hair off his forehead, her finger tracing the furrows
in his brow that hadn't been there when he'd been with
her mom. Unlike many mobsters who married for political reasons, or wanted Mafia princesses as trophy

wives, he had loved her mother deeply, and he had never been the same after she died.

After sitting with him for half an hour, she left to find a nurse to discuss her father's care. When she returned to her father's room, Rocco was standing beside her father's bed, hands in his pockets, staring at him with a thoughtful expression. At first, she was taken aback by his presence, but then she remembered that her father had hired Rocco as a driver in the beginning and continued to call on him over the next few years when Grace or Tom needed a ride.

"How did you get past the mean nurse?" she whispered.

"Tied her up and put her in the closet."

She glanced over at him, slightly disconcerted when she didn't even see his lips twitch. "Don't forget to let her out before we leave."

Still no response. When a quick visual search of the room didn't reveal a closet, she relaxed. "Do you think he needs a guard? The people who are after him might come back to finish the job."

"I called Nico and asked him to send two men to keep watch in the hallway, and another two outside."

Her tension eased the tiniest bit. "Thank you."

"Pleasure."

"Did Nico know why someone wanted to kill my dad? It's not like anyone in Vegas can take over as underboss in New York."

He stared at her and it took her a moment to remember that Mafia business was never discussed with women. But this was her father and she couldn't help him if she didn't know what was going on. She felt the flame of anger flicker bright inside her again and welcomed it in.

"I have a right to know if he's still in danger. He's my father."

His jaw twitched almost imperceptibly. "I don't have an answer for you."

"Who benefits if he's gone?" She mused out loud as they walked down the hall. "Most likely one of the New York capos. Some of them are very powerful. Maybe one of them sent someone out here. Or hired someone." She stopped mid-step. "That would make sense. Get someone to do the dirty work, and with Papa out of the way, whoever it is can take over as underboss."

She glanced around as they left the ICU. No sign of the mean nurse. Her heart kicked up a notch, but before she could voice her concern, Rocco's warm hand clasped hers, pulling her out of her thoughts. "I'll handle it, but I think it is better if you don't go home just yet. You can stay with me."

"You don't need to protect me, Rocco. Papa has friends here—the Forzanis. And once the don finds out . . ." One of the benefits of becoming a made man was that your family was cared for by the mob if something happened to you. So much for not getting involved. If Papa died, she would be swarmed by mobsters.

They walked in silence to the vehicle through the hazy afternoon. "I didn't protect you before," he blurted out. "I need to protect you now."

"There wasn't much you could have done," she said softly, bile rising in her throat at the reminder of the night at Newton Creek. "Cesare would have killed me and felt nothing. I looked into his eyes, and I saw evil. When he was holding the knife at my throat, he whispered in my ear that he hoped you would refuse him because he wanted to feel my life trickle through his fingers." She didn't tell him what else Cesare had said, that he didn't love his adoptive son, that Rocco was nothing but a tool, and that he could have as easily pulled the trigger and taken Rocco's life as he had slashed and disfigured her face. She suspected Rocco knew it, but if he didn't, who was she to take that illusion away?

"Fuck." Without warning, Rocco turned and slammed his fist against the brick wall.

"Rocco. Stop." She grabbed his wrist, her heart aching at the sight of the blood and torn skin.

"I should never have been with you. I should have pushed you away. I was old enough to know better."

She opened his hand, pressed a kiss to his palm. "And I was old enough to know what I wanted. I wanted you. I wanted to fix you, heal you . . ." And love. She wanted to give him love.

"There is no fixing me," he said bitterly. "Cesare made me exactly as he wanted me to be."

"An enforcer."

When his jaw went slack, she shrugged. "Yes, I knew. I went to see my father after I got back from being stitched up at the hospital that night and he told me about the De Lucchi crew and who you were."

"So you left."

"Yes." She swallowed hard. "I'm not proud of that. Running away seems to be how I always deal with things that are too difficult to handle. But I didn't see any other option. I wasn't going to stick around and let Cesare use me against you again. And I was done with the Mafia, done watching everything I ever loved be destroyed."

His face tightened. "It was the right thing to do. It had to end. Who you are and who I am . . . light and dark . . . it would never have worked."

Not then. She had been too innocent, too naive, too sheltered. Rocco had protected her so well she'd never really had a chance to live, to understand that the world wasn't black and white. Good people did bad things, and bad people did good things, and not everyone in organized crime acted like a stereotypical criminal. Living away from home, making a new life for herself, and doing her degree had helped her to understand people on a different level, to look beyond their actions to their motivations and deeper into their hearts.

"Because of me," she said. "Not because of you." She cupped his face in her hands, felt the bristle of his beard against her palms. "I know you, Rocco. I see you underneath all the scowls and black leather and the fiercesome reputation that makes a man as big as Mike quake in his boots. I know your heart, and it's a good one. I don't know how you've done what you do, but I do know it is killing you inside."

He wrenched away so violently her hands dropped. "You don't know anything about me. The man you knew is gone. What you think you see is a fantasy. I didn't choose to become part of Cesare's crew, but the night at the river I chose this life."

"To set me free. Your motives were good ones."

He shuddered and his hand came up so suddenly she thought he might strike her, but instead he gripped her jaw and jerked her head to the side.

"You're still so naive," he said coldly. "So trusting. So fucking good it breaks my fucking heart."

If he'd said that to her six years ago, she would have curled up inside and run away. But she understood trauma now. She understood the lasting effects abuse had on children. She knew when the walls of self-protection rose up and how to get them down. For the first time, she wondered if this was the real reason she'd gone into psychology. Not just to help others, but to help the one person she had cared for the most.

Although understanding made his words hurt less, they still hurt. Pulling away, she took a step back. "I'm going to catch a cab and stay at a hotel."

"You're not going to a hotel."

"Yes, I am." She walked away, slowing down only when he called out.

"Gracie."

Hope fluttered in her chest. She looked back over her shoulder, raised a questioning eyebrow.

"You're not getting into some fucking stranger's car."

Well, didn't that just ruin what could have been a perfect movie moment. "For your information," she bit out. "It's a cab. I take them all the time. They are perfectly safe."

He closed the distance between them with easy strides of his long legs. "Whoever is after you could be looking for you right now. What if one of them is behind the wheel?"

"Driving the random cab I call to get me the hell away from you?" Her hands found her hips and she turned to face him. "Don't you think that stretches the realm of coincidence?"

"Not when I think about the first time we met and discovering we both lost our moms, listened to the same music, followed the same sports team, and had the same interests. Not when I think about how you needed to save people and I needed saving and there we were for each other at the perfect time."

Her anger fizzled faster than the dick of the last guy she'd gone out with who had taken off her mask after a costume party and discovered something he hadn't expected to see.

"Don't pull the nostalgia card with me." She mocked a frown. "You said I was naive."

"You are." He cupped her face in his hands.

"You said I was too trusting."

"It's true." He tipped her head back until she could see nothing but the caramel depths of his beautiful eyes.

"You said I break your fucking heart."

"You do. You destroyed me then and you destroy me now." His lips found hers and he kissed her.

Softly.

Gently. Oh, so gently.

His teeth grazed her bottom lip. His tongue whispered along the seam. She opened for him, and he took her mouth like they had fallen into the middle of a kiss that had been going on since they had last been together. It was raw and honest, and so filled with desire that her blood turned molten in her veins. Sensation crashed over her and she moaned into his mouth.

Rocco growled. A real, honest-to-goodness growl that vibrated through her body right down to her toes. One hand fisted her hair, holding her in place while the other ran along her temple, her cheek, her jaw, and down her throat to the pulse that pounded the evidence of her desire against her skin. He ravished her, devoured her, until she didn't know night or day, up or down. She only knew him. Rocco's hard body against her. Rocco's mouth. His taste. His fire. Her fantasy made real.

"Beautiful." His fingers threaded into her hair, pulling her back to him, grounding her in his heat before she could feel the chill of fear that he would reject her. "Just wait until I get you home."

She splayed her hands against his chest, remembering every time she'd touched him after that night in Prospect Park. How he'd leave her a message about where to meet and her heart would pound when she went to him. He would let her strip off his clothes, touch and kiss and lick and suck his beautiful body to her heart's desire. And then he would remove her clothing piece by piece until she was bared to him. He would whisper, *beautiful,* and she believed him because he was her everything and he had made her dark world bright again.

"Is this how you get girls to your place?" she murmured against his mouth. "Flattery and seduction?"

She felt desperate need to know about the other women in his life: how many girlfriends he'd had, what he did with them, whether he crooned Rat Pack hits when they held each other in the dark or made love to them under a tree in the rain. She wanted to know six years of things about him, even though part of her screamed NOT A GOOD IDEA.

Because where was this going to go?

He took lives, and she saved them.

"You can sleep in the bed. I'll take the couch." Rocco offered Grace the T-shirt he had given her the night before, while giving himself a mental pat on the back for his fortitude. He didn't want to sleep on the couch and he didn't want her to wear any clothes. If he'd had his way, they would have been naked in the bed shortly after he took her for lunch, or, at the very least, following her afternoon visit to the hospital when her father had awakened and asked to see her.

Naked and in bed right now would be ideal, but with Tom still missing and her father in hospital, he didn't want to push.

"I brought my own PJs."

Rocco bit back his disappointment. The image of her wearing his shirt last night was burned into his brain, and if he couldn't have her naked, the next best thing would be to see her wearing it again. There was something about a woman in a man's shirt with nothing else underneath that appealed to his most primitive possessive instinct, as if the shirt, his scent, marked her as his and would keep other men away. "Keep it anyway."

"And I don't want to take your bed again," she said, her fingers curling into the shirt. "You must not have gotten any sleep last night. I'll take the couch."

"Don't even think about it."

"I have to get up early and go to the studio. I'm recording a radio jingle tomorrow morning. I don't want to wake you so, really, the couch would be better—"

"Gracie." He cut her off with an irritated bark. "Take the bed."

He stared at the TV while she unpacked her bag and flicked through the channels trying to focus on the screen. He was tempted, so tempted to climb into bed with her, but she had a new life now, and the last thing he wanted was to taint her goodness with his shit.

But, God, he wanted her like nothing he had ever wanted in his life. When he was with her, it was like all the pain and torture Cesare had put him through to learn to lock away his emotions had never happened. She opened him up, revealed him, leaving him emotionally raw and vulnerable inside. But it was a good kind of pain.

While she changed in the washroom, he threw a few blankets on the black leather couch, grabbed a pillow from the closet and lay down, facing away from the bed. He wasn't going to turn around. He wasn't going to talk. He wasn't going to think about the fact she wouldn't be wearing a bra or wonder whether or not she was wearing panties. He wouldn't think about her beautiful long legs or her long, thick silky hair and how it would feel wrapped around his hand when he pushed her onto the bed, tugged her head back and—

"Rocco?"

He didn't realize he'd squeezed his eyes shut until he heard her voice right beside him. So he opened them and there was his fantasy come to life. "Sinatra" spread right across her breasts, his shirt—HIS SHIRT—barely skimming the tops of her bare thighs, her hair loose around her shoulders, his dick so fucking hard he thought he would die from blood loss to the brain.

"Yeah?"

"Would you like a glass of water?"

There was only one thing he wanted right now and water wasn't it. "I'm good."

Then he forgot everything he'd told himself and watched her walk toward the kitchen, the cheeks of her ass just peeking out from under the hem.

Breathe. Breathe. Breathe. He fisted the blanket in his hands, but he couldn't tear his eyes away.

Gracie.

Gracie was in his apartment. Naked, beneath his shirt.

"Are you sure you're okay with this?" She walked toward him, and he tried not to notice that the shirt rode higher on the side where she held the water glass, so high he swore he could see the shadow of her pussy.

"Yeah." He threw an extra blanket over his midsection, and gave a satisfied grunt. There. He'd done it. He was still in full control. He wouldn't inflict his ugliness on beautiful Grace. After he'd dealt with who was after her, and her dad recovered, they would go their separate ways, and she would be free to find a man to make her happy. A nice civilian who didn't beat and torture people for a living and could give her a house and kids and the normal life she'd craved after finding out the life she'd lived hadn't been normal at all.

He folded his arms behind his head, closed his eyes, and tried not to think of Grace asleep in the bed behind him.

Naked.

Beneath his shirt.

Fuck.

Rocco didn't know how long he'd been sleeping when he was awakened by a scream.

He rolled off the couch, grabbing the gun he'd placed under his pillow, and rose to a crouch, quickly assessing the room. Door locked. Windows closed. No intruders. Heart pounding, he looked over at the bed where Grace was writhing and twisting in the sheets.

"Grace." He put the weapon down and sat on the bed beside her. "Gracie. Wake up."

When she didn't respond, he stretched out on the bed and curled his body around her, holding her tight. "Wake up, *cara mia*. I've got you."

"So much blood," she whispered. "Blood in the water."

Rocco didn't know if she was asleep or awake, but he felt her words like a knife in his gut. The night he lost her was all about blood.

Forgive me father for I have sinned.

"Rocco."

She turned in his arms, and he stroked his hand down her back until he felt her body soften against him. How could something that felt so right be so wrong? His hell on earth was finding the other half of his soul and not being able to keep her.

He felt her lips on his throat, her breath warm on his skin. Was she . . . ? No. She was still half asleep. But he suddenly became acutely aware that the T-shirt she was wearing had ridden up, her bare legs were twined with his, and only a thin piece of cotton separated him from her naked body. All his blood rushed to his groin, but as he tensed, preparing to move away, she rocked her hips slowly against him.

"Rocco," she whispered. "Make the nightmares go away."

"Turn around and I'll hold you."

"I don't want to be held." Her voice was clearer now without the soft murmur of sleep. Her arms slid around him, and her breasts pressed against his chest. "I want to be together."

He wanted to be together, too. He wanted his cock inside her pussy, his mouth on her breasts, his hands on her ass, her hair, her curves. He wanted to go back to the secret nights when the world didn't matter and it was just Grace and him and all the fucking pleasure in the world.

One hand curved around the side of her neck, and he pulled her in for a kiss. Soft lips. Sweet lips. He rolled until he was on top of her, taking his weight on his elbows. She fit perfectly beneath him, her breasts pressed up against his chest; her thighs parted to accommodate his hips. He'd been with many women since he'd been with her, but he had never felt this kind of connection, a bond that went deep into his soul.

He was weak. Cesare had cursed his weakness every day of his training until he turned fifteen and finally realized that physical pain could not compare to emotional pain, and that nothing Cesare could do to his body would ever compare to the pain of knowing he hadn't been adopted to be loved, but to be turned into a monster.

The night that message hit home, he grieved the family he lost and the family he might have had if Cesare hadn't adopted him. The next day, he skipped school and went to church to be secretly confirmed by a priest, making him personally responsible for his faith—an unbreakable covenant with God that would connect him to his parents forever, no matter what Cesare did to him.

He had almost died for that show of defiance. Cesare had stopped short of beating him to death, only because his right-hand man reminded him that every member of the De Lucchi crew was required, on pain of death, to train a son or an orphan to take his place so the crew would exist in perpetuity. Cesare had already spent four years grooming Rocco and five years training him. Did he really want to start all over again? Cesare agreed. But he was in killing mood so he dropped the whip and shot his right-hand man instead. That was the first death on Rocco's conscience. After that, he locked the emotional pain away and bore every torture in silence, until the day Cesare ripped out his heart.

He had been drifting since he'd lost Grace. He'd lost faith and accepted his fate. But now he'd found her again, and she had awakened something in him he had buried long ago.

Hope.

Grace had made a new life out of the ashes. He could make a new life, too. A future without pain. Only Cesare stood in his way. Once he was gone, Rocco would be released.

Grace moaned softly and Rocco turned his attention to the beautiful woman in the bed and his desire for release of another kind.

He slid his hand up her bare leg, teased the bottom of her nightie, searching for panties and coming up bare.

"Do you usually wear nothing to bed?

"Only when I'm hoping not to sleep alone." She nuzzled his neck, and his cock hardened.

"You won't be sleeping alone tonight." He wouldn't make that mistake again. She needed him to keep the nightmares away. And he needed her to fill the emptiness in his soul.

Pushing himself down, he kissed her belly, breathed in her scent, sweet and floral. "I want to taste you, *dolcezza*. You know where to put your feet."

She placed her feet on his shoulders, lifting her hips, opening herself to him.

He had always been a dominant lover, and Grace had been more than willing to follow his lead. Although he was certain that she had been with other men since him, he felt no small amount of satisfaction that he had been her first, that he had introduced her to this kind of pleasure, and even now, after all these years, she remembered how he could pleasure her best.

Her gasp melted into a sigh when he took his first lick, and her legs fell open. Rocco shuddered when he tasted the salty sweetness of her arousal on his tongue. He loved how wet she was for him, how she responded to his touch. For a moment, he dared think of what it would be like to have her in his bed every night, to indulge himself in her beautiful body, to hold her softness in his arms, to finally know peace.

Redemption.

Pain sliced his body as her heel dug into his shoulder, still raw and sore after his visit to Hellfire, yanking him back to harsh reality. There was no redemption for him. A future with Grace, bought with Cesare's blood, was a fantasy he couldn't have. That future was tainted by darkness, and he didn't want it to touch her.

She rolled her hips, arching up to get more from him. He wanted to take his time, tease her until she was begging him to come, but with the realization that this had to be a one-time intimacy came a need to put up the walls that protected his heart.

Pushing himself back, he knelt between her spread legs. "Up on your elbows." His voice coming out even sharper than he had intended. "Legs open. Show me your pussy."

Confusion flickered over her face, making his gut clench. But this was for the best. They could indulge their burning chemistry without the risk of emotional involvement. He had hurt her once, almost destroyed her. It couldn't happen again.

Of course, she did as he asked. She trusted him. And in a way, he was about to betray her by making this solely about sex, when he knew Grace was all about emotion.

"Touch yourself. Use your fingers. Show me how you make yourself come."

Her mouth opened in protest and closed again. In the games they used to play, she followed where he led and talked when he allowed. Clearly, she remembered the rules, which meant she also remembered the punishment for breaking them.

She tentatively stroked her clit, her hand gliding over the soft down between her legs. He was glad of the darkness because if he had to look into her eyes, he would be lost.

Or maybe he was lost already.

TEN

Something was wrong.

Grace slicked her wetness up and around her clit, trying to balance on the bed with one arm. She'd felt something change in Rocco, like a wall slamming into place between them. One minute he was holding her, soothing her, his tongue warm between her legs, and she'd felt like they were back in New York, hiding away in Rocco's small apartment, making the most of the few hours they had together. The next minute, he was gone, and in his place was the cold, efficient Mafia enforcer she had seen at the restaurant.

"Give me a show that will make my dick hard."

They'd played this game before, but always she could feel the connection between them, hear the warmth behind the sternness of his voice. Now, there was nothing and she felt a curious emptiness deep inside.

Pushing away her uncertainty, she pushed her finger inside and then rubbed her clit. God, that felt good, and it turned her on knowing it aroused him.

"Keep going, sexy girl." His rough, husky voice pushed her past her misgivings, and she rubbed short strokes until she felt the burn of climax. A small rush of pleasure took her breath, making her toes curl.

"That was hot, babe." He shoved his pajama pants down and grabbed a condom from the dresser drawer. "Over on all fours."

Babe. He never called her babe. In all the time she'd known him, he'd only ever used Italian terms of endearment.

Nausea tugged at her belly. It was stress combined with the orgasm making her light-headed, she decided, as she got in position. She hadn't slept well last night alone in his bed. Once he was inside her, their connection would snap back into place. She would feel him in every part of her body and down in her soul.

"Down." One heavy hand pushed her head to the bed, as the other lifted her ass in the air.

"Legs apart." He shoved her legs apart with a thick thigh and she heard the harsh rip of the foil packet as he removed the condom.

Thwack. Pain sheeted across her ass, yanking her back to the moment. She tried to look back but his heavy hand held her down.

"This is for not paying attention." His hand cracked over her ass again and something broke inside her.

"Rocco . . ."

The blunt head of his cock nudged her entrance. "You want that, babe?"

Babe again. Not *bella* or *dolzezza* or *cara mia*. Not Gracie. It was like he was purposely trying to push her away.

He smacked her ass again and her mind and body had a disconnect. She had wanted this, wanted to feel him inside her. Pinned to the bed by the weight of his hand, legs held apart by his wide hips, her body open to him, she tried to surrender to the pleasure building up inside her, and although part of her was on board, the other part stood at the edge of a cliff and saw only darkness.

"Rocco . . ." She couldn't find any other words to express her feelings, because she'd never had to. He had always been a careful and attentive lover. And yet tonight, it was like being with someone else. Someone she didn't know. Someone she didn't completely trust.

"Stop." It felt good to say it. Empowering. She could impose her control over chaos. She didn't have to be a victim. Especially not here.

He froze. "Did I hurt you?"

Grace fisted her hands in the covers and tried to breathe through the knot that had formed in her chest, the sickness in her soul.

"You okay?" he asked.

She drew in a shuddering breath through lungs that had to fight for air. She felt empty inside and consumed by a wave of utter desolation. How could she feel lonely when Rocco was right here, the way she had imagined all the years they had been apart?

Trauma? She was tired. Stressed. She'd been involved in a shooting. Papa was in the hospital. Tom was missing. She wasn't thinking straight. But the psychologist in her knew that wasn't the answer. She had been seeking emotional release through physical pleasure, but the connection wasn't there, because this was Rocco from the night at the river, and not the Rocco who had been part of her heart.

"No." She sat on the edge of the bed and pulled down her T-shirt. "This isn't working for me."

"What's wrong?" He followed her across the room, wrapping a towel around his hips, as she made her way to the couch.

"I want you," she said, bluntly. "That wasn't you. I couldn't feel you. I didn't trust you. It felt wrong."

His face tightened. "That was me. That's who I am."

"That's not who was in the elevator. That's not who came for me at Carvello's or brought me to the hospital or kissed me in the parking lot." She couldn't believe the words coming out of her mouth. As much as the man in the bed hadn't been him, this strong, bold, confident woman wasn't her. Or at least, it wasn't the her she used to be. The old Grace would have kept quiet and run away, but she didn't want to run. Rocco was broken and she wanted to fix him, and to do that she was going to have to take some emotional bruises, but they would come on her own terms.

"I want the real you, Rocco." She tapped her chest. "The Rocco I can feel in here. The Rocco I can see beneath your mask. You've hidden him away and I understand why, but I'm not the same girl I was in New York. I'm not a victim. I'm not helpless. I'm not dependent on anyone. I know what I want and I'm prepared to fight for it."

His shoulders slumped the tiniest bit. "I can't give you what you want."

"Then I'm going to bed." She curled up on the couch that he had been sleeping on and pulled the blanket around her.

"Why aren't you running away?" he said coldly.

"Because you're doing enough running for both of us."

Rocco startled awake, his heart pounding from yet another nightmare about the ten years he'd spent training to be an enforcer. Deprivation had been the first lesson, followed by discipline. His toys, games, and books had been taken away, his bedroom stripped down to just a bed and dresser, the housekeeper who had acted as a surrogate mother dismissed without a chance to say good-bye. He went to school, did his homework, then spent his free time doing martial arts and fight training. Weekends were spent with Cesare and a few members of the De Lucchi crew in the soundproofed training room in the basement, and that's always where the nightmares took place.

He pushed himself to sit, frowned when he saw the empty couch. When he heard no movement in the apartment, he got up to investigate, his heart slamming into his ribs until he heard the shower.

Breathe.

What a fuck up. She'd spent the night alone on the couch. Had he really thought Grace wouldn't notice when he emotionally disengaged?

"Fuck." He swept his hand over the counter, knocking a water glass to the floor. This was what he had wanted. Enforcers needed emotional and physical strength; they needed to be free of attachments and the burdens of law and morality. They needed to be able to take a life and walk away and never give it a second thought.

In that regard, Rocco had failed. He needed the sting of Clay's whip and the sanctuary of the confessional to help him bear the burden of the life that had been forced upon him. And before that, he'd had Grace.

Grace who he'd just treated like every other nameless, faceless woman he paid for a moment of pleasure.

His phone buzzed just moments after he'd pulled on his clothes. Nico wanted him at the clubhouse for an early morning meeting. *Christ.* Although Rocco was a De Lucchi, Nico treated him like one of his capos, but in return he expected Rocco's loyalty and that meant coming when called. Rocco didn't want to jeopardize his relationship with Nico or the benefits that came with his association with the powerful Toscani family faction. Not only that, Nico would need to be briefed on the situation, and he might have information that would help Rocco find out who was after Grace. But right now, she was in danger and he wanted to be by her side.

He sent Nico a text to let him know he was on his way. Then he called Mike and told him to come with four more associates to guard Grace on pain of death. Despite the threat, Rocco had no intention of offing five Toscani soldiers. He had a code that he followed when it came to his work that made his job easier to bear. First, gratuitous violence was never in the cards, nor was harming civilians or innocents. If a dude was stupid enough to get involved with the mob, then that was another story. Beatings and broken legs had to be expected if you borrowed from the mob, and if you were a rat (wiseguys who sold out to the cops), cheater (wiseguys who slept with the woman of a made man), or anyone stupid enough to hurt, kill, or steal from a made man.

Not that he thought the code would convince the "big man" to cut him some slack when he showed up at the Pearly Gates. But it helped him deal with the ugliness in his soul, and maybe his eternity in Hell might be a few years shorter because he was helping the Devil do his job.

"I've got an early morning gig at the studio," Grace said, walking toward him. "And then I need to get back to the hospital and see my dad." Her hair was wet, the ends dripping on her shoulders. Rocco had a sudden painful memory of the last night they'd spent together in New York. After hours of sex, they had showered together before collapsing on his bed. Grace sang along to the bad covers of Rat Pack songs that he'd made into a playlist, her voice vibrating against his chest, her body soft and warm against his, the scent of sex and her perfume filling his head. Her hair had dripped over his chest, each small drop trickling over his skin, and he'd tried to memorize all the sensations he wasn't supposed to have in case he never saw her again. Somehow, some part of him had known it was the last time.

"I have to go to a meeting, but I've got some guys coming who will stay with you until I'm done," he said, like they'd had an ordinary night together and not one in which he destroyed the tentative bond between them. But what else could he say? How did he make it right? He didn't have the words.

And apparently neither did she because the ensuing silence was almost deafening.

Finally, she sighed. "Okay. Although I can't imagine why anyone would want to kidnap me. Papa's in no condition to pay any ransom, and I don't know what happened to Tom. Maybe they took him instead . . ." Her voice caught, broke. Rocco gritted his teeth against the urge to go to her. The last thing she probably wanted was more of his fucked-up shit.

"I'm going to talk to Nico. We'll figure it out."

"Sure." She wiped away a tear, and he felt something crack inside.

After Grace was safely away with Mike and the soldiers, he rode his motorcycle to the clubhouse located at the back of an abandoned garage just off the 95 on the outskirts of North Las Vegas. Luca was getting the chairs ready for the meeting when he walked in the door. From the front, the clubhouse looked like every other small warehouse in the semi-industrial area, but inside, the place had been gutted and rebuilt to accommodate an office for Nico, a games area with a pool table, a small kitchen, and a lounge with a big-ass TV. Despite the reno, the place still smelled of diesel and oil, and with bars and black-out blinds on all the windows, there was no way to air it out.

"How long is this gonna take?" he asked throwing himself down on the worn, leather couch.

Luca gave him a puzzled look. "Why? You got somewhere you need to be?"

"Yeah. At the funeral home, getting a tombstone engraved, *Here Lies Luca. Nosy as Fuck.*"

"Ah." A smile tugged at Luca's lips. "It's about a girl. I hear you've been seen with the lovely Grace Mantini."

"Fuck off." He pulled out his cigarettes and lit one while Luca pulled up a chair. Mike must have told him about Grace. Fucking bastard.

"Still trying to kill yourself?" Luca asked.

"Maybe I'll save myself some money and just carve the words into your chest instead." Rocco blew a ring of smoke, and Luca laughed.

"I've been there, my friend." Luca settled on a chair across from him, a smirk on his lips. "Trust me when I say, it's not easy. Women will make you do things you never thought you'd do, and you'll do them with a smile."

Rocco's hand tightened by his side. The only reason his fist wasn't already in Luca's face was because he was Nico's underboss and part of the Toscani family administration—boss, underboss and *consigliere*. Charlie Nails, an attorney who had no issues working for the mob, was Nico's *consigliere*, a senior family advisor who had worked for Nico's father before he died. He knew the dirty secrets of everyone who was anyone in Vegas—judges, district attorneys, politicians, police chiefs, bankers, and investors—and, as a result, he had collected many favors.

"Since when did my life become any of your concern?"

Luca grinned. "Since you finally decided to have a life."

Charlie Nails joined them in the make-shift lounge, and Luca turned to chat with the *consigliere* leaving Rocco to stew. The noise level rose as the capos filed in, and Rocco gritted his teeth. They were always joking around, giving each other shit, but Rocco had never joined in the banter. He wasn't an associate, soldier, or capo. He was an outside. Other. Not part of the family. And he'd made sure everyone knew to stay away.

"So, Luca says you're with Nunzio Mantini's daughter," Charlie Nails said quietly when Luca left him to greet one of the capos. Charlie Nails was a good guy, although getting on in years, and no one knew more about the *Cosa Nostra* than him.

"What the fuck? Not seeing how my personal life is any of your business." Rocco glared at Luca's departing back, planning a long, slow, tortuous death for the man who professed to be his friend.

"Girls are business," Charlie Nails said. "And political alliances are good for business. Unfortunately, in terms of politics, the De Lucchi crew doesn't bring anything to the table."

Rocco's top lip curled in disgust. There was a stigma attached to the crew that would never go away. They were a necessary evil that the rest of the mob pretended didn't exist. Only Grace's father and Nico's crew had ever treated him like an equal. "She's a grown woman. She does what she wants to do."

"Mantini needs allies to hold his power." Charlie Nails lowered his voice so only Rocco could hear. "If he had them, he wouldn't be lying in a hospital bed. If he lives, he's going to have to face the fact that only a political marriage can save his family. If he dies, his son—if he's still alive—will need allies if he wants to take Mantini's place—allies who can be bought with the pretty face of Mantini's daughter."

"I thought this was Cosa Nostra and not *Game of fucking Thrones*."

Charlie Nails laughed. "Same game, different players. You need to figure out where you fit in—if you want to fit in at all."

Rocco didn't fit in. The political machinations of the Gamboli family were nothing to do with him, and he should have no feelings whatsoever about what was going on. And yet, the thought of Grace being forced into a political marriage flooded him with a wave of uncomfortable emotion. Another visit to Clay would sort him out, but for the first time since he'd found the underground club, the idea of being beaten into a state of emotional numbness didn't hold the same appeal.

Nico finally arrived, and Rocco briefed the crew on the shooting. Everyone had questions, and he answered them carefully, hyperaware that he was sitting in the circle, instead of lurking outside like he usually did. People asked his opinion, considered his ideas like he was one of them. In the end, they all agreed that despite the leadership dispute with Tony, this was Nico's town, and the attempt on Mantini's life was an insult to the Toscanis and a disrespect to the Gamboli family that had to be addressed.

"I haven't been able to get in touch with Don Gamboli or his *consigliere*," Nico said. "But Frankie suspects, and I agree, that Tony is involved. This visit from Nunzio was to give the appearance of fairness so Tony wouldn't complain, but the decision was all but made. Nunzio was going to confirm me as boss of the entire Vegas faction. I wouldn't put it past Tony to try and whack Nunzio and his son if he found out ahead of time."

"But he gains nothing from it," Charlie Nails pointed out. "Except to invite the don to send a De Lucchi to his house in the middle of the night for attempting to whack the underboss without permission."

Everyone looked at Rocco, and the illusion shattered. In the end, he was a De Lucchi, and they all knew what that meant.

Charlie Nails offered some information about the politics in New York and a debate ensued about whether the Toscanis should even get involved in what appeared to be a New York matter. Nico quickly put the debate to rest. He arranged for more guards at the hospital, organized a search for Tom, and agreed that Rocco should continue to protect Grace with as much back up from the crew as he needed.

He excused himself to take a call and returned a few minutes later, pulling up a seat beside Rocco and Luca. "Mia just texted to let me know Grace and Gabrielle are at her office," he said quietly. "Grace had the idea of trying to find her brother by tracking his phone and Mia and Gabrielle are helping her."

"Fuck." Rocco stood abruptly, and Nico gestured for him to wait.

"She's fine. You know Mia's got the best security system in the business and she said you have Grace well-guarded. If anything, this is a lesson in how to deal with headstrong women. It's about respect. Mia texted me because she knows who Grace is and she knows I would want to know what was going on. If they find something, she will, of course, text me right away. Mia is not the type of woman to go running headlong into danger. We have an understanding. She focuses on her cyber security and hacking work and leaves the dangerous jobs to me."

Rocco wasn't sure Nico's assessment of Mia was

entirely accurate. As far as he could tell, Mia wasn't really a rule follower, even if they were Nico's rules. She was fiercely intelligent, a skilled hacker, and a woman who wasn't afraid to stand up for what she believed in. In some ways, she was very much like Luca's new wife, Gabrielle, an ex-cop who had done exactly what Luca told her not to do in order to save his life. She also kicked ass with a gun and when she and Mia got together, Rocco stayed the fuck away.

He supposed the similarities between them made sense. Strong women were attracted to strong men, and Nico and Luca were probably the most powerful men in the Toscani crime family, save for Tony. The problem was, strong woman were difficult to control, and it was becoming abundantly clear that Grace had an inner strength that he had never had a chance to see before. She wasn't an innocent, trusting girl anymore. She was a woman, and she knew her own mind. Hell, he wouldn't be surprised if she decided to go looking for Tom on her own. Or with Mia and Gabrielle. Christ. Just the thought of the three of them together made his pulse kick up a notch.

"Tell me again, about that understanding," Luca said, holding up his phone. "Gabrielle just texted to let me know they've located Grace's brother in a trailer park, and they are on their way to meet him."

When Rocco's phone buzzed with a similar message from Mike, who was now following the girls down Las Vegas Boulevard, he'd had enough. Fuck Nico and the meeting. He wasn't bound by the rules of Nico's crew. He was other. And for the first time, he was damn glad.

ELEVEN

"I think that's it up ahead." Grace leaned forward from the back seat of Gabrielle's Mazda CX-3. Together Mia and Gabrielle had managed to find Tom's phone using his number and they had pinpointed his location to a trailer park on the outskirts of the city using some sophisticated software that Grace was certain wasn't available to the public.

"I know this trailer park," Gabrielle said. "And it's definitely a good place to lie low if that's what he's doing. The people here mind their own business, and they don't rat on each other no matter what they are involved in."

An ex-cop and now a partner in a private investigation firm, Gabrielle had insisted on coming along as back-up even though Mike and Paolo were following behind in a black Chrysler 300C that screamed Mafia, much to Grace's amusement. Dressed in pregnancy grunge, with a flannel shirt, rock band vest, and ripped pregnancy jeans, Gabrielle had been eager to come along, welcoming the opportunity to get out from under Luca's overprotective thumb.

"But Tom doesn't know anyone in the city who would

live in a place like this." Grace's niggle of worry became a full-on roar as they neared the trailer park. As far as she was aware, Tom didn't know anyone in Nevada besides their family friends, the Forzanis. If he was lying low after the shooting, why would he come here instead of staying with them, or returning to New York? Was he not concerned about their father? And why hadn't he answered her messages? According to Mia, his phone was charged and still on.

They pulled up into the parking lot, and Mia studied the map on her phone. "Looks like he's in one of the trailers at the far side."

Grace sent a text to Tom and they sat in the car waiting while Mike and Paolo paced up and down in the parking lot. After ten minutes, she reached for the door handle. "I'll go to talk to the manger and see if he'll let me in."

"Take Mike with you," Mia said. "You can't be too careful when you don't know who's after you."

She couldn't believe this was happening. How had her normal life spiraled out of control so quickly? And all because she'd let her father back into her life. But then that was the mob. Once you opened the door, the chaos and insanity blew right in.

"And you'd better get a move on," Gabrielle said. "Frankie was at the meeting with Luca and if you guys are really together like Luca said, and given what we know about him, he'll already be on his way, and it won't be pretty. He came with Luca to meet the new partners at my office and had them quaking in their boots with just a scowl."

Grace feigned a smile, but her heart ached at the thought that no one knew the real Rocco—protective, possessive, and hiding a gentle heart beneath his stony exterior. Even last night, which should never have happened, he had stopped when she asked him to stop. And his concern afterward was genuine. But she couldn't be with him without an emotional connection and last night that part of him was missing.

Mia cocked her head to the side. "Are you together or just friends?"

"We were together a long time ago," she said. "But we had to keep it a secret. I was sixteen and he was twenty-six. I was the underboss's daughter. He was a De Lucchi. It was all sorts of dangerous, although I didn't know it at the time. I just thought he was a guy who worked for my dad. But he knew, and he took the risk anyway."

"I can't even imagine what he went through as a child," Gabrielle said, her hand dropping to her belly. "Or that you went out with him."

"He wasn't like how he is now." Grace mentally compared the gentle lover he had been to the cold, harsh encounter last night. "Some part of me knew he was suffering, although I didn't know why, and I wanted to bring some joy into his life. He never talked about what he was going through, and I remember thinking that he was just having a hard time at home."

After she learned her father was in the Mafia, she guessed Rocco had some connection with them, too, but she didn't want to know so she never asked the question. Finding out he was not just in the Mafia, but involved in the very worst way, and having to witness exactly what that meant, had been too much of a shock to bear.

"I thought maybe the Rocco I knew was still there, hiding behind the mask," she continued, still half in and half out the door. "But last night I started to wonder if I was wrong."

Or was she? It was almost as if the closer they got, the harder he tried to push her away. Matthew had done the same, she remembered, when she first started counseling him at the orphanage. Abused by his foster family, he didn't trust easily, but Grace had been able to get through to him because she understood his fear. After losing her mother, her father, and Rocco, she hadn't wanted to get close to anyone because she couldn't go through that loss and betrayal again.

The roar of a Harley engine filled the air. A few moments later a motorcycle raced into the parking lot. Grace didn't have to wait for the rider to remove his helmet to know who had come looking for her. And for the first time since they'd met again, she felt a flicker of fear when she saw Rocco's face.

"Now that is one pissed-off alpha male in a protective frenzy," Mia said, watching him stalk toward the vehicle. "If you weren't sure about how he feels about you, I think your answer is right there."

"But don't worry." Gabrielle looked back and grinned. "I have a gun."

Jesus fucking Christ.

If he had to guess, he would say Grace was about to go into the fucking trailer park and start asking about her brother like there was no one after her, and she wasn't at the worst fucking scum hole in the city filled with criminal slime, some of whom wouldn't think twice about indulging in a little . . .

Breathe.

Breathe.

She was okay. She was okay. Mike and Paolo were here and would never have allowed her to go in alone because they liked having their limbs attached. Sometimes having a reputation as a vicious sadistic bastard had its advantages. Not only that, Gabrielle was an ex-cop and not only could she keep a cool head in dangerous situations, she was damn good with a gun.

Although she was six months pregnant.

And where the fuck was Luca to talk some sense into his woman? If Rocco had a wife who was six months pregnant, she sure as hell wouldn't be joyriding to a dangerous trailer park with her friends looking for a man who didn't want to be found. Hell, he'd lock her in the house where she would be safe, and the baby would be safe, and he wouldn't have to worry every second of every day if they were okay. And if they did have to go out, he'd be packing at least eight weapons, and she'd be wearing head to toe body armor, if they made that kind of thing for pregnant women.

Not that he could or would ever have a wife. Or a kid, for that matter. Definitely not a kid. And most definitely not a son because a son would be bound to the De Lucchi crew and he would never put a child through the hell he'd been through, even if it meant his own life. Cesare was already harassing him about finding an orphan to take his place, but there was no fucking way, and if it meant his days were numbered then he would look forward to the Hell waiting for him on the other side.

"Grace." He shouted, more out relief that he had found her in time, than anger. "Stop right there."

Of course, she didn't stop. His commands didn't seem to have any effect on this new Grace. Nor did his scowls or his shouts. To her credit, she didn't appear to be afraid of him, although right now he was frightening himself. If Tom was in this trailer park, chances were things were about to get ugly. He would have to make a decision that would either cost him his life or his connection to Grace, and he wasn't prepared to give up either one.

"Tom."

That's all she said. *Tom*. Like it explained why she

decided to leave the safety of his apartment, why she decided to seek out Mia, and why the fuck she thought driving out here with two chicks, one of whom was pregnant, albeit she was a better shot than most dudes he knew, was a good fucking idea.

Luca and Nico drove up a few minutes later, but he wasn't interested in hearing all hell break loose as they had it out with their women. Gabrielle, in particular, did not take kindly to Luca interfering with her work, but her pregnancy had sent the underboss into an overprotective frenzy, and every time they were together sparks flew.

"Grace." He jogged across the parking lot toward her. "What the fuck are you doing?"

"Tom," she repeated. "He's in there and I need to know he's okay."

Rocco's gaze swept over the trailer park, and he took in the dilapidated trailers, broken awnings, and rusted-out cars. He knew the place. It was a refuge for people who were on the run, a place where no one asked questions and every fucking week the newspaper reported another body rotting in the sun.

"I'll deal with it." There was no point trying to take Grace away without making a token effort to find her brother. Grace was a nurturer, and she felt too much. When God had been handing out the empathy, he'd given her a triple helping. The only problem was, sometimes she was so busy feeling, she forgot about practical things like how getting involved in mob business was not something she had ever wanted to do. And this had the stink of mob all over it.

"We can go together."

"Are you fucking kidding me?" The words exploded from him. "Do you seriously think I'm going to let you go in there? They will eat you alive."

"I'd like to see them try." She pulled a .22 from her purse and took a step toward the gate. Christ almighty. When had Grace become so damn stubborn? And brave? And when had she ever not listened to his advice? He was older and wiser and she had always done as he said.

"Jesus Christ. Put that away."

"Then stop bossing me around. My brother has been missing for two days, and if he is in there, something is wrong because he's not answering his phone. I need to find him. If I want to go in, I'll go in, and after I talk to the manager and find out if he's there . . ." She looked around the parking lot. "Mike will come to the trailer with me."

"Mike?"

"I'm not an idiot. I'm going in there alone. And Mike's a nice guy. He talks to me respectfully. He doesn't swear and shout. He does what I say, and he doesn't complain."

"Mike's a nice guy?" Should he tell her how Mike killed two Albanian hit men with his bare hands by smashing their heads together? Or how he had once re-enacted a gruesome scene from *Reservoir Dogs* with a drug dealer who had killed two of his friends?

"Yes, he is."

He pulled out his gun, tagged Mike standing near the manager's trailer. If that bastard had touched his woman . . . "Are you fucking Mike?"

That stopped her in her tracks. "Oh. My. God. No, you idiot. If you could get over yourself, I would be fucking you. But since you're all wrapped up in thinking I need to be saved from your badassness, I might as well do something useful with my time and find my brother. Now, unless you have a death wish, leave me alone."

"Are you . . ." His brow scrunched in a frown. "Threatening me?"

"Call it what you will. I won't be stopped."

Who the hell was this woman with the spine of steel, and what had happened to the sweet, submissive girl from New York? Or was it really such a surprise? He had seen that core of strength first when she left the family home, and then when she moved across the country to make a life for herself away from the Mafia world when she was only eighteen years old. He just hadn't recognized what it was.

"Is this because of last night?"

Thwack. She slapped him.

His breath caught, not because of the pain—her blow had barely registered on his cheek—and not because he didn't deserve it—he did—but because she'd gotten past his guard. No one had ever gotten past his guard.

The parking lot fell silent, the sounds of arguing fading away as everyone turned to stare. No one slapped members of the De Lucchi crew. They didn't clap them on the back, squeeze their shoulders, or even throw a mock punch in jest. Rocco had knocked men unconscious for less without even a second thought.

Not that he would ever raise his hand to a woman.

Grace glared at him. "That's for being such a bastard last night and today."

He stared as she walked away. Damn. She was still the Grace he'd loved, but now she was a whole lot more— more courage, more strength, more attitude. For the first time, he felt a flicker of hope that maybe there was someone in the world that could handle all that he was, that maybe this time she could accept the ugliness inside him.

"Gracie. Fuck. Wait. I'll come with you." He looked back over his shoulder and gestured for Mike and Paolo to follow.

"We're looking for someone in one of the trailers on

the east side," Grace said when they reached the manager's trailer.

The manager, a bald, portly dude wearing a Mickey Mouse T-shirt, looked over from the desk where he was watching a game show on TV. "Is he expecting you?"

"Unlock the fucking gate," Rocco growled. "It's a fucking surprise party. And a bullet going through your fucking head is gonna be another fucking surprise if you don't do it now."

Grace groaned loudly. "You don't have to kill him. I'm sure he wants to help us."

"You gonna unlock the gate?" Rocco asked the manager.

"Not unless your name is on the guest list." Seemingly unfazed by Rocco's threats, the manager made a show of looking at the empty guest list on the clipboard on his desk. "Doesn't look like there are any guests scheduled for today."

Rocco reached for his weapon. "There you go, *dolcezza*. He wants to die."

"Please unlock the gate," Grace said softly to the manger. "He hasn't shot anyone in days and I can't control him once he gets the itch."

The manager looked from Grace to Rocco and back to Grace again. "I get all types in here saying they're gonna blow off my head if I don't open the gate. They never follow through."

"Obviously," Rocco muttered, "else you wouldn't be talking, 'cause you'd have no fucking head."

Grace jabbed him in the ribs and he shot her an irritated glance. She was dragging out what should have been a simple discussion. If he'd been alone, the stupid manager would be unconscious or dead and the gate would be open.

"They're probably intimidated. You're a very impos-
ing guy. I'll bet you could take a bullet and still take
down anyone who tried to break in." She batted her eyes
at the manager, laughing softly.

Jesus Christ. Was she flirting with that dirtbag?
Rocco didn't like how the bastard's eyes had dropped to
half mast, or how his thick tongue was licking his big,
rubbery lips.

"I did take a bullet once."

"Wow." Grace breathed out the word, like she had
when they'd been in the elevator and she'd said his name.
"Was it from something like this?" She opened her
purse and pulled out her .22, pointing it seemingly idly
at the dude's chest.

How goddamn fucking smooth was that? His girl.
Leading the fucking slime ball on and turning his lust
against him with a subtle threat. For a moment, Rocco
wondered if his badness had rubbed off on her, but as
he watched the dude at the counter pale, he realized it
was a badness all her own.

"Did you show that to my brother when he came in?"
she said, still waving the gun. "He's always impressed
by guys who can take a bullet and carry on."

"Who's your brother?"

"Tom Mantini. A couple of inches taller than me.
Dark hair. Dark eyes. Kind of slim. Looks like me, but
a boy. He was supposed to meet me for lunch but he
didn't show and I got worried so I came out to see him."

"Yeah." The dude stared at the gun. "I suddenly remember him. Came here with the guys from trailer
twelve." He glanced over at Rocco and back to Grace.
"I guess I can let you in to check on him, but you guys
need to leave the weapons behind."

"Thanks. That's so kind." She gave him a big smile
and placed her weapon on the counter.

Rocco snorted as he removed the magazine from his gun and placed it beside hers. He had six more weapons strapped to his body, and he was damn sure the dude at the counter knew it.

"What the fuck was that?" he asked as they walked through the gate.

"That's called a non-violent solution to a problem."

"How is it non-violent if you point a gun at his sorry ass?"

She sniffed and tossed her hair like he'd irritated her by pointing out that simple fact. "I wasn't going to use it unless I had to. Anyway, I hope you took notes."

Rocco pulled another weapon from the holster behind his back and looked over his shoulder to check that Mike and Paolo were in position. "You want me to fucking come on to guys to get things done? Not gonna happen."

"Why?" Her lips quivered at the corners. "It might loosen you up."

Cazzo. "I don't like dudes. You know that."

"You didn't seem to like me much last night."

Whoa. He felt those words like a slap across the face. How did women so effortlessly turn any conversation back to the thing that had irritated them in the first place? He scrambled to keep up, his brain struggling to segue from him sleeping with dudes, to the bastard he'd been in bed last night.

A light breeze swept dust devils across his path as he made his way through the park. He heard the creak of an awning and the rattle of a can. Curious eyes studied him from behind torn curtains, but no one ventured outside. The kind of people who holed up here knew a wiseguy or three when they saw them.

If he wanted out, this was the perfect chance. He could tell her it was just sex. She would be hurt, but she'd get over it because she was strong and brave and beautiful, and he was damn sure there were dozens of men willing to take his place. He could nip this illicit relationship in the bud and send her back to her normal life, the way he'd done that night at the river, except this time he could do it without staining his soul.

"It was . . ." He looked at her beautiful face, the lines of worry in her forehead, the faint scar following the line of her jaw, the lips that had never been kissed until she had broken down his walls and pulled him through. Fuck the dozens of men. She was his. And he was hers, with all his ugly, tortured soul.

"Wrong," he said, releasing a breath he hadn't realized he was holding.

"You pushed me away." She threaded her fingers through his. "This isn't easy for me, either. I don't know if I want this or where I see it going. You know how I feel about the Cosa Nostra. It took me years before I was ready to reconcile with my father, and look what happened. I've been dragged back into a world I've run from twice already."

Yes, she had, but this time she wasn't running from it; she was owning it. She wasn't hiding; she was walking by his side.

They reached the far east corner of the trailer park and he studied the two trailers in front of him. One had flowers planted around it, a broken statute of a gnome and a tiny sprinkler watering a small patch of grass. The other one was covered in dust and had nothing but a broken lawn chair outside. He sent Mike and Paolo to investigate and tightened his grip on Grace's hand, forcing her to wait beside him.

"You got a minute, boss?" Mike gestured him away from Grace and lowered his voice so only Rocco could hear. "Two voices in the trailer with the chair," Mike said. "Maybe three. They aren't speaking English. If I had to guess, I'd say they're Albanian."

"Gracie." Rocco looked over his shoulder to where he'd left Grace waiting a safe distance away. "Mike thinks he might have found your brother. I'll go in first and make sure it's safe. Wait sixty seconds then send Tom a text."

"Okay." She pulled out her phone and damned if his heart didn't seize up at the hopeful expression on her face.

"Stay with her," he said to Mike. "Remember what I said."

Without waiting for a response, he walked up to the trailer and kicked open the door.

Within seconds, he had assessed the situation. Three men. Weapons. Drugs. No Tom. He heaved a sigh of relief and turned his attention to the shit-for-hire Albanians who, like him, did the jobs no one wanted to do. They worked for Cosa Nostra families who didn't have their own enforcers, as well as the Russian Mafia, drug lords, street gangs, and any other pussies who didn't want to get their hands dirty.

If Grace hadn't been outside, he would have just shot two of the bastards, and then used some creative interrogation techniques to get the information he needed from the third before sending him to join his friends. The Albanian Mafia were the worst of the worst—career criminals who specialized in death and torture—and the world would be a better place for their absence.

But he'd already almost lost Grace when she'd witnessed his violence before. Now he had a second chance, and he wasn't going to blow it.

He grabbed the first dude he saw and smashed his head into the wall. He threw a spinning sidekick, slamming his boot into the mouth of another dude sitting at the table. Out of the corner of his eye, he saw movement to his left, but by the time he turned, the third Albanian had drawn his gun.

Stalemate.

"Who the fuck are you?" the Albanian asked.

"I'm looking for a fucking missing person." He glanced around the trailer, taking in the gym bag full of cash, blood smears on the floor, a few needles and packages of powder, and three phones.

"No one here by that name." The dude with the gun laughed at his own joke, clearly thinking he had the upper hand because he had a gun.

Idiot.

Rocco had a gun, too, and he could get off three shots before the bastard even pulled his trigger, but today was the Albanian's lucky day because he was going to find a non-violent solution to the problem.

Right on cue, one of the phones vibrated on the table. He glanced over and saw Grace's name.

"Where did you get the fucking phone?"

"Who wants to know?"

"Rocco De Lucchi wants to know." He grabbed the nearest guy off the floor, and put his gun to his head. "Three seconds and he's gone."

Crack. The Albanian shot his friend, and the dude became deadweight in Rocco's arms. Rocco dropped to the ground as a second bullet shattered the silence, pulling his own trigger as he fell.

Outside, Grace screamed his name.

"Fuck." He rolled out from under the dead body and stared at the two men on the ground. "I didn't want to fucking kill anyone today."

The third guy was unconscious on the bed, his mouth a mess of blood and teeth. Unfortunate. But he would still be able to talk. He grabbed the bag and money as well as Tom's phone as he headed out the door.

"Oh my God." Grace ran over to him. "What happened? Are you okay? You're covered in blood. Was Tom there?"

His body still thrumming with adrenaline, he had an unexpected reaction to Grace's soft warm body pressed up against him as she drew him into a hug. He shifted his hips, gritting his teeth as his erection ground against her. How fucking inappropriate. He'd just killed two Albanians. This wasn't the time to get hard. But then he'd never had a hug after a hit, and it felt damn good.

"Tom wasn't there. Found his phone."

"Oh no." She sagged against him and he wrapped his free arm around, pulling her just a little tighter against his hips.

"There's a guy inside . . ." He gave Mike a pointed look. ". . . who might be willing to talk."

"I heard shots . . ." She looked up him, her brow creased in consternation.

"He . . . didn't like being . . . surprised." Rocco's heart thudded harder than it had when he'd been in the trailer. He didn't want to lie to her, but he also didn't want her to know two men were dead because of him. She wouldn't believe he'd tried not to kill them, and he couldn't even imagine losing her again.

"Oh." Her shoulders slumped the tiniest bit. "Well . . . let's go talk to the guy who is interested in talking."

"Mike will take care of it. He's good with that kind of conversation." He felt no small amount of satisfaction when her eyes widened with the realization that fucking "nice guy" Mike wasn't so nice after all.

She looked over at Mike, and then back to him. "Can Mike . . . get . . . the information we need? Or is it something you should . . . maybe . . . handle yourself?"

For a few seconds, he forgot to breathe. Was she serious? She wanted him to do the interrogation? "I thought you wanted non-violent solutions."

"I mean . . . I'm sure Mike is very competent," she said quickly. "And, of course, you know the best man for the job. But it's just . . . it's Tom . . . and he's been missing for two days, and you're . . ."

He was the best and she knew it. Not only did she accept what he could do, she wanted it, wanted him.

His chest swelled with pride, and his voice dropped to a satisfied growl. "You want me to handle it, *dolcezza*?"

"Yes."

He felt that word in his heart and in his fucking cock. Damn.

Just.

Damn.

"You gonna promise me you'll be okay with me doing what needs to be done?"

"Yes.

And fucking damn again.

"Consider it done." He nodded to Mike. "Call the cleaners for the trailer. Take him to the warehouse. Wait for me there."

"Sure thing, boss."

Rocco froze mid-step, his mouth opening to correct Mike. It was the second time Mike had slipped up. Rocco wasn't a boss. He was nothing. Outside. Other. But he liked how it sounded, liked the idea of having men of his own to help him with his work, and, when he caught Mike's smirk, to throw out the occasional joke.

"Thanks."

He almost laughed at Mike's sharp intake of breath.

The De Lucchis never said thank you. They never said please. They never said sorry.

His hand went to the cross around his neck. He was a De Lucchi, but before that, he had been someone else—maybe it was time to find out who that was.

TWELVE

By the time Rocco pulled his motorcycle up in front of her house, Grace was so aroused she was afraid to dismount in case that small amount of pressure made her come right there.

It didn't make any sense. Rocco had just beaten or possibly killed someone. His clothes were stained with blood. After he dropped her off, he was going to interrogate a man in a warehouse, and she knew exactly what that would entail.

Six years ago, just the thought of violence would have sickened her. But she knew Rocco. Trusted him. He wasn't a man who enjoyed gratuitous violence like his father, Cesare. He wouldn't have done what he had done without reason. If she wanted to find Tom and discover who had tried to kill her father and was after her, she would need to learn how to navigate this life instead of running away, and part of that was understanding that their world was not black and white; it was infinite shades of gray.

Watching Rocco kick in the trailer door had been all kinds of hot. The sheer raw, animal power that exuded from him, the intensity of his features, the confidence with which he moved, captivated her in a way nothing else ever had. She had never met a man with such a forceful and commanding presence. Even Nico, who was every inch a Mafia boss, had seemed positively civilized in the face of Rocco's raw, wild masculinity. On a primal level, he was simply irresistible, and the aura of danger he carried with him only seemed to heighten her desire.

Not to mention the hour-long ride pressed up tight against his back, her hips grinding against his perfect ass, the relentless vibration of the motorcycle rumbling between her thighs.

Gingerly, she slid off his bike, shaking out her hair as she removed her helmet.

Her skin prickled with awareness and when she looked up, she caught his hungry gaze.

Without a word, he cupped the side of her neck and yanked her toward him, kissing her so hard and fierce she almost lost her balance. His arm slid around her waist, holding her firm, and a moan vibrated low in her throat.

"Do you want to come inside?" she asked, when he let her up for air. "Ethan, Olivia, and Miguel are at work. Trevor's with the dog sitter."

"Got a job to do for you, *cara mia*. Gonna get it done. Just waiting for some guards to get here to keep you safe."

"Couldn't it wait?" Reaching down, she clasped his hand and placed it on her breast, hoping he could feel the tight bud of her nipple, the swell of arousal. His hand closed over the soft swell, and he kissed her again, plundering her mouth.

"You want me to wait?"

"God, yes." She arched her back, offered herself to

him. His was strung tight, every muscle like corded steel, and the heat coming off him . . . Lord she wanted to melt against him.

Rocco massaged her breast, rubbing his thumb over her taut nipple. She didn't care that they were standing on the street making out like a couple of teenagers or that there might be someone nearby wanting to snatch her away. She could feel his need, the energy humming in his body, his shaft thick and hard beneath his fly.

With a groan, he pulled away, his nostrils flaring, his eyes so dark with arousal they were almost black. "I tried for you, Gracie." He cupped her jaw, stroked his thumb over her cheek. "Today. In the trailer. I tried."

Her throat tightened and she swallowed hard. Part of accepting him was accepting that violence was part of the Mafia world. And yes, it had taken the person she loved, but it had also given her him.

"I know."

"I have a code." His voice caught, and she brought her fingers to his lips.

"Don't tell me. I know you well enough that I can guess. You're not Cesare."

"But I'm not a nice guy either." His lips quirked at the corners, and he pinched her nipple as if to emphasize the point, and dragged his thumb over the tip. She shuddered, a whimper slipping from her throat. And when his lips grazed her earlobe, sucked the sensitive skin at the base of her neck, she rocked her hips against him, seeking the pressure of his thigh between her legs.

"I can live with that. I'm beginning to wonder if I'm entirely a nice girl."

"Jesus Christ." He dismounted the motorcycle, releasing her long enough to set it on its kickstand, before wrapping his arms around her again. "Don't say things like that. I'm wound up pretty tight."

She knew exactly what he meant because they had often played rough, but as long as she could feel their connection, she had no hesitation giving him what he needed because he always made sure she enjoyed it, too. Not once had she ever felt unsafe with Rocco, even when they'd taken their encounters past her comfort level.

"Then let me unwind you." She clasped his hand and led him up the walk. When she reached for the key, he snatched it from her hand and unlocked the door, pushing her into the house.

Before she felt the first rush of cool air, he had kicked the door shut and propelled her backward. Her ass hit the door first, followed by the thick, hard bulge of his erection pressed up against her. And still he kissed her, now fucking her mouth with his tongue, hips grinding, teasing her with a taste of what was still hidden beneath a layer of denim.

"You don't waste any time, do you?" she murmured.

"Not when it comes to you." His hands smoothed down her body and under her shirt. Without hesitation, he shoved her bra up and captured her naked breast in his broad, warm palm. She moaned when he pinched her nipple, gasped when he unclipped her bra and tugged it, along with her shirt, over her head, tossing them both on the floor.

"Beautiful." He leaned down and his mouth, warm and wet, captured her nipple, and he sucked hard while his other hand made short work of the fly on her jeans.

Grace wound her arms around his neck, pulled him closer. She could feel his heat, the bunch of his muscles, the power thrumming beneath his skin, barely restrained. She ached to have him use his full strength on her, to unleash his passion, indulge his darkest desires, the way she wanted to indulge hers.

She had fantasized about him countless times as she

drifted off to sleep. She had dreamed of him taking control, surrendering to his most basic instincts to conquer and claim. Although she had tried to deny it, he was a predator, and she wanted to be his prey.

He released her nipple with a pop and drew the other one into his mouth. Without warning, his hand dove into her panties, fingers exploring the curve of her bare ass, the lacy material, the hidden puckered hole of her rear end. She shuddered at the unexpected contact, a mixture of fear and arousal sending a shot of pleasure straight to her core.

Rocco groaned against her breast and dropped to his knees, sliding her jeans and panties over her hips gently at first, and then, as if he couldn't wait, he yanked them over her feet one at a time until she stood naked before him.

She couldn't help but drink in the sight of him kneeling at her feet, fully clothed, his eyes intense, face taut with arousal. Her hands slid through his hair, as gentle as he had been violent only moments before, and then over his powerful shoulders, feeling his muscles shift beneath her fingers. She wanted to touch him like this when he was inside her, driving her wild.

"Lift your leg for me, *dolcezza*. Show me that beautiful cunt." He hooked her leg over his shoulder, giving her only a second to gain her balance before he plunged his tongue between her thighs, one long warm wet lick that went from her most intimate place through her labia and ended with a flick over her clit.

From out of nowhere, the stirrings of an orgasm caught her in a tide of white-hot heat. Her fingers tightened in his hair and she angled her hips—

"No." He pulled away, disengaging her fingers.

Grace looked down at him, confused. "No?"

"You don't come until I say."

Her cheeks flushed at his candid remark and the fact he had known she was so close to climax.

"I can't control it. When you do that . . . with your tongue . . ."

"Learn."

That word, his sharp tone of voice, the intensity of his gaze all had her quivering inside, hot and achy. This was better than her fantasies because she had never imagined he would deny her or that she would be able to deny herself. "Learn," she repeated taking deep breaths as the orgasm receded.

"Now, tell me what you want." He licked his lips, blew a hot breath on her aching pussy. "I want to hear dirty words coming from that sweet mouth. I want to get hard just listening to your voice."

"I want to come." She tightened her grip on his hair and pulled him forward. Dammit. She had been so close, and she wanted to be there again.

"How?" He inched forward, using his broad shoulders to spread her obscenely wide as he parted her folds with his fingers.

"With your mouth."

"Like this?" He flicked his hot, wet tongue over her labia, circling her entrance until she was rocking her hips trying to get his tongue where she needed it to go.

"My clit." She panted her breaths, her reticence fleeing before a tidal wave of desire. "Lick my clit."

"Not dirty enough. This is all you get." He rolled his finger over her clit, gently at first, and then faster, enough to drive her wild but not enough to send her over the edge.

"Oh God, Rocco." She panted her breaths. "More. I need more."

"Tell me."

"Lick my pussy. Suck me. Fuck me. Make me come."

"Good girl." He nipped her clit with his teeth, sucked it into his mouth as he plunged two fingers into her entrance.

She cried out, her nails digging into his scalp, her head banging against the door, as he licked and sucked while his fingers pounded inside her.

"I'm going to—"

He stood, sliding her leg gently off his shoulder. Stunned, still lost to the pleasure of his mouth, she watched as he yanked his shirt over his head and threw it aside.

"I want you to come on my cock," he said as he shoved his clothing over his hips. "I want to feel that hot, wet pussy. I want to hear my name on your lips."

Her gaze dropped down to the piercing glistening at the end of his cock, and her mouth watered remembering just how it felt rubbing against her sensitive inner walls.

He pulled a condom from his pocket and sheathed himself, rolling it slowly over his hardened length. He was inside her before she could speak, stretching her, filling her, the cold steel of his piercing a delicious burn. With one hand, he drew her leg up and around his hip, fingers digging into her ass, while the other tangled in her hair drawing her head back to bare her throat to the heated slide of his lips.

She cried out as he thrust into her, clung to his shoulders, begged with all the dirty words she had never dared say for him to give her the release he had been holding out of reach.

Rocco growled into her throat and devoured her with hungry kisses and hard sucks on her skin that she knew would leave bruises. But she didn't care. She wanted to remember this. She wanted to feel the burn and remember all his wildness.

"So fucking sexy." One hand slipped between them and he circled his finger around her clit, rubbing over the tight nub in time to his long, deep thrusts.

"Now, *cara mia*. Come with me." He sealed his mouth over hers and she came with a deep, guttural groan, his name tearing from her throat as he continued to pump inside her. And then his cock thickened and the sound of his release, low and primal, send another climax shivering through her.

For the longest time, they held each other, arms intertwined, hearts thudding together. Grace closed her eyes and thought back to the nights she had fallen asleep warm and safe in Rocco's bed with his body curled around hers listening to the sound of his voice as he whispered beautiful things in her ear.

"I like the bossiness when we're having sexy times," she said softly, looking up to trace the outline of his jaw with her finger. "It turns me on. But the bossiness outside the bedroom . . . not so much."

He caught her finger, drew it to his lips. "I'll keep that in mind the next time I want to watch you come."

"When would that be?"

"After I find out what our Albanian friend has to say about Tom." He kissed her finger and pulled away, leaving her bereft. While he disposed of the condom, she pulled on her clothes, their sweet moment destroyed by her guilt over what she was sending him to do. Once he walked out the door, there would be no going back. Whatever happened to the man in the warehouse would be on her shoulders, even if she wasn't there to throw the first punch.

"What if he doesn't talk?" she asked when he returned.

"He will." Rocco cupped her jaw in his hand and tipped her face up to his. "I promise he will walk away when I'm done, or if he can't walk, he'll still be breathing."

Grace let out a sigh of relief. "Thank you for understanding."

"Pleasure."

"I want to come with you if you get a lead."

Rocco snorted. "Not in a million years."

"He's my brother."

"And he's in some deep shit right now, and I don't want you involved. Either he's hiding and won't be happy to have both of us show up on his doorstep, or he's been kidnapped, in which case you would be a liability. This is business, *cara mia,* and women don't get involved."

"Someone wanted to kill my dad and brother and kidnap me," she said, bristling. "That makes me involved. And I'm not going to sit around playing victim when I could be doing something. I'm not stupid. I'm not planning to take unnecessary risks, but we have a lead because I had the idea to trace Tom's phone. So don't just dismiss me as a 'liability.'"

His mouth opened and closed as if he were going to say something and thought better of it. "Fair enough."

She heard footsteps on the porch and pushed Rocco toward the living room, hoping to hide any signs of their illicit activity. "Look casual."

Rocco snorted a laugh and sat on the couch, putting his feet up on the table just as Ethan and Olivia walked in the door.

"Grace! What's going on? Who are all the guys outside?" Ethan spotted Rocco on the couch and took a step back. "Whoa. Dude. You gonna break down the door again?"

"It's okay," Grace said. "He's under control. We're . . . um . . . together."

Ethan's face fell. "Together together?"

Creak. She didn't need to look over to know Rocco was off the creaky sofa and was on the prowl. Moments later she felt his heavy possessive arm on her shoulders. And although he didn't speak, the message was clear.

Mine.

"Yeah." She glanced up. Rocco's expression hadn't changed. But was that the faintest ghost of a smile on his lips? One less crease in his perpetual scowl? "Sorry, Ethan. I should have told you earlier but . . ."

"Hey. It's okay." Ethan shrugged. "If it was going to work out between us, it would have worked out long ago. Just glad you found someone who makes you happy, even if he does like to break down doors."

Rocco gave a satisfied grunt and shook Ethan's offered hand. "Gonna have some security at your place for a bit, but you just carry on as usual."

"Security for what?" Ethan glanced over at the guard standing near the window. "Is Grace in danger?"

"Classified."

"Classified?" Ethan's brow creased. "If she's in danger, I need to know. Are you in the secret service? FBI? CIA? Undercover police? Military?"

"Something like that."

Ethan folded his arms across his chest, and for the first time she realized he had an alpha side. "Something like that isn't an answer."

"The guys who put my dad in the hospital are still out there, and Rocco's worried they might come after me," Grace said by way of explanation. "I'm going to stay with him for a bit, but when I'm home I guess his guards will be here with me. It's just a precaution."

"Which one can I have?" Olivia murmured, half to herself. "I prefer blondes but I could make do with either of the guys on the porch."

"Can you still go out?" Ethan looked from Grace to

Rocco and back to Grace. "Our last gig was a disaster. Sunita was totally wrecked. Her voice was gone from all the smoking and she had no idea what was happening on stage. After two songs, I pulled her off and we just went instrumental until the end. I apologized to the manager and told him he didn't have to pay us, and this morning I kicked her out of the band. Now I have no vocalist and we have the Stardust gig booked for tonight."

Rocco gave a curious grunt of irritation, and Grace looked up at him and frowned.

"Anything you wanted to say?"

"No."

"Could you help us out?" Ethan begged. "Just for one night. I've been auditioning vocalists, but I haven't found anyone yet."

"I can't, Ethan." Her hand went to her cheek and she realized she rarely thought about her scar anymore. But that didn't mean it was gone. "I'll be there to support you, but I just can't go on stage."

Rocco washed the lingering traces of blood from his hands in the men's restroom at the Stardust, listening to Danny introduce the band. He knew all the musicians now after meeting them last night. Grace had convinced him to stick around for dinner when the other members of the band showed up. Although he didn't have much to say, he'd enjoyed chilling out with them, listening to their stories about gigs gone bad, having a few drinks and playing with the dog with Grace curled up beside him on the couch.

He'd stayed the night with her, indulging himself in her deliciously naked body until they'd fallen into an exhausted sleep. It had almost been normal, at least until dawn, when he'd had to leave her in the care of the guards and go out to the warehouse to spend the day torturing information out of an Albanian hit man who didn't want to talk.

In the end, however, the bastard had talked. They always talked. No one left a De Lucchi interrogation without spilling his guts—in every sense of the word.

Fuck. He hadn't meant to kill the guy. He had tried his very best to fulfill his promise. He really had. But what the fuck was he supposed to do when Mike and Paolo had forgotten to search the bastard before they tied him up and he'd jumped Rocco with a knife in the middle of questioning?

Lesson learned. He couldn't make that promise again because if he hadn't been so focused on trying not to kill the bastard once the torture got underway, he would have seen the subtle movements of the Albanian's arms that would have alerted him to the fact the dude had a knife down the back of his jeans.

Death was inevitable once the guy rushed him. Although he hated what he had become, he was a member of the De Lucchi crew, and the insult could be addressed in only one way.

By the time the clean-up crew arrived and he'd dumped the body in Lake Mead, it was too late to go back to Grace's house and he'd sent her a message— after finally exchanging numbers—that he'd meet her at the club.

He wasn't looking forward to giving her the bad news that Tony had hired the Albanians to find Tom, or that Tony had given them Tom's phone, because it meant that Tony or his guys were likely responsible for the Carvello shooting. The only people who had the power to give permission to whack the New York underboss were the don and his *consigliere*. But the *consigliere* had already given the contract to Cesare who had given it to Rocco, which meant the only person who could have ordered Tony to whack Nunzio and Tom was the don himself. But it didn't make sense. If he wanted them out of the way, why wait until they were in Vegas? Why go through Tony? And what did he want with Grace?

Rocco checked his hands under the restroom light. Blood had a nasty way of getting under his nails and he didn't want to touch Grace with blood-stained hands.

When his hands were finally clean, he left the restroom and walked down the hallway. Stormy Blu had just started their set, and the first few bars of Sinatra's "Strangers in the Night" drifted down the hall, bringing back memories of Grace and the first time they met. But when the vocalist sang the first line, he froze.

Christ. He'd never heard anything so bad. The dude sounded like he was being tortured, and Rocco knew all variations on that theme. His teeth clenched at the butchered sound.

"Go." A woman's voice echoed down the hallway. "You have to get out there. He's going to destroy the band's reputation. They'll never get another gig in the city."

"I can't go on stage."

His heart skipped a beat. Grace. And that had to be Olivia with her.

"It's like someone's pouring shattered glass in my ears," Olivia said. "Please. Put him out of his misery. No, put the audience out of their misery. Any moment now, there's going to be a stampede out the door. You know the songs. You rehearsed with them when Sunita couldn't make it. You have a beautiful voice. It's just this one time. Think how desperate Ethan must be to sing on stage. I know he's auditioning vocalists this weekend. I'm sure he'll find someone."

"Why didn't he just go instrumental?"

"Apparently the manager wasn't happy with that suggestion. It was sing or lose the gig, and he didn't want to let the guy down."

Rocco heard Grace curse. "It's been six years since I sang in public. And last time I didn't have the scar. They're just going stare at my face."

Pain spiked through his body at the thought that his beautiful Gracie was too ashamed to sing. And it was because of him, because he'd wanted her too much, because he'd been too selfish to let her go until it was too goddamn late.

"I bought this, just in case," Olivia said.

He heard the rustle of a bag and then, "What is it?"

"A mask of sorts. Half a mask. Really it's just a little lace and crochet work with some beads, but on the model it looked very sexy and mysterious. It doesn't really hide much, but I thought it might be enough to give you a small measure of comfort."

The tinny sound of feedback echoed down the hallway, and Rocco cringed. Fuck. Even though he hadn't signed the papers, he felt no small measure of responsibility for the club. Ethan was going to destroy the Stardust's reputation as well as that of the band. And what if Rocco did take over the club one day? Damned if he would own a club that was known for hiring bad bands. If this didn't end soon he would get Danny to put an end to the travesty.

"What do you think?"

Rocco walked down the hallway and pushed on the partially open door. Grace stood in front of a mirror in what he assumed was the band's backstage space. She wore a loose, flowery dress that was way too short for his liking, and a pair of cowboy boots that made her long, toned legs seem even longer. The delicate mask, all soft woven string and lace hid none of her beauty and instead made her look sultry and mysterious and sexy as fuck.

"I like it." Grace's eyes widened as she caught sight of Rocco in the mirror, and she gasped.

"What are you doing here?"

"Just got off work."

Her eyes widened, and her mouth formed an *oh* of surprise. But it was "work." Although this time he wasn't getting paid.

"Sing," he said. "You've got a beautiful voice. You should share it. You make people feel . . ." He thumped his chest. "In here."

Grace stared at him, her gaze burning a path to his soul. "I don't know . . ."

"I won't let anything happen to you up there," he promised, knowing this was a promise he could keep. "Anything goes wrong, you feel uncomfortable, anyone even looks at you the wrong way, I'll end it."

"You'll end it?" Olivia snorted. "How? You'll rush the stage?"

"I own the club." The words fell from his lips before he could stop them, but he could make it a truth with the wave of a pen.

Grace frowned. "You own Stardust?"

"Almost. All the paperwork is done. Just gotta sign on the dotted line. You go up there tonight, and I'll sign."

Her face softened. "I didn't think you could . . ." She trailed off, her gaze flicking to Olivia and then back to him. "That's kind of cool."

"That mean you'll sing?"

She drew in a shuddering breath. "You'll be here?"

"I'll be right here, Gracie. Just like I used to be. I never missed one of your performances and I'm not gonna start now."

She looked from him to Olivia and back to him. "Okay, since it's your club, and it's just this once. And I'll wear the mask."

After Olivia helped her tie on the mask, and Rocco gave her a kiss for luck, she walked out to the stage.

Rocco thought he'd almost burst from pride as they followed her. "She's singing," he said to Olivia as if she hadn't just been standing there when Grace agreed to sing.

Olivia looked up at him and glared. "There's something I've been meaning to say. I don't know what you did to her in the past, and it seems she's forgiven you, but I'm still watching. And I'm telling you right now that if you put that scar on her face there is nothing I won't do to keep her away from you."

He pressed his lips together, feeling no need for a response. Although he hadn't wielded the blade, he was responsible for everything that had happened that night at Newton Creek.

"I've lived in Vegas all my life," Olivia whispered, slowing her steps as Grace walked onto the stage. "I have connections. I know people. Scary people."

His gaze sliced to her, and he gave her a glimpse of what lay just beneath the surface of his otherwise expressionless face.

Olivia paled, but didn't back down. "Maybe not quite as scary as you, but you get my point."

"Yeah." His lips quivered at the corners. He wasn't afraid of any man or woman. But she was a protector, and he liked that Grace had her for a friend.

Grace joined Ethan at the front of the stage, and relief flickered across Ethan's face. He stepped back to give her the floor and picked up his guitar. Grace easily segued into the song, and Sinatra's "Something Stupid" became something beautiful.

Just like her.

She was the epitome of everything Rocco wanted but could never have. She was all the goodness in the world, and listening to her exquisite voice ripped something loose in his heart.

He didn't move while she was on stage, but he did make a decision, and when the band was done and he was waiting in the back hallway to see her, he was ready when his phone rang with the call he had known would come.

"Cesare."

"What the fuck is going on out there?" Cesare's voice rose to a shout. "It was a simple fucking job. Whack Mantini and his son. Now I hear Mantini is still alive. What went wrong?"

"Someone else got there before me. Mantini must have a lot of enemies. Five guys in masks. Busy restaurant. Whoever it was had balls. The son escaped. Mantini's in the hospital and Nico's put a guard on him. Nothing I can do until he's out."

"What about the girl?"

Rocco's heart skidded to a stop. "The contract didn't include her."

"You've been seen with her. What the fuck?" Cesare's voice turned to ice. "I thought I made it clear that relationship was over. If this is about you not keeping your dick in your fucking pants—"

"Don't go there," he warned, a growl rising in his throat as he dared to disrespect the man who owned his soul.

"If I have to come out there and teach that lesson again," Cesare continued, as if Rocco hadn't spoken, "it won't be just that bitch's face I cut up. And it won't just be me getting a taste of the pussy that's so sweet it's worth your fucking life. I'm going to give her to the crew if there's anything left of her when I'm done. And this time I won't let her run away."

Rocco's protective instincts surged to the fore and his hand tightened around the phone as he tried to breathe through the tidal wave of anger that had turned his vision red. "Save the fucking threats for your trainees. I'm done with all this shit."

"This 'shit' is your family," Cesare snarled. "And you are never done with this family until you're dead. You fuck up again, and you'll pay the fucking price. And if you thought I made you scream when you were a boy, that's nothing compared to what I will do to you now. I know you, Rocco, like no one else does. I broke you down until I saw inside your soul. I know what truly scares you. I can make you suffer in ways you never imagined. I can make you beg me for a death that will never come. I won't just destroy your body, I will destroy the essence of who you fucking are."

Until Grace had walked back into his life, Rocco hadn't cared if he lived or died. But now that he'd had a taste of the life he could have led if Cesare hadn't plucked him from the orphanage, he wanted more—more Grace in his arms and in his bed, more feeling like part of Nico's crew, more being part of the world instead of other.

He wanted out. Not just to ensure Grace's safety, but for himself. Fuck Cesare. Fuck the De Lucchi crew. Fuck the Mafia. Fuck the rules. After they were done here, he could call Nico and tell him to put more guards on Mantini. If he found Tom, he would hide him. And then he would go to New York and realize the fantasy he'd had since he was ten years old. For the first time, he had not only the skills and power to make Cesare pay for what he's done, but the will. He would have his freedom, and he would have his revenge. And then he would take back his life, just as tonight, his beautiful, brave Grace had taken back her voice.

It was on the tip of his tongue to tell Cesare to fuck the hell off, hang up the phone, and deal with the consequence. But he'd been too long in the life to make a rash decision that would end in certain death. He wanted to live. And to do that, he would have to play a careful game.

"You're getting melodramatic in your old age," he snapped. "I need some time. Nico Toscani is all over this shit. Mantini is untouchable in the hospital."

"You aren't my only soldier out there," Cesare said. "Even if you fail me, the job will get done, and if not by you, then expect to pay the price of failure."

Rocco ended the call, his blood pounding in his ears. Who the hell was Cesare talking about? He knew everyone in the De Lucchi crew, even the soldiers who had been sent out to other factions. There was no else in Vegas or in Nevada for that matter. Could Cesare be bluffing? Truth meant nothing to him. And his son, apparently, meant even less.

Adoptive son. One day he would trace his family and find out who he really was.

"Rocco!" Grace came running down the hallway. "I did it. I sang on stage!"

"Yeah, you did, *cara mia.*" He caught her on the run, swung her up into his arms. "You were magnificent. You have the voice of an angel."

"Can you believe it? A few weeks ago, I would never have imagined I'd be singing on stage." She wrapped her arms and hugged him tight. "Or that I'd have pulled a gun on someone or asked you to do what you do to help me find Tom. Or that I'd be with you again. There's no going back, Rocco. I'm a whole new me."

His heart felt like it was going to bust right out of

his chest. It wasn't just her. A few weeks ago, he would never have imagined disobeying an order, lying to Cesare, owning a fucking business, or sitting in a meeting with Nico's crew as if he were one of the guys. And he couldn't have imagined being part of Grace's life again, holding her in his arms, letting her into his heart. She was right. There was no going back. But nothing had ever scared him as much as the road ahead and the impossible dream that might not be impossible after all.

THIRTEEN

"*Put him on his knees.*"

Cesare folded his arms as Rocco shoved the Falzone crime family soldier down on the rocky shore of Newtown Creek. The soldier had shot up a Gamboli family restaurant, killing the don's aunt and nephew as well as two civilians. The don had called in the De Lucchi crew, and in a matter of hours they'd found the soldier hiding out in the basement of his brother's home.

"*Are you sure you caught the right man?*" *Cesare demanded.* "*Let me see his face.*"

Rocco worked loose the knot on the hood he'd placed over the soldier's head when he dragged him out of the house. Rocco had felt nothing when he pleaded for his life, nothing when his sister had begged Rocco to spare him, nothing when his son screamed not to hurt his dad. After years of torture and beatings, he'd learned to retreat into a cold, dark place when there was work to be done, a void without emotion or feeling, where all that mattered was obeying Cesare's commands.

"*Hurry up.*"

Rocco released the hood and ripped it over the sol-

dier's head, locking his hand on the man's shoulder in case he tried to get away. They always tried to get away, just like he had always tried to get away when Cesare took him to the basement for training. And just like Rocco, the victims quickly learned there was nowhere to go and no one to save them.

"Yes, that's him. Well done."

Rocco breathed a silent sigh of relief. It had been his first solo mission, and Cesare did not take failure lightly. Had he failed to capture the solider, or worse, brought the wrong man, he would have been expected to offer himself up for a beating by the five most senior members of the De Lucchi crew. The last time he'd messed up, he thought he would die from his injuries. If Grace hadn't gone looking for him because he didn't show up to pick her up at school, he wouldn't be here today. She had called an ambulance and saved his life, but as he stood on the bank of the creek knowing what Cesare expected him to do, he wished she had let him die in her arms.

"I trained you well," Cesare said into the silence. "But not well enough. You have a weakness, Rocco. A chink in your armor. Tonight, we repair it." He gestured behind him and Cesare's right-hand man, Benito, the most senior member of the De Lucchi crew, stepped out of the shadows holding Grace in front of him, one hand over her mouth, the other holding a knife against her throat.

"Grace." Her name was a strangled gasp on Rocco's lips as adrenaline surged through his body, the cold, dark void crumbling beneath a tidal wave of rage. He had been so careful. So very, very careful. He knew the risk, but he couldn't resist. Now he would pay for his selfishness with her life.

"You think I wouldn't find out?" Cesare sneered.

"*You think there is anything I don't know about you? I made you. I broke you. I know your most secret fears and desires. I know when you're hiding something. And this . . .*" He waved vaguely at Grace. "*This is what is holding you back from becoming the enforcer you are meant to be. This is the price we pay to hold the power of life and death in our hands. We don't have friends. We don't have lovers. We don't have relationships. Women are for fucking. They are cunts and nothing more.*"

Rocco could barely hear for the rush of blood in his ears. If Cesare knew him as well as he claimed, he had to realize that if Benito killed her, Rocco wouldn't stop until they both were dead.

He heard footsteps behind him. Turning, he saw another member of the De Lucchi crew with a weapon pointed at his back. Cesare had thought of everything, except the possibility that Rocco would welcome his death if Grace was no longer part of his world.

"*You can't kill the daughter of the underboss,*" he gritted out, trying to put an emotional distance between himself and the woman with the knife against her throat. *Senior members of the family, including blood relatives, could not be whacked without the permission of the don, and he knew Don Gamboli would never give his permission to whack Grace. First, women were protected by the Mafia code, and second, Grace was his goddaughter.*

Cesare laughed. "*I don't plan to kill her. This is about pain. This is about revenge. And this is about you, Rocco, and helping you overcome a weakness that is holding you back. I think the best way to do that would be show her who you really are.*" *He gestured to the soldier kneeling at Rocco's feet.* "*Finish the job.*"

Bile rose in Rocco's throat. Cesare was going to make Grace watch him take a life. He couldn't have thought of a better way to end the relationship or a worse way to hurt him. Grace had never gotten over watching her mother die in her arms or the revelation that her father was part of the same organization responsible for taking her mother's life. Forcing her to watch the soldier pay for his crimes tonight wouldn't just end things between them, it would scar her forever. For sweet, gentle Grace, his actions would be unforgivable.

"Let her go. She's not part of this."

"You made her part of this." Cesare gestured to Benito. "Bring her to me."

Rocco reached for his weapon, remembering too late that Cesare had instructed him to capture the soldier unarmed. He had only his knife with him, and there was little he could do from a distance when Benito's knife was at Grace's throat, and Cesare's man had a gun at his back.

Cesare changed places with Benito, replaced Benito's knife with his own.

"Get on with it," Cesare barked.

Rocco's stomach twisted in a knot. This wasn't the first execution he'd assisted with, but it was the first in which he was expected to deliver the death blow. It was his initiation into the Cosa Nostra. The night he became a made man. The thought of Grace witnessing his descent into darkness, the very moment he lost the soul she'd been trying to save, was a worse pain than any he had suffered at Cesare's hands.

He dragged his gaze to Grace, recoiling when he saw her face wet with tears. His fault. All his fault. He should have left her alone, resisted his longing, pushed her away. He tried to tell her with his eyes what was in his heart. He would always be the same man caught in a nightmare that he could never escape.

"Please let her go." He knew better than to beg. Weak men begged and there was nothing Cesare detested more than weakness. But it was all he had left to give her.

"Please?" Cesare sneered. *"You want me to spare her? Why? So she can keep pretending you're something you are not? So she can make you forget who you are and why I saved you?"*

If he hadn't been so distraught, he would have laughed. Until he was ten, he had believed the lie. Cesare had found him in an orphanage and saved him from a life of poverty and shame. He had given him a home, clothing, toys, food, and even a dog. He had sent him to school. He had given him female care in the form of a housekeeper who had pretended to be Cesare's wife to ensure the adoption went through. He had given him the De Lucchi name. But when the training started, he realized he hadn't been saved at all. He had been cast into Hell. His punishment for being a coward when he was six years old.

Over the years, Cesare had systematically destroyed every single thing he loved. Everything he owned had been given to him so it could be taken away. Enforcers didn't have attachments. They didn't love and were not loved. They existed solely to enforce the will of the boss to whom they were bound.

"You dishonor and disrespect me with your weakness." Cesare grabbed Grace's hair and yanked her head to the side. *"I can't take the temptation out of beauty, but I can take the beauty out of temptation."* Before Rocco could process what Cesare intended to do, Ceasre drew the blade down Grace's cheek from ear to chin, slicing open her perfect, creamy skin. Grace's scream pierced the night air, embedding itself like an arrow deep in his heart.

"*No!*"

Too late. Too fucking late. Blood dripped down her face, staining her white blouse and her scream went on and on, the sound reverberating in his heart.

"*Do it,*" *Cesare shouted over her screams, spittle flying from his lips. "Or I'll cut up her pretty face until not even her father will recognize her. She's the one thing holding you back from becoming what you truly are. We are De Lucchis. There is no room for emotion, no room for feeling, no place for love.*"

Rocco's vision sheeted red, every cell in his body screaming in rage and agony. He grabbed the soldier's hair and slid the knife across this throat—quick and painless, the only mercy he could give.

When the soldier dropped to the stones, he lunged forward, praying for death from the gun at his back, before Grace suffered more pain.

"*Release her.*"

Cesare let her go and she crumpled to the ground. It was over. Cesare had won. Rocco didn't need to look at Grace's face to see her horror and devastation. He was everything she despised—the worst part of the organization that had killed her mother. He would find no more sanctuary in her arms, no forgiveness in her heart or soothing beneath her fingers. He would never lie with her and hear her beautiful voice, feel the softness of her body or the sound of her laugh. She was everything that was good and pure in the world, and he was everything that was evil. In some perverse way, Cesare had done him a favor. He had saved Grace from the monster he had created—a monster who was too weak to let her go, and so had destroyed her.

"*If you were my blood, I would be ashamed to call you my son,*" *Cesare said coldly. "Of my three adoptees,*

you are my biggest disappointment. You'll resume your
training. Now that you have no distraction, I expect
you to excel."

And didn't that just drive the knife home. He had no
memories of his life before Cesare. No memories of his
parents or the orphanage in Vegas where Cesare had
found him. Cesare was the only father he had ever known.
His housekeeper, the only mother. Even when Cesare had
started training him as a Mafia enforcer, he had endured
the emotional and physical pain because he believed Ce-
sare's teachings were motivated by love.

He had been wrong. Just as he had been wrong to
think that he could have a normal life with a normal girl.
It was time to cut the ties. He had already done things
that had put him beyond redemption, things that tor-
mented his soul and kept him awake at night. Time to
stop fighting what he really was. Time to let her go.

"Rocco."

Rocco startled awake, instantly aware of the tremor
in Grace's voice. His hand slid under his pillow and he
drew out his weapon as he jumped off the bed, ready to
take down the intruder. "Where is he?"

"No." She shrank back against the wall, her arms in
front of her face, distracting him with the beauty of her
naked body. "No one's here."

He cursed himself inwardly for letting instinct over-
ride rational thought. After years of being woken, only
to be beaten, the slightest sound made his body react as
if it were under threat.

"What's wrong?" Adrenaline pounded through his
body, and he made a quick visual search of the apartment, disbelieving she could be so fearful when no one
was there.

"Your back." She stared at him aghast. "What happened to you? Who did that?"

Rocco let out a relieved breath and lowered the gun. Until tonight, he had been careful not to let her see his back, either by keeping his shirt on or positioning her in front of him, but last night, after he'd loved her properly—slowly and sweetly like he used to do—he'd stripped off his shirt to feel her against him and made the mistake of falling asleep with her in his arms.

"It's nothing."

"Nothing?" Her hand flew to her mouth. "Rocco. That's not nothing. And you didn't get those marks in a fight. It's torture. Someone tortured you. Was it Cesare?"

Words failed him. How could he explain the need to punish himself for every deed he did that tormented his soul? A lifetime of Our Fathers and Hail Marys would not be enough to atone for his sins. It was something too deeply personal to explain. Not even Clay knew why he visited the dungeon or what solace he sought under the lash of the whip.

"Come to bed." He slid his gun under the pillow and pulled on his shirt.

"I want to know what happened." She folded her arms over her chest, and it took him a moment to remember that this wasn't the same girl who had scrambled up the river bank, her face wet with blood and tears, screaming at him to leave her alone, the girl who had run away, left him without saying good-bye. This Grace had fight and courage, and she wasn't going to back down.

"I said leave it," he snapped.

"No."

"Jesus fucking Christ, Grace." His voice rose to a shout, and he slammed his hand down on the bed. He knew he was overreacting, but the nightmare was still with him, twisting its way through his heart. "It's nothing to do with you. Some things you just can't heal."

"Your pain is everything to do with me." She pressed her lips together and glared. "Pain and trauma are what I heal. And don't you dare speak to me that way again, or I will walk out that door."

His mouth opened and closed again. When he used that tone of voice with the Toscani soldiers and associates they almost pissed themselves in fear. When he scowled at the men he hunted down, they quivered in their boots. But Grace, less than half his size, one quarter of his strength, gloriously naked beside his bed, was not taking his shit, and he'd never been so turned on in his life.

"Nothing happens without my consent." It was as much as he was going to tell her, and even that revelation came through gritted teeth.

Her expression turned thoughtful. "Kink?"

"Fuck no."

She wanted more, and he could see her internal struggle reflected on her face, but mercifully she held back and climbed into bed beside him. "You'd better not introduce me to whoever did that to you."

Her fierce expression and her threatening words made him laugh. "I will never believe you again when you tell me you're anti-violence, *cara mia*."

"Not when someone I care about is hurt."

Damn. Her protectiveness made his heart squeeze in his chest. She cared about him. It was more than he had ever hoped for that night she ran away, more than he had dreamed about in the lonely years since.

"Come here, Gracie." A smile tugged the corners of his lips. "I have something else that hurts and you can kiss the pain away."

"Again?" She crawled across the bed and straddled his hips. "I didn't think you'd—"

"I would what?" He covered her breasts with his palms, squeezed them firmly.

"Be able to do it again so soon." Her legs widened and she rocked her wet pussy over his shaft, already rock hard and ready for her again.

"Why not? I have the sexiest woman in the city in my bed. And if I remember correctly, that was never an issue before. You used to beg me to take a break." He puffed out his chest, proud of his youthful stamina, as he reached over to the nightstand for a condom.

"You're . . . older now."

"What?" He froze with the condom packet in his teeth.

Her cheeks flushed, and she looked down. "Well, you're in your thirties now—"

"Jesus Christ." He ripped on the packet and sheathed himself, then lifted her, angling his hips so the head of his cock just breached her entrance. "You think I can't keep up? I am everything I was then and more. Bigger. Stronger. Faster. And I can go all fucking night long."

Grace's body shook, and he lifted her chin with one finger to see her laughing. "Little minx. You know just where to drive the knife."

"I love you like this," she said, running her hands over his shoulders. "You are beautiful to me. No matter how old—"

He cut her off with a kiss as he drove his cock into her warm, wet heat. Grace gasped into his mouth and he pushed her up. "Ride me, *dolcezza*. I want to hear you scream as your old man pleasures the fuck out of you."

"So romantic."

"Right now I am beyond romance. You are so damn

hot and wet, I can't think about anything else." He lifted her and slid in deeper, his hips forcing her thighs apart.

"It's your fault." She leaned back, grinding over his cock, her hands squeezing her breasts, and fuck wasn't that the hottest thing he'd ever seen. "The way you touch me, the way you talk to me and look at me. Everything about you makes me hot."

And everything about her made him hard. He understood now why Cesare said women made a man weak. He would die for this—not just the act itself, but the connection with her that took the encounter from just a physical act to something that nourished his soul. Cesare was dangerous to his body, but Grace was dangerous to his heart.

He cradled her face in his hands and kissed her gently, creating a steady, slow rhythm that threatened his self-control.

Grace squirmed on top of him, her hard nipples rubbing over his chest. "We did it slow last time," she complained.

Yes, they did, but he was reluctant to let go the way he had before. He wanted to learn her body again before he took her the way he really wanted—hard and wild and with utter abandon.

Sliding his hands down, he squeezed her ass as he pumped into her pussy. His middle finger stroking closer and closer to the cleft between her cheeks. When the tip of his finger brushed her rear entrance, she froze and her pussy clenched around him. He kept up the rhythm, waiting for her muscles to relax before he did it again. On the third pass, he slicked her moisture and drew gentle circles over her puckered opening.

"Rocco?" Her voice was thin with uncertainty but heavy with desire.

"I want you here, Gracie."

"We never did that before."

He didn't want to ask the next question, but he needed to know. "You ever had a man in your ass?"

Her voice was so quiet when she answered, he almost missed it. "No."

A satisfied growl escaped his lips. He had been all her firsts, and now he would be the first man in her most intimate place. Gracie would be his. In all ways, she could belong to him.

"I'm going to make it good for you, the way I made your first time. You're gonna love having me in your ass."

She gave him a half smile. "I like your dirty talking."

"I gotta whole lotta dirty waiting for my girl."

Grace pushed herself up and canted her hips, grinding her clit against his pubic bone as she twisted her nipples between her thumb and forefinger. "Your girl likes dirty."

His girl.

Riding his cock.

Wanting all the dirty he could give.

It was too fucking much. He grabbed her hips, bucked and grunted as they ground together. When her cheeks flushed and her pussy clenched around him, he slid his thumb over the hard knot of her clit and rubbed her hard. Her low guttural groan set him off, and they came together, her pussy rippling around his cock as he pumped his release in a rush of white-hot heat.

"Not bad for an old man," she murmured, collapsing over top of him.

"I'm not done with you yet." Utterly spent, he smoothed his hand up and down her back, and willed himself to revive quickly.

Neither of them spoke for a long time. Finally, he gently moved her to the side to dispose of the condom.

When he returned, she had put on his T-shirt and was lying on her side. Rocco climbed into bed beside her and pulled her over his chest. He liked the weight of her, the warmth, the softness of her body against his.

"You called me your girl," she said.

Rocco swallowed hard. "Yeah, I did."

"We never talked about . . ." She twisted her lips to the side. "I mean . . . I don't know."

He felt her hesitation like a knife to his gut. "I'm not asking anything of you, Gracie." His voice cracked, broke. "But to me . . . right here . . ." He thumped his chest. "You've always been my girl."

"And you've always been my man."

Rocco gave a satisfied grunt. "Your man wants you naked in bed."

"It's kind of cold," she teased.

"I'll warm you up." He placed her hand on his cock, already semi-hard, and she laughed.

"I take back everything I said about your age. You are a machine."

He wanted her again, but he was also content to just hold her, so he stroked his hand down her back and listened to the steady beat of her heart. "Your singing tonight was amazing," he said. "Your voice has changed. It's so much richer, deeper, and you've doubled your range."

"I took proper voice lessons when I moved here to help me land the radio gigs. I've also done some behind-the-scenes recording work. It was a way to keep singing without being in front of people."

Gently, he cupped her jaw and stroked his thumb over the scar. He remembered every brutal second of the knife slicing down her cheek, felt the searing pain as if it had been done to him. "And now, *cara mia*? Will you sing again?"

"I don't know. I might do local gigs if I can wear the mask. Ethan has threatened to play a recording of himself singing twenty-four hours a day unless I agree."

"You can perform on my stage anytime." He brushed a kiss over her forehead. "If it helps you gain confidence, you can sing there every night. You can have your dream, Gracie. I'll do anything to make it happen."

"I know being an enforcer was never your dream." She pushed herself higher, giving him a tantalizing view of her breasts. "What about owning a jazz club?"

"I'll have to let you know. I've only had one day on the job." He shifted her slightly, nudging her legs apart so his shaft was nestled at the juncture of her thighs.

"I suppose I've only had one day on the job too." She wiggled against him and fuck if he wasn't fully hard again. "I never thought I could make it big. At best, I thought I'd sing in the evenings after I finished my day job. But after I got my degree, the day job didn't happen. So I think in my heart I was secretly dreaming the impossible dream." She hummed a few bars of "Impossible Dream" and he felt a rush of pleasure like nothing he'd felt before.

"Sing it for me, *dolcezza*." He lifted her hips and thrust up into her wetness. "Live your dream as I live mine."

He flipped them over and licked and sucked her nipples as he withdrew and slid home again, over and over as her beautiful voice filled the room. She made it to the part about the unreachable star and then he slicked his thumb over her clit and sent her there. And they fell back to earth together.

FOURTEEN

"I'm so glad you're feeling better." Grace squeezed her father's hand. For the first time since the shooting, her father was able to sit up and talk coherently. She had rushed to the hospital after one of the nurses called to tell her they had stopped giving him the painkillers that kept him sedated and had moved him out of the ICU and to a private room on the recovery floor.

"It seems I have a lot of unfinished business," her father said, his forehead creased in a worried frown. "I decided I'd had enough rest. I've been on the phone already this morning with my capos and with Piero Forzani, who is still grieving his son's death. Tell me what's been going on."

"Tom has been missing since the shooting."

Papa paled. "No body?"

"No, Papa. I've been trying to find him." Grace filled him in on everything that had happened as well as the information Rocco had given her last night without mentioning Rocco by name—Tony hiring Albanians to hunt for Tom, her suspicions that Tony and his crew were responsible for the shooting at Carvello's, and Nico's efforts to keep him safe.

"I owe Nico a debt," her father said. "I was about to call him when you arrived. I've been trying all morning to get through to Don Gamboli to discuss this matter but I'm getting no answer."

"What about his *consigliere*, Luigi Cavallo?"

"Nothing." Her father shook his head. "I tried Don Gamboli's bodyguard and his wife and brother, and no answer from them either. I've sent some of my capos in New York out to see what they can find."

"Rocco said Nico was trying to get in touch with them as well and had no luck."

"Rocco?"

Grace swallowed hard. "Yes, Rocco De Lucchi. He was at the Carvello's. One of the shooters shouted something about taking me alive and Rocco has been protecting me."

Papa squeezed her hand so much she thought he would break a bone. "Why was he there?"

"I . . ." She sucked in her lips. "He came to see me. We were in—"

"Did you invite him?"

"No, Papa, but we—"

"Did you tell him who we were meeting and where?"

Grace twisted her hands together in her lap. "No."

Papa pushed himself up on the bed. "So he just showed up? When you were having dinner with your family and family friends? How did he find you?"

Grace's stomach twisted in a knot. "I don't know. I guess he followed me."

"He followed you." Papa's voice rose to a shout. "Jesus Christ. He's a De Lucchi. If he was there, he was involved. He probably had the contract on Tom and me, and he brought those men along to make sure the job got done."

"No." She pulled her hand away. "He shot at them. He protected us, protected you and Tom. He turned over a table, and he shot one of the guys in the chest. Then he got me out of there and took me somewhere safe."

"Did he kill the man he shot?"

Sweat beaded on her forehead. "No. Rocco said he was wearing a vest."

Papa snorted a laugh. "Was anyone dead when you left?"

Grace's mouth went dry. "No."

"Then they were his men. Have you ever heard of a De Lucchi leaving anyone alive?"

She pushed her chair away from the side of his bed and stood. "He left you alive. And Tom. And me. He saved me. And he's been helping me look for Tom."

"Helping you so you would lead him to Tom and he could whack him, no doubt."

"No. That's not how it was." Grace hugged herself, wrapping her cold hands around her body. "Nico's wife and his underboss's wife helped me track Tom's phone to a trailer park. Rocco showed up with some of his men, and he went into the trailer. I heard shots, and he came out with blood on him. He said there were three Albanians inside, and he could get one of them to talk. He brought me Tom's phone."

"Most likely they had Tom, too," Papa said. "Did you go inside? Did you look for yourself if Tom was there? Did you see this Albanian who was willing to talk? Did you talk to him?"

"No. I asked Rocco to"—her mouth went dry—"question one of them for me so we could find Tom, and he promised he wouldn't kill him."

"Cristo santo!" Papa exploded, throwing up his hands

and treating Grace to a string of choice Italian swear words. "A De Lucchi told you he wouldn't kill someone, and you believed him." Papa's voice turned cold. "You led him right to your brother and took him at his word that your brother wasn't there. And you let him convince you Tony was behind the hit. How naïve can you be?"

"I trust him," she said quietly.

"Well, you're the only person who does. The rest of us know who he is. He is a De Lucchi. They are not good men. A man is defined by the lines he won't cross, but the De Lucchis have no boundaries. Once they have a contract they will do whatever it takes to fulfill it. They will pretend to be your boyfriend, your lover, your friend—they will use you, betray you, hurt you—anything to get the job done."

A shiver ran down Grace's spine. "He's not like that. I know him. I was . . ." She fisted her skirt, steeled herself to reveal a truth she had kept hidden for so long. "We were together before I left New York. For two years."

Far from being angry or aghast, her father waved a dismissive hand. "It was nothing. A teenage crush. You meant nothing to him. The De Lucchis don't have relationships. Love, caring, empathy—all the emotions you seem to have too much of—are beaten out of them starting when they are ten years old. They are given things to care about when they are children, just so they can be taken away." His face softened. "The De Lucchi boys all get a puppy when they are adopted, *polpetto*. I'll bet you never saw him with a dog."

Grace's eyes watered. "Don't, Papa. Don't tell me that."

"And you." He shook his head. "Did you think Cesare wouldn't know about you? If you were with him for two years, it was only because Cesare allowed it for the sole purpose of breaking him by taking you away. Is that what happened the night you came back to me with bandages on your face asking questions about who we were and who were the De Lucchi crew?"

"Cesare said he would kill Rocco if I told you about what happened that night." Her hand went to her cheek. "I believed him."

"He would never kill his son, because if he did, he would have to adopt another boy and start again. It is required under their code. He doesn't have a son of his own. Few of them do, because it is not easy to find a woman willing to marry a De Lucchi, especially knowing that the relationship will be one without love."

"Rocco loved me," she blurted out.

"Maybe you loved him, but he didn't love you, *polpetto*. The De Lucchis don't know how to love."

"You're wrong." She trembled all over. "He did love me. I felt it." She tapped her chest, and a pained expression crossed her father's face.

"How many times do I tell you, those feelings you have, that your mother and the women in the family claim to have, are not real?"

"I felt something was wrong when we got to Carvello's," she snapped. "Tom laughed at me. But I was right. Look what happened."

"Rocco De Lucchi showed up with a contract to kill your family is what happened." Papa thudded the bed rail, wincing as he did. "And the comment about you being left alive . . . we don't involve women in our affairs. Even a De Lucchi won't harm a woman. No doubt he wanted them to take you out so there was no risk of you being shot."

"What about this?" She ran her hand down her face. "A De Lucchi did this to me."

Papa's lips tightened. "I don't have an answer, but once I get in touch with the don, you will be avenged."

Grace had never thought about revenge. She'd never once thought about making Cesare pay for what he'd done. All she'd ever thought about was Rocco, what he'd done that night at the creek, and how she'd felt sickened and betrayed. But now that she was with him again, knowing what he'd been through, she wanted Cesare to pay. Not for what he'd done to her, but for what he'd done to Rocco. Despite what her father said about the De Lucchis, she trusted her feelings in a way she hadn't before. What she had with him now was real. What she saw behind the De Lucchi mask he was forced to wear was a man strong enough to withstand Cesare's training. This time she would be strong, too. She wasn't going to turn her back on him and run away.

"What are we going to do about Tom?" she asked, changing the subject.

"You're not going to do anything. I'm able to think now that they aren't pumping me full of drugs, and I should be out of here in a few days. I'll ask Piero Forzani to coordinate a search for Tom, and I'll speak to Nico about getting some of his capos involved. We will find him, and after we do, and an appropriate mourning period for Benito has passed, you'll marry the Forzani's younger son, Dino."

Grace's brow creased in a frown. "What are you talking about?"

Papa sighed. "I had hoped it wouldn't come to this, but the family needs an alliance and the Forzanis are a perfect fit. Piero Forzani and I had hoped you and Benito would get together without any coercion, but now that Benito is dead, Dino will have to take his place. The capos in New York have gained so much power over the last few years that an alliance is the only way for both our families to survive. The Forzanis have a formidable presence in New York. Piero's brother is one of the most powerful capos in the Gamboli family. The alliance will secure the future of both families and keep our family safe from any more events like what has happened here in Vegas."

"You want me to marry a man I've never met?" She stared at him aghast.

"You'll meet him tonight. He will be your bodyguard until I can get someone permanent hired. I have it all worked out."

A shudder ran through her body. "First of all, I'm not meeting anyone tonight. I'm singing again, Papa. I have a gig at the Stardust. Second, I don't need a bodyguard. I have Rocco. And third, I'm not getting married to someone I don't know or love. You can't force me into a marriage. I thought you said you would never do that to me."

"I won't have to force you." He held out a hand. "You'll do it for me and Tom and the rest of your family. You don't want to lose your family, *polpetto*. It is all we have."

Rocco walked through the wide marble hallways of Tony's palatial mansion as he had done many times before, first as Tony's father's enforcer, and then as Nico's bodyguard when Nico was forced to kneel before Tony's father, Santo, then boss of the family.

This time, however, he was here as his own man, on his own mission, and with his own agenda.

Damn it felt good.

Using the power of the De Lucchi name, he had been given admittance to Tony's heavily guarded complex and obtained an audience with the man Nico most wanted to see in the ground. How easy it would be to pull the trigger during the meeting and end the civil war between Nico and Tony. But that one shot would not just end the war, it would end Rocco's life. And right now he had something to live for that made whacking Tony an unacceptable risk.

"Frankie." Tony looked up from his father's old wood desk. He hadn't changed anything in his father's office after his father died, and the dark heavy furniture, thick velvet drapes, and dark green carpet set Rocco's teeth on edge from the bad memories alone.

"If you didn't give your word of honor that you weren't here to whack me, I would never have let you in," Tony continued. "From what I've heard, Nico has you wrapped around his little finger."

Rocco tossed three gold rings on Tony's desk—He had removed them from the fingers of the Albanians before giving them a proper Lake Mead burial. Each ring bore the signet of the Albanian Mafia and they were only ever removed upon death.

"Is this a gift?" Tony stared at the rings but made no move to touch them.

"Your hires. I thought you'd like to have their jewelry back to send to their wives in Albania."

"If they were my hires, then those rings would indicate you were interfering in my business." Tony folded his arms and leaned back in his black leather chair. He had a bodyguard on either side of him, and two at the door, and yet he knew they wouldn't be able to save him if Rocco had come here on official De Lucchi business.

Rocco settled in the chair across from Tony's desk and stretched out his legs. "Since when does your business involve trying to whack the New York underboss, hunting for his son and trying to kidnap his daughter?"

"Since when is my business of interest to the De Lucchis?"

Rocco didn't even flinch when he lied. "You interfered with my contract at Carvello's."

"Ah." Tony smirked. "I heard the Bianchis lost two men that night. What's the problem? They're dead. Does it matter who pulled the trigger?"

"They weren't my contract."

Tony leaned forward. "So you were after the Mantinis? I hear Nunzio is still alive and his son is on the run and you are escorting his daughter around. Someone didn't do his job. What does Cesare think about that? I can't imagine he's very happy right now." He tilted his head to the side, put a finger to his lips. "Has a De Lucchi ever not completed a job? I can't remember hearing about a single instance until now. But then I can't remember ever hearing about a De Lucchi thinking with his dick instead of his gun. How's your ugly duckling?"

If Rocco hadn't been trained to hide every trace of emotion, he might have curled his hand around the armrest of the chair, broken into a sweat, or thrown himself over the desk and wrapped his hands around Tony's throat. Damn the fucking Mafia and the fucking eyes that were fucking everywhere.

"Why the fuck did you hire the Albanians to go after the boy? What's your interest in this?"

Tony laughed. "Everyone thinks I'm the bad guy, but I have a good heart. When I heard you were looking for him, I thought Nunzio might appreciate having someone step in to save his sorry ass." He opened his hands. "Who knows how he'll repay the favor? Maybe he'll go back to the don and tell him I would be a better boss in Vegas than fucking Nico who just sat back and let you rampage around his town."

"Not if you shot up a restaurant and killed two Bianchi capos."

Tony's dark eyes gleamed. "Maybe it wasn't me."

"Maybe it was."

"Why would I incur the wrath of two families, including the family of the underboss who gets to make a decision about who rules this town?"

Rocco snorted a laugh. "Because this is Vegas and you're hedging your bets."

"No betting man would take those odds."

For the first time in his career as an enforcer, Rocco felt a stirring of unease. Usually he knew how every situation would play out before he walked in the door. Today, he'd expected Tony to reveal he was working for one of the New York capos, and give him a name, but he was beginning to get the feeling that Tony was telling the truth.

"I shot the leader in the chest. You're saying that wasn't you?"

"I like you, Frankie, but not so much that I'm going to strip for you." Tony patted his silk shirt. "And if you'd shot me in the chest, we would likely not be having this conversation."

"Unless you were wearing a vest."

Tony nodded. "That would be prudent if one were going out on a hit. I'll remember that for next time. Thanks for the tip."

"Do you have the boy?"

A slow, sly smile spread across Tony's face. "Unfortunately, I can neither confirm nor deny that he is a guest in my home. If I were to find him, I would certainly look forward to the reunion of father and son and the ensuing reward for my selfless act of kindness in tracking him down and keeping him safe. Now, if I could get the girl away from you, there is nothing Nunzio wouldn't do for me."

Unable to sit another minute, Rocco pushed himself up. "She's in no danger from me."

"You're a De Lucchi." Tony laughed. "Everyone is in danger from you. I've seen what you can do, Frankie. I was here for every contract my father gave you. I was here every time you reported back. I saw the pictures. Sometimes I even went to view the bodies. Maybe you think she's not in danger from you, but she is, and I'm not the only one who thinks so. You can hurt people many different ways. But I don't have to tell you that. No one knows more about pain than you."

"Do you love me?" Grace rested her chin on Rocco's chest and looked up at him through the thicket of her lashes.

"Yeah, cara mia," he said softly. "I love you." He had no other word for the feelings he had when he was with Grace. It was like he had overdosed on the most powerful drug in existence—and he'd tried a lot of them— and his whole body was flooded with pleasure. If love meant he would die for her, that no matter what he was doing he thought of her, that he felt her hands on his body when he lay alone in bed, that he didn't wash his clothes because they smelled of her, that his heart felt like it only beat when she was with him, then yes, he loved her.

A smile spread across her face, and fuck, there was nothing he wouldn't do for that smile. He reached up to touch the gold cross around his neck, silently thanking his parents for giving him something that had enabled him to shield a small corner of his heart from Cesare so that he had been open to the love Grace had offered him, and he'd been able to love her in return.

She shifted on top of him and a growl rose in his chest as his cock responded to the gentle slide of her hips. He liked her in this position, her heart thudding softly

*against his chest, every inch of her body on every inch
of his. He'd never imagined two people could be so
close, and the feelings he had in these stolen hours in
the darkness were so powerful they made him believe
he could withstand anything Cesare did to him.*

"Will you always love me?"

*He swept a hand through her beautiful hair and
down her back.* "Always."

"Do you promise?" *Grace pushed herself higher.*

"Yes, I promise." *He leaned forward to kiss her so
she wouldn't see the flicker of pain that he knew would
be reflected in his eyes. He would always love her
because he had loved her already for seven years and
he couldn't imagine loving anyone else. But this couldn't
last. One day, Cesare would find out, and Rocco didn't
know what he would do. He could no sooner give up
Grace than he could stop breathing, and if it meant he
had to die, he would die knowing that he'd held perfection in his arms. She was everything that was good and
beautiful and innocent about the world, everything Cesare had stolen from him when he had plucked him from
an orphanage in Vegas and brought him to New York.*

"When I'm finished school, we can get married," *she
said with the certainty of youth.* "Papa won't be happy
about our age difference but when he sees how much
we love each other, he'll come 'round."

*Rocco was pretty damn sure Nunzio Mantini would
never come 'round to the idea of a De Lucchi marrying
his daughter, and especially one ten years older than
her, but he wasn't about to extinguish the light in her
eyes by telling her the truth. And even if Nunzio were to
agree, which was as remote a possibility as another di-
nosaur walking the earth, Cesare would find a way to
destroy them. But even the knowledge that this would
never last, that one day he would have to break her*

heart, couldn't stop him from taking what she offered. He was a selfish bastard, but he'd rather have a short time with Grace than never have experienced the emotion she had awakened in him at all.

"Anything you want, Gracie. I'll do anything for you."

"Will you wear a tux instead of your leather jacket?"

"If it makes you happy."

"Can we get married outside?"

"Sure."

"When you ask me, can you make it romantic so that when I tell our kids I can cry like my mom used to do when she told us how my dad asked her to marry him?"

Rocco swallowed past the lump in his throat. "I don't know anything about romance, dolcezza. *I just know how I feel about you."*

"Then tell me that."

"Okay."

She leaned up and pressed her lips against his. "Do you want anything?" she asked.

"Only you."

"You have me. I'm not going anywhere. I mean something at our wedding."

He didn't want to think about the wedding that would never happen, the dress she would never wear, the tux he would never rent, and the romance she wanted that he didn't even understand. But he forced the image into his mind so he could come up with something to see her smile again. "I want you to sing."

"What?"

"Something from your heart."

She kissed him again, her lips warm and soft. He wrapped his arms around her and held her tight.

"That's easy," she murmured. "Every song I sing

comes from my heart and my heart is full of you. I'll never run out of songs to sing."

He wished that were true. The world would be a darker place without her beautiful voice and it would be a Hell he couldn't even imagine when she was gone.

FIFTEEN

"How's your dad?" Rocco walked around Grace's room without even bothering to knock on the door. She cringed as he took in the piles of clothes and magazines on the floor, the shelves stuffed with knick-knacks she'd picked up in thrift stores, and the sewing patterns and pieces of material strewn across every surface. Yes, her room was a disaster. Some day she would get around to cleaning it, but she never seemed to have the time.

"Better, thanks. He's out of the ICU and in a recovery room." Her voice felt tight, and she took a deep breath and then another. If she didn't relax, she wouldn't be able to sing, but how could she relax after what her father had said? He had planted a seed of doubt, and despite her best efforts it had taken root over the course of the day.

"Has he talked to Nico yet?" He picked up a picture of Grace and her mom together, both of them dressed in blue, their hair up, identical smiles on their faces.

"He was about to call Nico when I got there. I'm sure he's talked to him now. He said he would get the Forzanis out looking for Tom, and he wanted to handle my security."

Rocco put the picture down and turned slowly to look at her. "What security?"

She sucked in her lips and shrugged. "He wanted to give me a bodyguard. I told him I didn't need one because I had you."

"I'm sure that didn't go down well."

"No." Her heart drummed in her chest as she tried to work up the nerve to ask the question she didn't want answered.

"Dolcezza?"

"Yes?"

"You're going to wrinkle your dress." He gestured to her hand, tightly fisting the skirt of her dusty rose-colored dress. It had a cream lace overlay that would hide the damage she was doing to the silk beneath, but still, she didn't want to go on stage feeling like she was hiding anything—even if it was just wrinkled silk—when her songs came from a place of honesty in her heart.

"Right." She smoothed down her dress.

"What's wrong, Gracie?" His voice was so soft, so gentle, her eyes watered with the force of the emotion she'd been holding back since this afternoon.

"Nothing."

"Are they not taking good care of your dad? You want different doctors? A different hospital? I can talk to Nico. You just tell me what you need."

"He's good. He's recovering."

"Is it the gig tonight? You know I won't let anything happen to you. Anything goes wrong and I'll stop the show."

The vehemence in his tone eased some of her anxiety, and she blinked back the tears, knowing he'd seen them and he wasn't going to let her distress slide. "I know. You own the club."

"That's right."

"Maybe you should wear a jacket and tie." She tried to put a teasing note in her voice. "There aren't many jazz club owners in leather jackets and jeans."

"Don't own a jacket."

"Ethan could lend you one. You're about the same size."

Rocco snorted. "Not borrowing a jacket from Ethan."

"Why not?"

"He wants you. If I borrowed his jacket, I'd have to return it in pieces so he'd get the message that you're mine."

Mine.

Her heart ached with longing. For the last few weeks, she had been living a fantasy, when the reality was there was a chasm between them so wide she didn't know if one word was enough to bridge the distance.

"I'll tell you what," he said. "You sing without the mask and I'll wear a jacket."

A smile tugged at her lips. "And a tie?"

"Don't push it."

She'd sung with only half a mask before, and in Rocco's club, with Rocco there, she was pretty sure she could manage to go without. "Okay. But I have to see you in the jacket first before I go on stage."

"I'll be right there, *cara mia*. Just like I promised."

"Papa said I should stay away from you," she said, watching him.

"If I had a daughter, I'd tell her to stay away from me, too." He folded his arms, leaned against her dresser. With her pastel shabby chic furniture, flowery prints, and white lace curtains, he stood out for his darkness.

"He said you didn't have any lines you wouldn't cross."

"I have lines." Rocco stared straight ahead. "I would never hurt a civilian or a woman."

She smoothed down her dress even though the damage was done. "What if that person was a threat? What if they meant to hurt someone you cared about, directly or indirectly? Would you hurt them then?"

He answered so quickly she wondered if he'd even heard the question. "Yes."

"So it's not really a line you won't cross, it's a line you prefer to not to cross, but under the right circumstances you will."

"What happened to you will never happen again." He crossed the distance between them, cupped her face in his palms. "I failed you, *dolcezza*. I will never fail you again. I won't let anything hurt you. I will keep you safe. And if that means I have to break the rules, then I'll break them."

"What about here?" She touched her heart. "What if you had to do something that would hurt me inside?"

"Never."

"But what if you had no choice? What if . . . you . . . Cesare gave you a contract that would hurt me?" It was as close as she could get to asking him the question without suggesting she didn't trust him.

"I wouldn't do it." His arms slid around her body, pulling her close.

"I thought death was your only way out."

"It doesn't have to be my death." He bent down and kissed her, his mouth moving against hers so softly and gently she almost couldn't believe he was suggesting he might kill Cesare.

"But . . . what will you do?"

"You." He groaned into her mouth, and she wove her fingers through his hair, pulling him toward her. She wanted more. More kissing. More of his hot body against hers. More strong arms holding her tight, protecting her. He kept her safe. He had always kept her safe.

And yet her father's words were an irritated niggle in her mind.

They are not good men.

A man is defined by the lines he won't cross.

They will pretend to be your boyfriend, your lover, your friend . . .

Her head spun, and she clung to him, savoring his taste, the illicit thrill of being wrapped around a mobster in her bedroom even after her father had warned her away, where there was nothing but the faint sound of traffic, the rumble of the bass as Miguel practiced in the living room, and the occasional thud of footsteps as Ethan got the equipment loaded for the gig. Why couldn't she have this, have him? Why wasn't it enough that she knew his heart and accepted who he was inside?

"I want you." She ground her hips against his, feeling the hard length of his erection beneath his fly. "Here, Rocco. Now."

She needed to feel their connection, to know she was right and Papa was wrong.

A growl of pleasure rumbled in his chest. His hands slid up her thighs to her hips and under her skirt. "That's a dangerous wish. I'm not in a gentle mood."

"I don't want gentle." She nipped his bottom lip and his fingers curled into her ass.

He cupped her sex with his warm palm, and she felt an almost frantic need to connect with him and wash her father's words away.

"This isn't you," he said softly.

No, it wasn't her. She had never been sexually aggressive. When she'd been with Rocco, he had always taken the lead. He had been her teacher in all things and she had been a willing pupil. After she moved to Vegas and started dating other men, she'd tried asserting herself, but it didn't give her the same kind of thrill, and she had never met a man as dominant as Rocco.

"I'm discovering a whole new me. I'm embracing the chaos I've been running from all my life."

His lips quirked at the corners. "I'm chaos?"

"Yes, you are."

With a low growl, he shoved her panties aside and slicked a finger through her wetness. His eyes darkened almost to black. "You're wet."

"For you." She rocked her hips against him, pressing into his fingers.

"Grace . . ." His voice cracked on a moan, broke.

"Please. Right now. I need you. I need to feel close to you."

"Fuck. I could never say no to you." He pushed a thick finger inside her and she gasped.

It must have been the gasp that broke him, because he crushed her mouth in a fierce kiss and pumped his finger hard and deep into her wetness.

"Oh God. Yes."

"Tell me what you want, Gracie." He added a second finger, curling them to prime the sensitive spot inside her that his piercing would stroke when he finally got around to fucking her.

"More." She didn't just want his fingers or the rough way he handled her; she wanted his dirty talking, the unfiltered words that made their every encounter seem dangerous and sordid.

"More what?" His voice was a sensual whisper in her ear. "You want more fingers in your slick pussy? You want my cock pounding into you? You want my teeth biting your nipples? You want my mouth on your hot, tight, wet cunt?"

She moaned as his words ratcheted her arousal up one hundred degrees. No one had ever talked to her the way Rocco did. His words made her feel desired and dirty at the same time. "I want it all."

"Greedy girl." He added a third finger and thrust harder, his palm rubbing against her clit, his other hand sliding under her shirt to cup her breast.

Grace arched against him, rubbing her breast against his hand, grinding into his fingers. She felt wanton and wild and desperate for release.

"Jesus Christ, you're on fire, *dolcezza*. I could play with your body all fucking day." He leaned in and took her mouth, his kiss fierce and passionate, his tongue sweeping every inch. Demanding. Dominating. She'd missed it. Missed him. Missed everything they had together. Six years she'd lost by running away. Now, she wanted it back.

"Give it to me, *cara mia*." His voice dropped low and husky. "I want to feel you come all over my hand. I want your juices all over my fingers." He increased his rhythm, firmly pressing his palm over her clit with each stroke. Grace writhed in his grip, widening her legs to accommodate his hand, just as he'd taught her the first time he'd used his fingers to bring her to climax.

"You close?"

"Yes," she whispered.

"Let it go." He pressed his palm hard against her clit, and her orgasm slammed into her, rocking her body from the inside out. Rocco swallowed her scream with a kiss, his skilled fingers drawing out her orgasm until her knees went weak. Before she had fully come down, he had pulled a condom from his pocket and freed his cock from its restraint.

"You ready for me?"

"Yes." Her heart was still pounding from the rush of orgasm, but she still ached for more.

Rocco tore away her panties like they were made of tissue. Then he curled his hands under her ass and lifted her easily, bracing her against the wall as she wrapped her legs around him.

"Tell me you want it." His eyes, fierce and hard, burned into her. "Use the words I like to hear."

"I want it, Rocco. I want your cock. I want you to fuck me. Make me yours."

She wanted to be his, to be anchored to the ground because the urge to run away after her father had warned her about the De Lucchis was almost overwhelming. But this time was going to be different. She believed in him, believed in herself. If it felt right between them, then nothing else mattered.

His big hands clasped her hips, the smooth head of his cock teasing her entrance. Her breath caught in short, wild gasps and she clung to him, nails deep in his shoulders as he held her up, cool night air brushing her heated flesh. Waiting. Waiting for the anchor to come.

"Rocco. Please." She levered her hips up, tried to push down over the head of his cock. His hands tightened on her hips in warning, and he retreated just enough that she could feel the heat of his flesh near her entrance but nothing more.

"Shhh. Let me enjoy you."

"I don't want to be enjoyed. I want to be fucked." This time the crude words slid easily from her lips.

Slowly, he pushed into her, inch by thick inch, his piercing a mouth-watering erotic burn against her sensitive flesh. She shifted her weight, widened her legs to take him all in.

He groaned, then slammed all the way in, stretching

her, filling her so deep her breath caught, and yet she took him, reveled in his power and strength, felt the climax build and was determined to hold back until he could come with her.

"Yeah, baby," she whispered. "Fuck me hard. Give me all that hard, thick cock."

His strangled cry encouraged her, made her feel the strength of her femininity. She leaned down and kissed the sensitive spot between his neck and shoulder and then bit down hard.

"Jesus Christ." Rocco pounded into her, his body taut and hard with restrained power. Faster, stronger. Her body trembled as he gently rubbed his fingertip around her clit, dipping down to her wet pussy for moisture, then stroking up again.

Grace moaned out loud. She'd never felt so tightly connected with anyone as she did with Rocco.

Her orgasm peaked without warning. A scream exploded out of her and she buried her face in his shoulder as she came around his cock.

With a fierce cry, he slammed into her and joined her in climax, his cock swelling against the clenching muscles of her pussy as he pumped his seed inside her.

"Grace?" Ethan thumped on her door. "You ready to go?"

"Fuck," Rocco murmured. "Perfect fucking timing."

"I don't remember you swearing quite so much when we were together before," she said as he released her.

"There wasn't as much shit going on that needed swearing at." He turned to dispose of the condom and then they quickly straightened their clothes. Grace held her arms out by her sides and twirled in front of him.

"How do I look?"

"Like you've been well fucked."

Laughing, she ran her fingers through her hair, straightening it out, her fingers brushing over the smooth skin on her cheek. Every time she was with him, she forgot about the scar. He didn't see her ugly, so why couldn't she stop seeing the scar?

SIXTEEN

"That's so good, baby. Keep going."

Mike ran his fingers through Tiffany's silky hair as her head bobbed up and down in his lap in the alley behind the Stardust. In the back of his mind, he knew he shouldn't have invited her to sit with him when he was supposed to be keeping watch, but when she called to see if he wanted to get together, and she was just around the corner from the damn Stardust where Mike had been sitting for the last two hours, he couldn't resist. She'd bought his story of making extra money doing surveillance and she'd been excited to keep him company and try and guess who they were watching. So fucking cute. Every time he looked at her, he felt like he was living a dream.

Mike moved his seat back one more notch so she didn't hit her head on the steering wheel. His mother had always said he was thoughtful, and he'd done his best to make sure she was comfortable when she lay on his lap and tugged open his fly. He'd put his jacket over her and angled her seat down to accommodate her long, lean legs.

Frankie wouldn't understand, but guys like Mike didn't usually catch the attention of girls like Tiffany. And even if he did get to hook up with them, they didn't call him again. Or beg to spend time with him even though he was stuck in a back alley staring at a black metal door. Or give him a "little treat" in the car so he didn't get bored. What universe was he living in that he'd found the perfect girl?

It wasn't like Frankie needed him, anyway. There was nothing the enforcer couldn't handle. Yesterday, he'd sent Mike and Paolo away from the warehouse where they'd tied up the dude from the trailer park, telling them he'd handle the interrogation himself.

Usually, Frankie would do the dirty work and the To-scani family soldiers or associates would clean up the mess and handle the disposal of the body, unless they were giving the dude a pair of concrete shoes, in which case Frankie would deal with the concrete work. Over the last few weeks, however, Mike—and Paolo because Mike had taken him under his wing—had been work-ing almost exclusively for Frankie at the behest of Mr. Rizzoli who told them to treat Frankie with the same respect they would give any boss.

Mike didn't mind. Frankie had been different in the last few weeks. He didn't scowl as much. He talked oc-casionally, and not just to bark out orders, and the few times Mike had seen him with Grace, he could swear he'd seen the enforcer smile. It was almost like they were Frankie's crew, although the De Lucchis didn't have any crew outside of themselves. Frankie even paid them, and as a result, Mike's bank account was in the black for the first time in years. To celebrate, he'd bought something special for Tiffany—a two-week anniversary present that he could hardly wait to give her when his shift was done.

Tiffany did a mind-blowing suck and swirl move that made his eyes close involuntarily and his body jerk back in the seat. Damn she was good. He was at once appreciative of her skill and jealous that she'd gained that experience with someone else. Maybe more than one someone else. Fuck. That was not a question he wanted to ask. He hadn't asked her many questions about herself. He knew now that she was a nurse and she was half Italian. She lived in an apartment in Henderson with a female roommate and a Bichon Frise. She loved his muscles, the fact he owned a chain of gyms, and having lots of sex. He wanted to know more, but she always started kissing him when he asked questions and he'd finally given up, afraid to fuck up what was turning out to be the most incredible hook up of his life.

"You like that, Mikey?" She looked up, licked her lush lips, and he almost blew right there.

"You're fucking amazing." He gently pushed her head back down. "Don't stop now."

"Close your eyes," she whispered. "I've got another surprise."

Oh man. He didn't think he could handle any more. He was right on the edge and holding back simply because he wanted it to go on forever.

Stroking her hair, he watched her get to work. This time she cupped and squeezed his balls with one hand and pumped him with the other, her mouth working in counterpoint until he was worried he was going to come so hard he'd choke her.

"Your eyes aren't closed," she said pulling away.

"I like to watch you."

Her lips tipped at the corners. "Then promise you won't take your eyes off me and I'll take you deeper."

Mike wasn't saying no to that. "I promise."

She opened her mouth and took him so fucking deep his fingers tightened in her hair.

"Jesus Christ. Where did you learn to do that?" He regretted the question as soon as it dropped from his lips because she pulled out and looked up at him, her big blue eyes hazy with lust. "The same place I learned to do this." She took him in again and . . .

Holy Hell. He couldn't even see his own dick. Or his balls. Christ her jaw must have come unhinged to fit him all in. Pleasure built up at the base of his spine and it was all too much. Her soft, thick hair. Her beautiful face. Her hands. Her mouth. Her throat. The thrill of her going down on him in the car where anyone could see them . . .

Fuck. He was supposed to be watching the door.

"Tiff . . ."

She sucked harder. Fuck it all. How could he stop her now when she had worked so hard to get him off? She wanted to give him this, and it would be wrong of him to refuse. No woman had ever treated Mike so good.

"Harder, baby." He fisted her hair, holding her still as he pumped his cock into her mouth.

Fucking heaven.

SEVENTEEN

Rocco did a quick visual sweep of the club, making sure the soldiers and associates he'd called in were still in place. Mike was out back, and he'd put two men on the front door. With both Mia and Gabrielle in the club, Rocco wanted more security, so he'd brought in another two guys to keep watch, and he marked them standing near the various exits in the club.

Satisfied with his security arrangements, he ordered a glass of bourbon and reached into his pocket for his cigarettes, realizing as he did, that he hadn't had a smoke in days. Maybe he wasn't addicted after all. Or maybe he'd lost the desire to prematurely end his life.

Tucking the cigarettes back in his pocket, he checked out the club, looking for potential threats. For the most part, the crowd consisted of couples, a few groups of women, and a few single guys at the bar. There was a skinny guy hovering near the pool table, who was watching Mia, but he had no doubt she would put him in his place if he made a move. Gabrielle was in good form, although her belly kept getting in her way.

Rocco chuckled when she missed an easy shot, but

his smile faded when she put her hand on her lower back like she was in pain. He'd never spared much thought for the girlfriends and wives of the Toscani crew until he'd gone on a rescue mission with Gabrielle. She had impressed him with her skill and courage and amused him to no end with her kick-ass attitude. Still, he didn't go out of his way to talk to the Toscani women, but tonight Grace had invited them to hear her sing, and he'd felt uncharacteristically protective. It made no sense. He wasn't part of the Toscani crew and he wasn't responsible for their women.

Longing gripped him hard and it took him a full minute to realize that he'd been heading this way ever since the first day he'd walked into the Toscani crime family clubhouse. He'd done a job for Nico, and then another, and another until the jobs he accepted for Tony's father, then the boss of the Toscani family, became fewer and fewer. When Tony's father was whacked in the massacre that led to the current power vacuum, Rocco had cut all ties with that side of the family and made it clear he was working exclusively with Nico—save for the assignments that came directly from Cesare and Don Gamboli.

They were family—albeit bound by crime and not blood—the kind of family he'd thought he was going to have when Cesare had adopted him, the family he had given up wanting when he lost Grace.

Now he'd found her, and she'd opened his eyes to the desires he'd been forced to hide away—family, in every sense of the word.

Fuck Tony and his stupid warning. Now that the underboss was on the mend and Tony had as good as admitted Tom was with him, whether as a guest or prisoner Rocco didn't know, and Nunzio would be sending guards to watch over Grace, he needed to turn his attention to how to break his ties with Cesare. He had accepted the situation for far too long. Grace had the strength to make a change. She had faith in him. He needed to have faith in them.

He slid off his seat and made his way over to the pool table. The skinny guy had been joined by two cowboy types wearing belts with big buckles and brand-new boots. Rocco would have pegged them as tourists, except they were too tense. Jazz lovers were usually a laid-back bunch. Tourists even more so. They came to shoot a little stick, have a few drinks, and enjoy the music. Those two looked like they were strung up tight.

"You okay, Gaby?"

Gabrielle startled, her eyes going wide like he'd grown a second head, but he wasn't surprised. He'd never made any effort to check up on her before, or Mia for that matter, but things were changing and they were going to have to keep up.

"Um." She shared a quizzical glance with Mia, and then shrugged. "Yeah. It's just . . . um . . . backache. From being pregnant. It happens if I bend over too much. I just need to sit down."

"I'll get you a chair."

"Thanks." She looked over at Mia again and then back to him.

"Something wrong?"

"I've just . . . we've just . . ." She looked over at Mia again. "Never seen you in a jacket and shirt before. You look . . . nice."

"I signed the papers this morning."

"Luca told me," she said. "Congratulations."

He nodded. Danny hadn't been happy when Rocco paid him a visit to tell him about the new ownership, but Rocco was confident the relationship would work out well simply because Danny was never going to forget what would happen if he tried to screw them over again.

He got her a chair and took up a position against a pillar where he could watch both the girls and the hallway where Grace would come out. Gabrielle would have lots of time to rest because it was Mia's turn and she was so damn good she could clear a table without losing a shot.

Grace joined them a few moments later for a quick visit before the gig. Fuck she was sexy. With that beautiful chestnut hair spilling over her shoulders, the tight jeans that hugged her curves, the flowery feminine top and the kick-ass boots she was something straight out of his deepest fantasies. He'd liked the dress she was going to wear, but he liked her in jeans better.

A wave of possessiveness slammed over him. No one knew Grace like he did. He'd had her for eight years, watched her change from a girl to a young woman, shared her hopes and dreams, held her when she cried, listened when she sang and encouraged her to follow her gift. He'd been the first man to touch her, the first man to kiss her, the first man to introduce her to the world of sexual pleasure. He wanted to share more firsts with her in a future free of threats or obligations. He wanted her to belong to him in every damn sense of the word and to know in her heart that no one could tear them apart.

"Nice jacket." She stopped only a foot away and he breathed in the floral scent of her perfume.

"Very restricting." He shrugged his shoulders, trying to find a comfortable place for the jacket to sit.

Her lips quivered with a smile. "The band is all ready. We're on in half an hour."

"They'd better provide an adequate accompaniment to your beautiful voice."

She laughed out loud, and Christ he loved that sound.

He cupped the side of her neck with his hand and drew her close. "You don't need them, *cara mia*. Everyone will be listening to you."

"I'm nervous." She pressed her body up against him. "But it will make all the difference to see you there, especially in this jacket. Where did you get it?"

"Borrowed it from Ethan."

Her breath was warm in his ear as she leaned in to whisper. "If you give it back to him in one piece, I'll make it worth your while."

Leaning down, he took her lips in a possessive kiss, one hand around her neck, the other holding her tight against him where he liked her best. He didn't fucking care if Gabrielle and Mia told every damn person in the family that they were together, or if everyone in the bar was watching. His girl was in his arms and there was nowhere else he would rather be.

"Do you have time to help me take on Mia in a new game?" Gabrielle asked Grace, interrupting. "She just cleared the table again so we're starting over."

"Your game is over, honey," the taller of the two cowboys said. "It's our turn."

"We paid for three games." Mia pointed to the tokens hanging on the wall.

"Your chubby friend scratched halfway through. That's one game. You playing fancy tricks and clearing the table is games two and three. Now move the fuck out of the way, and let a real man show you how to play."

"Seriously?" Gabrielle pushed herself to stand and grabbed the rack. "Chubby?"

"I'll handle this." Rocco gently unwound himself from Grace's warm arms.

The tall cowboy grabbed the rack from Gabrielle's

hands, pulling her off balance, and only Mia's quick reflexes saved her from falling.

The tension that had been simmering beneath Rocco's skin ever since his conversation with Tony erupted in a bark. "What the fuck? She's pregnant. You don't shove pregnant women around. And the girls have another game to play so I suggest you get the fuck out of here before I rearrange your face."

Clearly too stupid to heed the warning, the cowboy spat on Rocco's new jacket. "What the hell? She yours? I thought you were with the ugly one."

He didn't need to look at Grace to feel her pain, and he didn't feel the need to explain to the cowboy that Mia and Gabrielle were under his protection. They were family and although he'd never felt like part of the family before, he did tonight.

He drew back his fist, only to feel Grace's hand on his arm, her voice an urgent whisper in his ear. "You start something in here, the police will show up."

Rocco felt no small amount of satisfaction that she hadn't asked him not to pulverize the stupid fucker who had dared insult her, because there was no way the dude was going home tonight with all his limbs attached.

"She's right," the stupid-as-fuck cowboy said. "Let's take it outside."

"Outside." He yanked the dude away from the wall and shoved him toward the back entrance.

The cowboy looked back at his friend and smirked. "This'll be quick."

"Stay here." Rocco fixed each of the girls with a look that said he meant business and motioned for the guards to stay put and watch the girls. Then he followed the cowboy and his friend down the hallway and into the alley. He felt no fear. Instead he felt a curious sense of calm. This was his fight. He had picked it. It wasn't a contract. No one had sent him on this job. He could do what he wanted with them, the way he wanted to do it, and the cowboys deserved what they were about to get.

Something niggled at the back of Rocco's mind as they stepped out into the alley. Who threw around loaded insults at women for no reason? Gabrielle was clearly pregnant, and Grace was beautiful despite the scar. The dudes hadn't been in the bar long so it wasn't as if they'd been waiting all night for the table, and the girls had three tags on the wall showing they'd paid for three games. Even if the cowboys were drunk, it was all too convenient. Too predictable. But with adrenaline pumping through his veins and an unprecedented sense of righteousness in his heart, Rocco ignored the warning.

EIGHTEEN

"How was that?" Tiffany straddled Mike's lap, settling her moist heat over his spent cock.

"Christ, Tiff. You're wearing me out. I thought you were just wanting to suck me off that once."

She wrapped her arms around his neck pressing her warm breasts against his chest. "I didn't know you could recover so fast. I didn't want that big, delicious cock to go to waste."

"You're fucking amazing." He pulled her into a hug and buried his face in the soft down of her hair. She had the most glorious hair of any woman he'd met, a cascade of thick golden waves scented with summer sunshine that blocked out his vision of everything but her. "I wanna get you off now."

"How about we go to my place where we can be more comfortable?"

There was nothing at that particular moment that Mike wanted to do more than go to Tiffy's place and give her back the pleasure she'd given him, but he'd already taken a risk by not keeping an eye on the alley and Frankie wasn't a forgiving kinda guy.

"I gotta check in with the boss first," he said giving her a gentle kiss. "Once he leaves, maybe then we can go to your place."

"Maybe you could get me off here then." She clasped his hand and drew it under her skirt. Her panties were soaked, and he could feel his cock stirring to life all over again.

"You're a naughty girl." He shoved her panties aside and fingered her pussy. "You like sucking my cock?"

"Yeah." She pushed back her hair and he got a glimpse of the alley he was supposed to be watching, and Frankie beating down two guys in cowboy boots.

"Holy shit." He tried to get Tiffany off his lap but she was wedged in tight. "Tiff. Get off. My friend is in trouble."

"Don't leave me, Mikey." She ground against his groin, but fear had taken care of his growing erection. He glanced up again and saw four more guys in the alley heading toward the fight. Christ. Frankie was being ambushed. He was good, but six against one was no fair fight.

"Fuck. Tiff. Off." He shoved her to the side and opened the door, remembering his pants were undone only seconds before he stepped out of the vehicle. Zipping up, he reached under the seat and grabbed his gun. "Stay here."

"Why do you need a gun, Mikey?" Her eyes went wide and he got a sick feeling in his stomach that maybe this would scare her away.

"Just like to be safe, baby. Promise you'll stay in the car."

"Tell me what's going on."

He looked up again and the situation had gotten worse. Grace, Mia, and Gabrielle had come outside and had pulled two guys aside. Mia was holding onto some skinny dude, while a pregnant Gabrielle kicked the shit out him. Grace was putting some martial arts moves on another guy. Frankie was still fighting the other four, now with the help of two of the guards, and his assailants were looking a little worse for wear.

And Mike was about to fucking die because he'd been busy getting sucked off in his car instead of doing his job. "Nothing, baby. Looks like my friend might have had too much to drink. I'm just gonna sort him out and we'll head to your place and I can make you feel as good as you make me feel."

"I'm scared. Don't leave." Her big, blue eyes went wide, and he felt like total shit for letting her come with him. It was a Mafia job for chrissakes. Of course, there was going to be violence. Frankie wouldn't have called for so many guards if he hadn't expected some kind of trouble. And where the fuck were the rest of them? Three Toscani women were fighting in an alley and only two guards bothered to follow them? Nico and Luca were going to go crazy. Heads were going to roll, and his would be the first.

"You'll be fine if you stay in the car, baby. And when we go to your place, I have a present to give you." He leaned in and kissed her cheek. Fuck. Every second he spent consoling her was another second one of the Toscani women could get hurt and if that happened his fucking life wouldn't be worth living.

She sighed and sat back in the seat. "Okay, Mikey. I'll wait here."

"Good girl."

He ran down the alley, adjusting himself as he went. Who did he help first? Frankie was outnumbered. Grace was one-on-one with her attacker. And Gabrielle was pregnant. Mike didn't know much about pregnant women, but he was pretty sure kicking and beating on dudes wasn't good for the baby, even if Mia did have the bastard in a chokehold. And even if it was, he knew for certain Luca would go fucking crazy if he found out.

In the end, the decision came down to who seemed to be in the most danger, and that was Grace.

He barreled over to Grace and grabbed her attacker's shirt. "Grace. Get inside."

"No. Go help Gabrielle. This bastard is mine." She used another fancy martial arts move and drove her foot into the dude's stomach.

"Look after Grace," Frankie shouted, slamming one of the cowboys into the ground. His jacket was shredded, one pocket hanging off, buttons on the ground, a slash from what looked to be a knife right down the back.

Mike put an arm around his dude's neck, cutting off his air. As Grace's assailant struggled and thrashed, Grace kicked him between the legs.

"It doesn't matter how you look. It's what's inside that counts," she shouted at him.

Mike didn't know what the fuck that meant, but when the guy went limp, Mike lowered him to the ground and held out a hand to Grace.

"C'mon. I'll take you inside."

"I'm going to help Gabrielle and Mia," she called out as she jogged down the alley. "You help Rocco."

Fuck. How the fuck was he supposed to help when no one did as they were told? He raced after Grace only to discover that Gabrielle and Mia had knocked their guy unconscious and were tying his hands behind him with his own belt.

Okay then. No help needed there. Toscani crime family women were clearly not like the typical Mafia princesses he had known in his years with the mob.

What about Frankie? He ran over to help and the enforcer waved him away. "Jesus Christ. Can't you follow a simple order? Get Grace and the girls inside."

"Don't kill them," Grace yelled as Frankie banged two dude's heads together with a sickening crack. "The one on the left is Dino Forzani. He was supposed to be protecting me."

Frankie looked up at the sound of her voice. Mike could tell from his eyes the enforcer was in the zone. Mike had been in the zone once or twice. It was pure instinct. Kill or be killed. The two dudes groaning at his feet weren't going to make it out of the alley alive.

"Rocco. I'm okay. Please." Grace walked right up to him as if she didn't understand that the guy in front of her was a killing machine, likely to hurt her if she didn't get out of his way.

One of the other two assailants took advantage of Frankie's distraction and smashed a board over Frankie's head. Grace screamed and Frankie went down on one knee. The one guard left standing rushed the dude with the board and grabbed it out of his hands.

Shit. Shit. Shit. Mike didn't know what to do. "Go get the other guards." He pushed Mia and Gabrielle toward the door, praying they would go inside. Thankfully, this time they went and he turned back to help Frankie who was already up and pounding on the dude who had dared hit him with the board.

"Grace. Come on. Inside." Mike opened the door and stepped inside, waving for Grace to join him.

He heard the sound of footsteps. The wail of a police siren. Red lights flashed, momentarily blinding him. He breathed in the scent of summer sunshine mixed with the dank smell of blood and stale piss from the alley. And then he heard Tiffany's soft voice.

"It's okay. I called the police."

NINETEEN

"How can you be so calm?"

Grace looked over at Rocco, leaning back on the bench beside her, legs spread, cuffed hands resting behind his head like he was lounging on a bench in the park and not in the hallway of a cold, dreary police station waiting to be processed and printed. "Well?"

When she didn't get an answer, she sat back in her seat and tried to stop her body from shaking. She'd been okay when the police arrived, simply because she couldn't believe she was being arrested. After all, they were defending themselves so they hadn't done anything wrong. But when one of the police officers read her Miranda rights off a card and snapped a pair of handcuffs around her wrists, she realized that no one believed her. That's when the shaking started, and even Rocco's presence in the seat beside her hadn't been able to calm her down.

It would have helped if he'd talked to her. Told her what was going to happen. After all, he'd been arrested before. Jail time was a right of passage for made men, and Rocco had once told her about the two months he'd spent in jail after getting into a fight at a bar.

Grace, on the other hand, had never been on the wrong side of the law, and she was pretty sure that a criminal record would destroy any chance she had of getting a job as a psychologist. She couldn't even think about actually going to jail. And as for calling Papa in the hospital . . .

Bile rose in her throat, and she let out a soft moan.

"Calm down, *cara mia*." Rocco reached over and clasped her hands, his handcuffs rattling as he moved.

"Oh, you *can* talk." She glared at him. "Thanks for not saying anything in the police car when I almost threw up from being so scared."

"I'm pissed. The kind of talking I want to do right now is not the kind of talking you want to hear."

Heedless of the anger in his voice, she continued, desperate to distract herself from the fact that tomorrow she might wake up in a cold prison cell. "Are you mad at Mike for bringing a civilian with him? I couldn't believe it when she told the police that he was only trying to stop the fight, and that you and I were the instigators. What kind of bullshit story was that?"

"Dunno."

"Dunno? That's it? We might go to jail because of her lies."

Rocco's jaw tightened, and he stared at the ceiling. "Wouldn't have been a problem if you'd done what I fucking told you to do and stayed inside with Gabrielle and Mia."

"What?" She stared at him in shock. "Is that your way of saying thanks? If we hadn't followed you, it would have been six to one, and then six to three when the guards arrive. You might be dead. They set you up. Those guys were waiting outside. I know you're good—"

"Coulda handled it without breaking a sweat."

"But—"

"Next time I tell you to stay inside," he gritted out. "You stay infuckingside. The man protects you. That's how it works."

"Oh really." She moved to fold her arms and then realized she couldn't, so she thudded her cuffed hands on her lap for effect. "If I think you're in danger, I will come to help you. I'm a healing kind of person. That's how it works."

Rocco snorted a laugh. "Didn't see much healing going on when you kicked that dude in the balls."

Grateful to now have a focus for her anger, she huffed a breath. "We're not talking about that. We need a lawyer, Rocco. I know the . . . family . . . has lawyers, but obviously I don't want to call my dad for names."

"It's taken care of."

"Taken care of?" Her voice rose in pitch. "How can it be taken care of when we haven't even had a chance to make a call?"

"Trust me."

She scrubbed her face in her handcuffed hands. "I do trust you. I just wish you could have told me in the police car."

"Not about to discuss our business with the cops listening up front."

Grace sighed and leaned back on the bench. "Why did you pick that fight anyway? It was just words, and Gabrielle was okay."

"He called you—"

"Ugly." She sighed. "It's not like I haven't heard it before."

"You're not ugly," he said vehemently. "You're beautiful. Inside and out."

"Maybe you only see what you want to see."

His jaw tightened. "I see the truth."

"Well, you could have handled it differently. Violence isn't the only way to solve problems."

Rocco's lips quivered at the corners. "Says the woman who is sitting here with me in the police station because she attacked a man in a dark alley. I gotta say, nothing is hotter than watching your anti-violence girl beat the shit of someone two days after threatening a guy at a trailer park with a gun and two weeks after almost shooting some bastard in the chest."

"I didn't 'beat the shit' out of him," she said indignantly. "It was self-defense. He was going to join his friends who were hurting you."

"Would have been fun."

Grace didn't like thinking of Rocco in a fight with six guys. Even now his eye was swollen and dried blood was crusted on his forehead from a long gash that she was sure would leave a scar. But she also didn't like how easy it had been for her to get involved in the fight. She hadn't hesitated to use her Krav Maga moves on one of his attackers, and if Mike hadn't arrived she would have kept fighting until everyone was safe.

"My favorite part was when you kicked the dude who called you ugly," he continued. "And told him it was what was inside that counts."

"This is a nightmare of epic proportions." She scrubbed her hands over her face. "Dino was supposed to meet me and act as a bodyguard, not attack you with five of his friends and try to kill you. At least now he won't want to marry me."

"Whoa. Whoa. Whoa." Rocco jerked up on the bench. "Marry you? What the fuck?"

"Papa's idea." She sighed. "Apparently he needs an alliance or the family will be destroyed. I always thought he was kidding when he had me meet the sons of his friends. Or it was just wishful thinking on his part. But no. He told me yesterday in the hospital that he had intended for be to marry Benito before Benito got himself whacked, and now I'm supposed to marry his brother, Dino."

Rocco's hands curled into fists. "He's gonna force you into a marriage?"

"Not physically. He pretty much suggested the family would be ruined if we don't get the alliance, and people will die. He says, of course, I want to protect my family and that's how to do it."

Silence.

"Aren't you going to ask me what I'm going to do?"

"No." He leaned back, slightly away from her. "You do what you have to do."

"You won't fight for me?" She knew it was silly to ask, but after talking with her father, she needed to know where she stood with him and whether Cesare truly had the hold on him her father thought he did.

"If you feel you gotta marry that *testa di cazzo,* then I won't get in your way." He shifted on the bench, dropping his handcuffed hands between his legs.

"Really?" She huffed out a breath. "You'll just stand by and watch me marry Dino fucking Forzani? You'll be good with that? After everything we've shared?"

Rocco gave her a wary look. "You don't swear."

"I'll fucking swear all I want if you're going to act like a dick." She didn't know why she was suddenly so angry, but the thought he would give up on her so easily, that maybe he didn't feel the same way she felt about him lit a fire inside her. Maybe she should just ask the question that was on the tip of her tongue. If he didn't care, what was she trying to save?

"Grace." A pained expression crossed his face. "There's

stuff you don't know, stuff I've done since we've been apart. You couldn't accept it last time . . ."

"I just kicked a man in the balls and made him scream, Rocco," she snapped. "I almost shot someone. I made a life for myself out here when I was only eighteen. Do I strike you as the same woman I was in New York?"

"Yes. Inside you're the same," he said softly. "Beautiful and brave. You just never saw what I saw."

"This is what I get for reconciling with my dad," she muttered, turning so he didn't see her eyes water. "I opened the door to the Mafia world and now I'm handcuffed to a bench in the middle of a police station, about to go to jail, or if I get out I'll be guilted into a marriage with a man I don't love, and the man I do care about is going to just let me go."

"You have choices, Gracie. You always did."

She snorted. "You mean run away? I'm not that person any more. I think I realized that tonight in the alley. I'm a fighter. And it's not the violence that really bothers me. It's violence for the sake of violence. Violence where innocent people suffer. But if you're protecting someone you love or care about, or you're defending yourself, then it's excusable. There's a grey area that I couldn't see after my mother died." After her mother died, she wanted nothing to do with violence—no play fights, no violent video games, no toy gun fights with Tom. She couldn't watch shows with guns or bloodshed, and finding out her father was part of a violent criminal organization—the same organization that had been responsible for the death of her mother—had devastated her. And then she'd found out Rocco was the epitome of everything she'd rejected in her life.

But after running away one last time, her face scarred

and her heart broken, she hadn't given up. She'd learned to defend herself. She'd put herself through college, put her singing gift to use, and she'd reconciled with her father. Maybe she hadn't taken the final steps of getting a job or becoming professional singer, and she had made it clear to her father she was never going to be part of the mob, but she had made something of herself. She wasn't drifting, like she'd thought. She was at a crossroads in her life. A gray area. She just had to decide which path to take.

"I'm supposed to be a psychologist," she said, still mulling over her thoughts. "Obviously not a good one if it's taken me this long to figure out what my problem is. I'm beginning to realize it isn't my true calling."

He laughed, a deep, rich, beautiful sound that made her body tingle. She'd never heard him really laugh before. In all their years together, he had never fully let down his guard.

"I'm glad you can laugh when we're about to go to jail." She squeezed his hand, remembering where they were. The station was a never-ending stream of activity— uniformed officers coming and going, the benches filled with people of all ages cuffed or chained, some angry, some drunk, some terrified like her, people shouting, doors slamming, keys rattling . . . and was that the sound of a metal door?

"You won't be going to jail." He kissed her scarred cheek, and she felt the sensation as a burst of warmth inside her. Usually she felt nothing when anything touched her scar, just an awareness of pressure on her skin. "We'll be leaving here soon."

"You sound so sure."

"I promised to protect you and I will." He pressed his lips to her ear and murmured. "Nico's *consigliere* is an attorney. He's got everyone in his pocket from the DA to the police chief to the judges and a good handful of cops. He specializes in digging up dirt on people in power and trades it for favors."

Her heart skipped a beat. "You're sure? I mean, you're not a Toscani. Will Nico help you?"

"Yeah. He will. If I didn't think so, I would never have allowed them to put those handcuffs on you." His voice dropped husky and low. "Although they give me some ideas . . ."

Grace's cheeks flushed and Rocco gave a low growl of approval.

"You like that."

"Not when I'm sitting in a police station."

"When we get home."

She edged closer to him, bridged the gap he had placed between them, leaned her head against his shoulder. "Too bad we weren't arrested that night in New York. Maybe if we'd been handcuffed to a police bench we would have talked things through, and I wouldn't have run away."

"It wouldn't have changed anything. Not then. Not the people we were. We weren't ready."

"I felt like I'd failed you," she said quietly. "From the day we met, I could feel your pain. I knew Cesare was doing something to you. Each week you were a little bit different, a little more distant, sadder, like you were being torn apart. I knew you were hurting inside and I wanted to fix you. It made me happy that I could make you smile. I thought I could save you in a way I couldn't save my mother."

"You did save me, *bella*. In every way a man can be saved."

"De Lucchi and Mantini." A police officer stopped in front of them and jangled a set of keys. "You're free to go."

"That's it?" Grace lifted her hands so he could undo her cuffs.

"That's it. Apologies for the inconvenience." He looked back over his shoulder at an elderly gentleman wearing a smart, navy suit. "Your attorney says you agreed not to go public. Much appreciated."

Rocco nodded as his cuffs were removed. With one hand pressed against Grace's lower back, he led her down the hallway to the man in the suit.

"Charlie."

"Frankie."

"You want a smoke?" Charlie held out a packet of cigarettes. Rocco stared at them for a long second and then shook his head.

"Trying to quit."

Nothing else was said until they were out of the police station and half a block down the street.

"This is Charlie Nails," Rocco said stopping beside a shiny black Mercedes parked at the side of the road. "He's an attorney and a friend of ours."

A friend of ours told Grace that Charlie was a made man and connected to the mob. She figured him for Nico's *consigliere* given his age and their earlier conversation. "Thank you for your help." She held out her hand. "I wasn't looking forward to spending the night in jail."

Charlie gave Grace's hand a firm shake. "Grace Mantini. You're as beautiful as your mother was at that age."

"You knew my mother?" Her pulse kicked up a notch. Other than the aunt she'd lived with after leaving the family home, she hadn't met many people who knew her mother, and none from the mob.

"Everyone knew your mother," he said. "I used to live in New York until I was sent to Vegas to watch over the Toscani family rebels, and I knew her well." He sucked in an appreciative breath. "So beautiful. Every man wanted her. And it wasn't just because she was the daughter of the underboss. She was an amazing singer and the life of every party."

Grace had never heard any recordings of her mother singing. She had only her memories and a few photos of her mother on stage. "You heard her sing?"

Charlie nodded. "There was a club where our friends would go for a good time on Friday and Saturday nights. She sang there often. Your grandfather wasn't happy about it. He didn't like the idea of her up on stage, but she loved the spotlight and she always put on a good show. A lot of fights were started over her. But once she met your father, it was clear no one else had a chance."

"He never got over her death," she said.

Charlie's face softened. "It was tragic what happened to her. I never believed the story. It's a shame no one ever discovered the truth."

Grace frowned. "The story about Jimmy Valentino shooting up Ricardo's restaurant because Ricardo was having an affair with his wife? I was there. I saw a man come in and shoot."

"Jimmy's wife would never have cheated on him," Charlie said. "Some couples you just know are going to last. Your mom and dad were like that. Jimmy and Violet were, too."

"But he went to jail," she protested. "He has another eleven years to serve."

Charlie shrugged. "Maybe for a crime he didn't commit. But if that's true, he'll never say."

Omertà meant you went to jail rather than rat out another made man or reveal your affiliation with the mob, even if you didn't do the crime.

"Why would anyone want to kill her?"

"That's the wrong question." Charlie opened the door to his car.

"What's the right question?"

Charlie's gaze flicked to Rocco and then back to Grace. "That's something you need to ask you father."

"Grace! Your watchdog is on the front step," Olivia called out from the front door. "I gotta run or I'd bring him in to be fed. I'll see you at lunch."

Grace ran a comb through her wet hair and threw on a pair of cut-off jean shorts and a shabby cottage chic lilac tunic top with a see-through lace poncho overlay. She loved floral, romantic clothes although, with Rocco having disappeared for a day and a night, they didn't up-lift her like they usually did.

Ethan and Miguel waved to her from the kitchen as she headed for the front door, keeping her head averted. No amount of make-up could hide the dark circles under her eyes. She loved her father. Trusted him. But what she'd seen of Rocco since they'd met again didn't jibe with what Papa had suggested. He had done nothing except try to protect her and she couldn't believe he was doing it simply to get close to Tom and her dad so he could pull the trigger and end their lives.

She pulled open the door and studied Rocco on the front step, leaning against the porch. He was wearing the same clothes he'd been in yesterday when he'd left her to go for a ride after she'd finished at the recording studio."

"How long have you been out here?"

Rocco shrugged. "Most of the night."

Guilt speared through her chest. "You sat out here all night? Why didn't you come in?"

"You have some new security. Didn't want to disturb your neighbors by causing a fight." He gestured to the Forzani soldiers who had replaced Mike and Paolo and

Rocco's men outside her house. "We agreed I'd stay outside."

"I don't want them. I want you."

"Not willing to cause a political incident to have you in my bed, *bella*."

"What political incident?" Anger flared inside her. "I'm not marrying Dino Forzani. I won't be guilted into a marriage to a man I don't love, especially one so cowardly that he'd lure you into a back alley and attack you with five of his men."

"Aren't you cold?" Unable to stop herself, she knelt down beside him. "Did you eat anything? I can't believe you would sit here all night. You must be exhausted. Come inside."

"It's okay, Gracie." He pushed the damp tendrils of her hair off her cheek. "I'm good. I'll be here when you're ready to go."

Damn. She'd been up all night trying to reconcile her father's words with what her heart was telling her: Rocco wouldn't hurt her, and he knew nothing would hurt her more than losing the only family she had left.

"Inside." She clasped his hand, pulling on him as she stood. "Now. You can take a shower while I fix you some breakfast. I've got a studio gig this morning, and then I'm going to meet Olivia for lunch and visit the kids at the orphanage where I did my internship. If you want to come along, that's the plan."

"You worked at an orphanage?" He stood, still holding her hand.

"Yeah. I didn't feel that I could help adults if I couldn't heal myself, but I could help the kids, many of whom suffered abuse at home before they either lost their parents or were taken into care. I especially liked that I got a say in the adoption process, so I could help make sure the kids were going to a good home."

Rocco scrubbed his hand over his face. "Fuck. Grace."

She wasn't sure if *Fuck Grace* was meant to be a compliment or an insult or if he was expressing exasperation or pleasure, but he looked exhausted and hungry, and the part of her that just couldn't believe he would take a contract to whack her father and brother couldn't leave him sitting on the step.

After breakfast, he took her to the studio and then to Sunnyvale to meet Olivia for lunch. Matthew was in the courtyard shooting hoops and she joined him while Rocco parked his bike.

"You're really bad," Matthew said after she missed yet another basket. He dashed across the courtyard, neatly intercepting the ball before she could get near it.

"Maybe you're just really good. I have a feeling you practice every day." Grace ran to block him, but he was too fast and skirted under her arm.

"I do." Matthew jumped and made what seemed like an impossible shot. Father Seamus had installed an adjustable hoop, and even with it down on the lowest setting, Grace was losing by a wide margin. "I'm going to be a basketball star. I need something special about me so I get adopted, and if I tell people I'm going to be in the NBA they'll want me."

"Oh, Matthew." She left the ball and walked over to kneel in front of him. "The kind of special you need is in here." She tapped his chest. "And you already have it. The things we do don't define us; it's who we are inside."

"I'm an NBA star inside," he said, missing the point entirely.

She heard a chuckle and looked up to see Rocco with Olivia, watching them from the far side of the court.

"I found this hunk of manliness in the lobby," Olivia said, a smile tugging at the corners of her lips. "I was wondering what you'd do with the package on the doorstep."

Grace introduced Rocco to Matthew, smiling as Rocco shook Matthew's hand. How would he feel about being in an orphanage again? He'd once told her he didn't remember anything about the facility where Cesare found him, but sometimes situational experiences could trigger subconscious memories.

"Now we have a team," Matthew said.

Grace raised a querying eyebrow when Matthew offered the ball to Rocco. She had never seen Rocco play team sports, but then theirs hadn't been a normal relationship. After she turned sixteen, and their friendship became something more, their encounters all had to be kept secret. She had always thought he was concerned about her father's reaction to their age difference. But after she found out who Rocco was, she realized his concern stemmed from what could be considered a class difference as well. Outwardly, he was entirely wrong for her, and yet his sensitivity and need were a powerful draw, their shared love of Rat Pack music and art bringing them together despite their age difference, and they had a connection in a way she still didn't understand.

In response to her silent question, he removed his leather jacket and placed it on a nearby bench. "Me and Matthew against Grace and Olivia. Girls versus boys. How does that sound?"

"Great." Matthew beamed.

"What? Matthew? You're abandoning me?" Grace feigned a pout, and Matthew's face grew serious.

"He's much taller than you. He'll be able to reach the net easier." He gave her arm a gentle pat. "You can have him on your team next time."

Rocco laughed. "I have a feeling they are going to give us a run for our money."

"You'd better believe it." Olivia dribbled the ball, showing off her fancy moves. She played with the kids every day and had been on the basketball team at college. When it came to basketball, Olivia took no prisoners.

Five minutes in, and Grace had to admit Rocco was pretty damn good, too. Still, she'd played enough with Matthew and the other kids that she could hold her own, especially when he decided to shadow her around the court.

"Get out my way," she hissed in frustration as his huge body blocked her pass to Olivia. "This is supposed to be fun. Go block someone else."

Rocco laughed out loud. "Can't handle the competition?"

"I'll give you competition." She took a step and then bounced the ball sideways to Olivia who grabbed it and dribbled to the net. Quick as lightening, Matthew knocked it away and threw it into the net.

"Score!" He shouted as the ball sailed through the net.

"Good man." Rocco gave him a high five and Matthew beamed.

Grace's heart warmed to see them together. This was a side of Rocco she'd never seen before. The only kid she'd ever seen Rocco with was Tom and their interactions had been limited to brief conversations about sports and video games during their drives to and from school.

"He's really good with Matthew," Olivia said when they stopped for a water break. "And I like him, but he's kind of intense. I mean, sitting on the front step all night, following you around everywhere . . . it's kind of stalkerish."

Omertà means she couldn't tell Olivia that he was either following her around because he was worried she was in danger from a crazy Mafia boss or that he was just waiting for an opportunity to get close to her father and brother because someone had contracted him to kill them. Even if she hadn't been bound by Mafia rules, she couldn't imagine sharing that kind of information. Who would believe her?

"He's not a stalker type. Overprotective? Maybe. But he would never hurt me." So why was she even thinking about her father's words? But how could she not?

"I think you need some space," Olivia said.

"What do you mean space?"

"He's with you all the time. How can you sort out what you think and feel when he's always there? We're always telling our patients to establish boundaries, but it's not always easy to follow our own advice. Tell him to back off for a bit. No one's going to die."

Grace drained her water bottle. "He thinks I'm in danger," she said quietly.

"From whom?"

"Business associates of my dad."

"What kind of people is your dad involved with . . . ?" Olivia trailed off, and her eyes widened. "Is that the real reason he's in the hospital? I thought he was just in a wrong place at the wrong time kind of thing, and I didn't want to ask because you'd already been through something like that with your mom." She sucked in a sharp breath. "What's he involved in? Corporate espionage? Political scandal? Did he tell the company secrets to you? Did they find out, and now they want to punish you for his crime? He seemed so nice and mild mannered when he came to pick you up. Did he tell you something before they shot him? Crap. This is like the movies. Is it the mob? Or is it a big pharma thing?" She paused for breath and Grace held up a warning hand.

"I don't know how he's involved, but at the hospital the other day, Papa suggested it might not be in a good way."

"But he's trying to protect you?"

"Or maybe he's using me . . ." She trailed off because the words just didn't ring true. Rocco had never once used her, although given who her dad was, he could have asked for a favor many times when they were younger and he never did.

"Nah." Olivia shook her head. "I saw the way he was looking at you, and I saw him when I went out this morning for my run. He was wrecked. You don't do that to yourself if you're using someone. You do it if you care about them more than you care about yourself."

She looked over at Rocco holding Matthew up so he could dunk the ball in the basket. What kind of man would spend time playing ball with a little boy at an orphanage if his sole purpose was to get close to her father and Tom to whack them. He had been the one to arrange guards for her father at the hospital, and if he had really wanted to kill him, he'd had the chance the night of the shooting, and again when she'd found him alone in her father's room.

"You coming or are we winning?" he called out, tossing her the ball.

A smile spread across her face. "Why are you in such a hurry to lose?"

Rocco laughed out loud as he raced over to cover her. "I never realized you had such a competitive streak."

Neither had she, but ever since Rocco had come back into her life, she was discovering all sorts of new things about herself. And right now, there was no way she was going to let him beat her.

She spun around, as if shielding the ball from him and brushed her ass up against his hips. When she heard his soft grunt of arousal she tossed the ball to Olivia who slammed it into the basket.

"Interference." Rocco came up behind her and slid an arm around her waist.

"Doesn't feel like you mind." She wiggled against him, feeling the hardness of his arousal.

"Naughty girl." He pulled her head back against his chest and kissed her. "You know what happens to naughty girls?"

"I'm looking forward to finding out when priests and little boys aren't watching."

"Ewww," Matthew yelled from across the court. "Kissing is gross."

"Kissing means I get an extra basket." Olivia tossed the ball in again and then fist-pumped the air. "Looks like the girls win."

"Let's play again!" Matthew grabbed the ball and dribbled down the court, but Grace shook her head.

"Olivia and I have to grab something to eat, and I'm sure Rocco has places to go."

"I'm going where you go."

She shook her head. "I need some girl time with Olivia, and I've got the Forzani foursome on my tail. How about we meet at my place in an hour to go for a run. I am badly in need of some exercise."

"Wasn't the other night enough?" He licked his lips, and she laughed.

"Sexing me up all night is not the kind of exercise I need."

His smile faded. "It's not safe to run outside. I'll take you to Mike's gym. He's got a good set up and we can work out together."

"What do you do there? Something manly, I assume."

"I lift weights, work the bags, spar in the ring . . ."

"So, no cardio?"

Rocco snorted. "If you mean running on a hamster wheel, no."

"Too bad. I would have liked to see you break a sweat."

He spun her to face him. "I don't sweat."

"I do believe you were sweating the other night when you decided to bend me over your couch."

Rocco gave a low, sexy rumble of pleasure and tagged her around the waist with a strong arm. "That was a good night."

"Yes, it was." She leaned up to nuzzle his neck. "Maybe you'll want to test out my couch before we go to the gym. I have to go back to get my gear, and everyone will be at work."

She should have known better than to tempt him.

TWENTY

Two hours and three orgasms later, they walked into the aptly named "Mike's Gym" on East Tropicana Avenue. Located in a strip mall, with only a basic sign out front, the gym was surprisingly spacious and airy. Mike gave Grace a guest pass to get through the gate, and she changed in the locker room before meeting Rocco and Mike on the mats.

"I'm going to warm up before I hit the tread." She took a step toward the cardio machines only to feel a finger slide under the strap of her tank top and suddenly she was moving backward at rapid speed.

"You're not going anywhere dressed like that."

She looked back over her shoulder and sighed. "These are workout clothes. All the important bits are covered."

"This isn't covered." Rocco's hand slide around her waist, over her bare skin. "This isn't covered." He feathered kisses over her nape, down her back to the top of the tank sending a delicious shiver down her spine.

"Stop that. We're in public."

He spun her around. "Exactly. And this isn't covered."

His warm, wet tongue traced a path from the base of her throat to the crescents of her breasts.

Grace felt a rush of heat between her thighs. "Those bits are considered publicly acceptable to show."

"There's nothing left to the imagination." His hand curved around her hip to her Lycra-covered ass, and he squeezed her cheek, his thumb running up and down her cleft.

"Rocco." Embarrassed, Grace looked over his shoulder to Mike who had a smile plastered across his face.

"You meet the dress code," Mike said.

"And I'm sure Rocco can scowl the competition away." Grace leaned up to kiss Rocco's cheek. "Maybe I should send *you* back to change. Your ass is looking delectable in those shorts, and I can see every ridge of your lickable muscles under that T-shirt. I'm not really a jealous person, but I don't like the idea of all these women checking you out."

"Not interested in anyone but you." He leaned down to kiss her, and she felt warm all over.

"Feel free to use any of the equipment," Mike said. "We've got plenty of heavy bags, speed bags, weights, machines, and most importantly space. I always have at least three trainers on the floor in case people have any questions or need some tips, and I keep the music upbeat so we always have a good vibe going. We get all types here from people wanting to lose weight or stay in shape to professional MMA fighters and boxers who train here every day."

"What are you going to do while I run?" Grace asked Rocco. "Punch things?"

"Yeah. I'm gonna start with Mike 'cause he wasn't where he was supposed to be in the alley behind the jazz club."

His serious expression made her laugh, until she saw Mike pale. "You're joking, right?"

"This isn't my joking face."

"It's your forgiving face." She leaned up to kiss his cheek. "How about you punch something else, and I'll watch you while I run on the tread. Maybe learn a few tricks." Or she could watch his muscles ripple and fantasize about having that hard body and all that power focused on her in bed.

She heard a soft growl and suddenly she was plastered up against him, his arm a steel band around her waist. "You keep looking at me like that and we'll be working out in Mike's office out back."

"You didn't get enough at my house?" Grace laughed. "Seriously, Rocco. Your stamina is—"

"Legend."

"No."

"Magnificent."

"No."

"Incredible?"

"Exhausting."

His brow creased in a frown. "Exhausting?"

Grace pressed her lips against his ear and whispered, "How can you want me every minute of the day?"

"Because you're you."

A smile spread across her face, and she felt the slight tug of the tight skin on her cheek. When she was with Rocco, she rarely thought about her scar, never worried about how she appeared to him, or about the extra curves that she wouldn't have if she stuck to her running regime. He made her believe she was the most beautiful, most desirable woman in the world, and even if this didn't last, she would never forget how he made her feel.

"You make me want to skip the workout and go straight to Mike's office."

Rocco fisted her hair and kissed her hard. "Let's go."

"I was just joking," she murmured against his lips. "Workout first. Then hot, sweaty sex in Mike's office."

"Make it a short workout." He released her, and the smile faded from his lips. "Fuck."

"What's wrong?" Grace turned and followed his gaze to a blonde-haired woman talking with Mike at the reception desk. She looked vaguely familiar, and it took Grace a moment to place her.

"That's the woman who was with Mike last night in the alley. The one who called the police."

"Don't like her," Rocco said, his voice harsh.

"I'm sure she was just trying to help. She's a civilian. She saw a fight. Calling the police is what civilians do."

Rocco put a protective arm across her body, pulling her up against him again. "She lied to the police."

"She was trying to protect Mike."

"Something about her . . ." he muttered.

"You need to let things go," she said softly. "Miguel made that comment about your age and now you glare at him and mutter mean things about him under your breath every time he's around. It's not good to hold a grudge. Let it go. Lighten your soul."

"There is no light in my soul. It's all darkness."

Grace looked up and pressed a soft kiss to the underside of his jaw. "That's not true. There has to be a little ray of sunshine that gives you joy."

"Her name is Grace."

Her heart felt full to bursting as she headed over to the treadmill. Being with Rocco felt so right. There had to be a way to make it work, to reconcile what he did with who he was. She put in her earbuds and pulled out her phone to find her running playlist. A message flashed on the screen and her heart skipped a beat.

IT'S TOM. I'M OUT BACK. COME ALONE.

Grace didn't recognize the number, but then she had Tom's phone so it made sense that he had a new one. But anyone could have sent the message. If Rocco had let her know what was going on, she could have better assessed the danger, but all she had to go on was her knowledge of her brother and his knowledge of her.

WHAT TOY DID I SLEEP WITH UNTIL I WAS TEN?

His answer came within seconds. PIG PATCH.

A smile tugged at her lips at the memory of the stuffed pig with gray patches her mother had made when she was little. She'd slept with it every night after her mother died and even now it was safe in one of her dresser drawers.

"Forgot my water bottle." She jogged past Rocco and Mike, but when she got to the back hallway, she raced past the locker room and out the back door.

For a moment the sunshine blinded her, but after blinking a few times, she spotted Tom in a Toyota Camry parked in the shade.

"Tom!"

He gestured her toward the car. "God, Grace. I'm so glad to see you. Come inside so we can talk."

Grace jogged around the vehicle and climbed in the passenger side. After closing the door, she reached over and hugged him tight. "Where have you been? I've been trying to find you. I have some new friends who tracked down your phone, but the guys who had it were looking for you. Are you okay? Were you hurt in the restaurant? Are you safe?"

"A bullet grazed my arm, but I'm okay." He released her and leaned back in the seat. "I didn't want to go back to New York with Papa still in the hospital. Tony Toscani tracked me down and protected me. He said it would be better to keep a low profile because the De Lucchi crew is out to get us."

Grace's mouth went dry. "The De Lucchis?"

Tom's jaw tightened. "I was at Tony's place when Rocco De Lucchi came to see him. He admitted right in front of Tony he had a contract to kill me and Papa. I heard it, Grace. No bullshit. He was annoyed someone else beat him to it at Carvello's. He thought it was Tony, but Tony said it wasn't him. So actually there are two people trying to take us out."

She bit her lip, not sure how much to tell him. "We're . . . I'm . . ."

"Papa said you were together. I didn't believe him at first." His voice rose in pitch. "He's trying to get to us through you because someone messed up his hit at Carvello's. If Tony hadn't protected me, I would be dead. And Papa, too, if Nico hadn't put guards at the hospital."

"Rocco's the one who arranged for the guards," Grace protested.

"Probably so they would know him and not think of him as a threat the day he decided to take out Papa."

"No." Her heart sank in her chest. "No. That's not true. He's been trying to protect me."

"You're not made like Papa and me," Tom said, puffing out his chest. "He can only want you to use you."

Her blood chilled in her veins. "What do you mean, *made* like you? You're not . . . ?" One look at his face told her everything she didn't want to know. Her hand flew to her mouth and bile rose in her throat. "You're made? Oh my God, Tom. You didn't. You can't. Please tell me it's not true."

"Christ." He tipped his head back and groaned. "You

make it sound like it's something bad. I'm someone now. Papa just promoted me to capo. I've got my own soldiers, and my own associates. I've got businesses that bring in good money. Papa is proud of me. I'm following in his footsteps. When he steps down as underboss, I'm going to take his place."

Grace's blood pounded in her ears so loud, she could barely hear him. Tom. Her lovely, sweet, funny Tom was a wiseguy. No wonder he was targeted in the hit. He was officially Papa's successor.

"Nothing has changed between us." He put an arm around her shoulders. "I'm the same Tom, just with more power and more money and a chance at making something of my life."

"You killed someone," she said flatly.

"We don't talk about those things." His voice was uncharacteristically stern. "What happens when a man gets made is part of *omertà*."

"Did Papa make you do it? Did he force you? Or was it the don?"

"*Porco cane,*" Tom muttered, moving his arm away. "Don't be like this. You know the world we live in. You know about the family. And how can you judge me when you're with a goddamn De Lucchi enforcer? You don't like the idea of death, and yet you're fucking a man who has taken countless lives? A man who wants to kill me and Papa?"

"Don't speak to me like that." Grace twisted her hands in her lap, trying to get a handle on her emotions. "He didn't want that life."

"Well, for someone who didn't want it, he's damned good at it," he spat out. "And I do want it. I've wanted it all my life. It's part of our family history, passed down from father to son. I'm happy to carry on the family tradition, and part of that tradition is keeping our women safe. You are all Papa and I have left. And right now, you're in danger."

"He's not going to hurt me," she said.

Tom snorted. "He's a De Lucchi. He doesn't care about anything. He has no feelings. He is a cold, ruthless, heartless killing machine and right now he wants to kill Papa and me. You are a tool to him. He will do or say anything to fulfill that contract. In the end, we die or he dies and you don't need me to tell you which side he's going to choose."

Grace scrubbed her face with her hands, trying to untangle fact from feeling, but confusion flooded her mind, drowning her in doubt and questions. There were just so many little things that didn't add up. Rocco's insistence on staying with her after the gun fight in the restaurant, even going so far as to break down her door when she went home. The time she found him standing alone at her father's bedside in the hospital. How he'd followed her to the trailer park and insisted on going in alone. The cold rough sex they'd had at his place when she'd felt like she was with another man. And now, he followed her everywhere, refusing to leave her alone . . .

Had she been wrong? Was it all an act? Had she truly lost Rocco that night at the river or was she about to lose him now? "What do you want me to do?"

"Send him away," Tom said. "Tell him your family is protecting you and the Forzanis, because I hear you're going to marry Dino when Papa gets out of the hospital. You have people who truly care. You don't need Rocco."

"I do need him. I want him. I trust him, Tom."

"Christ. He's got you wrapped around his finger," Tom spat out. "Are you in love with him? That's what the De Lucchis do, Grace. They are master manipulators. They will do anything to get the job done, whether that means fucking the underboss's daughter to get close to the target, killing three Albanians who were trying to find me so Tony could protect me, or beating up the guys Mr. Forzani sent to protect you."

Her heart sank into her stomach. "They're all dead?"

"Yeah." His face tightened. "Tony had a camera at his place and Frankie walked in and handed him three gold rings with the Albanian Mafia stamp on them. I saw it. And he pretty much said he did it."

Her hand went to her mouth, remembering the blood on his clothes when he came out of the trailer. She'd suspected Rocco had killed them, but willful blindness had been her friend. "It's not true," she protested weakly. "He beat them up because they attacked him, and the one guy he questioned, he promised he wouldn't—"

"Well, he lied to you about that. Is it such a stretch to believe he lied to you about other things?"

Grace slumped back in the seat unable to hear anything else he was saying for the pounding of blood in her ears.

"I'm not your little brother anymore." Tom puffed out his chest. "I'm a made man, Grace. I know what I'm doing." He reached over her and pushed open the door. "You'd better get back inside. He'll be wondering where you are. And even though you don't believe me, we're going to protect you. Your family is going to protect you. Papa is going to ask the don for permission to whack Rocco."

"Why?" She stared at him aghast. "You are literally shooting the messenger. Someone hired the De Lucchis. Why doesn't the don make Cesare tell him who it is? If you kill Rocco, then Cesare will just give the contract to someone else."

"We're doing both," Tom said. "Petitioning the don and taking out the man who tried to kill us."

"He tried to save you in the restaurant," she said, shocking herself with the vehemence in her tone. "He tried to save Papa. He was right in front of you. If he wanted to kill you, he could have done it and no one would have known it was him." Grace slid out of the vehicle and back into the summer heat. "Let me talk to him. I'll find out what's going on."

"What's going on is that you've been seduced by a monster who wants your family dead," Tom said coldly. He started his vehicle and lowered the window. "But we're going to save you."

"Grace?"

Grace whirled around at the sound of a woman's voice and forced a smile for Mike's girlfriend who was standing in the open doorway.

"Yes?"

"I'm Tiffany." The woman smiled, her gaze flicking to Tom's car and back to Grace. "I'm with Mike. Frankie asked me to find you. When I didn't see you in the locker room, I thought I'd check outside. Everything okay?"

"Yeah." She looked over her shoulder as Tom pulled out of the parking lot. "I came out to see if it was too hot to run and bumped into a friend."

"I'm sorry about the other night." Tiffany fiddled with her ponytail as Grace walked toward the door. "I didn't mean to get you arrested. I was just worried that people were getting hurt. I guess I'm just oversensitive to violence. I work at a hospital, and I see so many people hurt I sometimes overreact."

Still reeling from Tom's revelation, Grace wasn't up for a conversation so she gave a dismissive shrug. "It's okay. They let us go in the end. We should get back to the gym."

"I'm actually not a big gym person," Tiffany said as they walked back into the cool hallway. She adjusted her barely-there skin-tight outfit on a body that belied her words. "But I came to surprise Mike with the ulterior motive of watching him work out."

Grace forced a laugh. "I had the same ulterior motive, although I've been desperate for a run all week."

"We can run together on the treadmills." Tiffany smiled. "I think the scenery is probably better in here anyway."

"Sure." The last thing she wanted to do was go back into the gym, but Rocco would be wondering where she was. She'd put it off for too long. There were questions that needed to be answered. And decisions that had to be made.

He knew something was wrong the moment she walked into the gym.

At first, he thought Mike's girlfriend had said something to upset her, but when the two of them laughed together as they walked past and she didn't even spare him a glance, his skin prickled.

What the fuck? She'd been fine before she went to get her water bottle. More than fine. She'd been happy, flirty, leaning against him. Now her cheeks were flushed, and she was suddenly best friends with a woman who had almost landed her in jail.

Maybe that was it. She was annoyed that he'd made negative comments about Mike's girlfriend. Good thing he'd held back on his true feelings, because something about that woman was definitely off.

"Everything okay, Frankie?" Mike gave an uncharacteristically obsequious smile that would have amused Rocco if he weren't so concerned about Grace. Mike must have figured Rocco was going to teach him a lesson after his screw-up in the alley. A few weeks ago,

Rocco would have considered icing Mike for what he'd done. But he didn't have the time or energy to discipline Luca's soldiers when he had to deal with the more pressing matter of Grace's sudden change of disposition.

"So that's your girlfriend?" Rocco pounded the speed-bag in front of him trying to work off the stress he usually relieved in his sessions with Clay. He had cancelled his last two appointments not just because he was wary about Grace seeing the marks when they were in bed together, but also because he didn't want to feel numb. With Grace back in his life, he didn't need to forget or hide his pain. She had opened him up, exposed him. Saved him. She made him want to walk again in the light, embrace his feelings and emotions instead of pushing them away.

He drum rolled the speedbag without missing a beat. Usually he enjoyed getting up a good rhythm and working up a sweat, but he couldn't focus with Grace studiously ignoring him as she ran on the tread.

"Yes, sir. I'm sorry I brought her to the club. With all the guards there, I never expected—"

Rocco held up a hand, cutting him off. "What's her full name?"

"Tiffany Oliver."

"What do you know about her?"

Mike's eyes narrowed and his muscles tensed like he was getting ready for a fight. "Why do you want to know?"

Protective. Rocco knew the feeling. Mike obviously cared for the girl and was willing to push even Rocco back if she was in danger. Rocco's gaze slid to the woman on the treadmill beside Grace and caught her watching him. There was more to Tiffany Oliver than met the eye, a darkness that matched his own.

"I like to know the people who are hanging around

my girl," he said trying to keep his tone light and casual.

Mike's tension eased. "She's a nurse. I met her at the jazz club a few weeks ago. She lives in Henderson with a friend, and she's got a dog. She was born here but her parents died in a car accident when she was six, and she went to live with her uncle in New York for a bit. She's half Italian and a sweet girl. Really sweet. She didn't mean any harm. She just got scared. If you've got a problem with her . . ." He tipped his neck from side to side, making it crack, sending the message that he was prepared to defend his girl, even though they both knew lifting a hand to Rocco would cost Mike his life.

Rocco smashed his fist into the bag. "I'm not going to touch a woman and especially not a civilian, but keep her the fuck away from our business and our friends. *Capice?*"

"Yes, sir. She's a real sweetheart, sir. I asked her to look in on Mr. Mantini and make sure he was getting good care, and she said she'd already been in to see him. She's assigned to his floor at St. John's. Isn't that a coincidence?"

Rocco's skin prickled in warning. He didn't believe in coincidence. Fate and chance had never been his friends.

"You don't break *omertà*. Not even with your woman."

"No, sir."

"You do, and you'll wind up at the bottom of Lake Mead wearing a pair of cement shoes that I will personally fit while you're still breathing."

Mike swallowed hard. "Yes, sir."

"I'm not done with you," Rocco warned as he drumrolled the speed bag. "I've got some shit to deal with, but when I'm done, you'll report to me at the clubhouse carrying a stick the size you think you need me to fucking beat you with so you learn not to be such a *cafone*."

"Can you lift a tree, sir?"

And that, right there, was why Rocco was letting Mike off easy. He was a good guy. Loyal. A good earner. And as honest as a man could be in this business. And he made Rocco laugh, although he never let Mike see it.

"I can lift anything you think will do the job." He gave the bag a final punch and turned to look at the now chastised soldier. "Word of warning. Don't think with your dick. When something seems too good to be true, it usually is."

Rocco wondered if he should take his own advice. His fantasy of leaving the De Lucchi crew and living a normal life was just that. A fantasy. The possibility of a future with Grace was too good to be true, and yet it didn't stop him from wanting it.

By the time he finished his workout, Grace was waiting in the reception area, talking to Mike and Tiffany. Rocco shouldered his bag, acutely aware that Tiffany was watching him. He could feel her gaze on him even when he put his hand on Grace's lower back to lead her out the door.

"I'm okay." Grace flinched and took a step away. "Let's go."

He followed her to his bike, waiting until they were out of earshot of anyone else, before he asked, "What's wrong?"

"Nothing." She straddled his bike, tightening the straps of her backpack although they didn't need to be tightened.

"Don't lie to me." His words came out harsher than he intended, but after an hour of being ignored, and his intuition blaring a warning, he wanted an answer and he wanted it now.

"I'm tired. That's all. I just want to go home and get some sleep." She dipped her head and looked away. "You can just drop me off—"

"I'm not leaving you alone."

Her shoulders sagged. "Well, I guess you can crash on the couch."

Damn. He'd fucked up big time if he was being sent to the couch. It had been a long time since he'd dealt with an angry woman, so he went with his gut instinct which was to shut the fuck up, get on the bike, and ride. Whatever was wrong had something to do with Tiffany because Grace had been fine when she went into the locker room and not fine when she came out. He'd already decided to do a little investigating into Mike's girlfriend. Now he had a reason to get started sooner rather than later.

After dropping Grace off and making sure the Forzani fuckers were in place watching her and keeping her safe, he swung by Gabrielle's new PI office, all steel and glass and giant windows overlooking a fake lagoon. After they'd shared a brief greeting, Rocco sat in front of Gabrielle's desk and stared at the pictures of tropical beaches on the wall, wondering if some day in his miserable life he might find his way to a place where he had nothing to do but lie in the sun.

"So what can I do for you?" Gabrielle took her seat and rested her hands on her pregnant belly. Rocco felt yet another twinge of longing for a life that was getting farther and farther out of reach. Out of habit, he reached for his cigarettes, realizing only as he felt his empty pocket that he couldn't even remember the last time he'd had a smoke. Hell, he'd finally kicked his addiction only to face losing the one person who had made it happen all over again.

"Wanna know about the girl who called the cops on

us in the alley. Mike's new girlfriend. Don't ask me any questions. I took a picture of her in the gym." He gave Gabrielle all the information he had, sent her a copy of the picture, and sat back while she ran whatever searches PIs ran to find people who didn't want to be found.

"Are you sure you have the name right?" Gabrielle looked up from her computer and frowned. "I'm not getting anything right off the bat. Let me try something else. It will take a few minutes."

"Sure." He needed to give Grace some space. He'd lived six years without her. He supposed he could live a few hours with her anger. Although, now that he thought about it, he hadn't been living all these years. He'd been existing. The last time he'd truly lived had been with Grace. Holding her. Kissing her. Loving her.

"You okay, Rocco?" Gabrielle's soft voice yanked him back to the moment, and he pushed himself out of his chair, disconcerted that he had allowed himself to be so exposed.

"Good. Just gonna grab some . . . water."

Water. Not cigarettes. He was clean and he wanted to stay that way.

"Make it a couple of hours. I need some more time." She tipped her head to the side and studied him. "Is everything okay with Grace?" she asked with the intuition that women seemed to have when it came to things that didn't concern them in the least.

"Yeah."

Rocco's head wasn't in the game when he returned to Gabrielle's office after going for a ride through the city. After the emotional rollercoaster of being at the orphanage, playing ball with a boy who had been the same age as him when Cesare took him away, the strange sense of déjà vu he'd had on the playground, and Grace's odd behavior since their workout at the gym, he was hoping for some good news, or at least something easy to handle—something that wouldn't send him back down to Clay's dungeon or into the nearest convenience store for a habit he didn't want to start again.

His hope faded when Gabrielle looked up with a grim expression on her face. "Sit down."

"Not in a sitting mood." He paced around her office, checking out the window, the framed certificates on the wall, a picture of her, Luca, and their son, Matteo, at their wedding, surrounded by family and friends. Luca had a huge family and most of them lived in Vegas, so he was tight with all his relatives—so tight he and Gabrielle had bought a new house across the street from his mother. Rocco had been invited to their housewarming party, but he'd given it a miss because the last time he'd met Luca's mother, she'd tried to stab him with a kitchen knife because she thought he was going to hurt her son. What would it be like to have someone who loved you so much they would die trying to protect you? He couldn't even imagine.

"Well, I'll stay sitting because my back is killing me." Gabrielle's hand dropped to her belly. "The baby is kicking. You want to feel?"

"Jesus Christ. No." He recoiled at the thought of touching Luca's wife in such an intimate way. Although he had no doubt he could take Luca in a fight under normal circumstances, he was pretty damn sure Luca would attack without restraint when it came to protecting what was his.

Kinda like how he felt about Grace.

"Sorry." She held up her hands palms forward. "I forgot you Mafia types aren't like normal people. All the rules and codes of honor—"

"The rules are there to protect you, and so wiseguys don't kill each other. Lotta deaths happened over women before the Cosa Nostra's ten commandments were put in place. Now, you don't touch another made guy's woman, and you definitely don't sleep with her. You do that, you might be chased." No one wanted to be cut off from the mob over a woman. "Chased" didn't just mean you lost your friends; it meant you lost your business, your home, and your livelihood, too.

"Well, I'm sure Nico and Luca don't want to lose a key member of their crew." She tapped on her keyboard, and the printer whirred to life.

He opened his mouth to remind her that he wasn't part of the crew and closed it again. Gabrielle wouldn't be helping him if that were true. Luca wouldn't allow it. And although he and Gabrielle had always been friendly, she wouldn't be spending her free hours doing him a favor that took her into a gray area of the law if Nico hadn't also approved. They were treating Rocco like part of the family—the Toscani crime family—and dammit he liked how that felt.

"So what did you find?" Rocco picked up the paper she had printed out and stared at the chart on the page.

"Nothing." Gabrielle leaned back in her chair. "That's a summary of all the databases and places I checked. She doesn't exist. Or at least, no one with that name and fitting her description and age bracket exists. And I'm not just talking about Nevada. I'm talking about anywhere in the U.S."

Rocco's skin prickled in warning as he stared at the result column of the chart, every entry marked negative. "What about St. John's Hospital? Mike said she's a nurse there." Mike had said some other things about Tiffany Oliver that he didn't want to think about because with every passing minute his pulse kicked up another notch.

"There is no one with that name registered on staff—I

have a source who checked all the databases including casual and contract labor. Everyone in the hospital has to have a security pass, so if she did work there officially, her name would show up."

Rocco scrubbed a hand through his hair. "What about her picture?"

"I ran it through the police visual recognition database, courtesy of a friend."

"And?"

She hesitated, and the prickle over his skin became a full-on glacial freeze.

"We got a hit. It's only sixty percent accurate, but it came up with a woman named Teresa Rossi, a career criminal from New York."

Fuck. Fuck. Fuck. Rocco ran through the corridors of St. John's hospital. He'd called Mike who'd told him he'd dropped Tiffany off at the hospital only an hour ago. Who was she? Was she working for the mysterious capo who had hired the De Lucchis? Or for the masked men who had shot up Carvallo's?

He slammed into a gurney and peeled off down the opposite corridor. He didn't know who was behind the scenes, but it was a genius plan. No one in the mob would be suspicious of a woman—especially a nurse, and one as pretty as Tiffany who had established a presence at the hospital. She would be able to get in and out of Nunzio's room without any problem and finish the job the assassins had started in the restaurant two weeks ago.

His worst fears were realized as he rounded the corner. No guards in the hallway. No guards at the door. No one to stop him from walking right into Nunzio's room where the angel of death was hovering beside Nunzio's bed with an ear-to-ear smile.

"Get the fuck away from him." Rocco closed the door and drew his gun, waving Tiffany away. She dropped a syringe into the pocket of her scrubs. With her long blonde hair tied up in a loose ponytail and in top-toe-pink, she looked as far removed from the lethal killer he now suspected her to be.

"Don't hurt me." She gasped and raised her arms over her head.

"What the fuck are you doing in here?" He glanced over at Nunzio, asleep in the bed.

"Just checking his vital signs and giving him his medicine." She peeked out from beneath her arms. "Please. I wasn't doing anything wrong."

"You don't work here." He nodded to her badge. "Your pass is fake."

Confusion flickered across her face. "I do work here. I was hired as casual labor from the Palermo Agency. You can check with them. I got my pass from security when I started a few weeks ago."

"I know who you are, Teresa Rossi."

"That's not my name. I'm Tiffany Oliver." Her big blue eyes glistened and her lower lip trembled.

Jesus Fuck. She was going to cry. Either she was a damn good actress or he'd fucked up big time by pulling a gun on an innocent civilian. He hesitated, gun wavering, as a tear rolled down her rosy cheek.

"You're Mike's friend." She drew in a ragged breath. "Is this about the other night when I called the police? I'm so sorry." Another tear followed the first and her face crumpled. "I thought you were going to get hurt. I explained it all to Grace, and she said she forgave me because everything turned out okay."

Grace. His brain fuzzed for a moment. Something had upset Grace at the gym and Tiffany had been there. Grace had gone into the locker room and had come out almost a different person, and the only person she had talked to afterward was Tiffany.

"Are you going to kill me?" She peeked out from under her arms again, her beautiful face a mask of fear. If she was Teresa Rossi, career criminal, she was very convincing as Tiffany Oliver, terrified nurse.

He opened his mouth to respond and only then did he register the change in sound. Instead of the steady blip of the heart monitor, there was only one long beep.

And that's when she smiled.

"What did you do?" His gaze fell to the underboss, his mouth slack, head tipped to the side, his body utterly still.

The monitor blared an alarm. Shouts and footsteps echoed down the hallway. Rocco's gaze flicked back to her and he saw something not so innocent in the icy depths of her big blue eyes.

"What the fuck?"

But it was too late. Tiffany drew in a deep breath and screamed.

TWENTY-ONE

"Did you kill my dad?"

Grace clenched the prison phone in her hand as she stared at Rocco through the glass barrier. She didn't expect him to answer—the phone lines were monitored and any admissions could possibly be used against him in court—but she needed to see his face, the shift in the color of his eyes. Even after so many years, she could read his expressions. She could see the truth even if she didn't hear the words.

No.

Her tension eased the tiniest bit. Maybe she didn't need to ask the next question. A nurse at the hospital claimed he had been tampering with her father's IV line, and he'd pulled his gun on her when she tried to stop him. He'd subsequently been arrested for weapons-related offenses, and on suspicion of murder pending results of the autopsy.

Not just a nurse, but Mike's girlfriend, Tiffany.

It was too much. Tom claimed Rocco had a contract to kill her father. Papa was dead. Rocco had been in the room. And now Rocco was in jail.

"Tom mentioned a contract," she said, trying to keep her words vague, but pointed enough so he would understand.

When he lifted an eyebrow, she nodded. "Yes, I saw him. He was at the gym the other day. He said . . . things. About you. He's been hiding out with Tony. He says Tony is protecting him."

Rocco stared at her, just as he'd done since she'd arrived. Was it guilt that had silenced him or disappointment that she would even suspect he was involved? But they'd been apart for a very long time. How well did she really know him? Where did his loyalty lie?

"Did you . . . have . . . a . . . ?"

A contract. She asked the question silently, knowing he would understand. *Did you have a contract to kill my father?*

Bile rose in her throat when she saw his expression tighten, the answer in the darkening of his eyes.

Yes.

"You okay, honey?" Olivia opened the car door and gestured Grace inside. She had insisted on waiting outside the jail while Grace talked to Rocco, and Grace was profoundly grateful to have her there.

Unable to hide her grief, Grace had broken down and told Olivia a version of the truth—Rocco had been found with a gun in her father's room and was now in jail, suspected of killing him as the result of a business deal that went bad. It had been a relief to share even that much of the story, and Olivia had gone out of her way to help—from driving her out to see Rocco, to making funeral arrangements for when the autopsy was done.

Grace shook her head, unable to lie. Her worst fears

had been realized. She'd gotten involved with the mob and lost yet another person she loved.

Two people.

Three, if Tom went ahead with his plan to take over her father's position because Tom didn't have what it took to survive in this world, even with the backing and support of his new best friend, Tony Toscani.

She'd been betrayed, yet again. Hurt, yet again. Had her heart broken, yet again. Why could she not learn the fucking lesson that there was nothing good about the mob—it destroyed everything.

"Did he . . . ?" Olivia raised an eyebrow in query.

"I don't want to talk about it."

"Of course, you don't. I'm sorry. I shouldn't have asked. I'll take you home."

Grace instantly regretted her abrupt tone. Olivia had been nothing but kind over the last few days. Grace didn't know what kind of arrangement Olivia had made with Father Seamus to cover her shifts at Sunnyvale, but she was grateful to have her there, reminding her that there was a world without guns or mobsters or death. A good world. And friends who cared.

By the time they reached the house, Grace just wanted to take a long bath and crawl into bed. She'd never visited a prison before, and even now she could feel the despair and hopelessness still clinging to her skin.

"We have visitors." Olivia pointed to the house as they pulled up at the curb.

Grace looked up, hoping it was Tom. She'd only seen him twice since their father died—once at the hospital, and then again at the police station, and both times he had been with Tony Toscani. Her heart sank when she saw Gabrielle and Mia sitting on the front step. The last thing she wanted was to talk with anyone involved in the mob.

"Keep driving."

"You want to go to the rehearsal space?" Olivia glanced over at Mia and Gabrielle but mercifully put her foot on the accelerator and drove past the house. "Ethan and Miguel are rehearsing with the band."

"Sure." She wasn't in the mood for music, but at least it would distract her from her grief.

"Miguel wrote a song and they're trying it out. Apparently, he's been secretly writing lyrics for years and Ethan only found out when he went into his room to borrow a charger and saw the music on his desk. I guess he's not just a pretty bass."

Grace forced a smile at Olivia's attempt to cheer her up. "Funny."

"Did you know those women?" Olivia asked a few minutes later.

"Yeah. I just don't want to talk to anyone involved in my dad's business right now. Actually, ever."

"Maybe you'll feel better after the rehearsal. You can sing something upbeat," she suggested.

"I'm not singing. I'm leaving Vegas after the funeral, and it's not fair for me to lead them on. Ethan needs to start auditioning for a lead singer again."

Ever the professional, Olivia didn't immediately try to talk her out of her plan. "Where are you planning to go?"

"Maybe a small town in the Midwest . . ." Anywhere without a Mafia presence.

Olivia twisted her lips to the side. "You're not really a small-town kind of girl."

"I could be."

"What about your singing? I thought you picked Vegas to do your degree so you could pursue a singing career on the side. And now you've finally done it. Ethan and Miguel have already planned all the recording contracts the band is going to get, what kind of tour bus they're going to buy, how they're going to split up all the fangirls who swarm them back stage after the gigs . . ."

"It was a stupid dream." She flipped the lock switch on the door. Off. On. Off. On. Kind of like her relationship with Rocco since he'd come back into her life. "Look at me. I can't be on stage without a mask and Rocco standing ready to shut things down if it all goes wrong. And there won't be much call for jingle singers in a small town that likely has only one radio station and one television station."

"So what are you going to do?" Olivia pursed her lips, the only indication that she didn't agree with Grace's decision.

"I'll do what I trained to do. I'm sure there's a small town in need of a trauma counselor. Small towns suffer traumatic events all the time."

"So do counselors," Olivia said gently. "And they should know that this isn't the time to make rash decisions. You need to go through the process, find out what happened and why, bury your father and go through all the stages of grief. When you come out on the other end, and the world isn't so dark, that's the time to think about change."

"I need to get away."

"Then we'll get away. But we won't run away."

Grace bit her lip to stop the tears. "We?"

"You aren't alone." Olivia reached out and squeezed Grace's hand. "You don't just have me. You have Ethan and Miguel and the rest of the band. You've got Matthew and Father Seamus and all the friends you've made in Vegas. You've got all the people in the city who you've touched with the beauty of your voice. And you've got Tom." Her lips pressed tightly together for a moment.

Olivia's family were always there for one another in a crisis, and she didn't think much of Tom's insistence on staying with "a friend" when Grace needed him most.

Grace felt Rocco's absence from Olivia's list like a black hole in her chest. Just like before, she had fallen for him hard and fast. She had trusted him. Opened herself up to him. Loved him, and lost him in the worst possible way.

"I know what you're thinking," Olivia said as she slowed for a stop sign. "Broken heart is written all over your face."

"Last time, Rocco did something terrible because he thought we couldn't have a future. He wanted me to be free so he pushed me away."

Olivia pulled into the parking lot behind the rehearsal studio and parked the car. "You wouldn't have left New York if you didn't want to go."

They exited the vehicle and made their way through the blazing sun to the shaded awning over the door. "You're right," Grace said, as she pulled open the door. "At the time, I didn't see any other option. But after a few years I began to wonder if I made a mistake. I was eighteen and scared out of my mind. I didn't talk to him about what happened. I didn't think about the person I knew. I ran away, just like I ran away when my mom died, and when I found some things out about my dad that I couldn't handle."

"Like you're planning to do now?" Olivia opened the door. "Of course, I guess this is different. I mean, Rocco's in jail because he was caught red handed—"

"They caught him pointing a gun at a nurse," Grace interrupted.

"I thought the nurse walked in on him when he was doing something suspicious to your father's IV line, and he pulled a gun on her when she tried to stop him."

Olivia stopped outside the rehearsal studio. "That's what I read online."

Grace groaned. "It was in the news?"

"Honey . . ." Olivia swallowed hard. "Organized crime is always big news."

Grace's head jerked up so fast her neck cracked. "I'm not . . ."

"You don't have to tell me anything, but *The Sun* reported your dad had ties to a Mafia crime family in New York, and some of the TV stations picked it up. They're calling it a Mafia hit. And Rocco . . ." She squeezed Grace's arm. "They said he was suspected of having Mafia ties, too. They found the ICU's head nurse tied up in the closet."

"I'm going to be sick." Grace slumped against the wall and then slid to sit on the floor. She could hear the steady thud of Miguel's bass from inside the studio, and the soft, swinging sounds of the band as they went through Sammy Davis Jr's "What Kind of Fool Am I."

"You didn't know?" Olivia settled beside her. "Maybe it's all fake news."

"I didn't know it would be all over the news." Grace dropped her head into the cradle of her arms.

"I don't usually say this kind of thing," Olivia said. "But if it's true, I think you could do better than a mobster, ten years older than you, who broke your heart once already, possibly killed your dad, and tried to kill a nurse at the hospital. Or maybe it's just me . . ." She shrugged, and Grace caught the hint of a smile showing her Olivia was trying to lighten the mood.

"I think you're probably right. I should have learned my lesson the first time."

And yet, part of her still couldn't believe Rocco had intended to kill her father. If he did have a contract to whack her dad and possibly Tom, someone had given it to him. So who wanted her father dead? The only people who would benefit from his death were in New York, and the most likely suspects were the Gamboli family capos. She didn't know them all, or how ambitious they were, or how powerful, but Tom did. Tom who was now under Tony's wing.

But it still didn't make sense. Rocco had had many opportunities to whack her father, especially when he was in the ICU, because he knew all the guards. He could have walked in, done what he needed to do and walked out without any of them batting an eye. And the whole thing about tampering with the IV line, possibly administering some drug . . . That wasn't the Rocco she knew. Yes, he was violent, but it was Mafia violence. The Mafia didn't use poison or deal in subtle or underhanded forms of death. There was a perverse honor in bloodshed. Physical violence was a statement, a calling card. Anything else was seen as cowardly. And Rocco was no coward.

The gun was more consistent with his personality. Getting caught wasn't. And threatening a woman with a gun violated his personal code. He was a professional. He would have known when the nurses were on shift, when the guards changed, who would be on the door . . . and what had happened to the guards anyway? Obviously, they had made themselves scarce when the police arrived. Wiseguys never talked to the police. *Omerta* meant that if they had a story to tell, no one would ever hear it.

"Do you want to see the article?" Olivia held up her phone. "They didn't publish any details about the nurse because she might be in danger. It says they'll probably put her in protective custody."

Grace looked at the screen and then over at the studio door. What was she doing? As if this wasn't difficult enough. Did she really want to start second guessing the police? Getting her hopes up all over again? Tom said Rocco had a contract. Rocco had confirmed it, albeit without words. Why was she searching for a reason not to believe the facts that were staring her in the face?

She was a psychologist, dammit. She knew, just as Olivia had so gently pointed out, that people didn't think straight in times of trauma. They didn't make rational decisions. But she also knew people were consistent. They followed their moral codes.

I would never hurt a civilian or a woman.

What if that person was a threat? What if they meant to hurt someone you cared about, directly or indirectly? Would you hurt them then?

Yes.

Gah. After the police investigation had wrapped up and she had buried her Papa and grieved his loss, she would think about Rocco. And she could grieve him, too.

"No, thanks. Ethan's destroying a big band version of 'Tainted Love' inside." She pushed herself up against the wall, feeling the vibration of the music through the painted brick. "I'll go put him out of his misery one last time."

TWENTY-TWO

"I was so scared." Tiffany wound her soft, naked body around Mike under the covers of his king-size bed.

"I know, baby. You were very brave." Mike lifted her on top of him, spreading her legs so she straddled his hips, her body bathed in the early-morning light. She had such a beautiful body—big, firm tits with rosy pink nipples, slender waist, and gently curved hips. She shaved her pussy, and when he spread her legs, he could see the pink folds of her cunt and the nub of her clit just waiting to be touched.

"I thought he was going to kill me." She shivered, and he stroked the creamy expanse of her thigh. This was the fourth night poor Tiffany had woken with nightmares about Frankie pointing a gun at her, and sex was the only thing that helped her get back to sleep.

"I'm sure it was just a misunderstanding." He didn't want to think about the conflict situation he was in. His loyalty was to his crime family, but Tiffany was the witness who could put Frankie in jail. Sweet, innocent Tiffany who had just been checking in on Grace's father as a favor to Mike. It was all his fucking fault. He should never have involved her in any way. Every time he tried to do something good, it got fucked up. Now he had fucking Mr. Rizzoli calling to remind him about the oath he swore to put his crime family above everything else. If there was no witness, there was no case. Big things were happening in New York that impacted the Toscani family in Vegas. Nico needed Frankie out of jail. Did Mike understand?

Yeah, he fucking understood. And fuck that. Frankie wasn't part of the Toscani crime family. Mike didn't owe him anything. Frankie had punched him in the face. He was going to beat him with a stick because he'd tried to alleviate the boredom of sitting in an alley for hours while Frankie panted after the underboss's daughter. So what that Frankie had given him most of the money to expand his gym business? Or that Frankie had given him responsibilities beyond those of any other Toscani soldier? Frankie was a De Lucchi. Other. And what the fuck had he been doing there anyway? If Mike had to guess, he'd finger Frankie for the one with the contract on the Mantinis. And poor Tiffany caught him in the act. Jesus Christ.

"Maybe I should go into witness protection." She drew in a ragged breath. "The detective in charge said I could call any time."

"You don't want that, baby," he said quickly. "You wouldn't be able to work or look after your dog. You wouldn't be able to go out. We couldn't be together. You'd be stuck in some safe house with a bunch of cops . . ." His gut clenched at the thought. His girl. Alone. With a bunch of men who'd be thinking exactly what Mike knew they'd be thinking when they had to look after a beautiful girl like his Tiffany. No fucking way. It was his job to protect her and mob or no mob he would find a way to keep her safe.

He trailed his finger along the sensitive skin of her inner thigh, but just as he got near the swollen folds of her pussy lips, she clamped a firm hand on his wrist.

"What kind of friends do you have, Mikey? He killed that nice old man and then he tried to kill me."

Mike wasn't about to tell her that his "friend" was a Mafia enforcer, or that Frankie must have had a damn good reason for killing the New York underboss, because even Mike knew he was going to lose Grace over it. No doubt Mr. Toscani would find out what that reason was when Charlie Nails bailed Frankie's ass out of jail later today.

"I don't know if he killed anyone. Maybe the old man just died 'cause that's what old men do." He eased her down until his cock was nestled against her hot, wet pussy. She was always wet for him. No matter what they were doing or where they were, if he wanted her, she was ready.

"Do you ever think about running away?" She cupped her breasts and squeezed them, grinding against his cock like something out of a wet dream. "Just getting in a car and leaving everything behind—your work, your friends, your apartment—and being someone new?"

"You mean starting over?" He reached for her breasts, covered her hands with his and watched her pink nipples harden.

"Yeah. You ever want to start over, Mikey?"

"Can't say I ever have." He'd been in the life as long as he could remember, and it had worked out well for him. He liked the crew, the work, and the benefits. Without the mob, he would never have been able to open his gym, or afford the nice bungalow he'd bought with the big back yard for his two rescue dogs, and he would never have had the respect he got as a wiseguy.

Mike knew he wasn't the brightest lightbulb in the

box, but he was a good worker, a good earner, and a loyal friend, which was why he wasn't saying much about Frankie even though his head was full of things he wanted to say. He knew Frankie didn't work exclusively for Nico. He was a De Lucchi, and he worked for anyone in the crime family who needed his help. Hell, Frankie had done work for Tony, and Tony's father, Santo, when he was alive, and the don had sent him all over the U.S. to help out other Gamboli family factions. If the don wanted his own underboss dead, the De Lucchi crew were the ones to handle the job.

But man, having to whack the father of your girlfriend had to suck big time, and given how close Frankie and Grace had become, Mike had trouble believing that Frankie had actually done the deed. Yes, he was a cold, hard, ruthless, vicious son-of-a-bitch, and even Mike, with his years of experience in the mob, couldn't stomach some of the things he'd seen Frankie do. But he had changed since Grace came into the picture. Mike hadn't thought Frankie was capable of feeling anything, but after seeing him with Grace, Mike was sure he cared for her. A lot. But more than that, the fact that Mike was still alive and with four working limbs after the fiasco at the jazz club said it all. Grace had turned the monster into a man. How could that man give up the one person who had brought him into the light?

"I wish you had been there." She lay over his chest, her breasts soft and warm on his skin, her face buried in his neck. "You're so big and strong. You could have fought him and saved the old man. You could have saved me."

He growled in pleasure at her appreciation for his size. Women usually thought he was overweight or too big. One woman had laughed at his barrel chest. No one had ever wanted Mike to save them.

"You ever need me, baby, I'll be there." He hugged her tight with one arm and reached for the condoms on the night table with the other. His gaze fell to the small gray box beside the lamp. He still hadn't given Tiffany her present. Every time he reached for it, something held him back. Maybe it was too soon. Or too late. Maybe she wouldn't like it. Or maybe she would refuse it because she had decided to leave him. He had come up with dozens of excuses, but in the end, it had never been the right time.

But now, after spending four nights with her, holding her while she slept, soothing her nightmares away, he wanted to give her something special—a little piece of him.

"I got something for you." He bypassed the condoms and picked up the box. "It used to be my mother's."

Tiffany opened the small gray box and her face ran the full gamut of emotions from wonder to tears as she stared at the little locket. "It's lovely," she said softly. "No one has ever given me a present."

"You're kidding me?" He stared at her aghast. "A beautiful girl like you? You never had a present? Not even from your parents before they passed or your uncle? What about boyfriends?"

"No." She shook her head. "I don't have many memories of my parents, and when my uncle took me to live with him, he made me leave everything behind. He lived in a tiny place and there was no room for my stuff. He wasn't a giving or sharing kind of person. I dated lots of guys, but it was just casual. You're the first serious relationship I've ever had." She looked up through the thicket of her lashes. "Are we serious?"

"You bet we are." His chest puffed with pride at knowing he was her first serious boyfriend, and he reached for the locket. "You can put something inside," he said, embarrassed that his fingers were too thick to open it for her. "Maybe a picture or something like that."

"A picture of you?"

"If you like."

"Could you hand me my phone? I'll take that picture right now."

He gave her the phone she'd placed on the nightstand and she took a few pictures of his smiling face.

"Put it on. I want to see it on you."

Tiffany took out the locket and fastened it around her neck. The slim gold oval hung just below the crescents of her beautiful breasts.

"You are the most beautiful girl I've ever seen," he said softly. "I'm the luckiest man on the fucking earth."

A pained expression crossed her face so quickly he wondered if he'd seen it. "What if I asked you to run away with me?" she asked, her fingers stroking the locket. "Would you leave this all behind? Would you become someone new and start over again . . . with me?"

Mike's phone buzzed beside the condom box, and his hand wavered between the two. He was hard to the point of aching and whoever was on the other end could wait long enough for him to get his rocks off and soothe his sexy little nurse.

Unless it was the boss.

Or the boss's boss.

Or Frankie calling him from jail.

He bypassed the condoms and picked up the phone. "Yeah?"

Tiffany slid her slick, wet cunt up and down his cock, making it almost impossible to focus on Paolo who was rattling off the address where Luca would be expecting him in half an hour. When Paolo finally finished he tossed the phone, and gripped Tiffany's hips.

"You're a bad girl. That was a business call and I

couldn't concentrate. What was that question you asked before we got interrupted?"

Her face shuttered for a moment, and then a slow, sensual smile spread across her face. "It wasn't important. Now I'm more interested in hearing how you're going to punish your bad girl."

Mike lifted Tiffany's hips and slammed her down over his cock. "She's gonna get fucked hard and long, and she's gonna come all over my cock."

She moaned and licked her lips. For a moment, he thought he saw something other than sweet innocence in her eyes, but then she started riding him, and all he could think about was the feel of her hot, wet pussy, the gentle sway of her breasts, and the long golden hair that spilled over her shoulders. He tried to think what he might have done in his life that God would send him an angel, but when she reached behind her to squeeze his balls, he stopped thinking at all.

And that's why he never saw it coming.

TWENTY-THREE

"Did you whack Mantini?"

"No." Rocco leaned against the corrugated metal shed in the middle of fucking nowhere and watched Nico pace up and down in the sand. The broken water tower behind him gave no clue what the property used to be, but the fact that they were meeting here instead of the clubhouse told Rocco everything he needed to know.

If he had whacked Mantini while the underboss was under Nico's protection in Nico's territory without approval from the don, his life was done.

Good thing then, he hadn't done his job. He pulled a pack of cigarettes out of his pocket. First thing he'd done when he got out of jail was buy a pack of smokes. Next on his agenda was a visit to Clay. He'd picked a couple of fights in jail, trying to find that cold, dark place that would help him endure the shit his life had become, but nothing beat the sting of Clay's whip.

"Why the fuck did Charlie Nails bail me out?" He was done with this shit. After the arrest, he had resigned himself to spending the rest of his life in jail. Seeing

Grace on the other side of the glass, watching her face fall when she saw the truth in his eyes had almost broken him. He could see her and not touch her. Listen to her, but not speak because the fucking phones were monitored. In that moment, she became the dream again, the embodiment of the longing that had filled his nights for six long years, the one thing in the world he wanted and was destined never to have.

"Do you mean, why did it take him four days?" Luca asked. "It's because you have a record and someone told a reporter you had ties to the mob. Charlie heard bail was going to be set at one million dollars. He needed time to work that down to something reasonable and then get the cash." He tipped his head to the side. "What's Henderson like? I did my time in Reno."

"It's a fucking country club. I wanted to stay. Only reason I came out was because Charlie said Nico put up the funds and he wanted a return on his money." He pushed a cigarette out of the package. Fuck. It was just too fucking easy to go back. The darkness. The numbness. The pain.

"Nothing has changed in six years, Rocco. Smoking is still addictive. It still causes cancer. And you are still going to kill yourself if you don't stop."

He shook his head to get Grace's voice out of his mind. This time he was going to fucking smoke until he fucking died so he wouldn't have to feel the pain of losing her all over again.

"I don't know if your scowling face is the kind of return I was hoping to get," Nico said. "But yes. I need you on the outside. I've been hearing rumors that Don Gamboli is dead, not missing. Cops found the bodies of two of his guards on a riverbank as well as the bodies of his two brothers. This is big. It's a fucking coup and we're in a dangerous position because Gamboli and

Mantini favored my claim to head the faction. Whoever is behind this is about to show his face and if he sides with Tony, we're going to have to make some difficult decisions. I need my best men beside me."

"If we live that long," Luca interrupted. "If Tony is made Toscani boss in Vegas, he'll whack everyone who stood against him."

"You need a bodyguard, not an enforcer." Rocco lit the cigarette and inhaled deeply, trying to get that nicotine down to the corners of his lungs.

"I need you," Nico said firmly. "But first I need to know what happened at the hospital."

"Dunno." Rocco folded his arms across his chest. "I got a bad feeling about Mike's girl when she called the cops on us outside the Stardust. Then she said something to Grace at Mike's gym, turned her against me. I gave her details to Gabrielle and she figured Tiffany wasn't who she said she was. When she told me she thought Tiffany was a career criminal from New York with Italian roots, and she worked at the hospital where Mantini was recovering, I went to check things out. All the guards were gone. I walked into Mantini's room and Tiffany was there, doing something to the IV line with a needle. Mantini's monitors were beeping and he looked okay, but I pulled my gun on her, told her to get away. She played it like she was scared, raising her arms, eyes watering. She was a good actress. So good I didn't drag her out of there right away like I should have. Then the monitor went flat and an alarm sounded. She fucking smiled at me, and then she screamed. The staff were already coming down the hallway because of the alarm. I couldn't get out. She told them she saw me doing something to Mantini."

Nico raised his eyebrows. "She lied."

"Yeah, she did. Just like she lied in the alley at the

Stardust." Rocco felt an unexpected burst of warmth in his chest. Nico believed him. No questions. No second thoughts. No long searching looks. No side glances to Luca. He believed him like he had been a loyal member of his crew since the beginning, and not for the first time, Rocco wished he was.

"You think maybe she realized she'd done something wrong and was trying to cover her ass?"

Rocco shrugged, remembering Tiffany's smile. "Or maybe she knew exactly what she was doing. Might be she worked for the same guy who sent the shooters to Carvello's, and he sent her in to finish what they started."

He should have just done the job he was supposed to do and none of this would have happened. Mantini would be long gone, someone else would have stepped into his role, and Rocco would be going home every day to his cold, empty apartment waiting for the next call with the next contract or the address of the next two-bit criminal who needed a beat down. It wasn't the life he would have chosen but it was a life in which he didn't have to deal with all the fucking emotions that were threatening to tear him apart. And wouldn't that have been better? No guilt or longing or desire. No love or the pain of loss. He would have been safe behind the walls he had built to protect his heart—the walls he needed now to get through the remaining time he had before Cesare came after him or he went back to prison.

"Fuck." He puffed on his cigarette, his nose wrinkling at the acrid fumes. Had his cigarettes always tasted like ashes? Or was it because Grace's sweetness had tainted his tongue?

He dropped his hand, letting the cigarette dangle. If he had done his job, he wouldn't have had the last few weeks with Grace. He wouldn't have held her in bed and watched her sleep. He would never have felt the connection between them snap back into place, shared those intimate moments, or heard her sing. He would never have played ball with her and the great little kid at the orphanage, never would have heard her laugh as she snatched the ball from his hands.

Fuck. That orphanage. It had triggered a memory of the orphanage he'd been at before Cesare took him—a playground with a climbing frame, a slide, and a basketball court. Happiness. Friends. Laughter. He wished he could go back and tell himself to run when Cesare walked in the door. That he wouldn't laugh again until Grace walked into his life.

"You had a contract on Mantini?" Nico pulled him out of his reverie.

"Yeah." He had a contract on Tom, too, but if Nico wasn't asking, he wasn't offering that information. Over the last year he'd been playing fast and loose with the De Lucchi crew rules. Time to get himself back on track. He was an enforcer. He had no friends. No family. No lovers. No relationships. He did the jobs he was assigned to do and then he moved on. Now that Mantini was dead, he had one job left to do before either the cops or the crew put him away for the rest of his life.

He tossed the bitter cigarette and pulled another one from the pack. This time the taste made him slightly nauseous, but he was already committed so he inhaled and blew out a puff of smoke.

"Authorized?"

"Apparently." If Cesare said it was authorized, it wasn't his place to question him. Cesare was the equivalent of a don in the De Lucchi crew, although in the wider world of Cosa Nostra, he still ranked lower than a Mafia associate.

"So someone else and maybe this nurse beat you to it?"

Rocco shrugged, uncertain where Nico was heading with his line of enquiry.

"That doesn't sound like you," Nico continued.

He was right. That wasn't him. Rocco did every job he was asked to do. When he hunted, he caught his prey. When he fired, he didn't miss. Over the last few weeks he'd been distracted, but this time there would be no mistakes. Tom wouldn't see him coming.

"Won't happen again."

Nico studied him as if seeing him for the first time. "What are you going to do about the nurse?"

"If the DA has no witness, then they have no case." His entire world was imploding, why not go down in flames and break his own moral code as well as the Cosa Nostra rule against violence toward women. He had traveled so far from the enforcer Cesare had trained him to be, he would need to plumb the depths of his depravity, sink deeper into the morass of the De Lucchi ethos than he had ever sank before to get back on track. If Mike's girl had set him up to cover for her mistake, or worse, if she had planned it from the start, then she deserved what was coming to her. That was who he was. Rocco De Lucchi. Enforcer. Not Frankie, valued member of Nico's crime family.

"Don't forget. She's Mike's woman." Luca threw out the not-too-subtle reminder that Cosa Nostra rules also prohibited touching another man's woman—fucking and killing both falling within the prohibition.

"Where the fuck is Mike?" Nico put a hand over his eyes and stared down the dusty road.

"I called a couple of guys to go check out his place and see what's up," Luca said. "They haven't reported in yet."

"You seem to have a problem with your guys not showing up." Rocco flicked the half-smoked cigarette across the sand. He couldn't take the fucking taste any longer, and he wasn't getting the buzz he usually got from his nicotine fix. There was just too much going on right now—too much to live for. Nico needed his help, and he didn't feel the need for even that small escape. "What happened to the guards at the hospital?"

"Mantini dismissed all our guys and replaced them with four Forzani soldiers," Luca said. "He said too many guards made him look weak. I talked to Piero Forzani and he said security threw the new guards out an hour before you got there. Someone complained that they looked suspicious and they couldn't provide a good reason why they were standing in the hall."

"Three weeks our guys were there and no one ever complained about them." Rocco snorted in disgust. Toscani soldiers knew how to make themselves invisible. They knew how to protect people. They could be relied on to do their job.

Unlike him.

"Convenient," Luca said. "I know."

"Maybe he didn't come out here because it's gotta be over one hundred fucking degrees," Rocco muttered, as sweat dripped down his body beneath his leather jacket. "Mike can't take this kind of heat."

"I talked to him this morning, and he said he'd be here." Paolo shoved his hands in his pockets, a worried crease on his brow. "You think maybe something happened on the road?"

Rocco had been thinking the same thing. Mike was as dependable as the sun coming up every day. He had never missed a meeting, never been late, never shirked his duty. He was the kind of guy who checked the traffic before he left and set out earlier if he thought things would be slow. He never complained, not even when Rocco had given him that unjustified punch in the face when he thought Grace was missing. He was a friend, Rocco realized. Even though Rocco had been a bastard to him sometimes, Mike always showed up when he called. He could have asked Luca to send someone else, but he never did. If he'd been held up, he would have let Rocco know. Paolo was right to be concerned.

"You go for a drive down the road. Check for an ambulance or a tow truck or see if you can find his car," Luca called out. "Give me a call if there's problem."

Rocco watched Paolo's lanky frame disappear into the glimmer of heat and dust. "Might not be a good idea to send the boy. Something's up, and he might not be able to handle it on his own."

Nico and Luca exchanged a glance. "Sounds like something an underboss would say," Nico said.

"Yeah, well, you got one right beside you, but if he doesn't hurry, Paolo's going to go out on his own."

"I mean you."

Rocco waved a dismissive hand. "You got Luca."

"Only because I offered the job to you and you turned me down. Luca doesn't like being in the administration. He's got too much going on with all his restaurants and nightclubs, his crazy-ass family, and now he's got another kid on the way."

"So what? I got no kids and you need someone new to kick around, so you want me to do the job? You forget I'm out on bail and looking at spending the rest of my life in prison? No thanks." He poured as much venom into his voice as there was longing in his heart. He couldn't have this. He was part of the De Lucchi crew and he would be until the day he died.

Seemingly unperturbed by his uncharacteristically disrespectful outburst, Nico shrugged. "It's a promotion. You go from nothing to underboss with the chance to build your own crew, set up your own businesses, and answer only to me. You even get to boss Luca around, and if that isn't a deal clincher, I don't know what is."

A deal clincher would be the chance to make Cesare pay for taking an innocent boy and turning him into a monster. Cesare's death would free him if he wanted to be free. But Cesare was untouchable. Not just by geography or because of the guards that surrounded him, but because if Rocco so much as lifted a fist to his adoptive father, the new De Lucchi boss would send the entire De Lucchi crew out to end his life. And Cesare knew him. He had stripped Rocco down to his very core and peered into his soul. He knew his strengths and his weaknesses; he knew what drove him, what scared him, what he feared most to lose, and how to cause him the most pain.

Luca's phone buzzed and he checked his messages. Thoughts of revenge and a future that could never be disappeared after he read the text on his screen.

"They found Mikey. Someone slit his throat."

Bang. Bang. Bang.

Grace startled awake, her mind scrambling to play catch up with her ears. She had barely slept, still numb over the death of her father, Rocco's imprisonment, and the revelation that he had a contract to kill her family.

"Grace!" Ethan shouted through the door. "You have a visitor."

Her gaze flicked to the clock. Ten A.M. Who would be visiting her at this time? And why wouldn't they just call?

She heaved herself out of bed and pulled on her jeans and a floral blouse, working the tangles out of her hair as she made her way down the hall. Miguel was already up and seated in front of the television watching a morning show, and Ethan was in the kitchen drinking a giant cup of coffee. Olivia, the only morning person in the house, would already be at work

"She's on the porch." Ethan pointed to the front door. "With Trevor the betraying and ineffective guard dog who is more interested in hugs and cuddles than protecting us."

Puzzled, Grace pushed open the door, but her smile faded when she saw Gabrielle sitting on the front step with Trevor draped over her lap.

"He's very friendly," Gabrielle said. "He almost knocked me over so he could have a hug. My dog, Max, is the same way, although he's not as accepting of strangers."

"He's supposed to bark at strangers." Grace fixed Trevor with a firm stare, and he buried his head under Gabrielle's arm. "Yeah, you know what you're supposed to do," she said to him, but she couldn't help squatting down to give him a pat.

"I got the impression you didn't want to see me the other day when you drove past the house without stopping."

"You're right," Grace said honestly. "But it isn't personal. I'm just done with the mob. They've taken everyone I loved—my mom, Rocco, my dad, and now that my brother has been made, I'm going to lose him, too."

"Do you love Rocco?"

"I don't think I ever stopped loving him. But he had a contract to kill my dad and my brother. I just can't—"

"But he didn't," Gabrielle said. "He didn't kill your dad."

Grace fought back the hope that surged inside her. "You don't know that. There still hasn't been an autopsy report."

"You know it." Gabrielle put a hand to her heart. "In here."

"It doesn't matter. He still had a contract to kill them.

My brother said Rocco was using me to get close to them. Someone just beat him to it."

Gabrielle's face tightened. "You don't really believe that, do you? He didn't need you. I know it's hard to hear, but he doesn't waste time with his work. He gets the job done quickly and efficiently, and then he moves on."

"I know what he does." Her hand flew to the scar on her cheek. "I had to watch him once . . ."

"Did he do that do you?"

Grace shook her head. "His father did it. He found out about us and did this to force Rocco to take a life in front of me. I guess he thought if he made us both ugly on the outside we wouldn't want each other anymore. It worked. I ran away and stopped loving myself, and if you don't love yourself, you have nothing left to give."

She touched the scar again, thinking about the years she couldn't bear to look in the mirror, the offers she'd turned down from agents who heard her jingles and wanted to see her on stage, even the night she'd joined Ethan's band wearing a mask to hide her shame. Rocco had made her look in the mirror and see the beauty beneath the scar. He had given her the courage to make her dream of becoming a professional singer real. And she'd almost done it. The night he'd been attacked by Dino Forzani's men, she had planned to go on stage without her mask.

"It took me a long time to get over the shock of discovering who he really was and what he did," she continued. "I felt betrayed so I ran away. It was a mistake. I knew who he was inside. I knew there was goodness in his heart. And I think part of me knew Cesare broke something inside of him that night. I just wasn't strong enough to fix it."

"I think you're one of the strongest people I've ever met," Gabrielle said. "You've been through hell and you've lost a lot of people, but you're still living your life, following your dreams, and opening your heart."

She had opened her heart again, and Rocco had jumped right in. The very essence of the man she had loved hadn't changed. He was still protective and supportive and giving and kind—all the qualities she'd put out of her mind when she left New York. He'd seen past her scars and given her the courage to get on that stage and live her dream. He believed in her. Why couldn't she do the same for him?

"I don't think he killed my dad," she admitted, relieved to say the words out loud. "I don't even know why I asked him the question. When I saw the truth in his face, I felt awful. But the contract—"

"That he had many chances to fulfill and didn't?" Gabrielle shook her head. "I talked to Luca about Frankie and his role in the De Lucchi crew. He doesn't get a choice with respect to the contracts he's given from New York. But he did have a choice about who he worked with in Vegas. He chose to work with Nico because he is as honorable as a mobster can be. Nico doesn't get involved in the drug trade. He enforces the policy preventing violence toward women. He doesn't kill indiscriminately. That's not to say he can't be a ruthless bastard when he has to be. But if Frankie really was the kind of enforcer Cesare wanted him to be, he would have continued working with Santo and then Tony when he took over."

"But he didn't."

"No. Once he started working with Nico, he told Santo and Tony he was done with them. That's when Nico and Luca realized he was different from the other De Lucchi enforcers they'd worked with before. They made him part of their crime family by treating him like he'd always been there. Nico gave him the privileges of a capo, and Luca treated him as an equal." Gabrielle laughed. "It wasn't totally altruistic on their part. Frankie has skills that are a great benefit to the family. It's a good thing Charlie Nails bailed him out of jail this morning. They'll need him to help deal with what happened to Mike."

"What about Mike?" She hadn't had many chances to talk to Rocco's friend, but she still felt bad that he'd taken a punch because of her.

"Someone tried to kill him this morning. He's at St. John's in the ICU."

Grace wrapped her arms around Trevor and buried her face in his fur. This was exactly why she wanted nothing to do with the mob. Too much death. Too much violence. Too many people suffering. "Do they know who did it?"

"No. But he was found naked in bed." She grimaced. "Luca is convinced it was his new girlfriend."

"Tiffany?" Grace's voice rose in pitch. "She seemed so . . . innocent. Normal. I thought she really liked him." She should have known better. One of the first things she'd learned when she started her degree was that there was no normal. People wore masks of all shapes and sizes, and the only thing you could ever know for sure was that the essence of the person was never the first thing you saw.

"I didn't like her after she got you and Frankie arrested," Gabrielle said. "And Frankie was suspicious, too. He had me check her out and it turns out she isn't who she says she is." She pulled out her phone. "I think Tiffany is actually Teresa Rossi from New York. She's done some time in prison for assault with a deadly weapon and had a few other charges laid against her. We only had a 60 percent accuracy rate on the profile, but it looked pretty close to me."

"She was the nurse in the room with Frankie," Grace said quickly, putting the pieces together. "If she tried to kill Mike, maybe she's the one who killed my dad. But why? What connection is there between Mike and him? Or between her and my dad? It can't be random." At least that would explain why Rocco had pulled his weapon. He had been trying to stop her. And Grace had almost run from him all over again.

TWENTY-FOUR

"Who the fuck is she?" Rocco kicked a chair across the ICU lounge, and Luca ducked out of his way. He'd lied to the head nurse and told her that Mike was his brother. Of course, it didn't fly and he'd had to tie her up and put her in the closet, just like he'd done to the other nurse who wanted to stop him from going to visit Nunzio Mantini. If he kept this up, St. John's would need more fucking closets.

"We don't know for sure it was Tiffany," Luca said. "We've got everybody on the street looking for her, and once we find her, we'll get the truth."

"He was fucking naked with a condom in his hand. One of the soldiers said the place smelled of perfume and there was an empty jewelry box on the floor. Doesn't sound like a dude to me."

"He might have come in after she left."

"Jesus fucking Christ." He took out all his anger on the only person strong enough to stand up to him. "It was her. I know it was her. There was something about her . . ." He shook his head, at a loss for words to express the darkness he'd seen in her eyes—something so familiar it had chilled his heart. "What the fuck is going on? She's always one step ahead of us. I'm tired of being a fucking pawn in this game. Nunzio knew what it was all about, and now he's gone. And Mike . . ." He grabbed the chair and smashed it on the floor. "Mike doesn't deserve to die like this. When I find the bitch, I'm going to make her suffer a hell you can't even imagine. The worst thing I've done is going to be too good for her."

"All you'll get out of that is the satisfaction of revenge."

"Looking forward to it."

Luca shook his head. "Come on, man. She's a tool, just like you are when you're given a contract. Someone else is pulling the strings. There's a bigger game going on here that we don't see. If you whack her, then we'll never find out who's behind this."

"She'll talk before she dies," Rocco spat out. "I can guarantee that. Woman or not. I'll have answers. What she did is sick. Slitting a man's throat in the middle of sex? She's like some kind of fucking black widow spider."

Fuck. Fuck. Fuck. He smashed everything he touched—mirrors, windows, tables, and chairs. Luca stood at the door and kept the staff away, letting him rage until his anger had faded to a quiet roar.

"Never seen you express anything more than a grumble," Luca said when Rocco stopped to catch his breath.

"I usually go see a guy named Clay. He beats the fucking feelings out of me so I can get through each fucking day. Haven't seen him in weeks. Maybe it's time." But even as the words dropped from his lips, he knew Clay wouldn't be able to help him. Suppressing small doses of emotion was doable, but ever since Grace had walked into his life, he'd been overwhelmed with the kind of feelings he'd never thought to experience again.

Powerful feelings. And good or bad, they made his heart pound and blood run hot in his veins. How could he go back to the cold empty void that had been his life for the last six years?

Luca shrugged. "I always prefer to hit things. Or shoot them. Punch out a couple of guys who deserve a beating. You bottle everything up inside and one day it rips you apart. Almost happened to me. It took meeting Gabrielle for me to get over Gina. Three words and I was free of all the bad shit that was eating me up inside."

"What three words?"

"You'll know them when the time is right."

"Jesus Christ. I don't have time for this shit." Rocco's hands curled into fists. "That bitch is on the loose. First Mantini. Now Mike. Who the fuck is she going after next? Is she the one who is after Grace and Tom?"

The answer came to him even as he asked the question. Of course she was. Her actions in Mantini's hospital room were deliberate. The look on her face triumphant when the heart monitor slowed. She had to be the one who was after Grace and Tom. There couldn't be a third player in the game trying to off the Mantini family. They'd both been contracted to take out the men, but she'd also been instructed to take Grace alive. Could they be working for the same person? Who would hire the De Lucchis and then send in backup—and a woman for that matter?

Only Cesare ever knew the identity of the contractor. And right now, Cesare was the last person he wanted to see. Once he found out Mantini was dead by someone else's hand, Rocco would be called home to account. Three weeks ago, he would have gladly made the trip back to New York. He would have offered himself up to Cesare's justice, knowing as he did that his death would be his revenge. Not only would Cesare have to find and train a new orphan to fulfill his commitment to the crew, he would have to admit his failure.

"We've got to catch her before she finds Tom or Grace," he said. "Or anyone else. She was at Carvello's. I'm sure of it. She owes the Bianchis two lives."

"So someone hired both her and you to take out the Mantinis?" Luca asked.

"Might be the same person, might be two people. But whoever hired her wanted the men out of the way and Grace for himself. No doubt he'll reveal himself when he becomes the new underboss, but that bitch is acting now and we don't have time to waste." And didn't that just make his fucking blood boil. He had promised to protect Grace. She had been his since she was ten years old, and he knew what he had to do to convince her to be his again.

"I thought you just wanted revenge," Luca said. "Now you're wanting to save the world."

"I want . . . out." He couldn't believe he'd said it but as Luca had stood watching him destroy the room, he realized he was a friend. Just as Nico was a friend. And Mike. All this time, he'd wanted out and the answer was sitting across from him at the clubhouse or riding beside him in the car or hauling bodies with him to Lake Mead. He couldn't break with Cesare alone, but if he had help in the form of some very powerful friends . . . maybe . . . just maybe . . . he could have a fucking life, and he could have Grace in it.

"So we'll start by finding the girl," Luca said without missing a beat, as if De Lucchi enforcers confessed to him every day that they wanted to break with the tightest crew in the Cosa Nostra. "We'll either make her confess or disappear. That will clear your name and lead us to whoever is behind this coup. Once we know, we'll be able to keep Grace safe while you find your way out with whatever support you need from us."

For a moment, Rocco couldn't speak. "That's it? You're gonna help me, no questions asked. No concern about the risk. Nothing in return?"

"That's what it means to be part of the family." A sly smile spread across Luca's face. "Also, we need an underboss. He needs to be a non-smoker, a good earner, and able to handle discipline in the family as well as teach the occasional lesson to guys who want to cheat the mob. Maybe break a few legs, chop off a few fingers, that kind of thing. Other than that, we'll do the usual and hire out the dirty jobs to the professionals."

"No one's ever gotten out."

"I'll bet no one ever tried," Luca said. "But then maybe they didn't have a family behind them, a beautiful girl who loved them, and a friend who's tired of breathing in second hand smoke. So what's the plan? What do we need?"

Luck.

Conviction.

Hope.

And bait.

Grace had never seen Rocco so still. From her vantage point in the doorway of the ICU room where Mike was just barely clinging to life, she couldn't even see his lungs rise and fall.

"Rocco?"

He didn't turn when she said his name, and since he hadn't asked her to leave, she invited herself inside.

"I hear you're his brother." She smiled even though he didn't look her way. "We should have tried that one with my dad and you wouldn't have had to stay in the hall."

Silence.

Grace had a sudden urge to turn and walk away, just like she had always walked away, leaving the people she cared about to suffer alone.

No.

She gritted her teeth and pulled up a chair beside him. This time she wasn't going anywhere. Although she still hated the mob, she had been born into it. Her family was a mob family, the man she cared about was a Mafia enforcer. And unless she was prepared to give them up, she needed to learn how to deal with the mob instead of letting it control her life.

"What can I do to help?" She reached over and covered his hand with hers.

"Nothing. I'm going to kill the bitch."

Grace took a quick look over her shoulder to make sure they were alone. "Are you sure it was her?"

"He was fucking naked. Condom in one hand. If someone broke in he would have reached for his gun, but it was under his pillow. No signs of struggle. Means he trusted whoever was in the room. Got naked for them. Let them get close enough to slit his fucking throat. Only reason he's still alive is 'cause he's such a big guy and he's got a lot of muscle around his neck. The blade missed the important veins, but if Luca's guys hadn't broken down the door when they did, he wouldn't have made it." His voice cracked, broke. "Jesus Christ. He was bleeding out all over the bed."

"I'm so sorry." She stood to wrap her arms around him and he pulled her into his lap, hugged her tight.

"She's no amateur," he mumbled into her hair. "The whole thing with your dad, that was set up for weeks. Everybody here knew her, trusted her. She could go anywhere in the hospital without drawing suspicion. She could sign out any medication she wanted, tamper with any equipment. Even fooled me. I didn't say anything to Mike about her after she called the cops on us in the alley. And if she hadn't made you sad at the gym, I wouldn't have investigated her."

"It was Tom," she said. "I saw him at the gym. He was at Tony's place and he heard you say you had a contract on my family. He said you were using me. My father had already said something similar. A lot of little things came together and I just . . . wasn't sure anymore."

"And now?" He stilled, his hands still around her, holding her in the cradle of his lap.

"You saw beyond this." She touched her scar. "I can see beyond the work you do as an enforcer. I know you, Rocco. There's good in your heart. I think you came to save my dad, not kill him."

"I could never hurt you that way, *bella*. I had the chance and didn't take it for that reason. But don't think that makes me a hero. I'm no saint. I've done things that would keep you awake at night, and no doubt I'll do more. But, I'm gonna try and get out."

"Out of the crew or the life?"

"I'll never get out of the life. I know too much."

Her lips tipped up in a teasing smile. "So you're going to be a regular mobster?"

"Yeah." He couldn't help but smile. "Just your average every-day wiseguy."

"I could handle that." She kissed his cheek. "Less drama."

"First I gotta find Tiffany." His hand curled into a fist beneath hers. "I'm pretty sure it was her at Carvello's along with some hired men. She has the Bianchi murders to answer for, as well as your father's and Mike's, if he doesn't make it. And I've got a feeling she's still after you and Tom. Whoever hired her wants to make sure Tom doesn't take your father's place, and he might want you for himself."

"Tell him I'm taken." Her face tightened. "And if she was responsible for killing my father, then you're going to have to stand in line." She hadn't meant the words to come out with such venom, but if she came face-to-face with her father's killer, she didn't think she could turn the other cheek.

"You'll stay the fuck away from her." His body stiffened. "I mean it, Grace. I'll lock you up if I have to. She's a fucking psychotic, highly intelligent, cold-hearted, vicious, ruthless cu—"

"I get it," she said interrupting. "Sounds like a description of you. Except for the last part."

"Luca's spread the word that we're looking for her, but our best chance of finding her is if she comes to us. We need someone to act as—"

"I volunteer."

Rocco scowled. "No fucking way. I almost lost you once. It's not happening again. I was thinking of Tom."

"Tom? He's still with his new best friend, Tony. I talked to him just after Papa died. He's planning to declare as underboss once everything shakes out. He's staying in Vegas because he thinks it is safer here than New York."

"And no doubt he'll make Tony boss of the Vegas faction," Rocco said bitterly.

"I suppose so. He'll owe Tony a favor."

"We need to get him out of Tony's house and somewhere we can lay a trap for Tiffany. I'll make sure he's protected. Nothing will happen to him."

Grace bit her lip considering. "I trust you, Rocco. I really do. But it would be in the best interests of the

Toscani family to whack Tom so Tony doesn't get declared boss. I think that's one of the reasons he's sticking so close to Tony. How can I offer him up as bait when the people who will be tasked with protecting him want him dead? I'm the better option."

"No."

"I want her caught. I want justice for Papa. I want revenge. I have skills. I can fight. I have a gun. And you'll be there protecting me, like you promised." A shadow fell across the room. She looked up and saw Luca standing in the doorway.

"No." Rocco stared at Mike, lying motionless in the bed.

"Luca agrees." She gave Luca a hopeful look and he nodded.

"It makes sense," Luca said. "The risk to Grace is low because whoever it is wants her alive, not dead. Tiffany won't take the risk of killing her, and neither will we."

Rocco's fingers dug into Grace's hip so hard she knew he would leave bruises. "No. And that's the end of the discussion."

"It's my choice," she said softly. "I'm not going to stick my head in the sand and pretend the mob doesn't exist or that I'm not a part of it. I'm going to use it. I'm going to make it work for me. I want her to pay for what she did to Papa and Mike. I want you out of jail and free to live your life. And I want Tom safe. If I have to go full mobster to get those things, then that's what I'm going to do even if it scares me more than anything has scared me since I lost you."

"The things I might have to do . . . to keep you safe . . ." His voice cracked. "I might have to be the man you ran from in New York, and there will be no hiding it from you. Can you live with that?"

"Can you live with this?" She clasped his hand and brought it to her scarred cheek.

"When I look at you, I see my beautiful Gracie with her kind heart, wicked laugh, sexy body, and the voice of an angel," he said softly. "I see the ten-year-old girl who messed with my radio to play the kind of songs only old people listened to—the songs I listened to. I see the twelve-year old girl who brightened my life when all I could see was darkness. I see the sixteen-year old girl who had never been kissed with the most perfect lips I ever had the pleasure of touching. I see the eighteen-year old girl who was so beautiful she broke my heart when she gave herself to me and trusted me to keep her safe. I made a promise to her that I didn't keep. But I mean to keep it now."

Grace leaned in and kissed him full on the lips. "I guess that's a yes."

"Yes. But the answer to using you as bait is still no."

TWENTY-FIVE

"Rocco? Are you awake?"

Curled around Grace's warm body, Rocco pressed a kiss to her nape. He couldn't sleep. Tomorrow they were putting their plan to catch Tiffany into action, and he wanted to remember every minute of what could be his last night with Grace. If the plan worked, then he would be free. But if not, and he made it out alive, he would spend the rest of his life behind bars, and if that happened he would cut all ties with her so she could live out a happy life.

"Yeah, *bella*."

"I was thinking if we don't catch her—"

"We will." Failure wasn't an option because failure meant a life without Grace and after six years without her, he had no intention of going through that hell again.

"But if we don't." She snuggled into his chest. "We'll have to go on the run. I'll miss Olivia, Ethan, and Miguel, but I'm sure they can find a new housemate. And, of course, I'll miss Tom. But I don't have a steady job, so that's not a problem, and I can probably make money singing so we can get by. I could wear different kinds of masks—"

"Jesus Christ. Is that what you're thinking instead of sleeping?"

"It's hard to sleep with something hard pressed against my ass." She wiggled against his erection, and he groaned. How the hell did married men sleep with their woman naked in bed with them? He was constantly hard, and when he wasn't hard he was either recovering or getting hard all over again.

"How 'bout I put it somewhere?" He chuckled. "That should help you sleep." He lifted her thigh back over his hip and nudged his cock against her entrance.

"Um . . . I don't think that's going to help me sleep."

"Maybe not, but maybe it will help you forget about going on the run." He cupped her breast in his palm and squeezed it gently. Her breath hitched, and he increased the pressure until she wiggled against him.

"Shhh. Stay still so I can enjoy your body." He feathered kisses along her neck as he gave her left breast the same attention.

"I can't stay still when you do that." She ground her ass against him and he gritted his teeth at the painful pleasure. "And I can't stay here without you. I'm going where you go."

"I'm going to jail if we don't catch her." He slid his hand down over her stomach to the soft down between her legs. "I won't have you living life on the run. You can stay here, meet a guy, have a house, kids, a dog . . . the normal life you used to talk about. Remember that, Gracie? You had our whole life planned from how I would propose to you right to how we were gonna be buried beside each other when we died. Except you kept forgetting I was ten years older than you and given my line of work, chances were I'd be in the ground for a long time before you joined me."

Grace looked back over her shoulder and glared. "Is this morbid talk supposed to be turning me on? Because newsflash, it isn't."

"I don't have to try and turn you on, *bella*. You're always wet for me." He slicked a finger through her folds and rubbed her wetness along her inner thigh.

"What's a girl supposed to do when she has a sexy mobster in her bed who always seems to be ready to get it on at a moment's notice?"

"She's supposed to open her legs wider so he can be inside her." He nudged her legs apart and she trembled.

"We've never done it like this."

"We haven't done a lot of things. If we were ever to have that life you planned for us, I'd fuck you in every way you could imagine and some you wouldn't even believe."

"We could do that on the run." She angled her hips to take him, and he entered her with one hard thrust. "Just think how exciting it would be to have sex in all sorts of different places."

"I'm thinking here." He ran a finger over her puckered back opening. "I still want to take you here. Every other bit of you is mine."

Grace tensed. "That's not what I meant. But I'll make you a deal. You stay out of jail, stop smoking and letting people beat you, and you can have my ass as a wedding gift if we ever have that wedding I planned for us when I was seventeen and we have a whole lifetime together to look forward to. How's that for an incentive?"

"I'm done with all that shit, Gracie. I don't need it when I have you." He increased the pressure on her rear entrance. "No waiting. I want to be incentivized now."

"Bad." She reached behind her and slapped his hand away. "That's not how incentives work."

"That's how they should work." He pulled out and thrust deeper inside her, this time teasing her clit with slick strokes around the swollen nub.

"Well they don't." She groaned and bucked against him.

Rocco pulled her closer so he could squeeze her breast with one hand and rub her clit with the other. He wanted to feel her go to pieces in his arms while he held her, keeping her safe.

"No more talk of going on the run." He kissed his way along her spine, his stubble scraping over her skin, making her shudder and arch against him. Fuck. He was driving them both crazy and he didn't know how much longer he could hold on.

"Okay. But it would be kind of exciting to go on the run with a wiseguy."

"I'm happy you're not afraid anymore of what we are, *bella*. But that doesn't mean you need to throw away the life you always dreamed about having. I like who you are and that's the kind of girl who dreams of romantic proposals and getting her man in a tux so he can tell her in front of the world what she already knows."

"What do I know?" She looked back again, and he leaned forward to take her lips.

"I love you. I've loved you since you were ten years old."

She looked back over her shoulder and a smile spread across her beautiful face. "I love you, too. But I suspect you're just saying that to get an early present in case the wedding never happens."

Rocco chuckled. "It's one hell of a gift, but I think I can make do."

Holding her tight, he flipped her to her front and pulled her to her knees, ass up, chest down. He sheathed himself quickly, then smoothed a hand over her beautiful ass before pushing into her slick, hot cunt, as far as he could go.

Grace sucked in a sharp breath. "Rocco?"

"Yeah."

"If we did get married, I want to be married outside and I want wildflowers at our wedding."

"Anything." He pulled halfway out and then pushed in again, sliding his piercing along her sensitive inner tissue.

She trembled. "And Italian food like my Mama used to make."

"I'll fly a bunch of nonnas over from Italy."

"And after it's over . . . if you did as I asked . . ."

"My present?" He hammered into her with long, smooth strokes, driving them both to the peak.

"Yes," she gasped. "Your present."

His heart squeezed in his chest. "If we were to get married, *bella,* there would be no present better than you."

"Safety Sam is your man. Catch a deal if you can." Grace sang the jingle for the twentieth time, trying to put as much enthusiasm into the tune as she had the first few times. The studio producer was new and trying to make his mark by insisting on absolute perfection, but after nineteen takes she was ready to throw in the towel.

"Can you bring the last note up a beat?" His voice grated through the headset.

"You asked me to bring it down three takes ago."

"I've changed my mind. I think it was better on the upbeat."

She could hear groans from the sound room where the techs had been working just as hard as her to get it right. At least this contract paid by the hour instead of the fixed session fee she was used to—a mistake she was sure they wouldn't make again.

By the time she had something close to acceptable, it was well into the afternoon. Rocco had replaced the two Forzani guards with two of Luca's soldiers, and they had switched shifts twice during her time at the studio.

"Ready to go, Miss Grace?" The taller of the two jumped up when she walked into the hall, folding her union paperwork into her purse.

"Yes. Finally. I never want to hear that jingle again. I'll be catching my deals somewhere else."

They followed her down the hallway to the elevator, but as she reached for the button the doors slid open and Tom stepped out.

"Tom!" She hadn't seen him in over a week, not since the day their father passed away, although they had communicated briefly by text with respect to making funeral arrangements for their father when the autopsy was done. "I never expected you to come. You just missed the session." She had invited him to sit in and see how the jingles were made, hoping to get a chance to talk to him alone without Tony hovering nearby. Rocco had come up with a plan to lure Tiffany into the open, but they needed Tom on board.

"I was making arrangements to fly Papa back to New York when the autopsy is done. It took longer than I thought." He ran a hand through his thick, dark hair, messing up the slicked-down style. His outfit—an ill-fitting dark suit, white silk shirt, thin black tie, and dark glasses—made him look like a caricature of a movie gangster, and she bit back a laugh. Sometimes she forgot he had only just turned twenty and was still hovering between boy and man.

Grace peered around his shoulder. "Where's Tony? I thought he was permanently attached to your side."

"I didn't invite him." He puffed out his chest. "I'm going to declare as the underboss after Papa's funeral service. I need to be hiring my own men, handling things myself, not relying on the acting boss of an outlying faction. I need to be putting Tony in his place and telling him what to do instead of the other way 'round."

Grace lifted an eyebrow. Where had that come from? Tom had never been one to put people down, and she had never heard him be disrespectful of anyone in the family regardless of their rank.

"Miss Grace, we should get going." One of the guards gestured to the elevator, and they all squeezed inside.

"So you escaped?" she asked Tom as the elevator doors closed. "You're here without anyone protecting you?"

"I wasn't a prisoner. I was a guest. It was just safer to stay at Tony's place because of the threat. But now that the De Lucchi bastard who killed Papa is in jail . . ." His voice cracked, and she put a hand on his arm.

"You mean Rocco? He's out on bail and he didn't kill Papa. The nurse did."

"No." Tom shook his head. "It was in the news. The nurse was a witness."

"Tom." She swallowed hard. "It wasn't Rocco. We don't know who is pulling the strings, but we're pretty sure the nurse pulled the trigger. We think she was at Carvello's, too, and the only reason we're not all dead is because Rocco saved us. If you're telling people you intend to declare as underboss, then you're still in danger. You shouldn't go anywhere unprotected."

He sucked in his lips and looked away, a sure sign that

he was rattled. "Well . . . you've got guards. Maybe we can grab a bite to eat and catch up. Tony didn't tell me any of this. I'm head of the family now. I should know what's going on."

She bit back a retort about him being head of the family. "That's why I wanted to meet," she said. "We have a plan to catch her, but we need your help."

"You're involved?" His brow wrinkled in confusion. "I thought you hated everything to do with who we are."

The elevators slid open and the guards stepped out, checking the hallway before waving Grace and Tom to follow.

"I'm not embracing the life, if that's what you mean. But I'm not going to stick my head in the sand either. There is only one way to deal with this problem, and it's the mob way. I'm going to take advantage of who we are and the power that we have and do what I need to do to keep the people I care about safe."

Tom's eyes widened and he barked a laugh. "Who are you and what have you done with my anti-Mafia sister? Next you'll be telling me you're not anti-violence anymore."

"I have a lot to tell you." A smile tugged at her lips. "And I know a nice Italian restaurant downtown where we can catch up. It's called Il Tavolino. Luca Rizzoli owns it, so at least we know we'll be safe."

"I was safe at Tony's place," he said, as they walked outside. "You wouldn't believe how heavily guarded it is. When I go back to New York, I'm going to sell the house and get a place like Tony's with high-tech security and lots of guards. And the girls . . ." His cheeks reddened. "He has a lot of parties and so many girls come. They're . . . very friendly."

"I'm sure they are," she said dryly.

One of the guards snorted a laugh. "I've heard about

Tony's parties. They're well-known and that's saying something in Vegas."

"I met a girl . . ." Tom's cheeks flamed, perking Grace's interest. She had missed Tom's foray into teenage dating, but she had never expected him to be shy when it came to the opposite sex. "She was at one of the parties. Her father is one of Tony's soldiers. She's . . ." He looked up at the guards and then leaned in to whisper as they exited the elevator. "She's beautiful like Mama was, but blonde. And she's sweet and nice. She knows who we are, and she's okay with that. She was impressed when I told her I was going to be underboss."

"I'd like to meet her."

"You will." A smile spread across his face. "I brought her with me. You can talk to her in the car on our way to the restaurant." He straightened his spine and looked over at the guards. "You two can follow behind."

Grace grimaced at his officious tone and shot an apologetic look at the guards. "We're going to Il Tavolino. Do you know where it is?"

"Mr. Rizzoli's restaurant? Sure do. We'll be right behind you."

Tony opened the door to a black SUV parked beside the curb and Grace slid into the passenger seat as he ran around to the driver's side door.

"Grace," he said, gesturing to the woman in the back seat. "Meet Tami."

"What do you mean you lost them?" Rocco's shout echoed through the Toscani family clubhouse. "Why the fuck wasn't someone in the car with them?"

Clearly distressed, the guard on the other end of the phone mumbled something about Tom declaring himself underboss and not wanting to disrespect someone in the administration. Reading between the lines, Rocco got the message. If Tom was the underboss, he outranked Rocco as a member of the De Lucchi crew, and his orders prevailed.

"He's not the fucking underboss. He's a stupid kid. Jesus Christ. Where were they going?"

"Il Tavolino, sir."

"Luca!" He yelled although Luca was no more than ten feet away, playing pool with Nico. "Call the restaurant. Tell them to call you right away if Grace walks in the door. She and Tom were heading there and never made it. Fucking stupid guards let them go on their own and lost them."

"What were they driving?" Rocco barked into the phone. "Don't tell me you didn't take down the license plate number."

"I'm sorry, sir . . ."

"*Vaffanculo!*" His vision sheeted red, and his heart pounded so hard he thought he would break a rib. If the stupid fucking guards had been standing in front of him he would have ended their miserable lives and enjoyed every second doing it. "Find them or don't bother showing your face again." He smashed his thumb onto the screen, ending the call, and pressed Grace's number. When he got her voice mail, he left a message, then sent a text before shoving the phone in his pocket.

"Christ. How am I going to find her?" he muttered half to himself. "Everybody's driving a fucking black SUV."

"You aren't." Nico put his cue into the rack. "But luckily you aren't alone. You're part of the Toscani family and we have your back, just like you've had our backs countless times. I'll get every soldier and associate out on the street looking for them." He turned to Luca. "Can Gabrielle track a car?"

"Not quickly, and especially not without the license-plate number."

Rocco scraped a hand through his hair. "Tony will have the number. He might even have a tracker on the vehicle. He has as much interest in keeping them both alive as we do."

"So we're going to work with Tony now?" Luca leaned against the pool table and folded his arms. "Never thought I'd see the day, but then I never thought I'd see our very own Frankie with a girl."

"They were last seen in a black Escalade heading north on the Las Vegas Freeway." Rocco ignored the comment because if he didn't find them fast, he wouldn't have a girl. And if he lost her again . . . His stomach churned and he pushed the thought away. "I'll call Gabrielle and see if she knows someone who can access the city cameras."

"We should get Mia involved," Luca suggested. "She could use that trick they used to find Tom and track Grace's phone. I'll give her a call."

Rocco felt the smallest bit of tension ease. "Appreciated."

"Our resources are your resources. Our people are your people. Whatever you need to find her is yours." Nico whipped out his phone. "I'll set up that meet with Tony."

"It's okay." Rocco held up his hand. "I'm a De Lucchi. He'll see me. No appointment required."

"I thought you were in jail." Tony leaned back in his chair, folding his arms behind his head.

"I'm out on bail."

"Well, then you can't be here to tell me you're planning to come back and work for me because last I heard

first-degree murder puts you away for a very long time."
He looked over at one of the guards standing by the door
and smirked. Tony didn't need to put on a show for
Rocco, and as a result, he had only two guards in the
room—one beside him and one at the door—instead of
the usual four.

Rocco forced his body into stillness. Only a short
while ago he was looking forward to a life behind bars
where he wouldn't have to spend his days staining his
already-tainted soul. But now that he had found Grace
again, prison would be just another form of hell.

"Wasn't me."

Tony smirked. "They all say that."

"It was a woman. The nurse."

"Since when do women get involved in Cosa Nostra affairs?" His tone was mocking, but he had leaned
forward slightly, and his dark eyes had widened with
interest.

"Since someone hired her to whack Mantini and his
son."

"I thought that was your contract."

Rocco shrugged. "Apparently the person who contacted Cesare isn't the only one who wanted Mantini
dead."

"So why are you here?"

"She's got Tom and Grace. Tom was driving a black
SUV. I assumed it was yours since he'd just come from
you place."

Tony pushed his chair away from his desk and walked
over to the wet bar in the corner. "Drink?"

"No, thanks."

"I need a little something." He lifted a bottle of whiskey. "It helps me think when unexpected gifts land on
my doorstep." He poured his drink and leaned against
the bar. "You need my help."

"I need the license-plate number of the SUV."

"License-plate numbers are confidential information. How do I know you won't misuse it? You're asking me to take a risk. A considerable risk. I'll need fair compensation."

Damn Tony, always angling for an opportunity. "You'll get Tom back. He managed to escape from your fortress of solitude and steal a car. You'll be able to start whispering in his fucking ear again about how you should be ruling Vegas."

Tony sipped his drink. "Or I let him get whacked and take a chance that this coup in New York results in a new don and underboss who are favorable to my claim."

"Didn't work out so good for you last time. You were about to lose Vegas."

Tony nodded. "True. It was going to become a blood bath. I would have expressed my annoyance. Nico would have retaliated. New York would have sent some guys to help him out. There would have been more dead bodies. The FBI would have become involved. And we would all have wound up in jail together."

"So, you help me out," Rocco said, standing. "I rescue them. I get the girl. You get the boy. You talk him around to your point of view . . ."

"And Nico loses Vegas." Tony swirled the liquid in his glass. "I like it, but I can't see it happening. You're Nico's man. Why would he approve a plan that means he loses the thing he wants most of all?"

"I'm a De Lucchi. We don't get involved in political games." Rocco dropped his hand to his belt beneath his jacket. He'd been relieved of his weapons when he entered the house, but not all weapons were easily seen.

Tony snorted a laugh. "De Lucchis also don't have relationships. They don't go on rescue missions. They don't save people. They don't negotiate. They don't have friends. You're no more a De Lucchi than I am. You're part of Nico's crew, and that makes you enemy number one."

"Is that a no?"

"You need me to spell it out? N.O."

In one swift motion, Rocco pulled out a knife and threw it, catching Tony in the upper quadrant of his chest. He was moving while the knife was in the air, and by the time Tony staggered back and the guard near the desk realized what was happening, he was behind Tony with a second knife at his throat.

"You forgot one." He yanked Tony's arm back and he screamed in pain. "De Lucchis don't take no for an answer. And neither do members of Nico's crew."

TWENTY-SIX

"I can't believe you." Grace glared at her brother who was tied up beside her in the basement of an abandoned, unfinished hotel just off the Strip. The last rays of evening light shone through the tiny window fifteen feet above them, illuminating the otherwise dark space. "She's so sweet and nice, he says. She's just like Mama, he says. I want you to meet her, he says—"

"Stop it, Grace."

"How could you possibly think she was the daughter of one of Tony's capos? How many fair, blonde-haired, blue-eyed Italians have you met?"

Tom's jaw tightened. "It's possible. With the right genetic mix . . ."

"Did you ask your BFF Tony?" she spat out. "Did you say, 'Hey, Tones. Which of your capos spawned the demon ice princess of hell?"

"She didn't act like a demon. She came across so . . . innocent."

"So did Norman Bates."

Tom huffed. "You don't need to get nasty about it."

"I don't need to get nasty about the fact that you were

sleeping with the woman who killed Papa?" Her voice rose in pitch. "That you let her stroke your ego until it was so big you left a place of safety and thought you could swan around Vegas when you knew someone was after us? Do you know what she did to her last boyfriend?"

Tom pressed his lips together and shook his head. "Don't tell me."

"I am going to tell you so you realize just how lucky you are. She slit his throat while they were having sex. He was found by some guys in his crew naked with a condom in his hand, bleeding out all over the sheets. How's that for nasty?"

"Jesus Christ." Tom snapped his legs together and grimaced. "It's almost impossible to believe."

"What's impossible to believe is how she shoved a gun against my skull and made you drive out here without those guards noticing what was going on."

"How could they follow us with all those twists and turns, back alleys drives and red light run-throughs?" He snapped. "She knows this city like the back of her hand." He yanked against the ropes. "Fuck. I can't believe I was taken in by a beautiful face and a sweet voice."

"I'm sure male black widow spiders say something similar before they're eaten."

His lips tightened and he looked away. "I don't want to talk about her any more."

"Papa is dead because of her. Rocco went to jail because of her. She tried to kill you. I want to know who she is, who she's working for and what they want. What is the end game that is so important she would destroy our family?"

"We'll have to wait until we get the fuck out of here to find out." Tom tugged fruitlessly on the ropes. "Or maybe Rocco will save us again like he did at the restaurant."

"If he does, I don't think he'll leave anyone alive. He's got a seriously crazy protective streak that I never saw when we were together in New York."

"I used to watch you guys laughing and joking around in the front seat," Tom said, leaning back against the wall. "I thought he was so cool. I was jealous because he hardly ever talked to me. I wanted him to be my friend, too. And then when I was twelve or thirteen I realized you guys weren't just friends. He would touch your arm or brush the hair off your shoulder and your face would go soft. Sometimes he would just stare at you and I'd be afraid he was going to crash the car."

Grace laughed. "I thought you were engrossed in your books or video games."

"Mostly, I was, but it was because I felt left out of what was going on between you guys." He shifted his weight, pushing himself up on the cement floor. "After you left New York, did you see him?"

"No. I didn't see him again until the funeral."

"Must have been hard," he said softly. "I only knew Tami a short time and I was having crazy thoughts about being together forever."

Grace swallowed hard, thinking of Mike. "You weren't the only one."

"I'm sure he'll be looking for you." His face brightened. "Maybe he'll bring help."

"I don't plan to sit around waiting for a miracle." Grace rubbed the ropes binding her hands along the edge of the wall using the jagged edges to wear through the strands. "We need to get out of here ourselves."

"Don't waste your time. There's nowhere for you to go." Tami/Tiffany walked toward them from the dark recesses of the vast space.

"Oh look, Tom. It's Tami, or should I say Tiffany?"

"You should say Teresa." She smiled an impossibly

beautiful smile from someone with such an evil heart. "Teresa De Lucchi."

Grace's blood ran cold. "De Lucchi? You're Rocco's sister?"

"Half-sister, and not by blood. We share the same adoptive father. Unfortunately, we never had the chance to meet in New York. Papa kept separate households."

Grace remembered Rocco mentioning that he had spent a good part of his teen years alone in the house with the housekeeper because his father was traveling. Maybe he hadn't traveled that far.

"Did he train you?" She stared at Teresa aghast. "As an enforcer?"

"The best." Teresa smiled. "They never see me coming. They're always too busy looking at my hair or my boobs or listening to my sad stories about my mean ex-boyfriend."

Tom groaned and turned his face away.

"Aww." Teresa laughed. "The truth hurts, doesn't it, Tom? You want to hear another truth? You'll never be the underboss. You don't have what it takes. You're too nice. You might make a good soldier, and in twenty years of hard living possibly a good capo. But you're not a leader. Not that it matters. The position has already been filled, and unfortunately, you've been made redundant."

"Don't touch him." Grace edged closer to Tom as footsteps rang out in the empty basement. She peered through the darkness, her heart thudding in her chest.

"Cosi bella." The deep, heavily accented voice turned her blood to ice. "You look even more like your mother than the last time I saw you."

"I've got it narrowed down to a five-block radius," Mia said over the phone. "The signal is too weak to pinpoint the exact location. Either her battery is running low or she is somewhere the signal can't get through."

Rocco looked over the vast, unfinished gaming resort taking up eighty-seven acres at the end of the Strip. Five hotels stood in various stages of completion, along with a partially finished casino, convention center, and theaters. The last rays of evening light crept through the skeletal frame of the interrupted construction casting it in an eerie orange glow.

"I need more than that."

"Gabrielle has a record of an SUV with that plate number going through an intersection on the west side of the Strip, so you might want to start your search there," Mia said. "She's working with her partners to see if we can get you some blueprints or plans—"

"We don't have time." Rocco fought back a wave of panic. "I need people on the ground, checking out all these buildings. There isn't much daylight left, and it doesn't look like the construction site is lit at night."

"Luca's organizing the capos and soldiers," Mia said. "They should be there shortly."

"Paolo." Rocco turned to the young associate who had volunteered to be part of the first wave of the search party. "We'll need flashlights, extra ammo, and as many weapons as you can carry."

"Got it all here, sir." Paolo lifted his pack.

"Good man." Rocco gestured to the first building. "We'll stay together. Look for a black Escalade or doors with a vehicle access. They'll have had to move Grace and Tom from the vehicle into the building and I doubt they would have risked a long, public walk with them, even at gunpoint."

"They? I thought they were taken by a woman."

"Tom's about the same size as you, maybe a bit bigger. And Grace won't have gone without a fight. Tiffany will have had help. Probably the same guys that were in Carvello's."

Paolo nodded. He was a good kid. Brave, strong, and he had more than pulled his weight when Luca had been kidnapped last year. He also had lock-picking skills, which came in handy in the most unexpected ways.

The first hotel had no visible road access. Likewise the casino. They had just started searching the second hotel when Paolo called a halt.

"Tire tracks." He pointed to the fresh prints on the dirt road.

Rocco drew his weapons and they followed the prints to a partially completed underground garage.

"There's the vehicle," Paolo whispered.

Waving Paolo back, Rocco studied the SUV parked alongside two other SUVs and a sleek silver Bentley. A rough calculation yielded a potential sixteen armed men inside plus Tiffany. Not good odds, but he'd faced worse. Still, if it was going to be a bloodbath, he didn't want Paolo involved.

"Stay here and watch for Luca and his men." Rocco took the pack from Paolo, and handed him an extra magazine and a flashlight.

"Don't you need back up?" Paolo tucked the magazine in his pocket.

"If those vehicles were all full, one extra gun isn't going to make a difference. Call Luca and tell him we might have sixteen assailants inside. He'll need to bring more men."

Moving carefully in the shadows along the wall, Rocco checked the vehicles. They were all unlocked and unoccupied. A quick search turned up Grace's phone on the front seat of one of the SUVs, and another phone on the driver's side floor. His pulse kicked up a notch and he took a deep breath and then another, reminding himself that whoever was behind this had wanted Grace alive in Carvello's and would surely want her alive now.

Although, with her father dead, and Tom now in enemy hands, she was no longer any use as a hostage.

No. He forced his thoughts off that path and reached down inside himself for the darkness that Cesare had taught him to embrace, the focus that cleared his mind and his thoughts of everything except the task at hand.

Calm settled over him, emotion receding under the memories of pain inflicted on a young boy who couldn't understand what he had done that could have made his Papa turn on him, destroying everything he cared about, and beating him until he learned to feel nothing.

Ten years of nothing. And then Grace had walked into his life and had undone it all with a smile.

Flicking on the flashlight, he made his way through the partially finished underground parking lot and into what he assumed would one day be the basement. Emergency work lights cast an eerie glow along the dark, dusty hallway. He turned off his flashlight and followed the dusty footprints until he heard voices. Pressing himself up against the cold, cinderblock wall, he listened, counting at least three men in the room beyond. He withdrew his knife and prayed Grace wouldn't see his handiwork on the way out.

It took only minutes to eliminate the threat.

Cesare had trained him well.

Making his way through the room, he came to a long, dark hallway. Reluctant to turn on his flashlight again, he took a minute to let his vision adjust to the darkness and followed the sound of footsteps until he heard a woman's voice.

Laughter.

A gasp.

And then . . .

"Cesare."

Countless times over the last six years, Grace had awoken at night, her heart pounding after yet another nightmare in which Cesare caught her again. She felt the cold steel on her throat, the blade splitting her skin, and always she saw Rocco's face—rage and anguish marring his handsome features. The nightmares had driven her to find a roommate when she moved to Vegas, and Olivia's presence at night had provided her with some measure of comfort—Ethan, Miguel, and Trevor even more.

But no nightmare could compare to the terror of seeing Cesare again. Her throat seized up, and for a moment she couldn't breathe. He had three men with him, all tall and heavily muscled, one in a suit and the other two wearing jackets without a tie.

"You knew our mother?" Tom asked, edging closer to her, his warmth and solid presence thawing the chill in her blood.

"I knew her well." Cesare walked toward them, his Italian leather shoes tapping softly on the cement. He wore a dark, tailored suit, crisp white shirt, and blue and white patterned tie. Perfectly coiffed, with his neatly-combed dark hair greying slightly at the temples, his jaw shaved, and only the most tasteful of gold cuff-links on his wrists, he looked every inch a distinguished gentleman and nothing like the soulless monster he truly was.

Grace continued rubbing the rope against the sharp corner, praying the slight movement of her shoulders didn't give her away. She was not going down without a fight, and she needed her hands free so she could wrap them around that bastard's throat and make him pay for everything he had done to the people she cared about most in life.

"We were engaged, your mother and I." Cesare stopped only five feet away, his gaze fully on Grace. "Did she ever tell you that?"

"No." She spat the word out, sickened at the thought of her mother with this man.

"I fell for her the first time I heard her sing. We dated secretly for a year because, of course, her parents wouldn't have approved. And then I asked her to marry me. We were going to run away together. I was going to abandon the crew, she her family. We had plans to travel the world. I would run my rackets; she would sing for money. It would have been perfect." He sighed. "And then she met Nunzio."

"You killed him," she snapped. "You killed my father."

"Teresa killed him. But yes, on my orders."

"Bastard." Grace had never felt hatred like she felt it now, never felt anger surge through her veins, giving power to each rub of her wrists against the blocks.

"He took everything from me," Cesare said. "He took Cristina and made her his wife. He took our dream of traveling the world together. He took my only reason to leave the crew. And then he became underboss and took something from me that I had only ever been able to dream about. De Lucchis can't hold administrative positions. We have no respect. Even if we kill more men, make more money, gain more power, or show more strength, we will never even have the rank of an associate in any crew. If I had come from any other family, I wouldn't have had to hide my relationship with Cristina. I would have married her right away. I would have had the power of her family to add to my own, and I would have become underboss. I would have had respect from the family and from the woman I loved."

"I thought De Lucchis didn't have relationships," Tom said bitterly. "I thought they didn't feel. That's what makes you so good at what you do."

"Unfortunately, there is one emotion that cannot be suppressed." Cesare's face tightened. "I thought I'd learned my lesson. I was harder on Rocco than I was with my other orphans and still it prevailed. He loved you, Grace, and no matter what I did to him, he wouldn't let you go. But that night at Newton Creek, I found the answer. Your mother never saw me as I truly was, but I showed you what Rocco had become, and not even love could keep you together after that."

She felt the ropes give way and forced herself to be still. With two De Lucchi enforcers between them and the door, their only chance of getting away was a distraction, and she had to be ready to free Tom when it came.

"We're together now," Grace shot back.

"Indeed." Cesare sighed. "It seems love prevails above all things, and I failed to save my trainees from my fate." He drew his weapon from beneath his jacket. "Teresa."

"Yes, Papa." Teresa came to stand beside him, and his eyes narrowed on her neck.

"Where did you get that necklace?" Cesare pointed to the gold locket hanging between her breasts.

Fear flickered across her face so fast Grace wondered if she'd seen it.

"It was a gift," Teresa said.

Cesare slid his weapon under the fine gold chain holding the locket around her neck and lifted it off her chest. "From whom?"

"From Rocco's friend. The one you asked me to kill as a warning to Rocco about the danger of getting too close to people."

He lifted the locket higher with the barrel of his gun. "Open it."

Teresa's hands trembled as she opened the locket.

"How lovely." Cesare's lips peeled back in a snarl. "I assume that is a picture of him."

"Yes, Papa."

Sweat glistened on Teresa's brow. Grace caught movement in the shadows, and then one of the men who had accompanied Cesare disappeared into the darkness without a sound.

"Is he dead?" Cesare's voice was low with warning.

"I thought he was, but he survived."

"How disappointing." Cesare slid the weapon through the chain and with a hard yank, ripped it off her neck. With a flick of his wrist, he sent the locket sailing into the darkness and it landed on the cement with a soft clink.

All the blood drained from Teresa's face, and the smallest whimper escaped her lips.

"You loved him, didn't you?" He shoved the barrel of the gun under her chin, forcing her head up.

"No." Teresa shook her head, but the near panic in her eyes belied her words.

"What did I tell you about love? What did I tell you about emotion? They will destroy you. They make you useless to me. I am about to become the New York underboss, Teresa, and I don't want to be surrounded by useless people."

Nausea churned in Grace's gut and she worked the ropes free from her ankles. If she'd harbored any hope that Cesare would spare her because of her likeness to her mother, it had disappeared the moment Cesare shoved his gun into his daughter's throat.

"He'll be dead by morning, Papa."

"I hope so." He grabbed her hair, yanking her head back even farther. "We have glorious days ahead and I want you to share them with me. Luigi Cavallo and I orchestrated a coup like nothing the Cosa Nostra has seen before. He helped me gain access to the don's house and I slit his throat in the middle of the same night you were supposed to whack Rocco and the Mantinis and bring me the girl." He gritted his teeth. "A failing you will remedy tonight."

Grace watched as another guard was swallowed by the shadows and hope burned bright in her chest. "Why?" she called out, trying to buy Rocco—she had no doubt it was Rocco—time to deal with the other guards. Who else would be in the shadows, working his way around the room? "Why would you want to kill your own son?"

"Because he suffers from the affliction of my youth," Cesare spat out. "I gave him a contract to take out Benito Forzani and it led him back to you. I knew he was done after that, so I sent Teresa to clean up the mess and get the Mantinis out of the way so there would be no one to challenge my claim to be underboss. Luigi has promised to change the rules so the De Lucchis are no longer exempt from holding positions of office. I'll have everything Nunzio stole from me, and you will be a substitute for your mother."

"If that's what you want, then let Tom go. He won't challenge you."

"I'm not worried about being challenged by an inexperienced boy." Cesare snorted a laugh. "I need Tom so you'll do what I tell you to do, willingly and without coercion. If I tell you to sing, you'll sing, or Tom will suffer." He released Teresa and fired at Tom, the bullet thudding into the wall only inches from Tom's head. "Do you understand what I'm saying?"

Shaken from the jolt of adrenaline and the near miss, Grace nodded.

"I can't hear you." He fired again, and this time Tom screamed. A red stain seeped through his shirt and Grace threw herself over his body, heedless of giving up the advantage of her unbound hands and feet.

"Don't hurt him," she screamed. "Don't hurt him."

"Then learn to behave or I'll finish him and end your life the way I ended your mother's."

Grace's hand flew over her mouth. "You killed my mother?"

"Of course, I killed her. She betrayed me. She knew I would come for her, so I waited, dragged it out. Ten years, I bided my time, and ten years they suffered, living in fear, unable to go to the don because your father had broken the rule about sleeping with a made man's woman. He thought it wouldn't matter. I was a De Lucchi. Nothing. The lowest of the low. He couldn't have been more wrong."

The third guard disappeared into the darkness. Grace tugged on the ropes holding Tom's wrists, working the knots until his hands were free.

"Love is a weakness. And it is a weakness that cannot be overcome." Cesare handed Teresa his weapon, and drew out his blade. "Keep your weapon on her brother. If she steps out of line shoot another limb, and keep shooting until she either behaves or he's dead." He gestured to Grace with his free hand. "Come. I see you've managed to free yourself so we don't have to waste any time."

"Fuck off."

He huffed a laugh. "Teresa."

Teresa aimed her gun at Tom, and Grace jumped up, putting herself between the gun and her brother. "Don't shoot him."

"Come, girl," Cesare barked. "Now."

Shaking with anger, Grace walked over to the man who had haunted her nights for the last six years and spat in his face.

A gunshot cracked the silence and Tom screamed.

"You're a slow learner," Cesare said as a dark red stain spread along the leg of Tom's jeans.

"Don't." She drew in a ragged breath. "Please. Don't hurt him again."

"Then behave." He slid the flat of his blade along the scar on her cheek. "I like this. It's my mark. Everyone who looks at you will know you're mine."

"I'll never be yours," she spat out. "I'm going spend the rest of my life planning a way to make you pay for what you've done to my family."

Another sigh. "Teresa."

"No."

Another crack. Louder this time. Grace looked over in horror, as the room echoed with a scream.

Rocco stepped out of the shadows as Teresa crumpled to the ground, her hand clutching her side.

He had a sister. All those lonely nights alone in the house with only the housekeeper to keep him company, and Cesare had been across town with her.

"I was waiting for you." Taking advantage of the distraction, Cesare grabbed Grace and held the knife to her throat. "I would have felt that I failed you if you hadn't managed to find us."

"Let her go."

Cesare laughed. "History seems to be repeating itself. We both fall for a woman. We are both betrayed. And now here we are at the same impasse we were six years ago, albeit the scenery is not as pleasant."

"And you are a soldier short," Rocco pointed out.

Although he had wanted to rush in and save Grace as soon as he saw her, experience had taught him to deal with the unseen threat before dealing with the obvious one. He had disabled all the guards in the room as well as the ones outside, although each painful minute he spent away from Grace killed him inside.

"But not a woman." Cesare gestured to Teresa who had her gun pointed at him, despite having to hold the wound on her side.

"Why her?" Rocco asked, genuinely curious. "Cosa Nostra doesn't allow women."

Cesare gave a smug smile. "That's why she's so perfect. She can go where men can't go. She is overlooked and underestimated and no less vicious or ruthless than the other members of the crew."

"So you destroyed her life as well as mine," he said bitterly.

"I gave you a life," Cesare spat out. "If not for me you would have grown up in that run-down orphanage in North Las Vegas."

Teresa groaned and dropped her gun. Cesare's face curdled.

"Finish her and I'll let your girl go. Teresa succumbed to the poison of love, just as you did. She's no longer any use to me."

Rocco made no effort to hide his disgust. "That's all we ever were to you, wasn't it? Not children. Not people to be loved. Just tools to be used." Rocco's gaze dropped to Teresa, now on her knees, doubled over in pain. He could have killed her with the shot, but he'd been careful because damned if he was going to make Grace relive that night at Newton Creek. He hadn't killed one damn person tonight, although no one would be getting up anytime soon to give Cesare a hand.

"As I was," Cesare said coldly. "And all the De Lucchis before me."

"I won't do it. She has suffered enough."

"I don't give a damn about suffering." Cesare's face twisted in a scowl. "She failed me so she pays the price. If you want to save your woman, then you need to extract that price for me. Grace won't complain if you pull the trigger. After all, Teresa killed her father, and she almost killed your friend." He leaned down and pressed his lips to Grace's ear, although his voice was loud enough to carry across the room. "Tell him, *bella*. Tell him you want her dead. Tell him how you want her to pay for killing your father."

"No." Grace's voice was firm and clear. "She can go to jail. That's enough for me."

"Maybe he needs a fucking incentive." Cesare dragged the very tip of his knife along her unscarred cheek. "Should we give you a matching set?"

"Do it." Grace reached up and grabbed across his wrist. "I'm not afraid of being scarred. I'm not afraid of looking ugly. Beauty is on the inside, but it took Rocco to help me see it." In one swift movement, she rolled his arm down to her chest, and raised her right arm to block the knife. Pivoting left and inward, she bit down hard on his wrist like a vicious dog.

Cursing and swearing, Cesare released her, and she bolted across the room before Rocco had even taken a step to help her.

Damn.

Just. Damn.

His moment of admiration was his undoing. Too late he saw Cesare draw a gun as the last rays of daylight faded away plunging the room into inky blackness.

"Get down." He fired into the darkness, knowing as

he released the trigger that the bullet he had waited a lifetime to shoot would find its mark. Cesare had trained him well.

Grace screamed.

A second shot rang out in the room.

And then everything went still.

"Grace?"

Silence.

"Gracie? Where are you? Are you okay?"

"I'm fine."

His heart thundered in his ribs as he pushed himself to his all fours and crawled in the direction of her voice. Although the urge to run to her was strong, he couldn't take the risk that he'd missed his target, or that Teresa or one of Cesare's men was waiting for him to make a move. "*Bella?*"

"Yes. I'm okay, Rocco. Really."

"Will you marry me?"

Silence.

"Gracie?"

"Are you serious?" she said after a long pause.

"Very serious."

"No."

He crawled until felt the familiar softness of her body beneath her hands. "No?"

"This isn't romantic." Irritation laced her tone. "This isn't a story I'm going to tell our kids. Oh, you want to hear about the day your father proposed? Well, we were in the basement of an unfinished hotel just off the Vegas Strip, and your Auntie Teresa had just shot your Uncle Tom, and your Papa had just shot your Auntie Teresa and then your grandfather tried to slit my throat." She paused and drew in a ragged breath. "But I had escaped because when I moved to Vegas, I joined a Krav

Maga class and learned how to defend myself against a knife attack."

"I'm proud of you," Rocco said, running his hands up her body to check for injuries. Grace put a finger to his lips.

"Shhh. I'm not finished the story you're expecting me to tell our children." She cleared her throat and changed to the same gentle tone she'd started with. "So then your grandfather tried to shoot me, and your Papa shot him, and the light disappeared and your Papa shouted in the darkness, *'Bella,* will you marry me?' and then he crawled across the floor and squeezed my breasts."

"I can hear you," Tom called out. "Except for the manhandling my sister part, it's kind of romantic."

Grace groaned. "It's not romantic to be asked to marry someone because he thinks you might be dead."

"I knew you were alive," Rocco huffed.

"How?"

"I could feel you." He placed her hand over his chest. "Right here."

"That's a bit better for the story." She reached up to touch his face. "I might skip out all the shooting parts and get straight to the good stuff."

"Is that a yes?" He kissed her gently.

"Yes, Rocco. That's a yes."

Shouts and then footsteps echoed down the hallway. Moments later the beam of a powerful flashlight swept the room.

"Frankie!" Luca's voice cut through the darkness.

"All clear," Rocco yelled. "We're going to need a cleaner, two ambulances and transport to Lake Mead. And I need you to take Grace home."

He had a special pair of shoes to make tonight.

And a past to bury forever.

TWENTY-SEVEN

"He was a nice guy."

"Yes, Tom." Grace crossed herself as the pallbearers carried the coffin of Dino Forzani across the grass of the Las Vegas Shady Rest Cemetery. After attending her father's funeral a few weeks ago, she wasn't happy to be back in the cemetery so soon, but when your once-prospective fiancée mysteriously turned up dead, you had to make a show of pretending to grieve his loss.

"He would have been a good husband," Tom said.

"Mmmhmm." She made a noncommittal noise at the back of her throat. Was she a terrible person for being relieved that the Mafia soldier her father had arranged for her to marry had been killed in a hit-and-run accident the day after he'd been overheard boasting to his friends over a meal at Luca's restaurant that he was still going to marry the "Mantini bitch" and "put her in her place" by "pounding her pussy" and showing her what it was like to fuck a "real man"?

Thoughts of "real men" took her to Rocco, who had promised to meet her at the service. She hadn't' dared to ask him if he was behind the hit on Dino—no one believed it was an accident—because she didn't want to know the answer. Rocco was utterly uncompromising when it came to her safety or matters of honor. Even if he hadn't been behind the wheel, as the new Toscani crime family underboss, and leader of the De Lucchi crew, he could have ordered any one of a number of soldiers to do the deed and no one would have dared disobey.

"He was into baseball," Tom said.

"Yankees?"

"Red Sox. And you'd better wipe that smile off your face. Your husband is a Red Sox fan. Better get used to being on the losing side."

"He's not my husband yet." And he might never be if he disrespected the family and failed to show up before the end of the service. "Weddings can't be planned in just a day."

Tom laughed. "He said you've been planning this one for years."

"I planned it for New York. I had to start all over again since we're having it in Vegas. Luckily, I have Olivia who knows everyone who is anyone in the wedding planning industry in the city. Apparently dealing with bridezillas on a day-to-day basis leads to a need for counseling when you try to have a stable relationship of your own."

He gave her a gentle nudge. "Please tell me you're not a bridezilla."

"I don't have to be. When you're a mobster's bride-to-be, people will bend over backwards to make you happy. No one wants to piss me off when the price of failure is a visit from Rocco in the middle of the night."

Tom cleared his throat and a shoved his hands in his pockets. "Olivia told me about the caterer who put down Italian food. She said his facility went up in flames in the middle of the night."

Grace was less interested in burning kitchens and more interested in the fact that Tom had offered to chauffeur Olivia around as she helped source flowers and decorations for the wedding. "You've been spending a lot of time together."

"Just trying to be a good brother and help out."

"Sure. I get it." She bit back a smile when she caught a few people looking in their direction. The graveyard was filled with members of the Toscani crime family—soon to be her family after she married Rocco—all dressed in black despite the blazing sun overhead and the unbearable ninety-degree heat. It was an almost perfect replica of the funeral she had attended for Dino's brother, Benito, only a few months ago except this time she was a stronger, more confident version of herself. She had embraced who she was and what she wanted. She was part of the "family" and her heart had finally been made whole.

"I never imagined you staying out here permanently," Tom said. "But then I never imagined me living here either."

Over the last few weeks, the huge political shake-up in New York had led to a new administration and shifts in alliances between the families. Once *consigliere*, the scheming Luigi Cavallo had become don after his coup and appointed two powerful capos as his underboss and *consigliere*.

Still recovering from his injuries, and deeply affected by their father's death and the events that followed, Tom had decided not to challenge the new regime and instead moved to Vegas to be near Grace. Nico had welcomed him into the Toscani crime family and he now worked as a soldier in Luca's crew.

"I like it here in Vegas." And for the first time, she meant it. Rocco and her closest friends were here, and with Tom's arrival, her family, too. Not only that, she had just landed a national jingle contract, and she had officially joined Stormy Blu. With her vocals, Ethan's contacts, Miguel's new arrangements, and some kick-ass playing from the rest of the band, they had been in high demand since their first performance at the Stardust.

"We've also just closed the deal on the house we were looking at in Henderson," she continued. "So it looks like I'm definitely here to stay."

That's what happened when your family was in the mob. You didn't get to choose the kind of life you wanted to live, but you could take the life you got and make it work for you. You didn't get to live in the city of your heart, but you got to live in the city where you'd found your heart. And you got to be with the man you loved.

"What about your psychology degree?"

Grace shrugged. "It wasn't really my calling, although it helped me work through everything that happened in New York. But I'm going to keep up my skills by increasing my volunteer hours at the orphanage and helping out the kids in need."

The priest finished the Rite of Committal and the crowd responded with the proper prayers. Grace felt the whisper of a breeze against her neck, the softest caress. A shiver trickled down her spine, but when she turned slightly hoping to catch the soothing air, the breeze died away.

"He's here," she said softly, remembering the shiver that had coursed down her spine at Benito's funeral. That afternoon, she had suspected. Now she knew. Their connection was a living, breathing bond that tied them together even if they were physically apart.

Although they spent every night together, she hadn't spent much time with Rocco during the days since the incident in the hotel basement. Now Nico's underboss, Rocco had also become defacto leader of the De Lucchi crew. Instead of stepping aside, as Grace had assumed he would do, he had accepted the position and was now in the process of making sweeping changes through the organization. He had eliminated the requirement that each member of the crew offer up a son or orphan to be trained as a replacement. Training was to be done only after the age of sixteen and then only with consent and in a facility where other crew members could observe and prevent any abuse. Enforcers were free to reject contracts for any reason. And members of the crew were expected to join with established crime families where they would move up the ranks and be treated as equals.

Although Rocco ran the De Lucchi crew, he left the hands-on enforcement work to his soldiers so he could focus on his work as underboss and the fight to overthrow Tony so Nico could lay claim to the city. He could never leave the mob so he had made the best of the world that had made him. Although she still had dreams of a life without guns and funerals, men with nicknames, and codes of honor, Grace had reconciled herself to being married to a mobster. Rocco had promised to keep his business out of their home, and losing him again wasn't an option.

"It's weird how you know he's around," Tom whispered. "When I was having delusions of a happy life with Tami or Teresa or whoever she is, I never imagined being able to sense her presence when she walked into a room."

"Did you go to see her in the hospital before they took her to jail?"

Tom shook his head. "I didn't want anything to do with her. She's a nasty piece of work. I'm just glad I didn't wind up with a scar across my throat like Mike. Even he didn't go to see her after he recovered, and I heard he'd fallen for her even harder than me."

"The mob is worse for gossip than high school," she muttered under her breath. Teresa was now in jail after being arrested on suspicion of murder. A mysterious informant had directed the police to a discarded syringe with Teresa's prints on it, as well as the video surveillance tapes from the hospital that had gone missing shortly after the event. As a result of the new evidence, Rocco had been cleared of all charges and Teresa was facing a lengthy prison term.

"I also heard that Dino's accident wasn't an accident." Tom glanced around to make sure no one could overhear them. "Was it Rocco? Or was it you?"

Only in a Mafia family would they have this discussion.

"I'm still a pacifist."

Tom barked a laugh and then immediately tried to cover it up by feigning a fit of coughing.

Grace caught movement in the crowd near where the priest was standing.

That's when she saw him.

Tall. Dark hair. Broad chest tapering to a narrow waist. Black T-shirt tight over a ripple of muscle. Jeans a feast of seams in all the right places. Thick-soled boots for riding. But instead of leather, he wore a casual suit jacket, and instead of keeping to the shadows, he stood with the Toscani crew.

Her body heated in places it shouldn't. Only one man would dare show up at a Mafia funeral wearing anything other than full formal dress.

She squinted, trying to make out his face, but by the time her eyes had adjusted to the light, he was beside her.

"*Bella.*" Rocco bent down and gave her an inappropriate, hand-in-the-hair, tongue-down-the-throat, this-is-my-woman, touch-her-and-die kiss.

"Nice jacket," she said when he let her up for air. "Is that your idea of following Nico's instructions to dress like an underboss for the funeral?"

"Yes."

"You're missing the suit pants, shirt, tie and Italian leather shoes." She patted his lapel as Tom moved a discrete distance away. "Look at Nico and Luca over by the trees. No jeans. No T-shirts. No boots."

Rocco scowled. "I'm a De Lucchi. I dress how I want to dress. Nico should be pleased I even went this far."

"I like the look." She leaned up to kiss his cheek. "Nothing says sophisticated badass like Gucci over Guns and Roses."

Rocco growled deep in his throat. "Nothing says 'fuck me now' like Grace wearing a dress made of material I can shred with my bare hands."

"We're in a cemetery," she warned.

"Then I'll fuck you to death." His hand slid around her waist and he yanked her against his hard chest.

"How was your meeting with Father Seamus?" She tried to distract him in case he got carried away, a distinct possibility because he hadn't made it back to her place until the early hours of the morning and then had to leave at the crack of dawn, which meant the intervening hours had been spent asleep and not engaged in the activity he liked best.

"He found the old records. Sunnyville was my orphanage. He even remembered me as a boy. The only thing he didn't have was a record of my last name or where they found me, but he's got some leads he's going to follow. He has a vague recollection that it was an Italian name." He puffed out his chest. "Maybe I'm actually a Gamboli or a member of one of the five founding families in New York."

"Or maybe your last name was Smith."

Rocco huffed in indignation. "I'm not a Smith, *bella*."

"Hey. I know some very nice Smiths. Ethan, for example. He says thanks for returning the shredded jacket, by the way."

His satisfied growl made her laugh. "He is very welcome. I'm sure he got the message."

"The only message he got was not to lend you any more jackets. You'll have to buy your own now that you're an underboss and you're going to be running the Stardust."

He bent down and brushed a kiss over her ear. "And the vocalist of my headlining band will be singing without a mask."

"About that . . ." She grimaced.

"No mask."

"It's not the mask. It's just . . ."

"What?" His brow creased in a frown.

"Well, since New York has washed its hands of us, and it's full-on with the war between Nico and Tony, and Tony's still crazy angry that you threw a knife into his shoulder, and the club is underground in a basement where it's kind of dark . . ."

"You don't think I can keep you safe?" He gave her an incredulous look.

"No. It's not that. Maybe . . . you could turn on the lights when I'm on stage."

"You want to sing with the lights shining on your beautiful face? There will be no light unlit in the whole goddamned club."

"You say such romantic things."

Rocco grinned. "It's my Italian blood."

She looked up at him, studied his face. Beautiful and

breathtaking. His sculpted lips were full and sensual, and his whiskey-brown eyes so dark they were almost black, but there was a softness in his face that she'd never seen before, a warmth that made her heart pound.

Once upon a time those eyes had looked into her soul, and those lips had touched every part of her body. Once upon a time all that beauty had belonged to her, and then the mob had stolen it away.

Now she had taken it back and it was hers forever.

"Say something else romantic."

He wrapped his arms around her and sang the last verse of Frank Sinatra's "Strangers in the Night" softly in her ear, taking her back to the first time they'd met when she'd found her soulmate in the words of a song about a love so right it would last forever.

"You stole Sinatra's words," she teased.

"He stole my words. He knew one day a man would meet a girl and fall in love the first time he met her, so he sang a song for us before we were even born."

Grace melted against him, safe in his strong arms. "Did he know that love would last even though we were apart?"

"I knew it, Gracie." Her pressed a kiss to her forehead. "When I fell in love with you, I fell in love forever."

EPILOGUE

One year later

The wedding had been perfect.

Outdoors. Wildflowers. Sunshine. Friends. Family. Good Italian food. Great music. Everything his Gracie had wanted.

Rocco got what he wanted, too. Grace was his. Forever.

Tom had walked Grace down the aisle. A fully-recovered Mike had been Rocco's best man. He had a scar across his throat that had turned him into a chick magnet. Every time Rocco saw him he had a woman on his arm and a smile that went from ear to ear.

Squeezed into a tux, Rocco had almost lost his shit when he saw Grace in her curve-hugging white dress with some kind of beaded corset on top and a long layered skirt made of that easy-to-shred material he liked. She had a crown of flowers in her hair, and when she walked down the aisle she looked so goddamm beautiful he'd choked up and Mike had to thump him on the back so he could recite the words the priest asked him to say. Grace had written some beautiful vows, but when it came time for him to make his pledge, he had only three words to say. Three words from the heart. Three words he'd known from the first day they'd met.

Apparently, they were sufficient, because ten minutes later she was wearing his ring and they were walking down the aisle and his heart was full to bursting because the girl he had loved since she was ten years old had become his wife.

Then the party started.

That had also been perfect. When the Toscani crime family was involved, nothing went wrong from the tent to the food, or from the entertainers to the booze. Grace had coordinated everything and he had been happy to cede control to see the smile on her face. Security, however, had been his domain.

Weapons had been checked at the gate of the estate the Toscanis had recently acquired from a man who had come up three hundred grand short on the loan he had been given to keep his used-car business afloat. Rocco had been in a good mood after a night of sexing up his bride-to-be so he'd given the dude a choice of broken legs or giving up the three acres of prime real estate near the glistening waters of Lake Mead. Although he no longer worked as an enforcer, old habits died hard, and sometimes messages were more effective when bones were involved. He didn't share his occasional forays back into enforcement work with Grace, but even if he did, she wouldn't ask him to change. It was part of the job and she accepted him for who he was.

And right now, he was a man on a mission.

He spotted Grace talking with Father Seamus near the stage where Stormy Blu was getting ready for their next set.

"When do I get my wedding present?" He smoothed a suggestive hand over her ass, out of view of the priest, his mouth watering in anticipation of the gift he'd been waiting for all year. He had kept his end of the bargain, but she'd held firm on her promise despite his frequent attempts to change her mind. He wanted to own every inch of her beautiful body and tonight she would be his in every way.

"Rocco. Not okay." Grace slapped his hand away. "Father Seamus was just telling me the adoption papers will be ready to sign next week. He says Matthew is so excited about coming to live with us, he's already got his bag packed and waiting at the door."

Rocco's throat tightened at the thought of the boy they had decided to adopt. Matthew was around the same age he had been when Cesare had taken him from the orphanage, but the life he planned to give Matthew would be nothing like what he had endured. He wanted to give a child the one thing he had so desperately wanted all those cold, lonely years he'd spent in Cesare's house—the gift Grace had given him—love.

He glanced over at the wedding tent where Matthew was running around the dance floor with the other Toscani crime family kids. He'd been the ring bearer in the wedding party, but his little suit jacket and tie had long since been discarded. Rocco didn't blame him. Unused to ties of any form, he felt like he was choking to death. All the more reason to get Grace alone so they could take off their clothes and get down to the giving and receiving of presents.

"Father Seamus wants to know about the house." Grace gave him a gentle nudge, pulling him back to the present. "Olivia told him you had some friends help with the renovations."

Rocco bit back a laugh. Grace knew exactly what kind of "friends" had helped fix up their new ranch house in Henderson—men who owed him favors and were happy to help him out instead of losing a few fingers.

"The house is all ready," Rocco said. "I did the final inspection last night." They had bought a house with a big back yard for the rescue dogs they planned to adopt as soon as Matthew had settled in, and for the children they would have starting nine months from today after he got Grace out of that dress.

Father Seamus smiled. "I have good news for you, Rocco. I won't share it today because I think you have enough to celebrate, and there are a few documents you'll need to check over at my office first."

"You found my family." A statement. Not question.

"I did, but we'll talk tomorrow." Father Seamus clapped a hand on his shoulder. "I think you'll be very happy with what we've uncovered."

"We're going to have a proud Italian name, *bella*." He puffed out his chest as Father Seamus walked away. "An honorable name."

"Or we might become the Smith family," Grace said dryly.

He slid his hand down her back and squeezed her ass. "When do I get my present, Mrs. Smith?"

"When the party's over, Mr. Smith. Now go and enjoy yourself." She wiggled against him and he bit back a growl. He was seriously close to firing a gun in the air and shutting the whole thing down. Although he enjoyed having his friends and around, he wanted to be alone with his wife, hold her in his arms, and lose himself in the miracle of a dream come true.

But more than that he wanted her to be happy. So he waited. They danced. He drank. He put Matthew to sleep in the back of Father Seamus's SUV. He talked business with the boys, ate too much good Italian food, and watched Olivia and Tom sneak off into the night.

He had waited for her since she was ten years old. He would wait for her forever.

Fortunately, forever came at 1:15am.

"Ready to go?" Grace walked into his arms and leaned up to press a kiss to his cheek, her lips curled into a smile.

"Was it everything you imagined, *bella*?"

"It was perfect."

His wife in his arms. His friends around him. A boy he could love. She was right. It was perfect.

And so was the present he got later that night.